OFFICIAL J.K. FRANKO
LAUNCH EVENT COPY

"WHO KILLED JOHNNY?"
The Mason
October 7, 2023
Dallas, Texas

# KILLING

## JOHNNY MIRACLE

BY J.K. FRANKO

Published in the United States and the rest of the world by Rum House Books (an imprint of Talion Publishing LLC)

Cambridge, UK.

A catalogue record for this book is available from the British Library

ISBN - 978-1-8382759-4-5

*For David and Monica Applewhite.*
*Soulmates.*

Nobody ever said it was going to be anything better than a round of poker on the raft of Medusa.

It's not who wins the game that counts. Nobody wins.
It's who gets out least lost.

From Memo, by Todd Hearon

# PART ONE

## MARY'S WORLD FALLS APART

# CHAPTER ONE

Mary Miracle would always recall with clarity the moment she decided to kill her husband. It wasn't a decision she'd come to suddenly. She had loved him at one point, with all her heart. But over the course of their marriage, there'd been an accumulation of things he'd done that—little by little, like a blowtorch burning paint off steel—scorched away chunks of her love.

Usually, once love is gone, only indifference remains. In which case, the logical thing for Mary to do would have been to get a divorce, not kill him. But in Mary's case, there was one final thing Johnny did to her that obliterated not just the love, but even indifference. And from the charred remains of everything she had once felt for him grew a revulsion so deep that she refused to live in a world where he existed.

After Mary decided that Johnny had to die, she spent the rest of the week working out the best way to do it, the 'best' way meaning how to kill him in the manner that was least likely to end with her in prison or—as they lived in Texas—on death row.

*As his wife, I'll be the prime suspect. The fact that we're in the middle of a divorce makes that even worse. Lord knows, I've got plenty of motives.*

*It needs to look like an accident. Poison? A hit and run? Maybe a burglary gone wrong?*

*And I'm gonna need an iron-clad alibi.*

It took Mary a few days to figure out the accident part. The more difficult piece was the alibi. She came up with lots of ideas. But in the end, she concluded that to pull off a foolproof alibi she needed help: an accomplice. There was only one person in the world she could trust with something like this. Abby Winehouse. They'd grown up together, shared secrets. They knew each other like sisters.

Abby also had the skills to help Mary put the finishing touches on her plan. The only downside was that she'd probably try to talk her out of killing him; Mary was almost sure of that.

She arranged to meet Abby at her place that Friday for some wine and cheese. The house was just west of downtown Austin and had been in Abby's family since the late 1800s. The two friends sat, as usual, on the wooden back deck in lawn chairs overlooking the small yard. Its perimeter was marked by a hurricane fence. The lawn was thick Saint Augustine grass. There was a small rock garden in one corner, in the center of which sat a broken bird bath; the bath part was dry and dusty. A couple of beat-up cornhole boards leaned against the fence by the gate to the alley. It was just past seven. A cool fall evening.

Abby was sharing some of the highlights of her week. She was on a bit of a rant. "And so, I told him, 'Don't be mansplainin' to me about what a rollin' stop is. You may have a badge, but I was runnin' stop signs while you were still on training wheels!'"

Mary nodded and smiled as her friend spoke, but she wasn't listening. She was rhythmically clinking her fingertip against the stem of her wineglass to disguise the slight tremor in her hands. Nerves. She had rehearsed what she wanted to say. And how to say it. Still, her neck felt tight. Could Abby tell that she was distracted? Abby was never one to pry. She had always been the type to chat, entertain, all while waiting for Mary to open up.

"So fiiiinally," Abby dragged out the word, "he agreed to let me off with a warnin'." She shook her head. "But I had'ta get all pissed off *and* tell him I'm a lawyer to get 'im to back down." She scoffed. "Imagine how they treat regular folk . . . " She stopped to pour herself some more rosé.

Mary decided to capitalize on the lull. The sound of cars rushing down Mopac highway nearby provided white noise that she felt protected their conversation from prying ears. But she reached out and turned the music on the Bluetooth speaker up a bit, just to be safe. A song by The Dixie Chicks was playing, the one about Earl. It was a song she knew well, but she was so focused on what she wanted to say that the irony was lost on her.

"I need to tell you something, Abby," she said. "Ask a favor, really . . ."

Abby finished refilling her glass. She turned to look at her friend, and her face fell. "Oh, shit! What's wrong? No. Don't you cry, girl," she reacted instinctively, then backtracked. "Or go on and let it all out if ya need to . . ."

Mary hadn't realized her eyes were watering. Tears were not on her agenda. She inhaled, seeking to extract confidence from the air around her. She wiped her eyes with the back of her hand.

"What is it, Mare?"

"I'm gonna need your help with something," Mary said. The tension in her neck eased slightly as she spoke.

Abby cocked an eyebrow, and Mary watched her eyes dart back and forth as if scanning through a spectrum of possibilities. Despite all her rehearsing, Mary couldn't help beating around the bush just a little. "It's a big one," she added, her eyes turning hard and her chin tilting up slightly.

The air around the two women suddenly felt almost electric. Mary saw that her friend felt it too; the hair on Abby's arms stood on end.

She leaned towards Mary, placing a hand on her knee. "You know you can count on me, hon." She unconsciously lowered her voice to a whisper. "What can I do?"

"I . . . It's about . . . him."

Abby inhaled deeply and sat up straighter. Her lips pursed, then she took a swallow from her wineglass. "Well, what's he gone and done now?" Abby's head tilted; her mouth set in a hard line. "It's high time you divorced that sumbitch. I know it's been a mess. But of course, you can count on me—"

"Oh, no. It's not about the divorce." She sat back, more confident now that she had gotten the topic on the table. "I mean, thank God, I found out *because* of the divorce. But . . ."

Mary had read somewhere that when the police deliver news of a family member's death, they use simple, direct language to avoid confusion. In the shock of the moment, brutal clarity works best. Mary had decided to follow that approach. That's what she had rehearsed.

She took a sip of wine, her gaze locked on Abby's. She breathed in, then exhaled slowly and, for the first time, said out loud what she'd been thinking, planning, what she knew she had to do.

"I'm going to kill Johnny."

Her tone made it clear that this was not a figure of speech.

Abby sat for a good while studying her friend. She was searching, hoping for some indication that she was misreading the moment—that Mary wasn't actually declaring her intent to commit murder.

When it became clear that Mary had nothing further to add, Abby started to speak several times. Mary watched as her mouth would form the tip of a word, before aborting the effort as new scenarios percolated out of her keen mind. Finally, Mary saw that look in her friend's eyes; her best friend was still there, but the lawyer in her was sharing control. Abby clasped her hands together, resting them softly on her knee, then spoke the best open-ended reply of them all.

"Why?"

# CHAPTER TWO

**Six years before Mary decides to kill Johnny.**
**Austin, Texas.**

Every failed marriage begins to fall apart well before the wedding vows are spoken. Seeds of failure are always treasonously mixed in with the blossoms of love. Those pretty, sweet blossoms can easily distract the unwary from dealing with the bitter weeds that will grow to strangle a relationship. Even after those weeds are good-sized, our natural tendency is to focus on the pretty. But pretty isn't permanent—there's always a catch.

Mary's journey towards murder began in a happy place. Her marriage was like many other modern marriages. It was built of popsicle sticks and cheap glue, motivated by a Hollywood-inspired belief in finding 'the one.' But her marriage was not doomed by the naive belief that mature love would magically grow out of childish infatuation once he 'put a ring on it.' No, Mary had worked hard on her marriage, and to be fair, it did have a splendid beginning.

Back in college, Mary shared an apartment with two other girls just south of the UT campus in Austin. On this particular day, her roommates had a late class, so Mary was home alone, having a glass of white wine while she dressed for a date with Johnny. It was the one-year anniversary of the day they'd met, and as he'd said nothing about it all day, she was sure he had a surprise planned for that evening.

She had butterflies in her belly. She'd had them all day. Her intuition told her that Johnny was planning something special. Since they'd started dating, she'd gotten to know him very well. In many ways, he was a typical college guy. But there was something exceptional about him. Something different. When they talked, he listened, and looked at her with his soft brown eyes, and it felt as if Mary was the only person in the world. As though they were sharing a bubble in time, just the two of them, that no one else could invade. He made her feel loved and safe.

*I can't believe it's already been a year!*

Although they both attended the University of Texas at Austin, they'd first met in Cancun (of all places) on spring break. Mary had gone with some of her friends, Johnny with some of his. They were all staying in the same mega-hotel but didn't cross paths until the next to the last day of the break. She remembered it well.

* * *

Mary had gotten up early to watch the sun rise over the Atlantic. She'd put on a bikini and a bathrobe and, leaving her friends to sleep off their hangovers, she'd made her way down to the easternmost pool, the one overlooking the ocean.

There were several staff members, dressed all in white, quietly milling about, cleaning up plastic cups and used linen.

Mary moved a few towels off a lounge chair and curled up to wait for the magic to happen.

As she sat in the dark, the rhythmic sounds of the ocean—waves breaking on shore then receding—and the soft rustle of palm fronds in the wind seemed to accent the whispered Spanish being spoken by the staff as they went about their work. The world slowly lit up as the sun passed through its different phases of twilight before sunrise. Mary could see that the sky was cloudless as shades of purple, orange, and red painted the firmament.

She felt so small there by the pool, with the immensity of the ocean laid out before her. She knew that straight ahead was Cuba and, beyond that, Africa. She was almost two thousand miles from home, which lay to the northwest in Texas.

The Earth felt so vast all around her. And beyond it was the emptiness of space—over ninety million miles from the sun, that orb of fire and gas without which life on Earth would not exist. She sat, waiting for the Earth to rotate just enough for that distant star to become visible once again as it did every day, as it had for millions of years . . .

*And suddenly, there it was* . . . that feeling she would sometimes get of clinging to the large sphere that was the Earth, a little speck of a thing in the universe. Mary fell into a trance of sorts and briefly connected with the immensity of it all. She felt tiny and insignificant, yet somehow a part of everything, comforted and at peace, positioned right where she should be in the scheme of things.

And then, just as the sun's edge was about to break over the horizon, Mary picked something up in her peripheral vision, moving to her left. Something where it shouldn't have been. Mary screamed. Her reverie shattered as the pile of towels on the lounge chair next to her shifted and sat up . . . before dropping to reveal a young man in a swimsuit.

"*YOU SCARED* . . ." she began in a shout, then lowered her voice to a hiss from embarrassment, "the crap out of me!"

"Sorry. I fell asleep." He stretched. Even in her anger, Mary noticed that the young man was her age, and very fit, lean. And unlike many kids at the resort who'd sunburned during the break, he had a deep tan.

He glanced at the horizon, then said, "Ah, you're one of the romantic types. Up to see the sunrise. Nice. How do you like your coffee?" Johnny raised his hand and waved, trying to get the attention of one of the staff, while glancing back at Mary, awaiting a reply.

"No. Thank. You," Mary spat and rose from her chair. The sun was fully up now. And her peaceful moment had been destroyed by the trespasser. As she walked away, she could hear the intruder get up to follow her.

"Wait! Where are you going?"

She walked briskly towards the beach, her flip-flops *slap-slap-slap-slap-slapping* angrily in pace.

"You sure you don't want anything? Not even water?"

She walked on and could hear him following behind her.

"I didn't mean to startle you. It was an accident."

She ignored him, though she slowed her pace just a bit. Inside, she chuckled to herself.

*I have always startled easily . . .*

"And why were you watching the sunrise from the pool?" he asked, catching up to her. "Wouldn't the beach be nicer?"

"Safety!" she snapped. "The beach is not safe at night . . ."

As they approached the steps to the beach, three musicians were leaving, carrying varying sizes of what looked like guitars. Mary's heart sank. She froze as she saw several couples on the beach sitting in the sand at a polite distance from one another. They had apparently been there to watch the sunrise as well.

"Look, I said I'm sorry. Why don't we get some coffee, some breakfast, while it's still quiet? Before all the meatheads and barbies wake up and start drinking again?"

A smile began to tease across her face, but Mary hid it by squinting at him, feigning annoyance.

"I'm Johnny," he said, holding out his hand. "Johnny Miracle."

Mary laughed out loud. "No way," she said. "Miracle?"

"I know. What can I say? It's my cross to bear." Johnny cocked his head, smiling coyly. He reminded her vaguely of Matthew McConaughey, Texas drawl and all. "Is that a 'yes' to breakfast? Come on. I'm famished." He patted his bare flat stomach with both hands and winked at her. Mary felt butterflies in her belly.

They'd had breakfast . . . and spent the day together . . . and watched the sunrise together on the beach the next morning. As the sun rose, the musicians, the same ones she'd seen leaving the beach the day before, played a song in Spanish—"Solamente Una Vez."

It was a magical memory.

* * *

*That was a year ago. Time flies.*

Johnny had been acting strangely for the last week or so. Nothing Mary could put her finger on, but she sensed that something was up. The last few months, they hadn't spent as much time together as they'd have liked; Johnny was working with his father in Buda, and Mary worked alongside her grandmother near Fredericksburg, about eighty miles between them. But they'd spoken almost daily by phone, gotten together most weekends, and now they were getting into a regular rhythm of spending time together. Tonight was a part of that rhythm—Friday night: date night.

The doorbell rang. Mary checked her face in the mirror and answered the door. She smiled.

"Hello, gorgeous," he said. Johnny was wearing khaki pants, loafers, and a nice blue Oxford shirt, tucked in with the sleeves rolled up—more formal than usual for him.

Two hours later, she was sitting with him in a horse-drawn carriage. They'd had an amazing meal, shared a bottle of wine, then skipped dessert. The carriage ride was Johnny's idea. The weather was just beginning to warm up a bit—not quite summer, but the frigid winter appeared to be in the past.

She curled up into Johnny. He had his arm around her. She felt again an inkling, the memory, of that sensation she'd had in Cancun, of being positioned right where she should be in the scheme of things.

Mary heard music playing as they pulled up to the corner of West Ninth. But not the typical musical sounds one hears leaking out of the bars on the streets of downtown Austin—country, rock, blues, jazz. This was different, more lyrical, more nostalgic.

Mary bolted upright.

There, on the corner, at the foot of one of Austin's Moonlight Towers, was a group of *mariachis*. They were playing "Solamente Una Vez," the song Mary and Johnny had listened to on the beach that morning after their last night in Cancun—also the night they'd first made love.

"Stop here, please," Johnny told the driver.

The carriage pulled up to the musical group, and Mary sank deeper into Johnny as she watched the musicians playing on the street to her left. He held her with both arms. She felt her heart swell to the point of bursting as the singer hit the final high note ending the song.

Tears welled in her eyes as she sat up and turned to face him. "That's amazing! Aren't we lucky?" Mary told him.

"There's no such thing as luck, babe . . ." Johnny said, giving the lead singer a thumbs up.

The singer tipped his hat to Johnny, and said, gesturing toward Mary, "You are a very lucky man, Mr. Miracle!"

Mary turned to Johnny, eyes wide at his surprise. "You arranged this?"

He smiled, nodding, and looked down. She followed his eyes and saw that he was holding something in his hand. It was a small pale blue box out of which peeked a sparkling drop of heaven.

"Will you marry me, babe?"

Mary's world expanded; she could hear every sound in all downtown Austin—the jingle of the tack on the horses, the roar of a motorcycle several blocks away, the wind blowing through the oaks in Wooldridge Square across the street. Then just as suddenly, all that sound disappeared, and all she could hear was the rhythmic thumping of her heart and Johnny's beside her, beating in sync. Then, she felt herself melting away . . .

"Of course, Johnny. Of course, I will."

Three months later in an intimate ceremony at Mary's Grandma Nellie's vineyard near Fredericksburg, Texas, Johnny and Mary became husband and wife.

And for a while, everything was grand.

As time passed, Mary didn't ignore the little weeds sprouting here and there from the pretty blossoms in her marriage. She was too smart for that. Her mistake was that she lied to herself about them; she told herself there really weren't that many and that they weren't all that bad.

There's a thin line between love and hate, so goes the cliché. What they don't tell you is this: the thin line between love and hate is self-deception. And self-deception is like suicide; we are both the perpetrator and the victim.

Mary's escape from self-deception took some time. It was a process that, she would tell you, began one weekend in August, about five years after she married Johnny.

# CHAPTER THREE

**Five years after Johnny and Mary's wedding.**
**The vineyard near Fredericksburg, Texas.**
**August 2015.**

In the Texas Hill Country between Fredericksburg and Austin lies a land of peach trees and honeybees, rolling hills, bluebonnets, dark earth, plentiful rivers, and infinite blue skies melting into burnt orange sunsets. Crabapple Creek Vineyard lay smack dab in the middle of all that bounty. Grandma Nellie had bought 500 acres of raw land in the early nineties, determined to turn it into her dream vineyard, despite the skeptics who said it couldn't be done. With tireless effort and an unwavering spirit, she had transformed the raw landscape. Acre upon acre of lush grapevines now stretched as far as the eye could see, their leaves rustling softly in the gentle breeze. It was a sight that made Mary proud of her grandmother, a testament to the power of determination and hard work.

Mary had shared much of that hard work with her grandmother. After her mother—Nellie's daughter—was killed in a car accident, Mary's father proved to be the no-account bum Nellie had always suspected, so the blessing of raising Mary had fallen to Nellie. The vineyard was the only home Mary had ever known. She lived with Johnny in the bedroom she'd grown up in, a large room with an en suite bath.

Johnny had risen much earlier to leave on a business trip. So, Mary had awoken to an empty room and gotten out of bed alone. She stumbled barefoot toward the kitchen in her tank top and boxers and as the room came into view, her groggy mind struggled to make sense of what she saw. As she took in the details, a jolt of adrenaline surged through her body; her stomach lurched with anxiety and the soles of her feet turned slick with sweat.

"Put down that knife!" she implored.

Her Grandma Nellie, already in jeans, a long-sleeved cotton shirt, and her work boots, was perched on the top cap of a metal ladder, teetering as she reached up over her head. She was inserting a medium-sized butcher knife into the light socket of one of the pendant lamps hanging from the family room's twelve-foot ceiling.

Mary could feel her heart pound in her ears as she watched her sixty-six-year-old grandmother jiggle the knife blade in the electrical socket. Memories of Nellie's past heart attacks flooded Mary's mind. Her throat constricted as she imagined the deadly consequences of 120 volts of electricity coursing through her frail body.

"Stop! You're going to kill yourself!" Mary said, carefully approaching the ladder.

"Oh, shush . . . I've almost got it," the old woman replied.

"What the hell, Grandma?" Mary answered, moving closer and positioning herself to break the woman's fall if she slipped. "You're gonna get electrocuted."

"Don't be thick, girl! I shut off the breaker at the panel," Nellie glared down at her granddaughter for a moment, then shook her head and focused on her task.

"You know, there are tools for this kind of thing," Mary scolded, arms still outstretched. "Better than a knife . . ."

Nellie twisted the knife counterclockwise slowly until the socket end of a broken bulb came loose and dropped out of the fixture into her hand. "The screwdrivers were all too thin, and pliers were too fat. This knife is just the right width to twist the socket loose. Now, hand me that bulb on the counter, will you?"

"Johnny could've changed that for you," Mary said, picking up a bulb from the kitchen island and handing it up.

Nellie scoffed, then gingerly leaned down and traded the broken socket for the bulb. "Johnny . . . That husband of yours—" Nellie bit her tongue. She tried her best not to meddle in her granddaughter's marriage, which included keeping her thoughts about Johnny Miracle to herself. Sharing her house, large though it was, with a married couple was complicated enough without adding fuel to the fire.

Right now, Nellie was trying to be extra careful. For the last couple of weeks, she'd noticed that there'd been something different in the air. Johnny was the same as always, but Mary seemed a bit more aloof when it came to him. And a bit preoccupied.

Nellie had always had suspicions about her grandson-in-law and had finally decided to act on them. She'd hired a private investigator. And just two days prior, she'd received a phone call with disheartening news confirming her suspicions. She was waiting on the written report with all the details.

For now, Nellie redirected her annoyance away from Johnny. "I'm not going to wait for anyone, much less a man, to do something I'm perfectly capable of doing myself." She twisted the bulb into its socket, then said, "There. All done. Now, here. Take this."

She leaned over to hand Mary the knife, handle first, but in the act, lost her balance. As she flailed her arms to recover, the knife fell from her hand. Mary had been reaching for it but missed it. She jumped into the air, trying to keep her feet out of the blade's flight path as it fell. The knife half-flipped and landed with a sharp *tunk* point down, nailing itself to the wood floor. Mary's feet landed about six inches to either side.

"Goddamnit, Mary!" the old woman exclaimed. "Be careful! You should be wearing shoes!"

"Me? You dropped it! And I was going to the kitchen, not to a goddamned construction site!" Mary glared up at her grandmother, who was glaring back . . . and possibly hiding a smirk?

Mary fought back a smile, then clicked her tongue. "Come on. Give me your hand, old woman, before you kill yourself." As Mary helped her grandmother down from the stepladder, she added, "Did Johnny and Pedro get out okay?" Mary asked the question to change the subject, but as the words left her mouth, her belly tightened as she recalled her 'Johnny problem.' She pushed the thought away.

"That they did, hon," her grandmother replied. "Headed to the airport at five. And to be fair, Johnny did offer to change the bulb, but I told him not to worry about it." Nellie lied to make peace. She studied her granddaughter—no makeup, sleepy-eyed, mussed hair. She reached out and gently pushed the hair out of her eyes. She looked so much like her mother, Nellie's daughter. She swallowed hard and smiled, then gently patted her cheek and asked, "You sleep well?"

"Yes, ma'am," Mary replied as she folded the ladder.

The two walked across the family room to the kitchen—it was an open design, where one room simply flowed into the other. Nellie picked out a red decaffeinated coffee capsule for the machine. Her blood pressure limited her to one 'real' cup of coffee per day. She flipped the switch on the kettle to heat water for Mary, who preferred tea.

Mary leaned the ladder against the kitchen island and took her usual seat at the counter.

"Johnny and Pedro ended up taking the van," Nellie said.

Pedro was the grounds supervisor at her vineyard, and he and Johnny were going to San Francisco to attend a seminar on new technologies in the wine industry. They were going to be gone for the weekend, and Nellie hoped Mary would open up and tell her what was wrong during Johnny's time away. If she didn't, Nellie had decided to tell Mary what she'd learned—once she had the written report, of course. Nellie planned to bring things to a head that weekend, one way or another.

"So," Nellie continued, "we've got the place all to ourselves. You given any thought to how we should spend our time? Maybe head into town and do a little shopping? We could even drive into Austin if you want. Or we could take in a movie?"

"Why don't we take a drive through the fields first and see how the shoots are doing? Then maybe we can head into town and get something special for dinner."

"It's a date." Nellie smiled.

They chatted over their drinks, which Mary finished first, putting down her cup and announcing, "I'm gonna get a shower."

While Nellie had her third cup of decaf and scanned the news on her iPad, Mary put the ladder away in the garage. She also took the opportunity to switch the breaker to the family room back on.

When she returned to the kitchen, Nellie was still seated at the island, sipping coffee and reading. Behind her grandmother, in the center of the family room, Mary noticed the knife, still planted tip-first into the floor, its blade gleaming ominously in the morning sunlight.

Mary retrieved the knife with an involuntary shudder and put it in the sink.

Shortly after, Nellie heard the distant drone of water running in the house.

Mary showering.

Nellie decided to head down to the service garage to retrieve a UTV. Utility Task Vehicles are all-terrain vehicles perfect for getting around on the vineyard—kind of like a golf cart on steroids. The ones Nellie had (she owned three) could each seat six people.

As she rose, she heard the *ping* of an email alert on her iPad. Scanning the 'From' and 'Subject' lines, she saw it was the *details to follow* email that she'd been expecting with some trepidation. She stood at the island, opened the email, and then the report. Her belly sank as she read the investigator's observations and conclusions. She flipped through the attached photos, and a wave of emotion washed over her, tears welling in her eyes. She could feel a fiery rage growing in her belly, fueling her determination to act. The images before her were a stark reminder of the cruelty and injustice in the world, and Nellie knew that she could not stand idly by.

"Goddamned sonofabitch Johnny!" Nellie hissed.

# CHAPTER FOUR

Mary finished her shower while Johnny sat in an airplane flying to California. She dressed in work clothes and roper boots, and put her hair up in a ponytail and threaded it through a ball cap. As she left her bedroom, she called out, "Grandma?"

Hearing no reply, she decided—per usual—to meet Nellie at the service garage. She left the house through the front door; as she crossed the porch, she heard the hum of a vehicle approaching, which she assumed was Nellie on one of the UTVs. As she listened, however, rather than coming from the service garage to the left, the sound seemed to be coming toward her from the main drive, a sound deeper than a UTV. This was a large vehicle.

Mary followed the sound and spotted a white SUV driving toward her. She squinted and crossed her arms defensively across her chest when she saw the blue and red light bar on the vehicle's roof, indicating it was some sort of law enforcement.

As the SUV pulled up, its tires crunching in the gravel and kicking up a light cloud of dust, Mary saw it was a Gillespie County Sheriff's Department vehicle.

A knot formed in the pit of her stomach. Mary swallowed hard, her mouth suddenly dry.

The deputy parked on the circular driveway in front of the house, stepped out of the vehicle, and ambled toward the porch, stopping about ten feet from the first step. He wore a standard beige uniform shirt, olive khaki pants, and black boots, to which he'd added a brown cowboy hat and a pair of aviator sunglasses. Mary noticed that he had a slight limp.

"Mornin', ma'am." He tipped his hat.

"Mornin'," Mary replied. "Can I help you, Deputy . . ."

The officer stood arms akimbo with thumbs stuck in his gun belt, hips thrust slightly forward. He studied the front of the house—and Mary—while biting the side of his lower lip. He took a few moments before replying, "Gripke," finishing her sentence. "Walter Gripke, ma'am."

"You're new around here?"

"That I am. Retired from the FBI up in Dallas. Joined the department here a few months ago."

"So, retired from the feds and working for the county now. Double-dippin'. Must be nice." The words were spoken matter-of-factly. "How can I help you on this glorious Saturday morning?" Mary asked without enthusiasm.

"Well, you see, ma'am, they've assigned me to cold cases. It's sort of my thing. Was, anyway, at the Bureau. I'm looking into a disappearance. You probably know what I'm talking about." He paused.

Mary didn't react. She waited.

"You're Mary Miracle, right?"

Mary nodded once, slowly, but said nothing.

"Well, Mrs. Miracle. I'm just chasing down some loose ends," he said. Then after a pause, he added, "You remember Zeke Fulton . . ." It was as much a question as a statement.

"I was a kid when that happened, Deputy. It's been years—"

"Thirteen," Gripke volunteered, interrupting.

Mary pursed her lips and nodded. "A lot of water under the bridge since . . ."

"You'd have been young back then, it's true."

"Sixteen years young, sir. It's been a minute, all right." Deciding to politely shorten the discussion, Mary started down the steps towards the deputy. "I haven't thought about all that in years. But like you said, I was just a kid back then. I heard about him, Zeke, disappearing, but I didn't know him. No more than just a name. And I don't know anything about it other than what I've heard around town, in the news, that sort of thing. I wish I could help you more." She shrugged. "Now, I'm afraid I've got work to do." She walked past him towards the service garage. "But you have a nice day, sir."

"I just have a couple of questions, ma'am. I'll only take a minute." The deputy turned as she passed him, then said a bit more loudly, directing himself at her back, "If you'd oblige me, I was hoping to talk to your grandmother, Nellie."

Mary stopped and turned. The pleasant smile she'd been feigning for the deputy before had hardened.

Gripke, unsure how to react, half-smiled, which, for some reason, pissed Mary off even more.

She took a step back towards him. "Do you have a warrant, Deputy Gretsky?"

"It's Gripke, ma'am. And no ma'am, I do not," he said, adjusting his sunglasses with his index finger. "I'm not here to search for anything. I just wanted—"

"And yet, you're on our property. Uninvited. And you're wanting to bother a sick old woman about police business . . . on a Saturday morning? Again, uninvited." She paused while taking another step closer to the deputy and staring at the reflection of her face in his sunglasses. "Am I being arrested or detained?"

"No, ma'am. I just . . ."

"Then please leave; I have work to do. If you have loose ends you wanna chase, you call ahead and make an appointment."

Mary turned and stomped off toward the service garage, looking for signs of Nellie and listening for the UTV. Nothing.

"I just need a few minutes, ma'am."

"Then call," Mary said, turning and holding her hand to the side of her head, pinky and thumb extended to mimic a telephone, but continuing to walk backward, "and make an appointment."

"Could you at least tell me if your grandmother is around?"

Mary stopped. "No! I am not going to have you bothering her over that . . . that ancient history."

"You know, ma'am," Gripke shook his head, "I get that you don't wanna be dealing with law enforcement. No one does. But most folks usually at least *pretend* to be cooperative. I'm just tryin' to do my job here. Tryin' to solve a murder, ma'am."

Mary considered correcting him by saying, *disappearance, not murder.*

"I'm not much for pretending," she said instead.

"Can I at least give you my card? In case your grandmother is of a different mind?" he asked.

Mary turned her back to him and continued walking. "You can leave it on the porch if you want," she replied, back-waving and adding, "Thank you for your service, Deputy. You have a blessed day!"

# CHAPTER FIVE

Mary entered the service garage, a large, corrugated metal building connected to the vineyard offices. Nellie was sitting in a UTV in the shadows near the back of the building; she had a clear view of the front steps and the SUV that Deputy Gripke was climbing back into.

"You heard?" Mary asked.

Nellie nodded. "I'm old, not deaf . . . not yet, anyway."

Mary climbed in next to her grandmother. The two sat quietly, waiting for the deputy to drive away. Once he was gone, Mary spoke.

"What should we do?"

"Nothing *to* do, Mare. That chapter closed ages ago. Probably just routine paperwork. Thirteen years. You know . . . dust off the file, ask a few questions, check a few boxes, and put it back on the shelf. It's how these government types justify their pay. That's all." She smiled at Mary reassuringly.

Nellie started up the vehicle and drove off toward the east hundred, where they'd agreed they would check on the work done on the trellises days before. But as she drove, the vines were the last thing on her mind. Nellie was on autopilot. She was thinking . . .

*Zeke Fulton! Dagnabit!*

Although she wore her 'happy and at peace face' for Mary's sake, her mind was racing. She could feel her scalp sweating under the large floppy hat she'd put on to protect her from the sun.

*Who's this Gripke sonofabitch?*

*When did he get hired?*

*Is this just a routine follow-up?*

*Or has some kind of evidence popped up?*

Big sins die slow deaths.

They drove along on the dirt road that ran between trellises and had just about reached the easternmost block of the vineyard when Nellie's thoughts were brought back to the here and now. Although she cringed a bit at first, she quickly saw the situation for what it was—a welcome distraction for her *and* Mary. She pointed ahead and shouted to her granddaughter over the engine roar, "Whoa! Check that guy out."

Mary had been riding along beside Nellie, also quiet, pensive. She perked up, replying, "Yep. I see him." Up the trail a ways, a good-sized snake which had been crossing onto their path hesitated, perhaps sensing danger, and turned its head towards the oncoming vehicle.

Nellie took her foot off the accelerator, rolling the vehicle to a stop and killing the engine. They sat quietly for a moment, observing.

Nellie sighed. "Do you mind?" The old woman looked at Mary, scrunching her nose sheepishly. "I just don't got it in me today."

"Not a problem," Mary replied, nodding and patting her grandmother's arm. Hunting was something that Mary had done a lot of, growing up in the Texas Hill Country. Mostly dove, quail, and deer, although she'd also shot the occasional javelina. She knew her way around firearms and bow hunting. Killing snakes was an afterthought.

Mary climbed out and removed a Winchester twelve-gauge short-barrel shotgun from the hood rack. She loaded four rounds of birdshot, then pumped one into the chamber while looking back up at her target.

About thirty-five feet up the road, the rumbling of the UTV had been picked up by the rattlesnake crossing the four-wheeler's intended path. It had stopped and was now coiled up defensively near the left side of the road. Mary approached slowly, looking around to make sure it was alone. The snake looked to be about four feet long—a decent-sized adult. Typically, a rattlesnake strike can reach a distance of about two-thirds its body length—in this case, about two-and-a-half feet.

"Don't get too close, Mare."

Mary nodded and replied as she walked towards the animal, "I won't," keeping her eyes on the snake.

"Diamondback?" Nellie asked.

"Naw . . . I'm pretty sure it's a timber rattler."

Mary stopped about fifteen feet away just to be on the safe side. She raised the shotgun and took careful aim. The viper's triangular head was perched about eight inches above the ground. Its thick, scaly body was tightly coiled and ready to strike; its yellow eyes—with vertically slit cat-like pupils—stared at Mary while its thin, black forked tongue sampled the air, searching . . . no doubt smelling her nearby.

As Mary looked down the barrel at the snake, she felt a mixture of revulsion and primal fear. The hair on her arms stood on end. The primitive part of her brain was firing adrenaline, and her pulse was racing. She lined him up in her sights. She took a deep breath, inhaling for four counts, holding it for four, and exhaling for four more—an exercise to control her heart rate. Intellectually, Mary knew that, although the animal was deadly, she was well out of striking distance. But deep inside her, something irrational, instinctive, didn't like the idea of standing at even a safe distance from death.

She prepared to shoot, and, for one brief moment, she thought of her husband. She was puzzled by the thought and pushed it away. Then she gently hugged the shotgun butt into her shoulder, became one with her tool, exhaled, and slowly squeezed the trigger until the end of the barrel erupted with a deafening *boom*. For an instant, Mary lost sight of the snake as the birdshot kicked up dust around it, and the animal jerked violently into the air then flopped back down.

"Nice shot," Nellie hollered. "Took his head clean off!"

The snake's headless body writhed futilely, nerves and muscles still firing in confusion, not realizing that the brain that ran things was lying several feet away. Mary took a cautious step forward, looking more closely. Her shot had obliterated most of the snake's head and cut off a portion of the tail end.

The rapid twisting of what remained of the snake's long body, combined with the smell of gunpowder, reminded her of burning hair.

To be safe, she got a small folding shovel from the four-wheeler, dug a hole by the roadside, and scooped the remains of the snake into it, burying it all. A dead snake's head is still highly venomous.

Killing rattlesnakes on sight at the vineyard was a given. Grandma Nellie had repeatedly told Mary how she'd learned the lesson the hard way.

* * *

The first time Nellie had seen a rattler on her land, it was in clear view, minding its own business, sunning itself on a rock just outside the white picket fence that separated the main house from the rest of the vineyard property. At the time, she had just moved to Texas and had owned the land for less than a month. Nellie would admit that she was still a bit of a tree hugger back then, very *pro-*

*everything.*

She'd admired the small, fat, ugly rattler from a distance and let it be. *Live and let live*, she'd thought.

About a week later, the same snake followed the sun around the house and decided to warm itself near the trash cans, still outside the white picket fence. Unfortunately, Nellie had taken out the trash without noticing the little creature. She'd dumped two bags in the trash can and closed the plastic lid with a loud *thwack*. The vibrations from that must have startled the snake; just after closing the trash can, Nellie heard that signature rattling sound that no one wants to hear—too, too close.

She found herself standing in shorts and flip-flops within three feet of the same snake. For what felt like half an hour, but was probably only five minutes, she had stood perfectly still, regretting she hadn't killed the thing the week before. Finally, the reptile had decided there was no threat and slowly uncoiled, moving away from her.

Once the snake was out of striking distance, Nellie ran back to the house. Returning in cowboy boots and armed with a long-handled shovel, she'd beaten and sliced the creature until it was dead. This encounter had taught her a valuable lesson about snakes and the importance of appropriate footwear in Texas. From then on, Nellie always carried a Colt .45 loaded with snake shot on her hip whenever she left the house, just in case a rattler surprised her.

* * *

Mary emptied the remaining shells from the shotgun and racked it on the hood of the UTV. She took no joy in killing the snake; it was a question of survival. As she climbed back into the four-wheeler, her grandmother said the same thing she said every time they killed a snake. "I hate having to do it, Mare. You know, killing rattlers. But—"

"I know, Grandma," Mary interrupted, then finished her sentence for her. "The *snake* you don't kill today may kill *you* tomorrow."

# CHAPTER SIX

That afternoon, the two women went into town to buy something special for dinner. It being August and plenty hot, they decided to buy the fixings to make a wedge salad with blue cheese dressing and crumbled fried pork belly.

While in the produce section, Mary spotted a new offering. "Check these out," she said. In her hands was a tin of dried Medjool dates from Israel. "Sleigh bells ring, are ya listenin'?" Mary sang.

"Are you thinking snowballs?" Nellie's face lit up.

Mary nodded, grinning from ear to ear.

Every Christmas, Nellie made huge batches of snowball cookies for sharing with clients, friends, and neighbors. It was a family recipe, handed down from Nellie's mother, Laura. The process began with simmering a decadent mixture of chopped dates, pecans, sugar, and butter in her cast iron skillet until it was just the right consistency. After it cooled enough to handle, she mixed in a secret ingredient that added fluff and crispiness, rolled the dough into little 1-inch balls, and then dunked them in powdered sugar. For Mary, this holiday treat struck the perfect note between rich and decadent—and it had a history. Snowball cookies reminded her of all the Christmases she and Grandma Nellie had spent baking them together and then sharing them with others.

As Mary held the tin, Vanna White style, Nellie saw a sparkle in her granddaughter's eyes that had been missing as of late.

"That's a great idea, Mare! What fun!"

When they returned home, they worked in the kitchen. Repeating the process they'd shared over so many past Christmases put them in a festive mood. Mary played holiday music to accompany them as they rolled snowballs in the summertime; it was silly . . . but fun. And for the first time in a while, Nellie saw that Mary seemed happy—her usual self.

"How about *that*," Mary said. "Christmas in August." She popped a freshly rolled snowball, thick with powdered sugar, into her mouth, letting the sugary dryness blend with the buttery warm dates and pecans as she savored not just the magical flavor, but the memories that came with it.

Nellie smiled. Mary was loosening up. "How about adding a glass of rosé to that *that*?" Nellie suggested, wanting to maintain the happy momentum.

"Well," Mary looked at her phone. "It's almost five o'clock. Why not? Any preference?"

As Mary rinsed her hands and went to the wine fridge, Nellie said, "I'm feeling nostalgic. Life is grand, isn't it? Why don't you open a Clos Mireille?"

Mary cocked an eyebrow. "Sounds great to me." The wine was a spunky, slightly citrusy rosé and one of Mary's favorites. When Mary graduated from high school, she and Nellie had toured southern France and northern Italy, visiting the Domaines Ott winery in Provence which produced the wine. They'd visited many wineries so that Nellie could expense the trip. The wine brought back memories—including of the flat tire they'd changed together two kilometers before reaching the winery. They'd arrived for their wine tour covered in tire soot, sweat, and dirt. What a sight they'd been! Mary loved not just the wine, but the memories it evoked.

Nellie picked up her glass using a napkin, as her hands were greasy with butter from rolling cookies. Her hands were aged but nimble—un-arthritic and elegant—accented only by a thin white gold band on her left ring finger, the hand with which she was holding her wineglass.

Despite her age, Mary had always thought of her grandmother as a spry woman. In the last couple of years, however, she'd noticed that Nellie was moving a little slower and had become slightly more hunched and fragile. Nellie's eyes, once a bright blue, had faded to the color of steel and were framed by wrinkles chiseled by decades of laughter, wonder, and anger. Yet, the lines around Nellie's mouth testified to her general tendency toward smiling rather than frowning. Mary had always thought that Nellie looked like Helen Mirren.

Nellie grinned widely at Mary, her eyes lively. She gave Mary one of her trademark half-winks with her left eye; almost barely perceptible, mischievous, joyful.

"To *what* shall we toast?" Mary asked playfully, knowing how Nellie would respond.

"To motivated women!" Nellie said, raising her glass up and towards Mary's. The phrase was shorthand for Nellie's favorite adage: *No man, no matter how smart or strong, can compete with a motivated woman.*

Mary smiled and clinked her glass against her grandmother's. "To motivated women!"

"Speaking of, " Nellie continued, putting her glass down and returning to rolling cookies. "You getting everything set for law school?"

A little cloud passed across Mary's eyes. She had always dreamed of becoming a lawyer. She'd studied pre-law in college, read law novels, and watched law shows on TV. She could name all the Justices on the Supreme Court and recite their voting record. Everything law-related fascinated her.

Her dream had come true, and two months after marrying Johnny she'd started law school at UT Austin. She'd finished her first semester strong but had surprised—shocked—Nellie with the news that she'd decided to take a 'short' leave of absence. She'd refused to say why, but Nellie had her suspicions.

One year turned into two, turned into three, and so on . . . And, after much nagging by Nellie, Mary had finally gotten approval to resume classes the coming January, just five months away. But lately, Nellie had noticed some hesitation in her granddaughter about the decision.

Mary shrugged and drank from her wineglass again before attacking the remaining cookie mix. "Law school? I don't know, Grandma. There's still so much that needs to be done around here. I may just wait. I mean . . . I can go back anytime."

Nellie stopped mid-roll. "Goddamnit, Mary! Enough is enough. No more excuses! If I have to sell this place to get you to go to law school, I will! If you're worried about the
money—"

"It's not that, Grandma. It's just that . . . I mean . . . the vineyard's a part of it, sure . . . but we're still kind of newlyweds. I dunno. It feels like adding law school to the mix may just be too much."

"Newlyweds? Five-year newlyweds?" Nellie shook her head. Just as she suspected: *Johnny getting in the way again. Maybe this was it . . . the thing that had been bugging Mary?*

"Mary, you can't put your life on hold because of me, or the vineyard . . . or *anyone else*," Nellie spoke carefully. Her granddaughter was as stubborn as she was principled, and if she got on the defensive, there'd be no changing her mind. Maybe now was the right moment to tell her what she'd learned about Johnny.

Mary was silent, excessively focused on the cookie she was rolling.

"Look, honey," Nellie continued. "This place, I know you grew up here, and it's your home. But this whole project, this vineyard, it's *my* dream. And I have to take the good and the bad of it *on my own*. If I can't make it work, I shouldn't be doing it. But, if you give up *your* dream to help keep mine alive, you'll kill both of them. I don't want *this,*" Nellie gestured at the property all around them with buttery hands, "if it keeps you from being happy. And, honestly, I just don't see you driving around here fixing trellises and pruning and suckering when you're in your sixties. I know you do it *now*, and I appreciate all of your help; *I really do*. But you have to do *you*, Mary. You can't let me . . . or anyone . . . stand in the way of that."

Mary knitted her brows and nodded, dropping a rolled cookie into the powdered sugar bowl. After rolling several more, she looked up at her grandmother. "It's not just the vineyard."

"I knew it," Nellie nodded. "This is all about—"

Mary's phone rang.

*Shitty timing*, thought Nellie, pursing her lips.

Mary smiled at her grandmother, relieved to have an excuse to step away from the conversation. She wiped her hands and looked at the screen of her phone as it lay on the counter.

"Let me take this," Mary said. "It's Johnny."

# CHAPTER SEVEN

Mary grabbed the phone and her wineglass, stepping away from the kitchen island and into the study for a little privacy. She smiled as she answered; she'd read somewhere that your voice when speaking over the phone was affected by your facial expression. She didn't want Johnny thinking anything was wrong.

*After all. Nothing is wrong . . . really . . .*

She could hear a cacophony of music, hawkers, and the low roar of a crowd in the background.

*He's calling from the convention floor.*

"Everything's good here, babe. The conference is fine. You know . . . only about twenty-five percent of it's worth seeing."

"Yeah, well, that's how those things are," she replied.

"So, listen, I was thinking . . . hey, is that Christmas music in the background?"

Mary smiled for real. "Yeah. Just doing some baking and reminiscing."

Johnny chuckled. "Oh. Okay. Chick stuff. Got it. Good for you two. So, listen . . . I may stay on an extra day. Drive up the coast. There's a company here that's making drones for vineyards. Instead of manually surveying everything, you can do it remotely. Huge timesaver. Can you imagine? So, I'm gonna go up and check out a demo Monday, fly back Tuesday instead."

"Oh. Okay . . ." she replied. "And Pedro?"

"Don't need both of us for that. He'll fly back Monday, as planned," Johnny replied.

Mary's tummy fell, as did her smile. "You really think the demo's worth the extra day?"

"Hey, I'm already all the way out here, babe. Might as well take advantage, you know? Unless you think it's a waste of time?"

"No. No. That's what you're there for." Even as she said the words, she wished she hadn't. "If it seems useful, take a look." She raised her voice slightly, trying to feign enthusiasm.

"Perfect. Then I'll touch base with you tomorrow and plan on a Tuesday flight," he replied. "Ooh. Yeah . . . be right there," he said to someone nearby. "They're starting a demonstration of this new leaf scanner thing. I gotta run. Love you!"

"Okay, Johnny—"

The line went dead.

Mary looked for a moment at her phone screen, confirming that the call had ended. She felt hollow inside. This was not the first time Johnny had extended a business trip for an extra day or two. Mary wasn't dumb; she just didn't want to believe that anything was going on. Leaning her forearms against one of the leather chairs facing the fireplace, she fought back tears.

Nellie had never liked Johnny; she'd thought her granddaughter's engagement was too fast and too short. In the end, when Mary made it clear that he was 'the one' for her, Nellie reluctantly accepted him. As a result, Mary was always careful what she told Nellie about Johnny and about their marriage. She really wanted to go back to law school. She felt like the timing was finally right. But a complication had arisen. Two weeks earlier, Mary had learned that Johnny's email address was on a hacked list from a website called sallymadison.com—a dating site for married people.

Cheaters.

Mary was conflicted. She knew that generally, where there's smoke, there's fire. But she also wanted to give her husband the benefit of the doubt. Maybe it was some kind of joke? Or there was some other explanation.

She'd spoken with a friend who she thought could help. Her friend was recently divorced. Mary had always considered her street-smart. And sure enough, she'd suggested a clever approach.

"Just give me a week or two, Mary. Let me reach out to him, flirt a little, and we'll see how he responds."

Now, Mary was anxiously waiting to hear if her husband was stupid—and horny—enough to come on to one of her friends. Meanwhile, Mary had begun to wonder whether she'd been too infatuated to see Johnny for what he was all along.

*God, could I have been so completely wrong?*

Although it was a bit dim in the study, with only dull afternoon light coming in through the windows, Mary knew the space so well she could see it all.

The room had always been a special place where Grandma Nellie had told Mary stories about her life and her family. Their family. So many stories. She felt safe here. It was a cozy room. The wooden shelves were filled with books and family photos, including pictures of Mary, Nellie, and Johnny, as well as one of her wedding photos. Two large, comfy leather chairs faced the fireplace which was made of black marble and had a large ornate mantle. Above the fireplace hung a small painting. A family heirloom. A masterpiece by Claude Monet.

Like all great art, the Monet had a story behind it . . . a story her grandmother had told her many times right here in this study. It was a story that always inspired Mary.

Mary sipped from her wineglass and admired the Monet. She could see its appeal as a work of art. Still, it was *so much* more; it had become a part of her childhood, life, and family.

Her grandmother was right: you have to do *you*. Nellie had always done what had to be done . . . get her Monet back . . . follow her dream and build her vineyard. Mary drew strength from those stories, inspiration.

She inhaled deeply. She was going to take back control of her life. Whether Johnny was on board or not. She knew she had it in her. Everyone does. *Every woman*, especially. Nellie lived by that creed, and it was Mary's turn to do the same.

She raised her glass to the Monet and whispered, "To motivated women."

* * *

While Mary took Johnny's call, Nellie took the opportunity to make a phone call of her own.

Pedro Gomez picked up on the second ring. "Nellie," he answered.

"Hey, Pedro. How's our boy behavin'?" Nellie asked.

"All business, so far. Professional. He's got a tchotchke bag full of brochures and business cards. I'm watching him right now, at a booth, some kind of mapping tech from the looks of it. But, like I told you, if he does anything . . . untoward, I'm on it. And I *will* call you," Pedro said a bit stiffly.

"Don't get your feathers all ruffled, Pedrito," Nellie said, using his nickname. "I'm not calling to check on you. Something else came up."

"Oh?" he replied, his voice softer, curious.

"A deputy came by today . . . name of Gripke. Asking 'bout Zeke. Said he's working cold cases . . ."

Pedro sighed. "Shit . . ."

"Amen, *hermanito*."

"And . . . ?"

"And nothin' . . . yet. Mary ran him off. I didn't even talk to him. I called 'Tweedle Dumber'," this was Nellie's nickname for the sheriff, "and told him, in the future, to make an appointment."

"For what that's worth . . ." Pedro replied.

"Yeah, I know. You heard of this guy? G-R-I-P-K-E." Nellie spelled the name reading from the card the deputy had left on the porch.

"Nah. But I know Scholz retired. I heard they were looking for a replacement. But that was a while ago . . . months." Pedro paused. "Shee-yit . . ."

"Shit is right. Well, we can chat more when you get back." Nellie wrapped up. "But, for now, keep your head down . . ."

"Yep," Pedro replied, "and your powder dry."

# CHAPTER EIGHT

Nellie was back to rolling cookies when Mary returned to the kitchen.

"I'm going back to law school," Mary announced.

"Oh, honey!" Nellie hugged her granddaughter, butter-covered hands in the air. "That's wonderful!" She cocked her head slightly as she pulled away.

"What's the official start date?"

"January 8." Mary then launched into a monologue about everything she had to do to prepare, books to be bought, and what her new schedule would be like.

Nellie listened, but also wondered.

*What just happened on the phone?*

*Why the sudden change?*

Nellie understood that, right now, what mattered was building on the momentum. Making sure the decision stuck. There'd be time later to discover *why* Mary had finally decided to take the plunge. And telling Mary what she'd learned about Johnny could wait as well.

*Right now would be terrible timing. But I can't wait too long . . .*

Nellie could envision her granddaughter finally in law school and Johnny packing his bags.

When they finished the cookies, while Mary set the table for two, Nellie snuck off to her room. When she returned, she held a small black velvet pouch.

Mary half-smiled as her grandmother approached her, beaming. "Okaaay." Mary eyed the pouch with curiosity and asked, "What's that, Grandma?"

"I know you don't remember your grandad too well, just from photos. But he loved you so much. And I know," the old woman's eyes watered, "I know he'd be so proud of the woman you've become."

Mary's eyes misted.

"When you were just learning to talk, I've told you how he used to call you 'Little Miss No.' For a while there, everything was 'no' with you. It was so adorable, but it also showed a bit of your personality. You're bullheaded—like me, I know." She laughed. They both did. "But your grandpa loved that about me. And he always joked that you'd make a great lawyer someday.

"So, I saved this for you. Something of his for when the time was right." Nellie winked. "And now that you've finally decided to go to back to law school, I think it's time."

As Mary opened the pouch, Nellie added, "I sent it in and had it cleaned and serviced. Good as new."

"Oh! Thank you, Grandma!" Mary put on her grandfather's Hamilton wristwatch. "You even set the time!"

"Like I said, *the time is right*!" Nellie chuckled. Mary laughed while faux-grimacing at all the puns.

"Now come on. This calls for champagne!" Nellie added. She opened a bottle of Pol Roger, and she and Mary toasted to law school and the soon-to-be new lawyer. Mary could barely contain her excitement, gushing about what legal specialty she might pursue.

Through her smile and proud eyes, Nellie studied her granddaughter. Just under half Nellie's age, Mary, at twenty-nine, looked nothing like her. Her eyes were dark, almost black, framed by a mane of flowing chestnut hair. Her face still gave off just the faintest glow of youthful altruism that was fading into the shadow of adult skepticism. But it was a healthy skepticism, one through which Mary's eyes and smile still communicated joy and somehow offered hope. Right now, she was beaming. This was clearly the right choice for her.

As she basked in Mary's happiness, a foreboding pulled at Nellie's heart. She could feel her iPad, the email she'd received from the private investigator, tugging at her from across the room, demanding to be revealed.

But Nellie was a wise woman.

*There is a time for everything.*

And the time for that would come soon.

## Great-Grandma Laura's Snowball Cookies

2 eggs
1 cup granulated sugar
1 teaspoon vanilla
3 cups Rice Krispies
1 stick butter
1 ½ cups chopped dates
1 cup pecans
powdered sugar

Combine eggs, melted butter, sugar, chopped dates. Cook in heavy skillet (about 15 min) until mixture rolls from sides of skillet. Mix in pecans and vanilla. Mix in Rice Krispies.

Let cool. Roll into small balls. Roll in powdered sugar. Serve with a smile and love in your heart.

# CHAPTER NINE

Walter Gripke was a messy child, pudgy, one of those kids who, no matter how his mother dressed him, always looked sloppy—shirt tails half-tucked, pants drooping, one shoelace untied. While he wasn't much to look at as a kid, Walter was smart. But growing up in a West Texas town with a population of two hundred fourteen, *smart* didn't get you too far. Walter had figured that out pretty quickly.

Gripke enlisted in the Navy at eighteen because, based on his research, they served the best food of all the military branches. He pursued a career in the Naval military police partly because he was naturally curious, though primarily because he liked the name of the job: master-at-arms. The role suited him well.

After twenty years in the Navy, he retired to take a job at the FBI, where he specialized in cold cases. As he approached his second twenty-year mark, this one with the Bureau, he answered an ad for a part-time deputy position in Fredericksburg, Texas. And so it was that at age 59, Walter Gripke found himself collecting retirement from both the Navy and the FBI while earning a salary from the county. Mary Miracle was only partly right; Gripke was actually *triple*-dipping.

During his time in the military and at the Bureau, Gripke had developed some eccentricities. He didn't look anywhere near his fifty-nine years. He exercised, not intensely, but daily—always some weights and a three-mile run. He only ate one meal a day and, even then, only on odd-numbered days of the month. In other words, he generally ate a full meal once every forty-eight hours. This meant he was often cranky.

"You sure you don't want one?" Sheriff Strauss asked. He was standing just inside Gripke's 'office' door, nibbling on the remaining half of a stiff glazed donut. His left arm rested horizontally on his ample gut; his right elbow rested on top of that, such that his right arm formed a perfect vertical line from his belly to his mouth, ending with the shrinking donut. The sheriff's eyes bounced between Gripke, seated at one of three desks in the back office, and the donut.

"That shit'll kill you," Gripke replied without looking up.

Through a sugary mouthful, Strauss replied, "Gotta die of somethun'." Then, after swallowing, "What're you workin' on, bud? Your shift ended an hour ago."

"Forms," Gripke looked up and sat back from his computer. His desk was small but neat, with folders stacked in perfect alignment.

"Fulton?" Strauss asked, cleaning his teeth with his tongue as he picked up the only open file on Gripke's desk with his free hand, labeled: "Zeke Fulton—missing person, pd." The "pd" was handwritten in blue ink, a shorthand note that Gripke had been told stood for "presumed dead."

Gripke grunted an affirmative, "Hmmm."

Strauss stood there, silently chewing and licking his teeth, until Gripke realized he was waiting for a slightly more detailed response.

"Went through the evidence locker. Sending some things off for DNA testing."

"Smart. Good thinking," the sheriff nodded. "You went out to Crabapple this mornin'?"

Gripke's only reply was a raised eyebrow.

"Got a call from Nellie," the sheriff said as if he were reporting on the weather. "Civil. Just asked . . . next time we pay a *surprise* visit . . . that we call first." The sheriff smiled at the obvious contradiction.

"She does a lot for folks 'round here. Well-liked. And *involved*." In his months at the department, Gripke had learned that "involved" was the sheriff's code word for folks who donated to political campaigns. In Texas, sheriffs are elected, and Strauss didn't like pissing off donors if he could help it. Apparently, Nellie was a campaign contributor.

"Didn't even see *her*," Gripke said. "Spoke to the granddaughter. Feisty," Not apologizing; just clarifying.

"Oh yeah. Mary's a piece of work. A lot like her grandmother." Strauss spoke absent-mindedly, flipping through the papers in the file, then closing and letting the folder fall with a *plop* on the desktop. He licked his fingers as he turned and strolled toward the doorway. Gripke shook the folder's contents straight, placing it squarely atop the other folders.

The sheriff turned at the doorway. "You do what you gotta do. If you ruffle feathers, ruffle feathers. Just keep it 100% by the book." Then the sheriff made his signature goodbye move, snapping the fingers on both hands together in a move reminiscent of the Three Stooges and ending with both hands in the form of guns pointing at Gripke. "Got it?"

Gripke chuckled. "Got it."

As the sheriff turned to go, Gripke added, "Oh. One thing."

Strauss turned.

"I'm meeting Al Scholz tomorrow to get his take on the case. Any advice?"

The sheriff hooked his thumbs into his belt and rocked back and forth, thinking, his tongue forming a bulge in his left cheek. "Good cop, Scholz. Thorough. But not good at the paperwork. Kept too much in his head. He always claimed he was just lazy, but I think there's some dyslexia or something goin' on there. He'll be able to fill in some blanks." The sheriff gestured toward the folders with his head. "Not a lot to go on there. But, hey," he grinned, "that's why you get paid the big bucks . . ."

# CHAPTER TEN

The floorboards creaked under Gripke's boots as he walked into the Mean-Eyed Cat. As the door clattered shut behind him, the sunlight that had followed him inside faded, then fled through the shrinking doorway. He removed his aviator sunglasses, pausing for a second to let his eyes adjust to the gloomy, dark bar, a bar that was larger inside than it appeared to be from the outside.

It was four o'clock in the afternoon, and a handful of patrons were scattered throughout the dive; a few were at the bar, hunched prayerfully over half-amber rocks glasses. Ghostly heads seemed to hover along the walls, which, as his eyes adjusted, Gripke realized were patrons seated in booths. It was relatively quiet. The only conversation seemed to come from the bartender's murmurs to a couple of customers seated at the bar—a small group therapy session. The place smelled of stale cigarettes and greasy food. The distant sound of billiard balls clacking punctuated the bluesy country music playing faintly overhead.

All in all, a very dreary happy hour.

Gripke strode through the bar, the soles of his boots sticking slightly to the dirty floor as he walked, making himself seen until an arm went up, which he followed into a booth, taking a seat across the table.

"What'll ya have?" Al Scholz asked.

"Beer's good," Gripke replied.

Scholz raised a gnarled hand, poking from beneath the cuff of a starched white western shirt (pearl snaps and all), and turned his head towards the bar, placing the order when the bartender came over.

"Thanks for meeting with me," Gripke began.

Scholz nodded. "How're you settlin' in?"

Gripke had been in his new role for almost nine months, but in small-town Texas, time passed at a different speed. He might as well have driven into town yesterday.

"Good. Good people. Hot though. Damned hot."

"July and August are the worst. Real scorchers. Should start to cool down here in a bit."

A hand materialized, thunking a sweaty bottle of Pearl beer on the table in front of Gripke, then disappeared. He took a moment to look around now that his eyes were beginning to see normally again. Scholz tracked his line of sight.

The Mean-Eyed Cat was an L-shaped space, with the bar running along one side of the long leg of the L, and booths on the other. The short end of the L contained a few high tops, a pool table, a dart board, and access to toilets.

"Ain't changed much all these years," Scholz said, "since Fulton disappeared. Menu's even the same. They don't serve the bloomin' onion no more . . . still on the menu, though." Scholz reached out, tipping the greasy acrylic displayette toward him, and briefly studied the menu, confirming.

"I came in here before, once," said Gripke. "Just to check it out."

Scholz nodded approvingly. "Gotta get into the space. Try to visualize how things went down. See what they saw. Feel what they felt." He continued as though it were in the same line of thought. "You were a fed."

Gripke took a sip from his beer and nodded, studying Scholz.

Cold case work was tricky, and not just because the crimes were old, the evidence stale, and the witness's memories were fading.

Every cold case is someone's failure. And while every failure has many illegitimate parents, usually, one person gets stuck with the kid. Scholz was this ugly baby's mother. And mommas can be very temperamental about their babies, especially the ugly ones.

"Yeah, well, we do the best we can here," Scholz took a sip. Gripke could smell the tequila from across the table.

"This is a real tough one. Fulton just kind of disappeared . . ." Gripke let the phrase die off. An open-ended prompt.

Scholz took his cue. "Ezekiel Fulton. Twenty-three years young. Left here a little after midnight, Saturday, May 4, 2002.

"Sam," Scholz nodded towards the bartender, "remembers what time Zeke left 'cause he had started cleaning up a little earlier than usual that night, 'round midnight. Zeke had been stewin' at the end of the bar for an hour or so."

"After the fight," Gripke said.

Scholz shrugged. "Not much of a fight, for Texas. Coupla' punches. Nothing broken . . . persons or property."

"You have any hunch as to what started the fight? Something Fulton said? Or Gomez? Nothing specific in the file." Gripke tried to make the statement matter-of-factly, not as a criticism of Scholz's police work. "What do you think?"

"Not much in the file 'cause nobody had much to say. Nobody saw nothin'. Who started it? Why? Nothin'. But my gut?" Scholz paused, eyes narrowing, a slight smile showing. Gripke sensed that he'd struck the right note. People were always eager to give you their insights. It was simple flattery, but it usually worked.

"Reaction formation," Scholz let the words hang in the air.

Gripke wasn't sure if the old cop was testing him or just watching for signs indicating that he was impressed, that maybe he had underestimated Scholz's level of sophistication. He played along. "Wow. There's a blast from the past . . . back to my psych training at the Bureau. As I recall," he paused, looking up and squinting, making a show of attempting to remember, "that's acting out in one way . . . that's the exact opposite of what you're feeling?" He had a sense of where Scholz might be going and added, "The example they gave us of reaction formation was when a boy bullies a girl on the playground because he likes her. But how do you think that applies here?"

"Well, that'd be sort of institutional knowledge. An inside tip. But, hey, that's why we're talkin', right?" Scholz signaled the barkeep for another tequila, then continued. "You won't find it written up anywhere, but Pedro Gomez is gay." He shrugged. "Wouldn't know it to look at him. Not a bear or nothing. And . . . not the flashy type, you know? Not flamboyant. More *Brokeback Mountain* than *La Cage aux Folles*, if you get me. But it's common knowledge. Lots of clues there, if you're lookin' . . . unmarried, never out with a lady, livin' with Old Nell. And, contrary to what you might think, or what you might see on CNN," Scholz added, "most folks 'round here don't give a damn. Generally, we're more Libertarian than Republican in Texas. Live and let live."

"Most folks," Gripke repeated.

Scholz nodded. "Now, Zeke," he continued, "he was the youngest of three brothers—"

"Isaiah and Jeremiah."

Scholz nodded again. "I seen them boys grow up. The oldest, Jerry, he's a criminal lawyer over in Austin. Isaiah's a State Trooper now. Good kids. Caroline, their ma, raised 'em strict. She was a Bible thumper; still is. Zeke was her baby.

You wouldn't know it to see him all grown up—big guy, tats, attitude—but Zeke was the sweetest little boy. His brothers, though, they were more rough-and-tumble. Growin' up, they 'beat the pansy' outta that poor kid. Toughened him up weekdays, while momma got him religion on the weekend."

He paused for a moment. Gripke nodded, taking in the information, waiting for Scholz to continue.

"Zeke played ball in high school. Defense. Had girls here and there, but never nothing steady. Didn't go to college like his brothers. Always seemed kinda lost. And lots of show . . . like he was trying to play a role, you know? Got loud when he drank. Hotheaded. Crude sense of humor. Nothin' dumb about him. Just, not quite right . . . socially awkward, if you know what I mean," Scholz concluded.

"Playing a role?" Gripke let the words hang. He wondered, *was there something going on between Fulton and Gomez?*

Scholz just stared back at him.

Gripke decided to take a different tack. "I saw in your notes, there was no reference to a specific witness, but you wrote 'suspect Fulton aggressor'."

"Just my hunch. Based on their personalities. You haven't talked to Gomez yet?"

Gripke shook his head.

"Smart," Scholz nodded his approval. "Get your bearings first. Then hit up the eyewitnesses . . . and suspects. When you do talk to him, you'll see. Pedro? Low-key, shoulder-to-the-plow kind of guy. Go along to get along. Not surprisin', really. The man's gay, Mexican, born here to a Mexican lady, no father around. These days, he's respectable and pretty important out at Crabapple, but back then, he was more of a farm hand. Hardly ever came in here. And never woulda' thrown a punch at Zeke, except to defend himself."

Scholz sipped from his tequila, pausing as if to let Gripke process.

"So . . . reaction formation . . . you think Fulton attacked Pedro because he . . . liked him?" Gripke summed up.

Scholz shrugged. "Maybe not that simple. I don't think Zeke was pullin' pigtails. I think maybe Zeke saw something in Pedro, saw something *of himself*, and maybe he didn't like what he was seeing."

# CHAPTER ELEVEN

Mary Miracle's life changed forever on Sunday.

Her alarm woke her at eight. She always slept in a little on Sundays. The sun had just risen, and a beautiful orange and purple glow lit up the bedroom. She checked her phone and frowned. Since their conversation the evening before, no phone call from Johnny. No voicemail. No text message "goodnight." Nothing. She sighed, went into the kitchen, and found Nellie in her robe, seated at the island with a coffee cup. Her iPad was propped in front of her on its stand.

"Mornin', Grandma." She ran her hand affectionately across Nellie's back as she walked by, then made herself a cup of tea. She still felt buoyed by her law school decision from the evening before. But her excitement was dampened slightly by not having heard from her husband.

"Sleep well?" Mary asked as she took a deep whiff from the cup before taking a sip. She loved the smell of peppermint to start the day.

"Your grandfather used to ask me that. Every morning . . ."

Mary sat on a stool at the island and looked at her phone, scanning messages and emails. She started typing a good morning text to Johnny, then paused. Then deleted it.

"What's going on in the world? Anything?" Mary asked, looking up. Nellie was always an early riser. By this time on Sundays, she had usually read through most of the overnight news and would give Mary an update. Her grandmother was sitting in front of her iPad, but her eyes had a distant look to them. She wasn't reading; she seemed preoccupied. She raised her eyes, taking Mary in.

"Oh, honey . . ." Nellie paused. "You know, " she winced, pressing her palm against her forehead, "blasted headache." Sighing, she shook her head, then walked over to the cabinets. "That's what woke *me* up this morning." She stood there, looking in the cabinet where they kept medicines and such. "I can't do the champagne like I used to."

"Grandma?" Mary called. "Are you looking for Tylenol? It's right here." Mary pointed at the kitchen island where Nellie had just been seated.

"Your grandfather loved champagne—huh? Oh, no. I want Advil. I took some Tylenol a while ago, didn't do the trick." Nellie took two pills with a swig of coffee and grimaced. "Coffee tastes like crap. Need to descale the machine, I think," she said, giving the coffee maker the stink-eye.

Mary glanced at the machine, then back at her grandmother. Nellie was bouncing from topic to topic; she usually did that when she had something to say but wasn't quite sure where to start.

Nellie pressed her palm against her temple.

"Headache that bad?" Mary asked.

"No. I'm fine. I'm gonna go get dressed. You do the same." She started toward her bedroom, then stopped and turned. She winked at Mary; her trademark half-wink. She paused, looking out the window, then back at Mary. "Looks to be a pretty day, Mare." She nodded, as if thinking to herself, then added, "Maybe we should take a walk. Out to the old well. There's something I need to tell you."

Mary perked up. There it was. "O . . . kay," She smiled back, studying her grandmother. A 'walk and talk' meant Nellie had something she wanted to discuss. "Can you give me a hint, at least? Good news? Bad news?"

Nellie's eyes were wide and soft. "You're doing the right thing, hon. Going back to law school." She blinked and her eyelids fluttered gently.

"Grandma?"

Nellie's lips and cheek twitched slightly, the beginnings of a grin. She nodded once. Then suddenly she collapsed. The sound of her body striking the floor was sharp and hit Mary like a punch to the gut. Fortunately, Nellie's arm flung out as she fell, and her head landed on it rather than smashing into the cold tile floor.

"Grandma! Grandma!!!"

Mary jumped up, knocking over her stool and ran to Nellie, dodging the coffee cup that had spilled and was still bouncing across the room. She banged a knee as she slid to the floor, checking Nellie's pulse. Her breathing was shallow. Mary smelled her grandmother's perfume and spilled coffee as she grabbed her phone and called 9-1-1.

"Help! I'm at Crabapple Creek Vineyard . . . at the main house . . . my grandmother's collapsed . . . Send an ambulance! Please! Please hurry!"

After what felt like an eternity to Mary—but was only seven minutes—she heard sirens in the distance. She jumped up, ran across the house, propped open the front door with an umbrella stand, and then returned to Nellie's side.

"HELLO!" she heard someone shout about a minute later.

"E-M-S! WE'RE COMING IN!"

Mary replied frantically.

"BACK HERE!

"IN THE KITCHEN!

"IT'S MY GRANDMOTHER!"

Two paramedics, a man and a woman, came in with their first responder bags, already wearing gloves. They carefully approached Nellie.

"She had Tylenol. And Advil. We were talking. And then she passed out!"

"We've got her, hon," said the female EMT, kneeling and shining a small light in Nellie's eyes while her partner put a blood pressure band on Nellie's arm.

"Pupils fixed . . ." she said. Her partner said something barely audible in reply.

Mary started to get closer to better hear when a police officer suddenly appeared and helped her aside to make room for the EMTs to work. He was talking to her, but she didn't hear what he was saying.

"I think she took Tylenol. I didn't see that—she just told me she did. But I saw her take Advil. She said she had a headache from the champagne yesterday."

The EMTs spoke in low voices to one another while they worked with Nellie, attaching something to her finger, removing equipment from their bags.

*I should have said 'no' to the champagne . . .*

While the EMTs worked, Mary stood by. Pacing. The police officer's radio crackled and she heard garbled communication to which he responded, "We're on the scene. Out at the vineyard."

"Is she okay? Oh, God! Is she going to be okay? What is that thing?" As Mary watched, the male EMT strapped a large jackhammer-looking device to Nellie's torso.

"It's a machine, for CPR," the police officer told her. "Automated compression."

As the EMT worked, the female was placing a device on Nellie with a mask and a squeeze bag, for breathing, it appeared. A few moments later, the cardiac machine began working. And the woman began squeezing air into Nellie.

Mary heard a squeaking noise behind her and turned to see a third EMT come in rolling a gurney.

"Transport?" asked the newcomer.

"Give us a minute," said the male EMT. He was looking at gauges, the blood pressure band. He checked the compression device. Then the device on Nellie's finger. He checked his watch. Then he looked up at his partner, with lips pursed. She squeezed the air bag several more times. He looked at all the devices again, then looked back at her and, almost imperceptibly, shook his head. The woman stopped squeezing the bag, and turned and looked at the police officer, not at Mary.

Mary studied her face and knew instantly.

It was resignation.

Surrender.

She was gone . . .

Nellie was dead.

"*NO!*" Mary screamed, and through her sobbing and tears, she felt as though she was suspended in the air. She was. She was being held semi-upright by the police officer, who let her slowly down to the floor, where she crawled on all fours over to her grandmother and took her in her arms. Sobbing.

And as she held her grandmother for the last time, she had that feeling again of clinging to the large sphere that was the Earth, a little speck of a thing in the universe. Only, this time it was different. She felt no comfort or peace.

Mary felt empty and alone—completely alone.

# CHAPTER TWELVE

*This trip just can't get any worse . . .*

Johnny Miracle shifted uncomfortably in his airplane seat, cold air blowing down from the tiny gray nozzle above him.

The phone call from Mary about Nellie had cut his trip short. He and Pedro had managed to get on an earlier flight back, and Pedro had somehow gotten upgraded to business class. Johnny was also eligible for an upgrade, but the monitor showed him sixth on the list; he knew his prospects were grim. So, he had approached the gate agent, flashing his best Johnny Miracle smile.

She smiled back with her eyes, and Johnny sensed he had a shot.

"Hi, sugar. I know I'm kinda low on the list, but I just wanted to check and see how it was looking?" He cocked his head slightly to the side, Brad Pitt style, and from the flush appearing on the gate agent's neck, he felt even better about his odds.

But there hadn't been any more seats available in business class.

So, Johnny was stuck in the cattle car, though at least he'd managed to get the gate agent to switch him to an aisle seat, preferring it since it gave him unfettered access to the head. Plus, he could people-watch as the plane boarded: the lawyer in the two-thousand-dollar suit, the business guy with the logo polo shirt and matching laptop bag, the college chick going home to visit mom and dad, the MILF wearing too much jewelry but nothing on her left ring finger. They were all interesting to him. But . . .

*Oh, God. Please no. She's slowing down and looking my way.*

Johnny's aisle seat was 12B, and he hoped the window seat, 12A, would remain empty. Or, if not, the next best outcome was either a quiet guy or a hot chick.

*Please, Lord.*

*Please.*

*Not the fatty.*

A large woman with a small carry-on stopped, put her duffle bag in the overhead bin, then pointed at the window seat next to him and smiled sheepishly, "Hi. That's me . . ."

*That's me . . . Fuck . . . that's at least five hundred pounds of me . . .*

Johnny stood politely and let the woman in. She barely managed to squeeze in between the armrests as she sat down. Moments later, a flight attendant came by and discreetly gave his seatmate a belt extender.

*They oughta make these fat fuckers pay for two seats. For Christ's sake .*

*Eat all you want. I'm not prejudiced . . .*

*Your life . . . your choices . . . your business.*

*I don't fuckin' care.*

*But why do I have to suffer for your sins?*

The armrest to his left was now taken by the woman's flabby arm and side, and her thigh—taut in distressed denim—pressed against his leg. Johnny tried to squirm toward the aisle and position himself as best as possible, but he couldn't get comfortable.

He wasn't a huge guy, just slightly above average height. But the seats felt like they were built for the same generation of men that wore those tiny little suits of armor you see in the museums.

*Seems like every time you get on an airplane, there's less legroom and shittier snacks.*

He tried to distract himself by people-watching the remaining passengers as they came aboard. About five rows forward, he spotted a nice-looking brunette coming up the aisle.

*Tanned. Great smile. Nice tight-fitting raw denim jeans. And that white t-shirt's gently nestling a nice pair of fake D-cups.*

*Like Hamlet said, 'Oh to be a shirt upon those boobs . . .'*

And, as luck would have it, she took the seat across the aisle from him.

Johnny always played it discreet. He shared a reticent smile with her, then avoided eye contact. It was approximately a three-and-a-half-hour flight back to Austin, depending on the tailwind.

*Plenty of time. Best not to seem too interested right away.*

As the flight attendants went through the safety drill, Johnny leaned back in his seat and tried to relax. He managed to drift off for a bit and slept through take-off, waking when he heard the tinkle of glass as the beverage cart came up the aisle.

"What would you like to drink?" the flight attendant asked.

Johnny looked up and smiled.

*Why the fuck don't they retire these dinosaurs and hire some younger stewardesses?*

Johnny remembered reading back in business school about the launch of Southwest Airlines. He'd seen photos of gorgeous young flight attendants serving drinks and peanuts in hot pants and go-go boots.

*I bet this old biddy was one of them back in the day,* he laughed to himself and, for a moment, imagined her punching her mile-high club ticket back in the '80s. Then he cringed as he visualized, imagined what the woman would look like now, naked.

"Just a ginger ale, please," he replied, smiling.

Johnny took the drink and napkin. "Thank you, ma'am . . . and, uh, could I please have the rest of the can?"

"Sure *can*," she replied, smirking at the pun.

After they'd both been served, Johnny's seatmate asked, "Where're ya headed?"

"Austin," he replied, with just enough sarcasm. *It's on the fuckin' ticket, elephant woman.*

The woman seemed to pick up his tone, nodded, and shrugged awkwardly.

*You got the message, lard-ass?*

Johnny took a sip from his ginger ale and, as he did, noticed that D-cups across the aisle was looking over. He nodded at her once, in greeting. She raised her eyebrows at him then continued reading on her iPad.

*Interesting,* he thought as he pulled a magazine out of the seat pocket. He tried to get comfortable and feigned reading a bit. But his seat was stiff, making his back ache, and he was feeling bloated. He decided to go the bathroom. But then, he had a better idea.

Smiling to himself, he leaned slightly toward the aisle and eased out a long-but-silent fart at his overweight seatmate. When the foul odor reached him, he turned away from her and glanced across the aisle. Making eye contact with the brunette, he raised his eyebrows and shook his head discreetly as he rolled his eyes toward his seatmate. About ten seconds later, the smell hit D-cups. She covered her nose and mouth with her hand, looked at him with pity, then turned back to her iPad.

*She feels sorry for me. That's a start . . .* He sipped on his ginger ale and let his mind wander, his thoughts returning to his ongoing predicament and the latest development.

Johnny had grown up a doctor's son in Buda, a small town south of Austin, which provided his family with a certain status that he'd grown accustomed to. When he'd met Mary in college, he'd figured that a family like that, with so much land and a vineyard . . . they *must* be loaded. And he assumed he would have that same status in Fredericksburg if he played his cards right and married into the family. So he thought. He'd been right about the status, wrong about the money.

So far, he'd managed to keep Mary in the palm of his hand. But he could never get through to Nellie. He'd tried every trick he knew: flattery, fawning, anger, cold logic, but he couldn't ever get her to listen to his ideas. He'd long ago run out of options.

*That old hag had never trusted me.*

Mary's call that morning changed everything. With Nellie dead, he could finally turn the vineyard into a money-making machine.

*We'll do the funeral song and dance. And then, with the life insurance money, I can turn the place into something major. An international success! No more fucking economy flights—we're talking private jets.*

*And I'll finally get rid of Pedro. Nice cost savings there, just for starters . . .*

Johnny imagined himself at wine shows in Paris and Napa. Parties in New York. Rubbing elbows with the wealthy. And maybe other body parts as well.

He glanced over at D-cups, who sensed him watching and looked up from her iPad. She finally smiled. Johnny knew an opening when he saw one.

"So, what takes you to Austin?" he asked. As he did, he leaned slightly toward the aisle and eased out another fart toward his seatmate. Not as long as the first, but satisfying nonetheless.

# CHAPTER THIRTEEN

"Mary?" Johnny called out. He and Pedro had come straight home from the airport. Hearing no reply, he walked slowly into their bedroom while Pedro unloaded the van. The curtains were drawn, and Mary lay in the fetal position in bed. Her eyes were open, red, fixed blankly on the wall.

She did not respond.

Johnny sat on the bed next to her and reached out, gently stroking her head.

"I'm so sorry, hon. So, so sorry."

Mary didn't react.

Did she even know he was there?

Johnny sat with her for almost twenty minutes, until his phone vibrated. "Be right back," he said. On the one hand, he was glad for the excuse to leave, but at the same time, he dreaded the call.

It was Sick Eddie.

"Hello?" he said.

"Johnny . . . how are you coming with my money?"

Johnny walked from the bedroom to the kitchen, not speaking until he was sure he was out of earshot.

"I'm good for it, Eddie. Trust me."

"I don't know, Johnny. You told me you'd pay everything off by the end of the month. And now I hear you lost three large on the Astros and another two on the Rangers this past weekend."

*Dammit!*

Johnny had placed a couple of big bets, confident that he would make more than enough to cover his debt to Sick Eddie. He'd lost.

"My thirty large keeps growin', and I ain't seen a dime from you in two months. And now I hear you're placing bets with establishments other than mine . . . which is fine. It's a free country, but . . . come end of the month, with the vig, you're lookin' at thirty-five thousand dollars, Johnny."

*Compound interest is a bitch. Especially when compounded weekly . . .* Johnny cringed.

"Don't worry, Eddie. I . . ."

"I ain't worried, Johnny. I know where you live; you—on the other hand—should be worried."

"Eddie. Man. Be cool. Everything's on track. I'll get you paid by end of month."

"End of month."

The line went dead.

Johnny was about to sit down at the kitchen island when the phone rang. The landline.

He glared at the phone, which he usually didn't answer, but with Nellie dead and Mary in bed, there was no one else to take the call.

On the fifth ring, he picked up.

"Hello," he sighed into the phone.

"Oh . . . Hello. May I speak to Nellie, please?" said a woman's voice.

"Nope. She's dead." He replied. Then, realizing he may have been a bit abrupt, he added, "Uh . . . Who is this? Can I help you?"

There was a long pause before the caller hung up.

Johnny put the phone back in its cradle. As he did, he heard the door to the house open. It was Pedro. He came in and pointed toward their bedroom with an inquiring look.

Johnny nodded.

Pedro knocked lightly on the door frame before entering.

Johnny slowly walked towards the room. Reaching the doorway, he saw Pedro seated on the bed, holding Mary, who was crying uncontrollably.

# CHAPTER FOURTEEN

For Mary, the days after Nellie died were a blur. So many preparations.

*The pastor . . .* "Now, I know Nellie wasn't religious in the conventional sense, but I think maybe for the reading, something from Ecclesiastes? 'For everything, there is a time and season.' You know it?"

"That sounds fine, Reverend."

*The funeral home . . .* "Our condolences, Mary. So sorry for your loss. What kind of casket would you like?"

"I . . . I don't know . . ." *Does it matter?*

"She was a wonderful woman. She deserves something nice as a final resting place. Of course, there will be a discount; we couldn't see doing otherwise."

*Is this an upsell?*

"I think she wanted to be cremated," Mary said.

"Oh, well, in that case, we should choose an appropriate urn; something special, maybe in marble with silver accents . . ."

*The medical examiner . . .* "The cause of death was cardiac arrest, a massive heart attack. She'd had two prior episodes, heart attacks, correct?"

Mary nodded.

"Did she feel unwell the night before? Or that morning?"

"Well, we drank the night before . . . Maybe a bit too much . . ." Mary admitted guiltily.

"Hmmm. Based on her bloodwork, the amount of blood pressure medicine in her system was high. Diltiazem. She was probably feeling unwell. Maybe took extra?"

Mary shook her head. "She hated meds. They made her feel old."

"But you told me she took Tylenol *and* Advil that morning?"

Mary nodded, realizing . . .

*She must have been feeling really bad . . . why did I let her have so much to drink?*

Even Mary's estranged father reached out, who communicated with her only by text message.

*Dad: Sorry to hear about Nellie.*

The worst part was the phone calls—from friends, from business associates—having to re-tell the story over and over through tears and sobs of how her grandmother, her only true living family, had collapsed and died right before her eyes.

Mary didn't eat.

She hardly slept.

She wanted to die.

Everything around her, in the house, the vineyard, reminded her of Nellie. She tried to console herself, looking at old photo albums, walking the property, trying to focus on working the vineyard. But everywhere she looked there were memories. And rather than providing comfort, each memory twisted in her heart like a jagged shard of glass.

Never again would she hear Nellie laugh with joy at one of her own corny jokes. Never again would she work next to her in the vines or see her wiping the sweat off her brow with a dirty glove while pride radiated from her smiling face at seeing work well done. She would never feel Nellie's hand gently pat her back or playfully muss her hair.

Nellie was taken so young. Just sixty-six years. Mary had expected her to live at least another twenty. All of that had been stolen from them both. All that time together. More adventures. All those memories that could have been.

Mary didn't feel ready to be alone in the world. She still looked to Nellie for advice. To kick her in the butt when she needed it. And what about taking care of Nellie? Mary had expected to be able to show her love for Nellie by helping her as she aged. That had been taken from her as well. From them both.

Mary would never see that joyful half-wink again. Never feel the warmth of one of Nellie's smiles again. Her grandmother was gone. Even worse. Her husband was on dating websites and probably screwing around on her.

Mary would later look back in wonder at those few days after Nellie died, shocked at how rapidly she had spiraled down into despair. While she never told anyone, not Johnny, not Pedro, not even Abby, she'd gone suicidal. She began to obsess about the shotgun, loading it with buckshot this time instead of birdshot and just ending the pain.

She was all alone. She had no one but herself . . . and nothing to look forward to. Everything about life had lost its appeal. It seemed like one long, painful wait for the inevitable. At least there would be peace in death. No more pain. Why *not* go there now?

During those days, Johnny was barely around. He seemed to be avoiding her, distracted, preoccupied.

Pedro was very worried for Mary. He doted on her. He brought the family doctor to see her, who prescribed some pills to help her relax and sleep. She took one on an empty stomach with some water but hadn't eaten in days and promptly threw it all up.

It was shortly after that that Mary gave up. She decided that she would set her sights on the funeral—she decided she would get through *that day*. She had to give Grandma Nellie that, the ceremony she deserved. And then, when that was done, she would get the shotgun and go out into the fields—she knew just the spot out in the east hundred—and end it all.

The day before the funeral, Mary was sitting on her bed in a bra and slip, two black dresses beside her. Pedro had told her she needed to choose one. Her phone buzzed. She'd placed it on silent the day before; its constant ringing was unbearable.

She saw who was calling and reluctantly answered, only because it was one of her two closest friends.

"Hello . . ." she sighed.

"Oh, honey. You sound terrible. Are you holding up okay?"

The call was a long one. Brief preliminaries. Then repeated condolences. Some reminiscing about Nellie. Questions about the arrangements. But it was all hazy. Mary remembered only a tiny portion of the call—the few words that brought her back from the brink.

"So, I owe you an update. It's good news. I tried, Mary. I called him. I flirted. I made it very obvious that I wanted him. But no dice. Johnny wasn't interested. He was offended, actually. So, bottom line, I don't think he's cheating on you. I don't know what the whole Sally Madison website thing was about . . .

maybe a moment of weakness? Or a joke? But, bottom line, I think he's a good guy. I think he really loves you."

No tears came. Mary was empty. But this was something. A tiny spark of hope. At least she had this. This one thread she could hold onto; this gave some meaning to her life after Nellie. She put aside all her doubts, choosing to ignore all the past inconsistencies, the little lies. She chose to believe that she could count on her husband. She was filled, if not with love . . . at least with relief. At least she wasn't alone.

She could get through this.

She would.

Shortly after the call, she heard Johnny's footsteps coming towards the bedroom. She sprang out of bed, wobbling a moment from the head rush. She hadn't eaten in almost a week.

As Johnny came in, he saw that she seemed unstable and reached out to help her. Mary buried herself in his arms.

"I love you. I love you so much!" she sobbed.

Johnny just held her.

This was a difficult time for Mary Miracle. And if a little self-deception helped her get through it, who could blame her?

But self-deception is like an adjustable-rate mortgage, a short-term blessing that doesn't solve any of your problems. It just bundles them up into a hermetically sealed yet internally festering package of shit that compounds daily. Until one day, it lands on your front doorstep, bigger and uglier than you remember. For Mary, that day was coming soon. But for now . . .

The day of the funeral went quietly for her, a smooth blur: the church service, Johnny and Pedro on her left, her two lifelong friends on her right, the wake back at the vineyard, all the faces and condolences, everything ran together.

With one exception. She saw him at the service, standing in the back of the church.

At least he didn't have the temerity to come to the vineyard.

Deputy Walter Gripke did not offer his condolences.

And he did not wear black, but his khaki uniform.

# RUBY YI

**San Francisco, California • 1969**

Ruby Yi touched many lives, including Mary Miracle's. To understand how she came to be in a position to help Mary, we need to learn a bit about her past.

Ruby began her life in poverty in San Francisco as the bastard daughter of a divorced Korean War bride. From these humble beginnings, Ruby went on to build a global business empire, dine with presidents and prime ministers, and receive the Presidential Medal of Freedom in recognition of her business accomplishments and humanitarian work.

Ruby's path to success was, as she put it herself in an interview with Forbes Magazine, "complicated." That said, Forbes was unable to find any information about her life before the age of twenty-three, other than a birth certificate. Ruby preferred it that way.

While she always claimed that she'd never met her father and knew nothing about him, that wasn't entirely true. This was probably the only thing that Ruby Yi had in common with Mary Miracle: her father had also abandoned her as a child.

Ruby's father was referred to as Little Tony back in Chicago. Between crimes and homicides, Little Tony became a moderately wealthy man, married three times, sired nine legitimate and several illegitimate children. One of his illegitimate children was born to a beautiful woman of Korean descent whom Little Tony seduced while on "business" in California. The mother named their daughter

Ruby, and although she tried to contact Little Tony about their child, he wanted nothing to do with either of them.

Ruby inherited her beauty from her mother, and her good luck and homicidal tendencies from her father. Some might argue it was *bad luck* that Ruby Yi's mother abandoned her in 1969 at the age of seventeen. Ultimately, as we will see, this was a good thing for Ruby Yi, who, from that point on, had to make her way in the world as best she could.

Which she did.

Not long after her mother disappeared, Ruby fell in with Mr. Jin Park of 1250 Ellis Street in San Francisco, California. Mr. Park had never heard of Little Tony. And even if he had, Mr. Park had no reason to know that Ruby Yi, the petite young woman seated across from him, was the mobster's daughter.

Mr. Park's home, which doubled as his office, was small, dark, and stank of dirty old man. Although Mr. Park was not that old, he was cheap, grubby, and unmarried. And *that* smell and 'dirty-old-man smell' are easily confused.

"Is the fishmonger coming around?" he asked from behind his desk.

"He will. He'll start paying next week. Standard rate," Ruby replied. The fishmonger had just opened his shop, and Ruby had gently explained that he needed to begin paying for Mr. Park's protection or 'bad things' might happen. "I told him. Rough neighborhood. Lots of young hoodlums. He understands now," she added, sitting upright, which she had learned made her look older.

Mr. Park looked up at seventeen-year-old Ruby over his bifocals, assessing, then nodded and returned to counting the money she'd laid on his desk. Between the protection money, the laundry business, and the bar, Mr. Park's nest egg was growing such that he anticipated he'd be able to retire in a few more years.

"Very good," he said after counting for the third time. "It's all here."

Ruby stood, bowed slightly, and said, "I'll get your tea." Tonight, of all nights, she needed him to follow his usual routine. As she went to the small kitchen, Mr. Park stood and stretched, his over-fifty-year-old bones creaking. He lit a cigarette and inhaled deeply.

"In here tonight," he said louder than necessary to ensure she could hear him. "I'll take you bent over the desk. My back's killing me."

Usually, the words would have caused Ruby to break out in a cold sweat. He'd been having his way with her for several months, though thankfully, he was old and not always up for it. Tonight, apparently, he was.

As she prepared the tea, she could hear him putting away his money—she knew exactly where—and getting ready for her. She heard the buckle clinking as he removed his belt, his pants unzipping. Thankfully, he always had his tea first.

With her gaze downward, Ruby returned to the room carrying his teacup in both hands, partly because that was how he liked for her to carry it and partly because her hands were shaking from nerves.

Mr. Park was seated at his desk, naked. She could smell him—sweat, body odor, cigarettes—as she placed the cup on the desk. He began to drink his tea and nodded, "Go ahead. Undress. Slowly."

Ruby did just that. She moved slowly.

Very slowly.

As Mr. Park watched Ruby that night and drank his tea, he began to feel very relaxed. And he sensed that Ruby also seemed more relaxed. More confident.

*She's finally learning to enjoy it,* he thought, smiling to himself.

Normally, this would have aroused him. But, by the time Ruby was fully undressed, he had swallowed the last of his tea. The cup fell from his hand to the floor, but he didn't care. He stared at Ruby. And oddly, though she was beautiful, the desire had left him. Instead, he slowly stood.

How had he never noticed them before? The little nubs?

*Ruby has horns!*

Tiny little horns at the top of her head. He wasn't frightened by them. Not at all. Jin Park was not afraid of a seventeen-year-old girl!

No, he was curious and amazed.

He moved slowly toward her with one hand outstretched.

"May I touch them?" he asked tentatively. Respectfully. "Your little horns?"

She looked up at him. Her eyes were huge, stunning. Beautiful purple irises with deep black pupils that a person could fall into. Her eyelashes fluttered like wings; he felt the breeze coming off them. How had he never noticed how big they were?

But the horns . . . the horns were amazing . . .

"So pretty . . . Such tiny, tiny little horns . . ."

They were the last words Jin Park ever spoke.

Two weeks later, Mr. Park's dead body was wheeled out of the house on 1250 Ellis Street. The neighbors had complained of the stench for several days before the police came around and discovered the cause. There was no evidence of foul play. The poison Ruby had used—undetectable after twenty-four hours—

caused hallucinations leading to cardiac arrest. The medical examiner would conclude that Mr. Park had simply had a heart attack.

Although Mr. Park was known to be involved in a number of illicit activities, and the police searched the house exhaustively, no money was found.

Business had continued as usual during the two weeks that Mr. Park lay dead in his house. By the time the neighborhood learned of his death, everyone had assumed that someone had replaced Mr. Park, and they all continued paying their protection money when Ruby Yi came by to collect.

It was about a month until the fishmonger became the first to challenge the status quo.

"What's the point? Park is dead! He cannot protect me now!" he shouted at Ruby. "Besides, I see no hoodlums around here!"

He shooed her out of his store, sending her away empty-handed. That was on a Friday.

Saturday morning, the fishmonger came to work and found the back door to his shop smashed open and all his inventory soaking in bleach. Ruby Yi came by that afternoon to express her sympathies at his loss, and he gave her the envelope with his payment.

Aside from that one hiccup, it was business as usual for Ruby. The laundry was no problem at all. The woman who ran the business for Mr. Park was competent and honest. She assumed that someone else had taken over from Mr. Park and kept giving Ruby his take every Friday.

In addition to the nest egg of cash she had stolen from Mr. Park's home, Ruby had also taken his account books. After an hour studying the entries, she was able to pick up on his bookkeeping system—which was extremely basic—and out of a desire to 'learn business,' she resumed the accounting entries where he'd left off. She understood everything except that Mr. Park allocated profits into two categories: tax and net. Ruby couldn't imagine Mr. Park paying taxes, and she had no idea what 'net' was. But she continued the practice and separated each week's funds into two distinct bundles, one for tax and one for net.

She immediately had the laundry and protection business in hand; it was the bar business that worried Ruby. That business 'belonged' to Mr. Park. But, as Ruby understood it, it was actually owned by Mr. Cho, a very important man who had his finger in many businesses in the neighborhood. Mr. Park didn't actually work at the bar, but he was 'responsible' for it. As Ruby had never dealt with the bar, she let it be.

The Friday morning after the bleach incident, Ruby arrived at the fishmonger's to pick up her weekly payment. She entered quietly and waited while he spoke with a customer. Ruby then saw the fishmonger nod his head toward her. The customer, a giant of a man, turned and walked towards Ruby. As he approached, she saw that he was placing a small envelope in his pocket.

*Her* envelope.

"Mr. Cho would like to speak with you," he said in a deep gravelly voice. It was not a threat, just a statement of fact.

Behind the big man, Ruby saw the fishmonger smiling with glee.

Ruby stood up straight. The top of her head was well below the big man's chest. She raised her chin, looked up into the big man's eyes defiantly, and said softly, "Did you count it?"

He studied her for a moment, then slowly removed the envelope from his pocket and counted the few bills in Ruby's clear sight.

"One moment," he said. The big man turned around. The fishmonger's face fell, and he held up his hands defensively.

"I'm sorry . . . It was a mistake! I miscounted. Here you go," he said, pulling out two more bills.

"You 'miscounted'? And you know by exactly how much?" the big man quietly asked. He took the bills, then in the same motion, backhanded the fishmonger across the face, making a loud *thwack!* The fishmonger fell to his knees from the force of the blow, a stream of blood running from his broken nose.

Turning, the big man nodded at Ruby with appreciation and said, "Now we will go see Mr. Cho."

"And . . . what is your name?" she asked.

"I am called Kong."

"Very well, Kong."

Ruby turned and walked towards the door. Then she stopped and paused, standing just to the side. She looked at Kong.

He hesitated for a moment, looking at her. Then, Kong understood. He stepped forward and opened the door and held it for her.

Ruby bowed her head slightly and said, "Thank you, Kong."

As she walked out, head held high, Ruby Yi looked back over her shoulder at the fishmonger who remained on his knees, sobbing, with his head tilted back, holding his now bloody apron against his face.

# PART TWO

## MARY MAKES A PLAN

# CHAPTER FIFTEEN

The week after Nellie's funeral, the consequences of her death became very real.

The lawyer's office was dark—wood-paneled walls, shelves filled with law books, the coffee-colored parquet floor barely visible around the edges of several large oriental rugs. In another universe, Mary would have been fascinated by the books, wanting to know what they contained. In this reality, she didn't even notice them.

"I am so sorry for your loss, Mary," said George Pringle, the estate lawyer.

The condolences sounded perfunctory to Mary. He probably meant them, but this meeting was about business, and his words rang hollow to her.

He shook her hand, then ushered her and Johnny in. Pringle looked like a lawyer out of a political cartoon, the farmer from that painting *American Gothic*, thin as a reed, spectral, round glasses, but wearing a blue pinstriped suit and black tie. He was quick in his movements, crisp and efficient as he sat down at his desk and flipped through the few pages of her grandmother's Last Will and Testament. Pringle cleared his throat as he looked up at Mary over his reading glasses.

Mary and Johnny sat down across from Pringle's desk. Johnny took her hand, and she held onto it fiercely for stability. She still felt overwhelmed by . . . everything. One minute, her grandmother was fine. The next, she was gone. And now *that life*, her Grandma Nellie's life, everything she had worked for, fought to build, accomplished, it was all reduced to an urnful of ashes and the thin little document sitting on the lawyer's desk.

"Well, there are no surprises here. Let's just get that right out of the way," Pringle looked up, half smiling. "She did want you to have this." Pringle slid a letter-sized envelope over to Mary. On it was written her first name, in Grandma

Nellie's hand. "I don't think it has any legal significance. She said it was of a personal nature."

Mary held the envelope, stifling back tears. Then she put it in her purse. She would read it later.

"Beyond that," Pringle shrugged, "you are her only family and her sole heir. Everything she had is now yours. Including her share of the vineyard."

"Her *share*?" Mary asked.

"Ahem . . . well, yes. Several years back, when things got tight, a rough patch if you will, she sold fifteen percent to help cover debts," Pringle replied.

"To . . . ?" Mary asked.

"To Clive Connard," Pringle replied. "I assumed you knew. It was all properly documented, with lawyers and everything. Nellie still owns . . . owned . . . 85% of the property and 100% of the voting rights. So, Mr. Connard is truly a passive minority owner."

"Well, that's good news, I guess," Mary sighed.

Pringle cleared his throat. "The issue . . ." As he said it, he drew the word out, which Mary took as an indication that the 'issue' was not a small one. She was right. "The issue is that the estate tax bill will be significant based on the value of her eighty-five percent of the business—and taking into account all other assets and exemptions."

"Estate tax . . . significant, like . . . *how* significant?" she asked.

Pringle slid a sheet of paper across to Mary, which she took after releasing Johnny's hand.

"Forty percent is the going tax rate," Pringle replied. "And . . . it smarts."

Mary's belly clenched. On the paper was a statement of assets and liabilities. She skimmed through the list, not focusing on details, but searching for the total. She found it. The number at the bottom. It was negative.

"One-point-two million dollars . . . in taxes?"

"That's the bottom line." Pringle nodded.

"But isn't there a huge exemption of some sort . . . like five million?"

"Yes, that exemption exists, and it stands at a little over five-point-four million dollars, but when Nellie gifted you the Monet, it was valued at six-point-five million. That gift essentially used up all of the exemption, leaving you with this estate tax liability."

Mary stared wide-eyed at the tax bill.

"But Grandma Nellie bought the vineyard outright, in cash," she shook her head. "She paid *all her taxes*—income tax, property tax, payroll tax, sales tax. How can the government ask for even more money from her now that she's dead?"

"Yes, well . . . A lot of people feel the way you do. But, that's *our* government . . . the tax rate is an issue for the ballot box, not my sphere of influence, I'm afraid," Pringle lamented. "Write your congressman. Or woman."

Mary glared at his sarcasm for a moment, then saw from his expression that he was serious.

"How am I supposed to pay that?" she scoffed.

"Isn't there life insurance?" Johnny asked. "I know Nellie had a policy . . ."

"She did. There is," Pringle responded. "But she borrowed against it some years back, around the same time she sold Connard his share to get through that rough patch, and she never repaid the debt."

Mary was watching her attorney and didn't notice that Johnny blanched. His face fell.

"The policy will still pay a little over twelve thousand dollars, which should cover the funeral expenses. It's all accounted for." Pringle pointed at the paper that Mary held, which she handed over to Johnny. He took the paper with a trembling hand.

"The one-point-two million tax debt is after taking everything into account."

"George, I don't have that kind of money. Can I . . . will the government take installments or something?" Mary's eyes burned. She'd wept so much lately that it had gotten to the point that she could only tell she was crying when her vision blurred.

"Um, no. The government doesn't do installments."

Mary stared off into the distance while Johnny looked blankly at the paper.

"When is it due?" Mary asked.

"It needs to be paid within nine months of her passing," Pringle answered.

"How generous of them." Mary looked at Johnny.

"Don't worry, Mare," he said robotically. "We'll figure this out."

# CHAPTER SIXTEEN

Marriages don't fall apart all at once. Although each is different, there is a general pattern to their decay. Typically, one partner invests more effort than the other in the relationship and, when things begin to sour, pretends that everything is fine. Friends and family are told that things are "okay," "good enough," or at worst, "going through ups and downs." This person is not lying to their friends and family. The problem is self-deception. This person is lying to themselves, *wanting* to believe that everything is okay when things are actually in decline.

It's like pushing a stalled car on a gentle slope. At first, movement is barely perceptible. Then we hear tires crunching gravel. Little slights, missed opportunities to be kind, and, of course, outright betrayal, keep pressuring the car further along the slope. But even then, if the pushing stops, so will the car . . . until it reaches a *tipping point* where enough momentum has accumulated that gravity takes over. Then everyone starts checking their seat belts because they realize and accept that they're accelerating downhill towards a brick wall.

Self-deception typically ends at that tipping point.

Mary reached that tipping point—her self-deception ended—ten hours after the meeting at Pringle's office, at just past 2:00 a.m. She was sitting curled up in one of the leather chairs in the study, sipping on a hot cup of Sleepytime tea, longing for sleep. As she did, she was contemplating the Monet. And the tax bill. And the vineyard that made no money.

*So much has changed, almost in the blink of an eye.*

The days since Nellie died had hammered Mary like an East Texas tornado. She'd experienced despair for the first time in her life, and she now cringed when she admitted to herself that she'd actually considered ending it all. She didn't know for certain if she would have gone through with it . . . if she could have pulled the trigger. But she'd been close enough to know that she never wanted to let herself go like that again. Ever. The important thing was that she had gotten through it. And that now that she was herself again, she knew she was better for it. Stronger.

*Now, if only I could sleep!*

As she studied the Monet, she thought of her grandmother. *You're doing the right thing, Mare. Going back to law school.* Those were the last words Grandma Nellie had told her before she died.

*Or were they?*

With the shock of the tax issue, she had forgotten about the envelope. Mary got up and went to the family room. There, in a corner on the sofa, was her purse. She dug through it and found the envelope Pringle had given her.

She returned to the study, switched on a small lamp, and opened the envelope. It contained a letter and a list. As Mary read the words, her eyes watered as her heart swelled. It was a goodbye letter.

*"If you're reading this Mare, it's because I've passed on . . ."*

If only she could have read it sooner, it would have helped her make it through everything. These words were from Nellie for Mary, for her eyes only. Words of love. Consolation. And encouragement. Hope.

*Oh, Grandma. You knew me so well . . .*

Mary cried again. But this time was different. She wasn't crying out of sorrow. Yes, of course she was sad. But these were also tears of joy at having loved and been loved so much by such an amazing woman.

*Well hell!*

*Now there's no way I'm gonna go to sleep!*

Mary scanned the second sheet: bank account passwords, email password, iPad password, etc.

*There you are!*

Since Nellie died, as she and Johnny took full control of vineyard operations, they'd had minor glitches as they couldn't access Nellie's email which meant that some business emails had gone unanswered since she passed.

Mary went to the kitchen and retrieved Nellie's iPad, which was still plugged into the wall in the kitchen corner where she'd always put it to charge. She entered the password, and the iPad opened.

*Finally!*

She flopped back down on the leather chair, opened the email app, and scanned, beginning with the most recent messages. She found a couple of unpaid bills and notices, which she forwarded to her email account. When Mary reached the day that Nellie died, she stopped, thinking that her grandmother had probably dealt with everything up to that fateful day. Then, she reconsidered.

*There may be some messages that came in before she died that she hadn't gotten around to yet . . .*

The day before Nellie died, there was an email from brad@hurtinvestigations.com.

*Subject: Miracle Matter*

Mary knitted her eyebrows, perplexed, then opened the email and the attached file. Her mouth fell open as she skimmed through the report and the photos. Photos of Johnny . . . photos of a woman named Summer . . . photos of them both.

*That son of a bitch . . .*

Mary looked up from the report. A photo of her with Nellie caught her eye.

*And you . . . you crazy old woman . . . Along with all the recipes and memories, you leave me a vineyard that barely makes money—a one-point-two-million-dollar tax bill—AND a report detailing my husband's infidelities. Thanks a lot, Grandma. I guess this is why you wanted to take that last 'walk and talk'? Was there any good news?*

Mary shook her head. She was staring, thinking, processing what this meant. Not the cheating, but the implications. For her. Her future. When she snapped back to the present, she realized that she was staring up at the Monet. Through dry eyes. No tears.

In the last few weeks, she had cried enough tears for a lifetime. And what good had that done? She wasn't crushed. She was mad as hell. If Nellie could have seen Mary's face, she would have noted that the faint glow of youthful altruism it used to bear was gone. This email presented evidence—clear facts as to the real Johnny.

No more self-deception. She was done with that. The glint in Mary's eyes was all grown up. She admitted to herself that things had been bad for some time now, and that they were going downhill fast.

*Some things around here need to change, that's for sure. A divorce, for sure. Sell the vineyard, I guess . . . But not the Monet. Then law school and a fresh start?*

She could practically hear Nellie's voice, "No man, no matter how smart or strong, can compete with a motivated woman."

*Oh, I'm motivated all right, Grandma. The question is, where to begin?*

# CHAPTER SEVENTEEN

A few days later, Mary was having her morning cup of tea in the kitchen, which felt empty without Nellie, when Johnny came in. He wore blue jeans, boots, and a crisp white cotton shirt with the blue Crabapple Creek Vineyard logo embroidered on the breast pocket. He was tanned, with sandy hair and a day's growth of stubble. A good-looking man—too much so, clearly.

*Cheating sonofabitch . . .*

Johnny had been supportive since Nellie died, but now that Mary knew the truth, her stomach turned at the sight of him. Still, she'd already decided she needed to play this smart, not emotionally.

"Penny for your thoughts, babe," he said as he kissed her on the cheek. She did her best not to flinch.

Mary sighed. *You're as stupid as you are good-looking. . .*

Johnny had felt Mary climb out of bed unusually early.

*Something must be bothering her. More 'missing Grandma shit,' no doubt.*

"Mornin'," she replied. *You ass-hat.*

She stretched her arms and yawned as Johnny made himself a cup of coffee.

"Is that new?" Mary asked.

Johnny looked at her, then at the coffee maker. "Yeah," he replied. "Coffee tasted like shit. Got a new machine."

"Another brand?" she asked.

He nodded as the machine came to life, spewing out brown liquid.

"I just can't get my head around the idea of selling this place," he said, looking at his wife with pursed lips and slightly squinted eyes. *If your dumb bitch of a grandmother hadn't drained her life insurance policy, we wouldn't be fucked right now, would we?*

Mary studied his face. *That expression . . . Is it sympathy he's trying to convey? He looks like he's constipated and about to sneeze. Is he actually expressing genuine emotion, or just pretending to?*

She replied, "I know. It's tough. But we've been through all the other options. Selling the vineyard is the best solution." She shrugged. "But . . . you really think *Clive* will offer enough to make selling this place worthwhile?" Ever since Nellie's death, Johnny had been dropping hints about a potential buyer for the vineyard: Clive Connard. Learning from Pringle that he already owned fifteen percent made him an even more likely buyer.

"He's our best bet," Johnny said. "I mean, not a lot of folks are interested in a business that doesn't make any money." *You can thank your grandmother for that.*

Mary nodded. She'd been through the numbers repeatedly; the vineyard made just enough to cover expenses . . . it wasn't really profitable. And although Johnny had always come up with ideas to increase sales, Nellie had never quite trusted his ideas. Or him.

*God, I should have listened to her!*

Johnny looked at Mary, then he glanced at the study.

Mary felt anger rise. "No, Johnny! Don't even start. We've discussed it *ad nauseam*. I am *not* selling the Monet to pay taxes. The vineyard, I can live without. But, that painting . . ." Mary shook her head.

*We'll see about that, you sentimental bitch . . .* Johnny grabbed his keys from the counter and said in his smoothest tone, "I get it, babe. It's your call. And I am one hundred percent on your side. I'm heading out. Gonna swing through town on the way in to see Clive. A/C in the Chevy's acting up again."

Mary glanced at her phone to check the time. Johnny's meeting with Clive was at eleven, in about two hours. They'd agreed that Johnny should meet with Clive alone; he was a bit of a pig and didn't work well with women.

*Yep,* she thought. *You've got just enough time to go get laid by your stripper friend before the meeting.*

"Okay," she said. "Let me know how it goes with Clive." *Asshole . . .*

Once she was sure Johnny was off the property, she picked up her purse to go to her own meeting, one Johnny knew nothing about.

# CHAPTER EIGHTEEN

As Johnny Miracle drove towards town, he tried to fight down frustration and anger. He'd thought that once Nellie was gone, he would naturally step in to run the vineyard, at last able to do with it as he saw fit. Finally, he could turn it into a successful venture.

And pay off his debt to Sick Eddie.

The whole estate tax and life insurance problem had thrown him for a loop. He hadn't seen that coming. He'd played the supportive husband while he tried to figure out what to do next, but inside, he was seething.

*Not only did I actually marry poor. The old bitch died and left us a liability. After taking all that crap from Nellie for years, now everyone's gonna think that we had to sell because I couldn't afford to keep the place. They'll all say that I couldn't make it work without her!*

"Fuuuuck!" he slammed both fists against his truck's steering wheel.

Johnny wasn't about to give up. He'd been trying to come up with a backup plan after finding out about the tax issue. But he was still pissed off and needed a release. At the first red light, he opened the glove box and grabbed his other mobile phone. He kept two phones, something he'd done for years: one for home and one for fun.

Johnny smiled to see that there were no more missed calls from Summer. He'd been ghosting her since just around the time Nellie died, and it looked like she'd finally taken the hint.

*That chick was stooopid! Even for a stripper.*

Johnny had screwed her for almost three months until he found a new, better-looking playmate. He wasn't good at break-ups, but these women were adults—they knew what they were getting into.

Over the years, Johnny had worked out his theory of what type of women were best for his little affairs. He'd learned to seek out women with flexible work schedules or that worked evenings and had daylight hours off: waitresses, bartenders, strippers, online workers, and even stay-at-home moms. Married women were great because they were generally just bored and looking for a temporary distraction. And they were as motivated to be discreet as he was. Single women could be more complicated, but if you avoided the young starry-eyed ones susceptible to 'falling in love,' they were manageable. Johnny thought older single women were the best—if you could find a hot one—because they were so "desperate" for a man you could "treat 'em like shit," and they'd still come back for more. Of course, you always had to be careful to not get caught. But then, for Johnny, half the fun was the risk.

Johnny's new go-to was named Karen. She ticked a lot of the boxes for him. She was single, and she was a realtor, so she had a flexible schedule.

*And an amazing natural rack.*

She'd also made a very big deal about wanting to be cautious. He'd been screwing her for around a month. In exchange, although it was unspoken so she wouldn't "feel like a whore," he'd give her money to "help with the rent" while she was "getting back on her feet." There were plenty of lies and clichés in this world of extramarital trysts. While Johnny had had a lot of flings, this one felt a bit different to him.

Karen had required a little more courtship than most, but once he'd finally gotten her into bed, the sex had been amazing; the woman was talented. But what had come as a big surprise to him was that she wasn't just tits and ass. It turned out she was smart too. She understood him and his predicament. He wasn't falling in love or anything. But he was pleased to discover that she could be useful out of bed as well.

Johnny called her, and she picked up on the third ring.

"Hey, Karen! How's the most beautiful woman in the world doing today?" He pictured her as he spoke, emerald green eyes, blazing red hair, and all the rest.

She giggled. "I'm doing great, cowboy. Perfect timing. I just got out of the shower. Hold on—let me put you on hands-free." There was a bit of clicking, and then he heard an increase in white noise coming over the line. "Okay. Can you hear me?"

"I can hear you just fine. What I need is to *see* you, babe. All of you . . ."

More laughter. "You *know* I can't stop thinking about you either. What's your day look like?" she asked.

"Goin' to see Clive about this whole 'sale' thing. Goin' through the motions, anyway."

"And the little wifey doesn't suspect anything?"

"Mary?" Johnny scoffed. "You shittin' me? Not a damned clue. She's still overwrought about the old bitch dying. Trust me. I'm all over this, babe. Mary won't know what hit her . . ." He turned left into an alley that ran behind a row of houses, one of which was Karen's.

"So, listen, I've got about an hour to kill, and guess where I am?"

"Ooh, naughty boy!" she answered seductively.

"Maybe we can try out that black skirt I bought you? And the heels?"

"But Johnnnny . . . That means I have to get dressed," she faux-pouted.

He chuckled. He was already getting hard.

"Oh! Wait . . ." Karen exclaimed as he pulled in and parked behind her house. "I think . . . I hear . . . you . . . coming . . ." she whispered.

Johnny locked the truck and headed up the walk to the back porch. He could see Karen in the kitchen wearing a white bathrobe, her red hair wet and slicked back.

*Time to drain the old evaporator,* he thought and chuckled to himself.

# CHAPTER NINETEEN

Clive Connard was a big man. Football big. He walked like an ex-football player—the Texas shuffle, his wife called it—but he'd actually never played. The walk was due to a car accident in high school that damaged his hip and left knee.

Clive's sport as a teen had actually been basketball. At almost six-foot-seven, he'd had the height; before the accident, he'd shown some promise. The car accident had ended all that for him and set him on a path littered with fried food, beer, and indolence that had left him in the state he was in, borderline obese at age forty, taking cholesterol medication along with Levatol for his blood pressure.

Clive fit the mold of the men in his family. The Connards had been in the Hill Country for four generations, and the Connard men were known for their appetites. They were also known for being in the land business ever since Clive's great-grandfather Virgil Connard, a woodworker by trade, had won two acres of land on Mayer Creek in a poker game and had to figure out what in the hell to do with them. His solution: peaches.

Clive was waiting for Johnny Miracle in the Connard Ranch Realty office in downtown Fredericksburg, where he spent part of his time managing the few peach farms owned by his family and the rest of his time as a ranch broker. Up on the wall behind Clive's desk hung a large wooden plank on which were burnt the words:

> *Land is the only thing in the world worth working for, worth fighting for, worth dying for, because it's the only thing that lasts.*
>
> *– Virgil Connard*

One New York couple shopping for a retirement property—actually the wife, so the story went—had dared to point out that the quote was oddly similar to what Scarlett O'Hara's father had told her in *Gone with the Wind.* They were promptly shown the door.

It was almost eleven, and Clive was on his fourth Coke Zero of the day—with just a splash of Jack Daniels . . . hair of the dog—when he saw Johnny's blue Chevy pull into one of the two visitor parking spots in front of the office.

"Kitty! Send Johnny up to the conference room," Clive bellowed.

The building creaked and shuddered as Clive made his way down the narrow hallway and up the stairs to the second-floor conference room that overlooked Main Street. Clive hated the climb, which always left him out of breath. If he could help it, he preferred to install himself in the conference room slightly ahead of his guests so he had time to recover from the exertion. Usually, he'd have met with Johnny in his office downstairs, but he didn't want Kitty eavesdropping on this meeting.

Kitty was sharp, sometimes too sharp for her own good.

"Will do, boss!" Kitty shouted back from her desk in the office foyer. She'd worked with Clive for almost three years, starting as a receptionist, promoted to office manager within two months, and recently earned her own real estate license. She knew the business as well as Clive did.

Kitty was a bit of an odd duck; she always had one earphone in her right ear. She claimed she used it to actively listen to (or, if she was otherwise occupied, "subliminally absorb") lessons from the motivational speaker Tony Robbins. Kitty also bedazzled everything she wore. Soon after she began work with Clive, folks began to call her the Rhinestone Realtor, though not to her face.

Clive was seated in the conference room and just catching his breath when he heard the stairs creaking as Johnny made his way up. He wiped his forehead on his sleeve as he arranged the few documents on the table before him.

As Johnny entered the room, Clive put on his interpretation of a game face, all smiles and 'aw, shucks.' He rumbled to his feet, the wood planks creaking under him, his chair scraping loudly against the floor as it slid back away from him, extending a hand the size of a baseball mitt and vigorously shaking Johnny's.

"Hey-hey! Johnny!" he roared. "What'cha no good for! Looking slim as ever. Don't know how you do it! Mary not feedin' ya enough, or what? Ha! Ha! Ha!"

Johnny smiled, gripping Clive's hand tightly. "Great to see ya, Clive. I appreciate you reachin' out."

After a bit of small talk, the two men took their seats, Clive loudly scraping his chair back towards the table several times as he repositioned himself in it.

"So," Clive began, "I've looked at the numbers like you asked, and . . ." He paused. "Look, Johnny. I wanna do right by you and Mary. It's terrible, Nellie dyin' and y'all stuck with this tax bill. But things are real slow right now. Real slow. Not a lot of cash out there lookin' for deals, and even if—"

"Cut the crap, Clive," Johnny interrupted. "This is the best kept, most improved vineyard land west of Austin. You and me both know that's worth a lot. And if you can't afford it . . ." he paused, letting the jab sink in, "I'll just find another buyer."

The words hung in the air while Clive sat, lips pursed, nodding slowly and studying Johnny.

"Look, Johnny. The problem is . . . this is a real specialized property. I mean, we're talkin' grapes here. This is basically a grape farm. You're not just selling land and a house. To get a really good price for it, you gotta find a buyer that sees value in what the land's producin'. And that's grapes, Johnny . . . and they ain't French grapes. They ain't California grapes. Them's Texas grapes. And, unless Nellie's been lying to me all these years, them grapes are barely making enough to pay expenses and feed your family. This deal's been a money loser for me ever since I bought my fifteen percent from Nellie . . ."

Clive paused. He wanted Johnny to think about that for a moment.

"Look," Clive said, picking up his pen and slowly tearing a sheet of paper from a small notepad, "I'm going to write down a number—"

"Oh, for fuck's sake, Clive," Johnny interrupted again, shaking his head, "this is real life, not a goddamned movie!" Johnny leaned forward. "Use your words, big guy. Just tell me how much you're willing to pay."

Clive sat looking at Johnny through narrow eyes. He was trying to hide the fact that Johnny had just ruined his plan. Clive had recently learned about writing down your offer on paper from listening to a negotiation book on tape. The idea was to build anticipation and because the written word is more powerful. That's about all he'd learned, as he'd slept through the rest of the book. He'd wanted to try the tactic out and see how it worked. So much for that.

"Two. I can pay two million, Johnny." Clive shrugged. "There. It's on the table. And that's all I got. I won't negotiate with you. You're like family to me, you and Mary. That's my best number. That's all there is. That's all the land's worth, Johnny."

Johnny sat stone-faced, studying Clive; the big man seemed uncomfortable with the scrutiny and swallowed hard.

Clive could feel sweat trickling down his back into his butt crack. He resisted the urge to scratch.

Finally, Johnny leaned forward and spoke.

"Clive, after taxes, two . . . well, that only leaves around eight hundred thousand dollars," Johnny said, shaking his head. "The vineyard is worth at least four million, and you know it!"

The words echoed in the room.

"Land is only ever worth what someone will pay, Johnny," Clive replied. "And right now, the market's tight. Real tight. Just bad timing. I'm really sorry."

Johnny stood up, the old wood floor creaking under his boots as he walked towards the windows and looked out over Main Street.

"Okay, Clive," Johnny said. "But you need to draw up two contracts. One is for Mary, for the vineyard—your two million dollars." Johnny turned and smiled at Clive. "And the second contract is between you and me. *My commission* for convincing her to take your piece o' shit offer."

Clive's eyes widened slightly. "So, that's how it's gonna be?" he asked.

Johnny nodded.

"Okay, how much?" Clive prodded.

"Another million."

Clive scoffed out loud. "You're crazy, Johnny! Another million? Three million? That's insane . . . that's . . . that's what that is. The market isn't . . . Johnny, it's just, there's . . . It's too much, Johnny, too much." Clive sat shaking his head from side to side, looking up at the ceiling. But inside, he was leaping for joy, his heart racing. Clive had been willing to pay up to three-and-a-half million for the property. Johnny's offer put the total price at three.

*Can I squeeze a little more?* he thought.

"Look, Johnny, like I said, you're like family to me. Family. And I know this is just bad timing. I could . . . maybe . . . I dunno . . . I could maybe pay you . . . I dunno . . ." Clive shook his head. "Maybe . . . two hundred thousand . . . for your commission." Clive slowly stood, holding out his hand. "But that's all I got. And that's only because—"

"It's a million or nothing, Clive. The property's worth four million, and you know it. You're getting it *well below market* if you take my deal."

The two men stood, staring at one another. In silence. The seconds ticked by.

Off in the distance, the office phone began to . . .

*Riiiiinnng*

Kitty was standing in the supply closet under the stairs in her stocking feet, with the door almost closed. From there, she'd been listening to the men's conversation through the air duct that led from that closet up to the conference room. She had heard everything so far, and then the damned office phone—clutched in her hand—rang!

Kitty slid out of the closet in her socks, taking shuffling baby steps so that the old floor wouldn't creak, into the reception area so as not to project her voice back up the air duct into the conference room.

*RIIIIINNNG*

Kitty answered in a normal voice, "Connard Ranch Realty, one moment, please." She put the call on hold and shuffle-baby-stepped her way back into the closet to listen.

". . . sometime early next week," she heard Clive say.

"Sounds good," Johnny responded.

"Goddamnit!" Kitty hissed. She heard the thud of footsteps accompanied by the creaking of floorboards moving across the conference room and towards the stairs. Again, she shuffled back out of the closet, this time all the way back to her reception desk, taking the call off hold as she moved.

"How can I help you?" she asked. It turned out to be FedEx calling to confirm the phone number for a package she'd sent out earlier that day. She got rid of the caller just as Johnny Miracle came into the reception lobby.

Kitty studied him closely, trying to guess the outcome of the negotiation.

"You have a great day now, Mr. Miracle!" she said as he headed for the door.

"Thank you, Kitty!" Johnny looked at the Rhinestone Realtor and couldn't help himself, "You're looking . . . dazzling, as always . . ." he said with a smirk.

Kitty's eyes narrowed slightly. But she repeated to herself Tony Robbins' words, *Nothing has any meaning except the meaning you give it,* and then replied, "Why thank you, Mr. Miracle! It must be my new eye shadow," Kitty blinked several times to show off the sparkly bright aqua shading. "It's called Northern Lights."

Once Johnny Miracle had left in his Chevy, and Clive was back downstairs and settled in his office, Kitty reached under her desk and slipped back into her boots.

# CHAPTER TWENTY

Deputy Gripke had watched from a spot down the road as Johnny Miracle exited the front gate to Crabapple Creek Vineyard at 8:41 a.m. in a blue Chevy and turned left, presumably heading towards town. Mary Miracle departed in a Jeep shortly after him at 8:54 a.m. and turned right, destination unclear.

Gripke wrote the particulars in a small notebook he carried for just such things, then hit the ignition button and drove onto the vineyard property. Records indicated that Pedro Gomez lived on-site, and Gripke hoped to interview him impromptu.

Nellie *had* asked Sheriff Strauss to have his people call in advance before visiting again, but then, she was no longer among the living. And while South Texas had a long history of dead people voting in elections, to Gripke's knowledge, none of them had ever made any campaign contributions. Nellie was dead, and given the changed circumstances, he didn't think the sheriff would consider this unannounced visit to be "ruffling feathers"—not any that mattered.

He parked away from the main house by the service garage and offices. As he exited his truck, he spied Pedro, who he recognized from file photos, leaving the building and coming towards him.

He wore neat but faded Wranglers, a khaki long-sleeved Dickie's work shirt, and work boots. A wiry man, he was clean-shaven, with sun-bronzed skin and dark green eyes. Black hair peeked out from under his old-but-well-cared-for, pinch-front cowboy hat. Gripke spotted a lock blade sheath on Pedro's right hip, but he didn't look to be carrying.

"Mornin'. Can I help you?" Pedro said as he approached.

"Mornin'. Yessir, you sure can. I was looking to talk with Pedro Gomez."

"Well, you can check that box done. If you made your bed this morning, then you're two for two on your way to changing the world," he held out his hand in greeting. "Pedro Gomez."

"Admiral McRaven . . ." Gripke chuckled, referring to Pedro's reference to bed-making. "You ex-Navy?"

"Long time ago. Another century," Pedro laughed. "Did four years before I landed here."

"Walter Gripke," he said, taking the man's hand. Its skin was rough, the grip firm, confident but not crushing. "I'm the new guy down at the sheriff's office. Nice to meet you." Gripke wondered whether the Navy reference was just a coincidence or if Pedro had been checking up on him.

"Why don't you walk with me? Headin' up that way," Pedro nodded toward the fields, "to check on an irrigation leak. We can talk while we walk."

The deputy nodded. As they began walking, Gripke got straight to it. "I'm looking into Zeke Fulton's disappearance," he said, turning his head and studying Pedro as he spoke, watching his reactions. "As you were one of the last folks that saw him, I wanted to see what you could remember about that night."

"Well, I don't know if I was the last person to see him that night, but I think I was the last to punch him." Pedro laughed.

Gripke did not. Pedro noticed.

"I'm not trying to make light . . . bad situation and all. But I know other people saw him after me 'cause I left the bar, and he stayed. I assume you're here because of the fight."

"That'd be a good assumption," Gripke replied.

"Well, all I can tell you now is what I said back then. I went in for a drink. I was sittin' at the bar. At around eleven o'clock, in comes Zeke. He sat on a stool one down from me and got himself a drink.

"After a bit, I get up to take a leak. When I'm coming back, just after I pass by him, he gets up and claims I bumped into him. Real loud. Aggressive. I denied it, because I hadn't. He came closer. I told him I didn't want any trouble. That's when he took a swing. He missed . . . well . . . I slipped it. Then I punched him in the gut, popped him in the face with my knee, and he went down. I paid my bill. And as I left, I saw that they'd helped him up onto his stool, and he had some ice on his eye."

"Where'd you go after that?" Gripke asked.

Pedro nodded along with the question. "Came back here. Took a shower. Went to bed. Next I heard about Zeke was that he'd gone missin'."

"He didn't come by here that night?"

Pedro stopped and faced the newbie. "Well, Deputy, that seems like a significant detail that I would have included . . . if it had happened."

Gripke nodded, scratching his head. "You know him at all? Before the fight, I mean?"

"You've been here what, nine months now, Deputy?"

Gripke nodded. Pedro *had* been checking up on him. *Interesting* . . .

"Well, this ain't Dallas. I was born and raised here and, except for four years in the Navy, I been here that whole time. It's a small town. You get to know people. So, yeah, I knew Zeke. His brothers. His mother. Everybody did."

"But, other than that night, no altercations?"

"Nope."

"So, if you knew him, what was your relationship like?"

Pedro studied Gripke for a moment, pursing his lips. "He was a guy I'd seen around town, like a lot of others. If I see you around a few more times, then I could tell you that my relationship with Zeke is the same as my relationship with you."

Gripke nodded. "You aware of anyone that had it in for him?"

Pedro shrugged. "I have no idea. Like I said, seen him around. But really didn't know him that well." Pedro turned and began to walk again. "I got things to do. We done?"

"Sure. Sure. Yep. We're done," Gripke replied. "I'll show myself out."

"Have a nice day!" Pedro said, not looking back.

# CHAPTER TWENTY-ONE

Gripke left the vineyard and drove about five miles west, pulling into the Stonewall Safety Rest Area, where Zeke Fulton's truck was found the day after the fight at the Mean-Eyed Cat. As far as rest stops go, this was a nice one. Well-kept. Clean.

Fulton's file contained a detailed description from two eyewitnesses as to what they had seen at the rest stop the night of Fulton's disappearance. Gripke walked along, recalling what he had read, trying to imagine how it had happened that night.

* * *

*Lionel Jaspers started his career as a long-haul truck driver when he turned thirty-four. During his first three years on the road, he'd gained ninety pounds and gotten hooked on a concoction he called "home-made no-doze"—a proprietary mix of amphetamines and cocaine that he took in (initially) small doses after every liter of coffee. This served him well as far as helping him put in miles, though slowly, his dosage increased, and towards the end of that third year on the road, he had his first heart attack. Given his obesity and drug habit, his doctor refused to give him the all-clear to return to work. Lionel ended up in rehab, where he met Debbie.*

*Debbie worked as an assistant in human resources at the rehab clinic. She was tiny, very quiet, and she was obsessively organized. Something blossomed between the two. Lionel got clean and wanted to stay that way for Debbie. And he lost weight, thanks to her food planning. But both lived in dread of the day when Lionel's cardiologist gave him the all-clear to get back to driving, because when he worked, Lionel was on the road more than 300 days out of the year.*

*The solution? Debbie got her Commercial Driver's License. And when Lionel was finally ready to go to work, they became a truck-driving couple.*

*The night Zeke Fulton disappeared, Lionel and Debbie were ahead of schedule on a run from Miami to San Diego that had taken them through Houston, and they had to make a stop in Fredericksburg to pick up some merchandise.*

*They arrived at the Stonewall rest stop in time to watch the sunset together (approximately 6:30 p.m.), after which they had grilled chicken and green beans for dinner and made an early night of it, going to bed in their rig's sleeper cab.*

*At 2:33 a.m., Debbie awoke when she heard a vehicle passing slowly by their truck. She peeked out the window just in time to see a second vehicle, a yellow pickup truck, pass by and stop behind the first. Lionel was up at this point, and he'd already gotten his handgun. Lots of strange shit happens on the road; best to be prepared.*

*The couple moved from the sleeper into the front of the cab, watching.*

*The yellow pickup stopped, turning its lights off. The vehicle in front of it still had its lights on, though as far as they were from it, they couldn't tell if it was still running.*

*The driver's side door to the yellow pickup opened, and a man got out. Average height. Not too big. Not too small. He walked towards the front of the vehicle and crouched down. It appeared that he was checking the front driver's side tire. Then he stood back up, put something in his back pocket, and walked away from the truck.*

*Debbie claimed she heard the muffled* thunk *of a door closing, and Lionel said he didn't, but that she was probably right. The first vehicle moved forward, pulled out of the rest stop, and got back on the highway heading west. It was another pickup. A dark color. Lionel could tell from the profile that it was a Ford F-150. And he could tell from the taillights that it was a pre-1998 model because, in 1998, Ford released the tenth generation of the F-150, which was less boxy, more streamlined, and as a part of the update changed its taillights from what he called candy-bar taillights—a long rectangle—to a stumpier, more compact shape. The vehicle was too far away for the license plates to be visible. Lionel couldn't even tell what state they were from, and this was a man who spent 300 days a year looking at license plates.*

*Lionel and Debbie went back to sleep.*

*The next morning, when they awoke, the yellow pickup truck was still there. Lionel, gun tucked in his pants at the small of this back, went to check it out, and found the vehicle empty. The front driver's side tire was flat.*

*Lionel was ready to go, but Debbie thought there was something strange about the situation; she wanted to call the police and report the abandoned vehicle. Neither of them wanted to be late on their run. They reached a compromise. Debbie called the police after they'd made their pick-up and were well on their way to San Diego, passing through El Paso.*

*Lionel and Debbie stopped in Fredericksburg on their way back from San Diego to Miami to be interviewed by the police about what they'd seen that night. The yellow pickup belonged to Zeke Fulton. Lionel and Debbie were honest and forthcoming about what they'd seen, though Debbie insisted they limit the interview to only forty-five minutes to keep them on schedule.*

* * *

The front tire of the pickup was flat due to a puncture in the tread. There were two data points of interest concerning this in the file (information that had not been released to the public). First, the diameter of the puncture made it unlikely that it was caused by a nail. And second, the hole was round, but, according to the experts, the friction mark was distorted, which meant that the tip of whatever caused the puncture was larger than the shaft. The expert's conclusion: a flat-head screwdriver was the culprit.

This meant that, whoever drove Zeke's truck to the rest stop that night probably punctured the tire in situ, then got into the Ford F-150.

Good news for Gripke—at the time, Pedro Gomez drove a dark blue 1997 F-150.

Bad news—the Ford F-150 is the one of the most common vehicles in the United States.

# CHAPTER TWENTY-TWO

While Gripke was interviewing Pedro and checking out the rest stop, Mary drove east on Highway 290 toward Austin. The scenery was lost on her. While she'd driven the road hundreds of times, if not more, she wasn't ignoring the landscape merely due to familiarity with the route —her mind was elsewhere.

She was driving to her friend David's office in Austin. They'd recently seen each other at Grandma Nellie's funeral.

They had known each other since junior high and had been close friends through high school and college at UT Austin, after which David had gone into the Army. He had returned to Austin about a year ago.

In addition to being close friends, they had briefly been boyfriend and girlfriend in high school, for half of her junior year. Mary had relegated those months to just a blip in her memory. But now, as she drove into Austin, she was thinking about how and why they'd broken up thirteen years gone.

* * *

*It was her sixteenth birthday, and Mary had invited a group of friends for a sleepover at the vineyard. Mary and David were lying together on the roof of her grandmother's house, staring up at the virgin night sky. The others were somewhere down below, taking shots and apparently getting stoned. Mary could smell the scent of marijuana when the breeze blew her way. For their part, Mary and David were sipping from a bottle of vodka that wasn't quite warm yet, but no longer cold enough to go down as silky as water.*

*"So, are things any better with your parents?" she asked.*

*David's father was ex-military and had given him the idea to join ROTC to help pay for college. His mother hated the thought of her son joining the military and blamed his father. His parents had been having issues on and off for some time, and this latest friction point had made things even worse.*

*"My mom's just completely stopped talking to him now. It's really uncomfortable at home. She's still super-pissed. Though, I guess it's better than the yelling." He sighed. "I'll be so glad when college starts, and I don't have to be around them anymore."*

*Mary sat, silent.*

*David cringed inside. He worried that he had accidentally stepped in it. Mary had not only had the misfortune to lose her mother in a car accident, but that tragedy occurred on her first birthday. Shortly after, her father abandoned her to Nellie, either due to the pain of losing his wife or because (according to Nellie) he was a poor excuse for a man.*

*For Mary, every birthday was . . . complicated.*

*"I mean, don't get me wrong. I love them and all—"*

*"It's okay, David. I get it." She reached into her bra and pulled out a crushed soft pack of Marlboros. "Just 'cuz I can't remember my mom and my dad abandoned me doesn't mean that if we were a family, we'd all get along. Who knows . . . maybe they'd be divorced, and I'd be a runaway or something . . ."*

*She offered a cigarette to David, who declined, then she lit her own and inhaled the sharp smoke, hoping David couldn't see the tears in her eyes. She wondered what it would be like not to live with this hollow feeling inside. And not to have to be reminded of losing her parents every year on what was supposed to be a happy occasion.*

*What kind of family* would *they have been? She thought of Grandma Nellie and how much she would miss her when she went to college. Mary was not looking forward to the change.*

*David tried a new subject. "UT's gonna be awesome. So many new people to meet. I've started looking at study abroad programs too. You know they even have one in China now?"*

*As Mary remembered it, that seemingly innocuous statement about 'meeting new people' was what set her off. She'd analyzed it from time to time over the years and had come to accept that what happened next—though at the time she didn't realize it—was, ironically enough, due to her fear of losing him.*

*On that night, through the fog of her usual birthday emotions further clouded by vodka fumes, what Mary had* heard *David say was that he wanted to meet new people, then go study in another country, after which he would join the military. Mary was sure that, whatever there was between them as two juniors in high school, it wouldn't survive all of that. Why suffer through it?*

*"Yes. It's going to be grand," she replied.*

*While David rambled on, Mary felt a tightness growing in her belly. She had always been slow to make friends. She cherished the safety of her life on the vineyard—her, Grandma Nellie, and Pedro. It was predictable and manageable. She had friends, but just a few. As she sat there, she could see herself in college, alone, fighting to adjust, while David was off meeting new people, trying to drag her along, and ultimately leaving her. As she imagined these things, she felt anger growing inside her. She took a swallow from the bottle and then a deep drag from the cigarette. David prattled on, with no idea what she was thinking. The more he talked, the angrier she became. She waited until he paused.*

*"So," she said, "I've been thinking. You're right. We* are *going to meet a ton of new people. And, you know, that's what college is all about. Expanding horizons . . ."*

*She'd blathered on about growing into their skins, and discovering themselves, and new experiences . . .*

*"Wait," David placed a hand on her knee. "Are you breaking up with me?"*

*"Well, I mean . . . it's not breaking up per se; I mean . . . we're in high school, dude. This is just a . . . you know . . . transitory . . ."*

*"Transitory?"*

*"You know what I mean. I mean . . . what? I'm supposed to keep the home fire burning while you're off in Afghanistan fighting al-Qaeda or whatever?"*

*"What the hell, Mary? Now you're starting to sound like my mom—"*

*"What? Screw you!" Mary got up. "You selfish prick! Your mother's worried about you. How can you even . . ." She shook her head. "Never mind." She threw what remained of her cigarette at him and left to climb down and find the girls.*

*David swatted at his shirt, ensuring he got the burning butt off him, then crushed it. "Wait! Mary . . . Come on." He followed after.*

*By the time he got down off the roof and found her, she was huddled protectively with several girls. Crying. Abby stared knives at him and hissed, "Really? On her birthday?"*

*"But . . . she . . . I didn't . . ." He raised his hands defensively. Looking from one girl to the next, he realized that there were no sympathetic ears.*

*For the rest of the evening, David and Mary avoided each other. And, although he had stayed the night, sleeping in the bunkhouse with the other boys, the following day, when Mary tried to approach him to make up, he was distant—aloof—and left without finishing his breakfast.*

*After that, things between them were awkward for several weeks. But their years of friendship far outweighed their dating interlude, and they slowly slipped back into being friends once more.*

*They'd dated other people through college, and neither of them ever happened to be single and available when the other was.*

*And then, Mary met Johnny.*

# CHAPTER TWENTY-THREE

"Come on in, Mary. You're early." David smiled and gave her a hug. "Let's go wait in my office. We can catch up." David's company occupied a very plain space. Rented. Beige. Commercial-grade carpeting. The furniture looked IKEA. Mary followed him down the hall and took the seat across from his desk. The only decoration, on the wall behind him, was one of those motivational posters—an image of an eagle flying with a fish in its talons. From where she was sitting, Mary couldn't make out the caption.

She looked at her friend's face, a face she'd grown up with. He looked good. He'd always been somewhat athletic, though he'd gotten leaner during his time in the military. Since returning to Austin after his stint in the Army, he'd let his thick dark hair grow out a bit, and it suited him.

His company, NetForce Analytics, was located west of downtown Austin in a nondescript office park. Mary had chosen the location for this meeting because it was discreet. While she was by no means a local celebrity, Fredericksburg is not that big. She knew a lot of people, and a lot of people knew her; the stakes were too high to be taking any chances.

In some sense, it had actually been right here in these offices where Mary's Johnny problem had begun, a few weeks before her grandmother's death. She'd gotten a call from David, asking her to come in because he needed to show her something, "as a friend," he'd said on the phone. What he'd shown her had left her speechless.

For quite some time, Mary had suspected Johnny of infidelity. There were clues: the increasingly overt glances at random women, the vacation trips to Vegas with the guys, the unexplained (or at least poorly justified) extra overnight stays on business trips. But Mary had always told herself that she was the jealous type, too suspicious. And she realized now that, subtly, Johnny had reinforced that thinking.

In this very office, David had proved the contrary. It seems that one of the tools that Johnny used for his infidelities was a website called Sally Madison—a dating website for married people. Mary had been shocked to learn that such a thing even existed. What was worse, the website had been hacked, and a list of user emails had been posted online. And it was there that David, while working on a project for another client, had found what he wanted to show Mary: on the list appeared j.miracle@crabapplecreek.com.

Mary had been crushed. After David showed her the evidence, she'd sat silent for a long time, numb, before thanking him for sharing the information with her and going home, unsure of what to do next. The hardest part had been pretending that nothing was wrong. Acting with Johnny and her grandmother as though everything was fine. But she'd had to. She'd needed time to think.

"So? How are things?" David asked.

Mary shrugged. "We're here, aren't we?" The reply sounded sarcastic, which is not at all what Mary had intended. David's smile wilted slightly.

But, before she could clarify, David's speaker phone beeped.

"David. There's a Ms. Beavers to see you?"

"I'll be right out," he replied. Standing, he said to Mary, "I'll bring her in here. You can use my office. That way, no prying eyes."

"Thanks," she said. "I really appreciate this . . . all of it," she effused, trying to undo the prior unintended sarcasm.

David smiled. "Be right back," he said. "And don't steal anything while I'm gone," he winked. Mary laughed as he gently closed his office door behind him.

As she sat waiting, Mary caught herself biting her nail, her left pinkie, so she sat on her hand.

A few moments later, the door opened, and a petite woman with jet-black hair and ice-blue eyes stepped in. She was professionally dressed; her only jewelry was two diamond studs and a thin gold wedding band. She smelled of a crisp, lemony perfume and something else; cigarettes?

"Hello. I'm Betsy Beavers," she said, extending her hand.

Mary stood, taking the woman's hand. "Mary Miracle."

"I'll leave you two to it, then," David said, closing the door behind him.

As if it were hers, Beavers walked behind David's desk, opened her attaché, and removed a small notepad and a gold Montblanc pen, then sat down.

Mary followed suit.

"So, tell me, Mary," the woman asked, "why do you want a divorce?"

Mary explained what she had learned in detail. She showed Beavers the investigator's report she'd found on Grandma Nellie's iPad. The photos of Johnny with a woman the investigator identified as Summer King, a stripper.

Beavers nodded. "That's useful in terms of helping *you* decide what you want to do. But a judge isn't going to care if your husband's cheating. It's a no-fault state. Sure, we can make him look like a sleaze, to try to gin up some sympathy, but in the end, divorce is about economics. It comes down to how long you were married and how we divide up the community property. Tell me about your assets."

Mary explained about the vineyard. About the estate taxes. About the meeting with Clive. She also told Beavers about the Monet.

Beavers gave Mary a form to fill out entitled "Inventory" to list all her assets and liabilities, bank and credit card accounts, and those of the marriage.

Forty-five minutes later, the meeting was done, and Beavers was gone.

As David walked Mary out to her car, she said, "That's one of the hardest things I've had to do in a while. It felt so . . . clinical. The whole getting married thing is all romance . . . planning, flowers, music, guest lists. And then the ending is just math, economics. Wow!

"And, you know, talking it through with a lawyer makes this whole mess feel *that much* more real, you know?"

David walked, listening, with his hands in his pockets. "When do you tell *him*?"

"If everything works out right," she replied, "not too long now. I have to fill out this paperwork for the lawyer; she needs a little time to put everything together. A few weeks at most, I'd guess."

David nodded. "So, this weekend . . ."

"This weekend, it's as if everything was normal."

They took a few steps in silence.

"That can't be easy," David said. "I mean, pretending every day."

"There are worse things in life, David. Right now, I've just gotta get through this without getting screwed. According to Beavers, lining everything up right in terms of assets and debts is critical. So, I'm gonna follow her advice."

David nodded. He looked somber. Mary appreciated his concern and felt that familiar belly lightness he always provoked in her. The last time she had kissed him, *really* kissed him, they'd been sixteen. She studied his face, now that of a man, as was his body, and she wondered what it would be like now.

"So, see you at AA Saturday night?" he said.

Mary laughed. From high school and through college, one of their closest friends was Abby Rhodes, now Abby Winehouse. During their second year of college, Abby started dating an older man, Arthur Winehouse. This continued on the sly for almost three years before they finally got engaged and married. But Abby's friends all figured out what was going on well before.

Because Abby had slunk off to see Arthur in secret for so long, even after her friends suspected something was up, they all joked that she'd been sneaking off to AA meetings—Arthur and Abby. The nickname had stuck.

"Yep. See you at AA," Mary smiled.

# CHAPTER TWENTY-FOUR

When Mary returned to the vineyard, she felt upbeat for the first time since learning about her husband's infidelity. Having spoken with the divorce attorney, Mary felt like she was finally re-taking control of her life. And as she'd driven back home, she'd come to another decision that she knew Grandma Nellie would have approved of.

She exited her car and saw Pedro coming over from the service garage. Mary waved as she approached. "Hey! Good morning! So, I wanted your opinion. I'm thinking about going ahead with the barbecue."

Every year, Nellie hosted a Labor Day barbecue. It had been her way of saying thank you to the community for its support throughout the year. But it wasn't just about thank-yous; it was also about connecting with neighbors and building social capital—a deposit in the "good neighbor bank," as she liked to call it. Folks were just more open to lending a hand or granting a favor if you'd recently fed and entertained their family.

"With Grandma gone," Mary said, "I wasn't sure what to do. But with the taxes now, and selling the place . . . it may be our last one."

"I think Nellie would want you to," Pedro replied, though not with the enthusiasm Mary had expected.

"Great!" She studied him. "Hey. Is everything okay?"

"That new deputy came by," Pedro stated. "Since you ran him off last time, I thought you'd wanna know . . ."

Mary's mood deflated. She crossed her arms over her chest, shaking her head, "Dammit. I hadn't thought about him since the funeral. So much other stuff goin' on . . ."

Pedro nodded. "He was asking how well I knew Fulton. And if he'd come out here after the fight."

"Shit." Mary pursed her lips, looking off towards the house. She made a conscious effort not to look out towards the fields, as though her gaze might betray guilt. "After all these years. You think there's something new? Some new evidence? Or a witness of some sort?"

Pedro shook his head. "That seems real unlikely."

"Well, I suppose there's not much we can do but hang tight." Mary sighed.

"Well, with Nellie gone, you and me are the only two people who know what really happened," Pedro said, studying Mary for a reaction.

Mary kept her face flat, nodding absently. But her belly tightened. What Pedro had said wasn't entirely accurate, and it was her fault.

# CHAPTER TWENTY-FIVE

Six months into their marriage—around the time that Johnny had begun to realize that the wine business, or at least Nellie's, wasn't as glamorous or profitable as he had expected—Mary noticed a change in him. He had seemed a bit detached.

Mary thought this was simply the beginning of the 'end of the honeymoon,' something she knew had to happen. She'd read about it. She knew that marriages had to be worked on, that they had to grow. So, she began to plan date nights. And little weekend trips—an overnight bed and breakfast, a weekend at the beach. Mary also started researching tips for building trust and intimacy in relationships.

And this was where she had screwed up.

On a weekend getaway to a hotel in Port Aransas, after a nice dinner and a couple too many drinks, Mary had gathered enough courage to propose trying a trust-building exercise. They were sitting in bed at the time, sharing a bottle of red wine—one of six they'd brought from the vineyard.

Mary had read directly from her phone:

***Tell one another secrets***

*We all have at least one deep, dark secret—the one we don't share with anyone. To strengthen your bond with your partner, make an exception. Share that secret with them. And have them share theirs with you. It will show how much you trust each other.*

"Are you sure about this, Mary? I don't think I have any deep, dark secrets . . ."

"Oh, come on, everyone does . . ." she'd replied. "If you want, I'll start. Since it was my idea, I already thought of one."

"Oooh. Okay. This *does* sound like fun!"

"Be serious. This is about our relationship. If you're not gonna be serious . . ."

"Okay. Okay. Okay. I'm sorry." Johnny's curiosity was piqued. *What secret could my perfect little wifey possibly be hiding?*

"So," Mary said. Suddenly, looking at her husband and thinking about what she was about to share, her throat tightened. Her eyes watered.

"Oh, shit, Mare," he took her hand. "Are you okay?"

She nodded, squeezing his. "It's just, I haven't thought about this in years. And I've never told anyone. It was at my sixteenth birthday party."

"At the vineyard. When you broke up with David?" Johnny leaned back a bit, loosening his grip on her hand. She'd already told him about her short fling in high school with David. Johnny didn't like it one bit.

Mary nodded. "I was feeling kind of down that night after we argued . . ."

". . . and after you dumped him . . ." Johnny was always double-checking the facts.

"Yes, after *I* dumped him. So, I went out for a walk, sometime after midnight, just to kind of clear my head. Out towards the east hundred. And as I walked, I saw a light on our property, out by the last set of trellises. So, I made my way along toward it. And it was Pedro. He was digging a hole. Which was kind of weird. I mean, who digs anything like that so late? So, I went closer to ask him what he was up to, and . . ." Mary stopped. *Maybe this isn't such a good idea.*

"And . . . ?" Now Johnny seemed intrigued. In his mind, Pedro wasn't all that useful at the vineyard, and he took down a really nice salary. Johnny had already decided he wanted to jockey to get rid of Pedro, maybe even take his salary for himself. *Mary's little story might be useful.*

"Maybe this isn't such a good idea," Mary verbalized her thought, then took a swallow of wine.

"What the fuck?" Johnny exclaimed. "Are you serious? You start this whole trust thing like there's something wrong with *me*. Like I'm not open enough or something, then when you have to share your secret—and this is all your idea, by the way—then you decide *you don't trust me*?!"

"It's not that, I just . . ." Mary was stuck.

"I can't believe this, Mary. This is just total bullshit! How do you expect our marriage to thrive if—"

"It was a body, okay?!"

Johnny gawked at her. Eyes narrowed. "A bod- . . . What do you mean, exactly?"

"I mean, there was a body, on the ground."

"He was burying a body?" Johnny laughed out loud. "Oh shit! Are you serious? Like a dead person?"

Mary shushed him. "Keep it down . . ."

"What did he say when you . . . Wait . . . *Did* you say anything to him?"

Mary shook her head. "I freaked. There was so much going on. And I was kinda drunk. I just went back to my room and went to sleep. I didn't know what to do. Whether to tell Grandma . . . or what. So, I just did my best to forget about it."

"Damn, man . . . That's intense. You think it was someone he killed? Some illegal on the property or something?"

"I have no idea," Mary shook her head.

Johnny was confident this information would be of use. He just didn't know how or when.

"Are you okay about it?" Johnny didn't care, but it seemed like the right thing to say. While Mary shared her feelings, Johnny started trying to come up with a secret of his own to share in return.

When she was done, she concluded, "Okay, now you."

Johnny nodded thoughtfully, then told her a long story about how, after drinking with friends one night, he'd kissed a guy on the mouth. It was total bullshit, but Mary wanted a secret. Johnny knew that to shut her up about all the intimacy BS, he had to tell her something.

*And chicks love that kind of gay shit. It makes them think you're sensitive and vulnerable.*

# CHAPTER TWENTY-SIX

For several weeks after sharing her "deep, dark secret" with Johnny, Mary couldn't get that image from her birthday out of her mind: the east end of the vineyard at night, a crescent moon periodically peeking out from behind inky clouds. It was dark, save one small circle of light, maybe ten feet across, coming from a kerosene lantern resting on the ground. She was probably a hundred feet away from it; the lantern clearly illuminated Pedro. He was visible from the knees up as he methodically shoveled dirt, slowly deepening the hole he was standing in. On the far side of the little island of light, just on its edge and fading into the darkness, on the ground, she thought she'd seen legs, jeans and boots, someone lying on the ground. She'd assumed it was a body the night she'd seen it. That's how she remembered it.

But, looking back, Mary wondered if she'd been mistaken. Why had she made that assumption back then? It *was* dark that night. She *had* been drinking. And . . . Pedro . . . she'd known him for years before—and years since—that night. He was a hard worker. A good man. He had a peacefulness about him. Why would he be burying a body in the wee hours?

The worst part was that if Mary was wrong—and the more she thought about it, the more she believed she was—she'd told Johnny a secret about Pedro that wasn't true. This made her feel miserable.

And so, one afternoon, about a month after having told Johnny about it all, when she and Grandma Nellie were alone out in the vines, Mary dove in headfirst.

"Can I ask you something, Grandma?"

"Sure, hon. What's up?" They were out on the east hundred picking up tools, done for the day.

"You remember my birthday party?" Mary asked.

Nellie appeared to tense up at the question. "Which one?" she replied, almost sounding nonchalant. Smiling innocently.

"My sixteenth. That night, late that night, I couldn't sleep, and I went out for a walk, and I could swear . . . I could swear I saw Pedro digging a hole. Over there." Mary pointed to a spot not far from where they were standing.

Nellie stopped and looked at her granddaughter; lips tightened into a thin pale line. Mary noted that Nellie did not look over at where she was pointing.

"Dammit," she shook her head, putting her hands on her hips.

Mary chuckled nervously, hoping her next statement was not true, "It looked like he was burying a body . . ."

Nellie did not laugh.

Mary swallowed. "I didn't see right . . . did I?"

Nellie shook her head, then walked about ten feet to the left, turned, paced back. She repeated this several times as she attempted to make a decision. Finally, she stopped in front of Mary.

"Honey, you know I don't believe in secrets. Not between me and you. Still, this is one you gotta take to your grave."

Mary nodded slightly.

"I don't know if you remember a big hullabaloo about the youngest Fulton boy, Zeke?"

Mary searched her memory, then shook her head slowly.

Nellie's eyes became distant as she continued, "Well, the short of it is, the night of your birthday party, he picked a fight with Pedro in town. He . . . Zeke, that is . . . was drunk. It was down at that bar, the Mean-Eyed Cat. He went after Pedro, not sure why, and got the worst of it. Pedro left the bar and came home. Zeke stayed and stewed on it, and prob'ly got more boozed up. 'Cuz he came out here lookin' for Pedro sometime after midnight, maybe 1:00 a.m.

"Well, with all you kids down by the house with your music, me and Pedro had come up here in his pickup, threw some lawn chairs in the cargo bed. You know, having a few drinks and whatnot."

"Whatnot" meant weed. Nellie occasionally smoked—though only medicinally, she claimed, "like Willie Nelson."

"And then, along comes Zeke. Drunk. He was stumblin', yellin', out of control. I told him he was trespassing. But he wasn't hearing none of it. He wasn't listening to anything but his own homophobia, I guess. I think he was mostly pissed that everyone drinking down at the Mean-Eyed Cat saw the gay Mexican beat him down. Zeke wanted to fix that. He got more and more riled up, cussing up a storm. And then he went for his gun. Started wavin' it around."

Nellie paused, shaking her head. Tears in her eyes.

"We tried to talk him down, honey. But he was drunk. So drunk. Finally, just when we thought he was leavin'—cuz he'd turned and started walkin' away—he spun around and took a wild shot at Pedro . . . well, at us. We fired back. Don't rightly know which of us hit him. But he went down. When we checked on him up close, we'd hit him three times. All in the chest. I suspect he died on impact."

Nellie sighed. "So, then, we had a decision to make. One I'll never forget. Go to the police? Or hide the body? Pedro wanted to call the cops. He's too good a man sometimes, you know? Not me. I wasn't born yesterday, hon.

"Small-town Texas. A young white man shot dead. Whose brother happens to work at the attorney general's office. Whose other brother is a state trooper. And mamma's a good *church-going Christian.* And he's shot by a gay Mexican and a Yankee fag hag?

"Sure, we could have claimed self-defense." Nellie scoffed loudly. "You'll appreciate that I just didn't like those odds . . . And once I explained, Pedro saw the logic to my thinking. So, Pedro buried the body. That's what you saw. Then, we took Zeke's truck up to the rest stop. We tried to make it look like he had a flat tire and left it there."

Nellie took a deep breath, then exhaled. "And that's all there is."

Mary was stunned. Her grandmother had killed a man. And he was buried . . . within fifty yards of where they were standing.

"Now, sweetie, you've gotta promise me that you won't breathe a word of this to a soul. Not anyone. If you do, it won't just be Pedro they'll throw in jail but me too and, honey, I can't be goin' to jail. I'm too old to be making license plates," she concluded with a wry smile.

Mary threw her arms around her grandmother. "I won't say anythin' to no one, I promise."

Mary held her grandmother for the longest time before the old lady broke the embrace. "Now, come on. Let's get some dinner. I'm starving!" she said, wiping her eyes with the back of her hand.

In one sense, Mary felt relieved. What she'd told Johnny was true; she hadn't lied about Pedro. On the other hand, she had brought Johnny into the circle of trust, something she knew neither Nellie nor Pedro would want. But there was no point in telling them. Besides, they had nothing to worry about.

*They don't know Johnny like I do.*

# RUBY YI – 1972

For the three years after Kong escorted her from the fishmongers to meet Mr. Cho, Ruby Yi lived well—the best she had in her life up to that point. She received a small monthly stipend from Mr. Cho and a bonus whenever she worked. And apart from work, her time was her own.

Mr. Cho had immediately recognized Ruby's talents, or so he believed. And over the course of her three years in his employ, Ruby Yi had killed many men.

Now, she was once again standing in Mr. Cho's office, the same office that Kong had brought her to those three years back. But oh, how things had changed.

* * *

The first time Ruby met Mr. Cho, he was seated behind his desk, which was decorated with, among other things, a small South Korean flag. As she entered the room, he did not stand, which irked her. He asked her politely what had happened to Mr. Park. And Ruby told him. Everything. Without remorse. She left out no detail.

Mr. Cho then asked where the money was, and she told him that as well; Kong took her to her apartment to retrieve her stash. She presented Mr. Cho with the account books, which were up to date, the stacks of cash that had been Mr. Park's nest egg, and the two smaller bundles of money she had created for 'tax' and 'net.' She also told him that she had no idea what this meant, but she had kept the funds segregated.

Mr. Cho laughed and explained. "I am tax." He smiled, sliding those bundles to one side. "You are net." And he pushed those bundles to the other.

He studied the large nest egg pile of cash and said, "Killing one of my men without my permission . . ." He looked up at her, then at Kong. "That normally does not end well for the killer. But you are fortunate in that Jin Park was a useless turd. I needed to be rid of him. So, in a way, you did me a favor." Mr. Cho picked up two small stacks of bills from the nest egg pile and placed them in Ruby's pile. He carefully moved the rest of the nest egg, which was a lot, to his side of the desk.

He studied the young woman. "You are tiny. But you are smart. You have strength where it counts—here and here," he pointed to his head and heart. "That is what matters. The rest you can buy. Look at me." He indicated his chair. "Look!"

From where she stood, Ruby could only see the man's torso. To her, he was a bust behind a desk. She took a small step forward and stood on tiptoes craning her neck so she could see the man's chair—a wheelchair.

"A cripple!" he roared, slapping the armrests with both hands. "I cannot walk, yet I run everything! Look at Kong." He pointed. Ruby glanced at the giant. "He is strong. He is a giant! But he will never be me." Mr. Cho pointed at himself with his thumb, smiling broadly. Then he pursed his lips and steepled his fingers under his chin, studying her.

"You will work for me . . ." A slight lilt at the end of the phrase made it just barely sound like a question, as though he hoped she would, but wasn't sure. He nodded with his head at the small pile of money on his desk, *her pile*, beckoning.

Ruby nodded. She stepped forward and took the money—irritated that Mr. Cho had kept the bulk of the nest egg. She bowed slightly and left.

Kong did not drive her home. Yet, during the next three years, Ruby's only friend, to the extent that she had one, was the giant Kong. They ate together regularly. And little by little, she learned from him about this new world—the underworld—everything he knew. He was quiet but observant.

She learned that Mr. Cho was one of a few men fighting to control parts of the area's underworld. That Mr. Cho had both licit and illicit businesses and did his best to keep them separate. That he had a son, Arvin, who ran the legitimate businesses, a man not at all like his father.

"Arvin would like to be his father someday," Kong explained. "But Mr. Cho does not think his balls are big enough."

Ruby laughed. "What do you think?"

Kong hesitated, then said, "Ruby Yi has bigger balls."

Ruby also learned that things had been relatively peaceful in the not-so-distant past, but of late, they'd been getting more heated. Mr. Cho ran the Korean underground. But as of late, there had been more conflicts—the Chinese and Italians were making trouble. It was in this respect that Mr. Cho put Ruby's talents to use.

During the three years she worked for Mr. Cho, Ruby started her own account book and kept track of the men she killed and the cash she earned. At one point, Mr. Cho began to call her "my little mosquito."

"The mosquito is small," he explained, "but it kills more people than any other animal on earth. Men will run away from a lion," he added, pointing at Kong. "But they never see the mosquito until it is too late."

Ruby didn't care for the nickname. After all, mosquitoes killed indiscriminately. She justified her killings, to herself, by the fact that she only killed *bad* men. True, Mr. Cho evaded taxes, laundered money, and ran protection and gambling. But the men she killed for him were far worse. They ran drugs and prostitutes. Mr. Cho did not.

Ruby was short-sighted in this regard.

* * *

When she arrived today at Mr. Cho's office, several barely-dressed women stood in the hallway, really just girls. Gaunt, malnourished, empty stares.

As she walked past them, in a flash, Ruby recalled when she'd killed Mr. Park and how everyone had continued paying her in the weeks after she had killed him, assuming that someone had taken his place. It dawned on Ruby that if Mr. Cho was having her kill off the men who ran drugs and prostitutes, someone had to be taking their place. It was becoming apparent to her exactly who that was.

She stood in Mr. Cho's office, waiting for him to explain what he needed. He was reviewing a document. While she waited, a young girl entered, head bowed, bringing him tea. She looked like the others in the hallway, hollow eyes, needle marks on her arms. The only difference was that this one was by far the prettiest.

Ruby looked at Kong. The big man did not meet her eyes but stared down at the floor.

"I have a meeting with a man next week," Mr. Cho said, finally looking up. "One of the Italians. His name is Buitoni." He slid a photo across his desk. "We have met before, but there is no reasoning with these people. They eat so much garlic—it addles their brains. They are too thick-headed. The meeting will be at the restaurant at the Palace Hotel. Very public and safe. That is the idea, anyway."

Ruby picked up the photo and studied it. A fat man in a suit with no tie. The fat ones were usually easy to kill. She was already estimating how much poison it would take. Probably a triple dose. Maybe quadruple, to be safe.

"Where does he live?" she asked. "Or will he be staying at the hotel?"

Mr. Cho shook his head. "This needs to be very public. I want to send a message." He leaned forward, resting his elbows on his desk, hands clasped. "I will not attend the meeting. You," he waved an arm at Ruby and Kong, "will instead. I need my little mosquito and my giant to kill this Chef Boyardee at the restaurant, in front of everyone."

For the next few days, Kong and Ruby planned. They had worked together for years but had never killed together. And neither had ever killed in such a public way.

"The fat man will be protected, Ruby Yi," Kong observed. "There will also be hotel security. There will be witnesses—"

"That's the point," Ruby told the giant. "Cho said, 'send a message.' There *have* to be witnesses. This is a suicide mission . . ." she frowned, shaking her head. "And for what?"

Between the two of them, they put together their plan.

The day of the meeting finally arrived. Ruby was armed with an ice pick. Kong carried his handgun. At 4:00 p.m., as agreed, Kong and Ruby arrived at Mr. Cho's house.

Mr. Cho's houseman answered the door, and Kong and Ruby went upstairs to Mr. Cho's home office. They entered without knocking and found Mr. Cho wheeling himself toward the office door.

"What are you doing here?!" he shouted, looking at his watch. "The meeting is in an hour!"

"Quiet." Kong pointed his handgun at Mr. Cho and said, "Back up."

Mr. Cho's eyes grew wide when he saw the gun. But he recovered quickly and half-smiled, then slowly backed up his wheelchair towards his desk, all the while staring daggers at Kong. Ruby quietly closed the office door, and she and Kong slowly walked toward Mr. Cho.

Mr. Cho's eyes narrowed. Behind them, his mind was racing, calculating.

Kong broke the silence. "This meeting tonight. It will happen. There should be peace. And the Cho Family should leave the drugs and whores to the Italians. There is no honor in that business. And there is no point in being greedy."

Mr. Cho was fighting to stay calm, but his pride got in the way. He was incensed that Kong would dare to speak to him in such a manner. His face burned red with anger, and he was about to shout in reply when he stopped short.

Mr. Cho smelled Ruby's perfume, then felt Ruby's delicate cheek against his. And he understood. While Kong was telling Mr. Cho what was to happen,

Ruby had come around behind his wheelchair and was now standing behind him, leaning down. She had wrapped her left arm gently around his chest in a half-hug, with her head softly resting on his right shoulder, right next to his cheek.

"My little mosquito," he whispered.

Ruby tightened her left arm in a deadly embrace, simultaneously bringing her right hand across Cho's chest in a quick, decisive stroke, plunging the ice pick into his heart. She paused for a moment. Then in an equally swift stroke removed the pick and pulled away from the old man.

Ruby stepped around and stood next to Kong, and the two watched. Cho looked down at his chest, his left hand pressing just under his breast. His heart was punctured. Failing.

He looked up at the two of them, no longer angry, but sad. Maybe even disappointed. His breathing became ragged. His lips parted, about to speak, looking at Ruby. Then old Cho's head fell limp against his chest.

Kong removed the body from the chair, laying it on a Persian rug, which he and Ruby then rolled up. Kong carried the package downstairs, placing it in the trunk of Mr. Cho's Cadillac limousine. They drove ten minutes down the street and made what would be their second of three stops that evening.

Arvin Cho was seated in the back office of the Lucky Three Pawn Shop reviewing the books when his office door opened. He was a small man with short-cropped hair. He looked up and saw Kong—who he knew—and a tiny sprite of a woman he'd seen around his father's office. She wore a simple black dress and two tiny pearl earrings. The little woman strode confidently into his office, saying, "You need to get dressed. Do you have a suit? We don't have much time."

Arvin was about to protest, but Kong, who he knew to be his father's confidante, nodded in agreement with the little woman. As Arvin put on a suit and tie, Ruby explained.

"The Chinese Mafia has taken your father. And," she looked at Kong, "we fear they may have killed him."

Arvin froze, dumbfounded. He fell into his chair. "That's . . . But, how . . . Oh . . . my God . . ."

Ruby put her hands on his shoulders and looked him in the eyes. "Listen to me." She paused, waiting for his wandering eyes to settle on her face and focus. Once she had his attention, she continued.

"We don't have much time. As we speak, the Chinese are on the move. If we hesitate, by tomorrow morning, everything your father owned, everything he built, will be theirs," she said. Then added, "Tell us what to do."

"We . . . we have to stop them . . . I . . . We . . ." he stammered.

Ruby waited, letting him wallow in indecision and uncertainty. She needed Arvin Cho to realize he had no idea what to do. She waited, watching as his mind tried to grasp what had happened and fought vainly to find a solution. Any solution. Even one.

When Arvin understood that he had no clue what to do and that all was lost, he sank back in his chair, the tension draining from his body in defeat.

Ruby waited a beat for the defeat to truly sink in. Then, she spoke.

"I have a plan."

* * *

Arvin Cho and Ruby Yi arrived at the Palace Hotel promptly at 5:00 p.m. After checking in with the maître d'hôtel, they followed a large man in a cheap suit to a table at the rear of the restaurant. The bodyguard advised the man seated alone at the table that Arvin Cho had arrived.

Buitoni nodded.

Arvin held the chair for Ruby, then sat down at the table for four across from the Italian. Arvin leaned over, whispered to Ruby, then turned his gaze back to Buitoni.

"My throat," Arvin said, barely audibly, pointing at his neck.

Buitoni leaned forward. "Ya wan' I can get ya some hot tea? Or a brandy?" Buitoni snapped his fingers, calling his man.

Arvin shook his head and pointed to Ruby. Then he leaned over and whispered to her again.

"Mr. Buitoni," she began. "First, our apologies that Mr. Cho was unable to attend this evening. But he sent his son Arvin with full authority to resolve all matters between the Cho Family and your people. Mr. Cho has given the situation considerable thought and would like to propose an accommodation."

Buitoni nodded and signaled his man to bring him another drink. "Would ya like somethin' ta drink? Anything, Miss . . ."

"I am Ruby Yi. But please, call me Ruby." She smiled broadly. "And yes, you are too kind." She turned to Buitoni's man. "I would like a chamomile tea—two bags of tea please, not one—with a half lime, not lemon, but lime, served on a separate plate. On the side, if you will."

Buitoni signaled with his head to his man, who shrugged and looked as though he was still trying to get his head around "chamomile."

Ruby didn't miss a beat and continued, "Mr. Buitoni, the Cho Family is interested in, to the extent possible, legitimizing its interests. This would naturally result in certain of their current businesses no longer being necessary. They need a steward, someone reliable to whom they could transfer these assets. Someone who can be trusted . . . and who would stand with them against common enemies," she paused, looking at Buitoni, "against the Chinese, for example."

Buitoni nodded, understanding. "If our interests . . . Mr. Cho's and 'dose of my associates . . . was to be properly aligned, in dat situation, it would clearly be to our . . . mutual benefit and advantage to present a united front in da face of da chinks—Mr. Xi and his . . . compatriots. To sue jointly for peace. A détente, if you will."

Ruby smiled, reached out, and delicately patted Mr. Buitoni's hand. "I see that we understand each other perfectly. And, because Mr. Cho's focus is, again, on legitimacy, the Cho Family would be willing to cede the business of drugs and prostitution to your care, provided, of course, that gambling, protection, and alcohol stayed in the family . . . the Cho Family, I mean."

Buitoni nodded slowly. "Da drugs and da girls is ours?" He looked at Arvin, who nodded. "But," he chuckled, "Ms. Ruby . . . wit' all due respect, if da Chos keep protection and gamblin', well 'dose ain't exactly," he made bunny ears, "'*legitimate'* businesses."

"Oh, Mr. Buitoni," Ruby giggled. "Semantics. Tomato, to-mah-to . . . as they say!" She laughed infectiously.

Buitoni nodded and chuckled. "Yeah . . . right . . . s'mantics . . ." He sat back, appraising Ruby, then said, "You're all right, li'l lady." Then he turned and shouted over his shoulder, "Hey, Sal! Get a bottl'a bubbly while ya'r at it!"

And so it was that, while old Cho's body lay wrapped in a Persian rug in the trunk of his Cadillac limousine, Ruby Yi cut a deal with the Italians, legitimizing the Cho Family businesses while placing the blame for Mr. Cho's disappearance on the Chinese Mafia.

# PART THREE

## MARY GETS PUNCHED IN THE FACE

# CHAPTER TWENTY-SEVEN

When Johnny told Mary about his conversation with Clive and his two-million-dollar offer, she'd exploded. Johnny wasn't sure if her anger was directed at him or Clive. But he concluded it had to be at Clive . . . after all, Johnny hadn't done anything wrong.

"Two million dollars?! That sonofabitch! The vineyard's worth twice that—just the land; forget about the business!"

Once Mary had calmed down, Johnny gave her all the 'whys.' The market was slow. Bad timing. The vineyard wasn't very profitable. There were better markets than Texas—California, Oregon, and Washington State—and there were more competitive properties on the market.

"That's all well and good, and it may even be true, Johnny. But I'll be damned if we're going to sell to Clive Connard before seeing if there are any other buyers out there," she'd said. "We need to find a realtor and put the vineyard up for sale. Even if we don't get a buyer, maybe at least we can scare him into paying us more versus ending up with someone else as his majority partner!"

It made sense, but Johnny wasn't crazy about the idea; another buyer wouldn't pay him the commission Clive was paying. But he really couldn't come up with a good argument against what his wife was saying, either. And he wanted to maintain as much control of the situation as he could.

"You're absolutely right, and I'm already on it," he'd replied, nodding in agreement with her. "The listing'll be up by the end of the day!"

Mary had eyed him skeptically.

Johnny scrambled. To make the most he could of the opportunity, he'd called Karen—his current booty call—and offered her the listing in exchange for splitting her commission with him on the side, to which she'd happily agreed. Karen had done her job, and the vineyard listing was live online that same day, PRICE AVAILABLE UPON REQUEST. Johnny reviewed the post to make sure all the details were correct. Then he'd shopped vineyards all afternoon, trying to see if any new listings besides theirs had come on the market. He checked for recent sales, not just in Texas, but anywhere, that would indicate the real estate market was improving. But, aside from one enormous sale of a winery in France to some Hollywood types, things were pretty slow.

*Maybe Clive isn't completely full of shit after all.* He sighed. *For years I tried to convince Nellie to sell while the selling was good. But the old crone was too selfish to let go of her baby. And now, look. This is what happens when you get greedy.*

Johnny's phone rang.

*Aw crap! Speaking of greedy . . .* "Hello?"

"You know, Johnny, when I was a kid . . ." Sick Eddie said, "we were poor. My dad bugged out before I was born. So, I was raised by my mom. Just me and her. An amazing woman. A very wise woman. She would always make sure that the rent was paid three days early. When I was old enough to notice, I asked her why, and she told me, 'Eddie, you never know when you'll need a favor from your landlord. If you always pay early, you're building trust.'

"It's almost the end of the month, Johnny. I was hoping that you'd be building some trust with me. But looks like you're gonna push everything till the last possible second, am I right?"

Johnny swallowed hard. "I'm gonna need a little more time, Eddie."

There was a long pause. Very long.

"That is *very* disappointing, Johnny."

"Look, my wife's grandmother died, and there was supposed to be life insurance money, but there wasn't, and . . ."

"You think I care about Nellie's life insurance?" Johnny cringed. He'd never mentioned Nellie before. How much did Sick Eddie know about his personal life? "I don't care about your excuses, Johnny. All I wanna know is when do I get my thirty-five large?"

"Can I please have an extension? Just one month, please? I'm right in the middle of something that's gonna pay off big, and there won't be any problem paying you. In fact, I'll pay you extra."

Silence.

"One more month. Sixty thousand dollars."

Johnny grabbed his forehead with his free hand. *Sixty thousand dollars!*

"Say, 'I agree, Eddie.'"

Johnny sighed. What choice did he have? "I agree, Eddie," he parroted.

"But as far as our relationship goes, this is a big strike against you. And Johnny, don't be confused. This ain't baseball. You don't get three strikes."

The line went dead.

Johnny put his phone down on the desk and took a deep breath. *God . . . what have I gotten myself into?*

There was a ping from his phone. He looked down.

*Mary: Dinner at Art and Abby's tonight . . . Don't forget.*

He sighed. He hated these college buddy get-togethers. He texted back a thumbs-up.

# CHAPTER TWENTY-EIGHT

Being the new person at a party is always a bit awkward. Being the new person at a party of close friends from college—where you are the only outsider—is *the worst date possible*. This is what Rio was thinking as she stood next to David on Art and Abby Winehouse's front porch waiting for the front door to open. Rio sent all her mental energy out into the universe, praying, *sinkhole, open now, below me, please!*

Once again, Rio's magical thinking failed. Instead, the door opened, and there before them stood a very large woman, wearing some sort of turban-y looking head thing and, despite her size, was decked out in a flowing gown of . . . horizontal stripes.

*Who does that?* Rio thought.

"David!" the woman yelled, and before Rio knew it, the woman had lunged through the doorway and devoured her date in a giant hug. After a few moments rocking back and forth, the woman—who smelled of Chanel and loyalty, there was no other way to describe the scent —released David and turned on Rio.

*Oh my God! No . . . please . . . I'm not a hugger!*

Rio found herself buried in a hug, all arms and bosoms, and up close, she also detected the scent of soap. When the embrace ended, the woman held Rio by the shoulders, smiling. "Let me have a look at'cha," she said.

Rio looked into the woman's eyes and immediately felt at ease. There was no judgment, cynicism, or reticence. Only love.

"I'm Abby, by the way." Then, before Rio could take a breath, the woman began firing words at her like bullets and dragged her into the house. A drink magically appeared in her hand, and before she knew it, she was planted on a barstool chatting in conspiratorially low staccato with her new best friend.

"So, Rio? Cool name. Why Rio?"

"It's short for Rhiannon."

"Wouldn't that be Ria?"

"My dad wanted a son."

The woman's infectious laughter filled the room, and Rio laughed with her.

"You're not from Texas, are ya?"

"No. Florida."

"Flor-gia? Or Miami?"

"I think it's simplistic to divide the state into just two regions, don't—"

"Got it, Miami. A Flor-gian would never say 'simplistic.' Big word . . . When did you come to Texas?"

"After Andrew. The hurricane . . ."

"So, you're a storm-dodger? Risk-averse. Sensible. Wouldn't know it from lookin' at your shoes."

"My . . . what . . . what's wrong with my shoes?" Rio looked down at her feet.

"Oh, honey, if you have to ask . . ."

And so it went. Rapid fire ping pong, back and forth. As they chatted, Rio could tell by the increased volume in the room that more people had arrived. But Abby wasn't letting her go.

"How long have you known David?"

"About three, maybe four months."

"Closer to three, yeah?"

"I . . . I think so. How'd you know?" *Aww, he's told her about me.*

"Because four months ago, he was dating Meghan."

Rio's heart fell.

"Don't worry, hon," Abby patted her leg. "David's a stand-up guy. Never cheats. And Meghan was never meant to be . . . would never work with *his* family . . ." Abby laughed.

"Huh? What do you mean, *his family*?"

Abby ignored the question.

"What do you do for a living?"

"I work at a museum," Rio replied.

"Oh! An artist? Front of the store or back?"

"Huh?"

"Ticket taker or curator?"

"Oh, ah, I'm a docent . . . is that front or . . ."

"Meh. It's technically 'front' of the store. But educated. Closer to back. So, you're book-smart, too."

"Too?"

"Well, you're obviously bright. Doesn't always translate to books, though. You know what I mean?" Abby paused to take a sip from her drink.

Rio saw the pause as an opportunity and seized it. "So, so, so, so . . ." she said, trying to take control of the ping pong match. "Tell me a little about who's here."

"Aaaahh!" said Abby. "Gotcha! Sure! The scoop. So," she looked around the room, choosing a target. "Over there, talking to your fella, David, are Mary and Johnny Miracle. Yes, *Miracle*. That's his last name. No. Shit. Her family owns a vineyard. Well, now *she* does. Grandma passed away." Abby made an exaggerated but kind frowny face. "Sweet lady. Ahead of her time. Oh, my . . . You . . . Museum . . . You should ask Mary about *the Monet* . . ."

"The Monet?"

"The Monet."

"Like the painter?"

Abby nodded. "It's a painting. A Monet. It was her grandmother's. Now it's Mary's, I guess . . . There's a story behind it. Fascinating. Beautiful piece of art. So—that's Mary and Johnny.

"Theeennnn . . ." Abby looked about. "Over there, talking to Art—"

"Who's Art?"

"Art? My husband . . . Art? Oh dear, have I not introduced you to Art? Come on!"

Rio was left looking at air. Abby was gone and had already sashayed halfway across the room by the time Rio got up and followed. As she did, she saw that Abby seemed to be bearing down on a smaller, thin man talking to a woman.

"This," Abby said, putting her arm around the little man, "is the love of my life, Arthur Winehouse . . . no relation to Amy. Art can't sing for shit . . . if you can't tell by looking, he's an accountant," Abby laughed. "And Arthur, this is Rhiannon. Rio for short."

"You can call me Art," the man said, extending his hand. "But wouldn't the diminutive of Rhiannon be Ria?"

Abby and Rio both laughed. Then Abby said, “Don’t be silly, Art. Everyone knows it’s Rio.”

Art shook his head, not understanding.

“And this,” Abby resumed introductions, “is our good friend, Karen.”

“David’s Angels, I call them,” Art chimed in. “These two and Mary practically grew up together,” he added.

“Pleased to meet you,” the voluptuous woman said, flashing a smile. “I’m Karen Kline.” Her emerald green eyes sparkled as she tossed her blazing red hair and held out her hand in greeting.

# CHAPTER TWENTY-NINE

An hour earlier, Karen had been smiling in the mirror with anticipation. That night at Abby's would be the first time she would see Mary since the funeral, and they'd spoken only briefly that day as Mary was so distraught.

As she'd sat in front of her make-up mirror getting ready, she'd been lost in thought. She'd puckered her lips in the mirror, checking her lipstick.

*Secret, secret, I've got a secret . . .*

Before Nellie died, when Mary called Karen about Johnny, she'd been shocked. The call had come while Karen was at work in the middle of the day.

* * *

"Karen," Mary said. "There something . . . Well, it's uncomfortable . . . But I was stupid not to see the signs. And, I still just can't believe it, but, well . . . I found out . . . it's about Johnny."

Karen's face flushed. She sat down—no, *fell* into her chair. She and Johnny had gotten together *once* for a cup of coffee. *Once.* And while there had definitely been strong vibes, a palpable sexual undercurrent . . . *How did Mary know? Who saw us? And nothing happened! Not yet, anyway . . .*

Mary then explained to Karen what she'd learned from David—about finding Johnny's email address in the Sally Madison website hack.

Karen sighed with relief. She knew Johnny had cheated in the past; it was obvious to anyone who cared to notice. *So, this has nothing to do with me . . .*

"I know it looks bad, but it could be a mistake," Mary added. "Not that his email was there at all, I mean, but maybe he created the account, then had second thoughts and never actually used it? I feel like I need to give him the benefit of the doubt."

Feeling that she was out of the woods, Karen scoffed inwardly. Mary had always been such a Pollyanna. She'd lived a perfect little life and just couldn't imagine anything *not* going her way. Karen knew better; she'd actually lived in the *real world.* And she'd gotten divorced just a year earlier . . . that wound was still fresh.

And then, Mary being Mary, she had to stick her finger right in that wound and dig.

"What did you do when you found out Ed was cheating on you?" Mary asked.

Karen felt her face burn. Her ex-husband's affairs still made her feel small. She took a deep breath, once again putting her emotions on the back burner to Mary's usual insensitivity.

Karen spoke to Mary the way she would to a friend. "Well, if you ask Johnny outright, of course, he's gonna deny it," she replied. "He'll tell you that he never used the account, or that he set it up as a joke, or that he got hacked . . . the list is endless. If he's cheating on you, he'll just fuckin' lie." As Karen spoke, an idea began to form, a half-baked plan. She sensed an opportunity, even though she wasn't quite sure how it would play out. And, deciding to give it a shot on the fly, Karen set the hook, adding, "No, Mary. You can't ask him about it. You have to do more."

Mary had always loved that Karen was so cunning. So street smart.

"Well, I guess you're right. I'll try to be more vigilant. I guess . . ."

Mary, half-assed, took the bait. *Typical Mary.* Karen pounced.

"Fuck that, Mary. You can't just wait and see. You need to find out!"

"That's easy for you to say, Karen."

"No. Not easy to say . . . easy to *do.* Just give me a week or two. Let me reach out to him, start a little flirtation, and we'll see how he responds," Karen proposed.

Mary paused. Thinking. That was a cunning idea, but sometimes Karen's little schemes backfired. "Isn't that . . . like entrapment?"

"Oh, for fuck's sake, Mary. I'm not the FBI. Besides, I'm not gonna force myself on him. 'Oh please, Johnny, fuck me, fuck me, fuck me!'" Karen smiled with relish at the thought. That's precisely what she would do.

Mary laughed in spite of herself.

"No," Karen continued. "I'm just gonna open the door. Hint a little. Make it known that I am . . . I'm available. And then we'll see what he does."

Mary warmed to the idea and ultimately agreed.

And after they hung up, Karen was thrilled. She could now meet with Johnny, and if they were seen publicly, she didn't have to worry if the news got back to Mary.

At that point, Karen wasn't sure what she would tell Mary about how Johnny reacted to her overtures. Given how he'd acted when they'd had coffee, Karen was *sure* that Johnny would go for her. She assessed herself in the makeup mirror, sitting tall so her cleavage showed above her low-cut top.

*Who wouldn't wanna fuck this?*

In the weeks following her conversation with Mary, Karen had begun sleeping with Johnny Miracle. Her plan had been to take Johnny to bed a few times, then tell Mary that there was nothing there, and let it go.

*The perfect revenge fuck! God knows Mary deserves it . . .*

But Johnny had surprised Karen. There was something more to the man beyond the physical that resonated with her. Sure, he was good looking. And strong. And had this sort of carefree way about him, a kind of frat boy charm. She had always been envious of her friends who had gone to UT, including Mary. Karen hadn't made the cut, and while she'd hung out with them during college and went to all the parties with them, she was always the friend that 'went to community college.'

The hot, dumb one.

Johnny, she learned, had suffered similarly at Nellie's hands. He hated that his ersatz mother-in-law treated him like an idiot. He claimed that Mary did, too, by association. This struck a chord with Karen.

She also liked the idea of *possession*. She knew something Mary didn't, something Mary was dying to know. She *had* something Mary didn't have, for once. Karen had wanted to relish the moment, she'd basked in it, and didn't want it to end. At least not too quickly.

And then, just like that, Grandma Nellie died.

It *would have* been the perfect moment for her to tell Mary that she *was* fucking Johnny and completely crush the bitch. Mary was apparently overwrought, and Johnny had told Karen how despondent she was.

What Karen hadn't expected was for Johnny to open up so completely to her. His marriage was not what he wanted. He was fed up and was going to leave Mary. He just needed time to get things in order, like ensuring a *fair* division of their assets. And then they could be together. If that was what she wanted too. Karen was ecstatic. Based on her own divorce, she gave Johnny advice on what to do. On how things should be handled.

Of course, Johnny didn't know about Karen's little deal with Mary. It was perfect. She could lie to Mary and, in doing so, buy Johnny time. Which is precisely what she'd done. Now, Mary believed Johnny was faithful. She trusted him. Meanwhile, Johnny could execute his plan to screw her over.

*Serves her right. It's all Mary's fault, really, for not keeping the man satisfied. She was always such a priss. And hell, she practically begged me to hit on him . . . I can't help it if I appeal to him in ways she doesn't.*

Karen winked at herself in the mirror.

*What a tangled web, Karen Kline . . . Or should that be Karen Miracle?*

She looked at the clock on her wall. She'd be at Art and Abby's house in less than thirty minutes. Tonight, she would see Johnny again. They'd both be together in the same room.

Something stirred in Karen's belly. There was something exciting about the whole mess. Who knows, depending on how the evening went, she might even let him fuck her in the bathroom.

*Kind of like giving Mary the finger behind her back again . . . only better.*

Karen put her lipstick in her clutch. If she left now, she'd arrive just a tad late. Fashionably so.

# CHAPTER THIRTY

As David watched the gang, he wondered what it must be like for Rio to meet everyone for the first time. Abby, so bubbly and personable. Mary, the girl next door. Karen, the sultry narcissist. There was so much history in the room that David marveled at the fact that they were all still friends. Of course, there were also a lot of secrets between them, and those secrets were probably the glue that kept them from falling out entirely.

Looking at Mary, David felt the usual pang of regret. He had screwed things up with her so royally, yet she'd always been stoic about it. Now that she was vulnerable . . . that her marriage was off the rails, David wondered. Of course, he'd be there to support her in any way he could.

*Is it just me, or was there a little spark between us the other day?*

* * *

*After throwing her cigarette at him and abandoning him on the roof at her sixteenth birthday party, David and Mary's breakup became the focus of the party, at least for the girls. They took turns consoling Mary protectively* and *glaring at him. The guys were oblivious and kept doing tequila shots. David joined them and got wasted.*

*He told them what had happened, hoping in vain for some advice. "I just don't get it, bro. One minute, we're fine, talking about college and shit . . . and then she just up and throws a cigarette at me and dumps me and runs off crying."*

*"Dude, who the fuck knows. Chicks are so unpredictable. Especially when they drink," said one guy.*

*"It's the birthday thing, man. Her mom. Her dad. It's my fault, dude . . . I blew it, opening that can of worms." David shook his head.*

*"Don't worry, man," said another guy. "Tomorrow's another day. Besides, prom's just a month away. There's no way she's not goin' to prom, and it's too late to find another date. Just wait 'til she sobers up. She'll come crawlin' back, man."*

*David hadn't had to wait that long. At around 2:00 a.m., they called it a night. The guys went to sleep in the old bunkhouse, and the girls went into the main house. David had been almost asleep when he felt a hand gently cover his mouth. It was dark, but he recognized that perfume.*

*He'd made room in the little bunk, and slowly, quietly, they'd made love. It was only the second time, and having to do it so slowly and quietly was amazing. They lay silently in the afterglow for some time when it was over, then got dressed and tiptoed outside.*

*And there, in the moonlight, David's heart fell to his feet.*

*"Karen? What the hell?" he hissed. "I thought . . ."*

*"Shhh," Karen placed a finger over David's lips. "It'll be our little secret. Besides, you guys broke up." She leaned forward and kissed him. And, although he was still in shock, he'd also just made love to this girl, and her lips were familiar. He kissed her back.*

*The next morning, at breakfast, he was overwhelmed by guilt. On the one hand, Mary no longer seemed angry with him. She actually seemed a bit regretful of the night before. But now David had the Karen problem to deal with. She was playing it low-key, but he caught her looking at him repeatedly. The tension was unbearable, and in the middle of breakfast, he made his excuses and left.*

*For the next few weeks, David painstakingly avoided Mary and Karen, occupying himself with his studies and soccer.*

*Eventually, the friends began to engage again, and several months later, things returned to normal between them all.*

* * *

As far as David knew, no one had ever found out about his one-night stand with Karen. It was so long ago, just a foggy drunken memory. But, from time to time, he could tell that Karen was thinking about it. Just something in the way she looked at him said that there was this secret between them—a secret that everyone around them was oblivious to.

He was getting that same feeling from Mary this evening. He knew she was ramping up to divorce Johnny, and, as far as he aware, they were the only two at the party who knew.

# CHAPTER THIRTY-ONE

After drinks and snacks, at Abby's behest, they'd split into teams to play charades, dividing themselves up into guys versus girls. Everyone seemed to be having a good time. Yet Mary picked up on a strange vibe. She sensed that something was going on with Karen. Initially she'd been fine. She had started acting oddly when it was Mary's turn to act out clues.

Mary had been standing in the middle of the living room in front of the sofa. She held her hand to her ear.

"It's a song!" shouted Abby.

Mary nodded but shrugged and pursed her lips. She held out her hand, making a 'so-so' gesture.

"Not a song? But musical!" shouted Abby.

"A musical group? A band!" shouted Karen.

Mary gave a thumbs-up, then paused for a second to think. She then held both hands on either side of her head, fingers extended upwards, smiling. Then she pointed at Karen.

"Oh, oh!" shouted Abby. "Queen!"

"Yes!" Mary replied, holding out her hand for a high five. Abby stood and slapped it. Mary turned her high five to Karen next and noticed her face had flushed red. Karen was sipping from her wine glass, and either didn't see Mary approach for the high five—or was ignoring her.

"I get the fingers on the head, like a crown," Johnny said, distracting Mary from studying Karen. "But why'd you point at Karen?"

"Because Karen," Mary gestured Vanna White style toward her friend, hoping to overcome whatever bothered her, "was our Prom Queen junior year."

Johnny looked over at Karen and said, "Impressive. We are in the presence of royalty."

Karen blushed even redder but ignored the conversation and leaned over the coffee table. "Come on," she had picked up a small bowl with folded papers inside, "the guys are up. Whose turn is it?"

"I'll go," Art said. He selected a paper, unfolded it, and after a few moments of thought, began acting.

Mary studied Karen, who took a swallow from her wine glass and a deep breath before looking up. Mary smiled and winked at her. Karen smiled back. *Maybe*, thought Mary, *I just imagined it . . .*

As play continued, Johnny kept stealing surreptitious looks at Karen but for a different reason. She was wearing a tight black leather skirt with a green top that matched her eyes. She looked amazing.

*That little number that David dragged in off the street—Rio—is a nice piece of eye candy, too.*

Johnny wasn't good at charades. He thought the game was stupid. So, although he sat with everyone and threw out a guess once in a while, he mainly watched Karen and Rio . . . imagining. As the evening wore on, Johnny grew depressed. He'd hoped for some flirtation with Karen. Exactly *what*, he wasn't sure. She wasn't avoiding him, but she acted like everything was normal.

So, he fantasized. About fucking her in Art and Abby's garage, their powder room, even—it was complicated, but he'd make it work—on a trampoline they didn't actually own. The few times he'd tried to corral Karen in conversation, she'd been polite and chatty but didn't seem to want to dedicate too much time to him. It soon became clear that nothing special would be happening between them that night.

*Smart,* he had to admit. *This group knows each other well. Someone might notice something. Better to be careful. I've probably had too much to drink . . .*

Still, for him, that was part of the excitement. And that excitement, plus the alcohol, made Johnny take a chance.

After one particularly raucous—why, he had no idea—round of charades, he saw Karen excuse herself to go to the restroom. He waited and then got up to go to the kitchen for another beer. Once there, he detoured through the dining room to find her.

As he made his way down the hallway, the din of the party faded. He reached the restroom, imagining her sitting on the pot with her panties around her ankles. He felt himself getting hard. He was about to knock gently when the door opened, and Karen walked out. She walked through the door and pushed her way through Johnny, her breasts intentionally rubbing across his upper arm, and said in a low voice, “It’s not polite to stare, Johnny.”

He watched her walk down the hallway. *God, what a great ass!*

At this point, he was too excited to return to the party. So, he went into the bathroom and masturbated.

# CHAPTER THIRTY-TWO

With charades over, the evening was winding down. Mary was wiped out. She was sitting on a barstool next to David and Art, listening to them talk about some sort of new network software *something, something, something* . . . and fighting not to yawn. It had been a long week, and she knew things probably weren't going to get any better any time soon.

So, she decided to excuse an early exit with an invitation. Using the nail on her index finger, she clinked sharply on her wine glass several times and stood. As she did, the room quieted down. "So, y'all know that Grandma Nellie passed recently. And thanks again for all your support and prayers during that time. You also know—most of you," she gestured at Rio, "or not . . . that in her will she left me Crabapple Creek Vineyards. But . . ." Mary couldn't believe it, but she had to pause for a moment to choke back tears. "Sorry," she cleared her throat and laughed nervously. "Too much wine," she said, holding up her half-empty glass.

"Anyhow, they say there are two things in this world you can't fight—death and taxes. And goddamned if I didn't get hit with both at the same time."

Abby shook her head and said under her breath, but loud enough to be heard, "It's a goddammed crime, is what it is." Art took her hand and nodded.

"Well, the bottom line, literally, is we can't afford the taxes. So, Johnny and I . . ."

At the sound of his name, Johnny stepped toward his wife and held out his left hand. *So glad I didn't wash my hands*, he thought.

*Asshole.* She took his hand and continued, "We've put the vineyard up for sale," Mary nodded at Karen, acknowledging that she was helping them list the property.

There were several murmured "Nos" and many heads shaking back and forth.

"I know. I know. But I feel super-blessed to have been able to grow up there and have the memories I have, of the vineyard and . . . of my Grandma Nellie." The tears came, and Mary paused for a moment, crying into the back of her hand before she composed herself.

"But . . . There's always a but . . ." she laughed. "We're still gonna do our annual Labor Day barbecue."

"Yes!" and "Good for you!" sounded out, and many heads nodded.

"And," Mary paused and looked around the room. "Well . . . the people in this room are like family to me. Not you, Rio!" She laughed, and everyone joined in. "At least . . . not yet!"

There was more laughter, and Rio smiled broadly.

"But seriously, I want . . ." Mary looked over at Johnny, whose hand she was still holding. *Ugh. This pig . . .* "Johnny and I want to invite all of you to the barbecue, of course. Saturday, Labor Day weekend. You're all welcome to come, though you know how hot it gets. But then, also, more importantly, we want y'all to come, or stay, for an after-party at the vineyard. One last night at Crabapple Creek. A sleepover!"

Words of approval and applause erupted.

Abby jumped up and took Mary into her arms. As they hugged, Johnny caught Karen's eye and winked. She rapidly scanned the room, confirmed that no one was looking, and shot him a coquettish grin and eye flutter.

# CHAPTER THIRTY-THREE

Everyone came to work early for the Labor Day barbecue at Crabapple Creek Vineyard. The preparation for the annual barbecue had begun in earnest a couple of days in advance, but there were always last-minute things to take care of.

Mary was dealing with entertainment. They always had a couple of live bands play, and as anyone who has dealt with musicians knows, even amongst local talent, there is always a diva or two. In addition, this year, Mary had the added task of ensuring things were in place for the after-party.

Johnny was off doing what he always did at the barbecue. He was responsible for food, specifically meat. Everything at the event was catered except for the meat. After all, it wouldn't be a Texas barbecue if you didn't smoke the meat yourself. The vineyard had invested in a giant trailer smoker several years back that was used three or four times per year, this being one of those times.

Pedro was responsible for everything else. Setting up tents, tables, and seating, managing staff, coordinating security, and having employees available to give tours of the facilities to those interested.

Opening the vineyard to so many people presented challenges. Several years back, some kids had hijacked one of the four-wheelers and run it into a ditch. Nobody got hurt, but from that year forward, Nellie took extra precautions to ensure the property was protected and everyone stayed safe.

The gates officially opened at 10:00 a.m., and Mary swung through the business offices just before opening the property to the public. She wanted to make sure that everything was locked up. Walking through, she found the main office door open. She went in quietly, listening, and heard some movement, noise, coming from the small windowless office that housed the vineyard's network rack and security systems.

"Hello?" she said, announcing herself.

"Mary?" she heard in reply. The voice she recognized as Pedro's. "Back here."

Mary stuck her head into the small office, finding Pedro crouched on the floor, holding his mobile phone before him.

"What's up?" she asked.

"Nothing. Well, nothing *now*. The security system was dead," Pedro replied. There were twelve security cameras on site. Mary hardly ever checked them. "The cameras were down, so I was troubleshooting."

"And . . . ?" Mary asked.

"The main power cord." Pedro pointed at an electrical plug attached to a surge protector. "It was still attached but not pushed all the way to, and it was loose, so the system wasn't getting power. But everything is coming back online now."

Mary frowned.

"Are all the cameras working?" she asked.

Pedro checked on a computer that sat on a small desk in the security office, then replied, "Yep. Everything's fine." He stood and stepped out of the room. "Strange," he said.

"Has that ever happened before?"

"Nope," he answered. He gave her a knowing look. Only four people had keys to the office and the security room: Pedro, Mary, Johnny, and Grandma Nellie. Two were present, one was dead, and one . . .

Pedro closed the security room door, then locked the deadbolt using his key.

"How could that plug have come loose?" Mary asked. She had her suspicions but wanted to hear Pedro's thoughts.

"Only if someone was in here doing something. *What*, I don't know."

"Or someone loosened it on purpose . . ." she said. Mary thought it too coincidental that the security system had gone down the very day they would have so many people on the property. She decided to make sure the system stayed up. She found her key in her pocket and inserted it into the deadbolt lock. "Everything is up and running now? You're sure?" she asked.

Pedro knitted his eyebrows, unlocked his phone, and checked all the security cameras again. "Yep. Everything is running fine."

"Good," Mary replied. Then she braced her left hand against the deadbolt housing and, using her right hand, bent her key to one side until it broke off in the lock. "First thing next week, let's get a locksmith out here to fix that, if you don't mind."

Pedro chuckled. "Sure."

"I'm gonna go check on the band. You'll lock everything else up?" she asked.

"Will do," he said.

# CHAPTER THIRTY-FOUR

A Labor Day barbecue in Texas is a thing to behold. To begin with, even early September in Texas is hot—extremely hot—like ant-under-a-magnifying-glass hot. The sun pounds the earth like a bronco's hooves. A breeze would be nice, but don't count on it. Spots under trees are highly prized, oaks and chinaberry trees, especially, as they provide the most shade. Tents are nice if available, the open-sided kind, essentially oversized umbrellas. And hydration—in the form of iced tea, lemonade, and beer—is a must.

Barbecues are about food, and the types and varieties typically served run the gamut. There is, of course, brisket, pork ribs, and sausage. Oftentimes turkey legs are served. The Mexican-American culture has become so ingrained in Texas that fajitas are also a common staple, as are corn and flour tortillas. To accompany the meats, there is always potato salad, coleslaw, corn on the cob, beans—usually pinto, often *borracho*—and finally, the desserts. Pecan pie. Funnel cakes. Snow cones. Ice cream.

While food is a significant draw to the event, socializing and games are as well. Everything from horseshoes to sack races, and entertainment for the kids. And finally, the music; live music is ideal. And at Crabapple Creek Vineyard, live music was a tradition.

A funky country rock band played classics while neighbors mixed and mingled. Some caught up after not having seen each other in months. Other studiously avoided one another, the barbecue forcing some involved in minor feuds within talking distance. A keen observer could learn a lot about a community by watching who spoke to whom—and who didn't.

The barbecue at Crabapple Creek Vineyard had at its focal point a small stage on which the live band played. Radiating out from that center point in a half-circle were tables and chairs, different game setups, and food and drink booths at the farthest arc from the stage. The event was staged to accommodate up to five hundred people, which was typical attendance based on years past. Given Nellie's passing, there were more attendees than expected and a neighboring vineyard helped out by bringing extra tables and chairs.

Mary was up near the stage, watching as the field filled up with guests. She'd dressed for the occasion, comfortable boot cut jeans, a white western shirt, brown goat skin boots, a matching belt with a silver Crabapple Creek western belt buckle Nellie had given her, and a straw cowboy hat, a cattleman. She would have to start to make the rounds soon, greeting, making small talk, and spending a little time with each guest so that they felt special—and also so that they knew that *you* knew that they'd enjoyed your hospitality. Such is community life in Texas. Usually, Nellie did this on her own while Mary dealt with organizational issues and put out fires. This year, it was all up to Mary.

As she plunged into the crowd, she initially felt that she just wasn't cut out for this. Nellie loved catching up on gossip and sharing the latest news from the vineyard. Almost everyone Mary met offered condolences. And while many shared stories and favorite Grandma Nellie anecdotes, at first she found the exercise exhausting.

Normally, she would have wanted—*insisted*—that Johnny join her and help. But she knew where their marriage was heading; for her, handling this on her own was a step toward independence. Little by little, she got into the groove. Soon, she began to enjoy the schmoozing. The more her head ached from small talk and the more her face cramped from smiling, the more she relished each conversation. She didn't need Johnny.

As she wrapped up a conversation with a neighbor, she looked up to see where her husband was, spotting him by the smoker, drinking beer, and laughing it up.

*Lousy piece of shit!*

Then, her stomach turned as she saw Deputy Walter Gripke walking toward him.

# CHAPTER THIRTY-FIVE

"Mr. Miracle?" Gripke asked, holding out a hand in greeting.

Johnny turned and smiled. "Hey, there," he shook the deputy's hand. "Welcome!"

"You responsible for the meat?" Gripke smiled.

Johnny held up both hands. "Guilty!" he laughed.

A sausage popped loudly on the grill. The deputy made small talk while he sized up his host. Gripke thought that the man seemed comfortable in his own skin. He was wearing a very nice pair of ostrich skin boots, Luccheses, if Gripke wasn't mistaken. Expensive taste. Not quite a good ole boy, but not much more than that, either.

Gripke cut to the chase. "I was wondering if you remember a fellow by the name of Zeke Fulton?"

Johnny's eyes narrowed slightly, but his smile didn't waver. He took a sip of beer. "Nope. Never heard of him," he said with a shrug. "Should I?"

"He's a local fella. Disappeared back in 2002. I'm just chasing down some leads. Wondering if you'd heard anything? Knew anything?" As he spoke, Gripke's eyes scanned the crowd until they came to a stop on Pedro Gomez.

Johnny followed the man's gaze. This was an interesting development. The gears in his little brain began to turn. "Well, I really can't help you there. That would be before I came to Fredericksburg."

"You're not from here?"

"Nope. I married into this little gem of a town."

Gripke made a mental note of the sarcasm in Johnny's voice.

"When did you say this was again?" Johnny asked.

"2002. May four, to be specific."

Johnny shook his head, but he was thinking. *Mary's birthday was May third, a day earlier.* "Well, now." He took a swallow from his beer. "I guess I'm curious why you'd be asking me. And why you were looking over at our groundskeeper," Johnny nodded in Pedro's direction, "when you mentioned 'leads.'"

Gripke half-smiled. "It's just that one of the last things he did—Zeke Fulton—before disappearing was get into a fight with Mr. Gomez. At the Mean-Eyed Cat."

Johnny chuckled. "With Pedro?" Then his eyes brightened. "That would make it a cat fight, right?" Johnny laughed hard, but when he saw that Gripke wasn't sharing his amusement, he stopped. Then, clearing his throat, he asked, "Who won?"

"It seems your man knocked Fulton down, or out, not clear exactly which, then left the bar. His truck was found up at the Stonewall Rest Area the next day with a flat tire." Gripke noted the surprise on Johnny's face. It seemed genuine.

"And the guy was never seen again?" Johnny asked absently. He was processing what he'd just learned. Fulton has an altercation with Pedro. Then disappears. Add to that the dark secret Mary had told him . . . She didn't necessarily have to have her birthday party on her birth date, depending on the day of the week it happened to fall.

"Never," Gripke said.

*This has to be connected.* "Well, now. Nothin' comes to mind," Johnny said. Then pointing at Gripke with his beer bottle, he added, "But if I think of anything, I promise . . . you'll be the first to know. You got a card or something? Just in case?"

Gripke handed Johnny a card. "I'd appreciate it. If anything comes to mind."

Johnny paused, studying the card.

"You look like a man that might have something to say," Gripke prompted.

"Let me think on that." Johnny nodded and did his best George Clooney 'much obliged' grin. "Deputy Gripke." He slipped the card into his back pocket. "You have a great day now. And thank you for your service."

Johnny scanned the crowd for Mary and spotted her up by the stage. He saw her glance at him, and he smiled as he blew her a kiss.

*Well, I'll be damned. And here I thought she'd made up all that shit about Pedro burying a body . . .*

# CHAPTER THIRTY-SIX

Johnny was sipping a beer with a couple of guys from town while watching fajitas grill when Karen sidled up.

"You boys watchin' the grass grow?" she ribbed.

"Makin' meat's hard work, ma'am." Johnny winked.

"You got a sec?" she asked.

Johnny excused himself for a moment and walked with Karen.

"I got good news, Johnny. We've got a bite on the vineyard. A possible buyer."

"Well, that's great," Johnny said, trying to muster enthusiasm he didn't feel.

"I checked 'em out online. They're legit. You ever heard of Bella Dona Winery? Owned by the Rosenbaum family?" Johnny shook his head while Karen continued, "They make wine in Sonoma. They have vineyards there and in Oregon. Well, they say they're looking to expand their footprint, and Crabapple Creek just might work for them."

"So, what happens next?"

"I've sent them all the information you gave me. They wanna come down next week and have a look for themselves. Walk the land. That kind of thing. They're apparently not that interested in the house, more in the land and the operations. But, if they like what they see, they'd buy it all."

"Any idea how much they've got to spend?" Johnny asked. If he was lucky, maybe they'd make a lowball offer, making Clive's deal look even better to Mary. Then Johnny could convince her to sell to Clive and still get his commission on the side.

"They haven't talked numbers yet, but wine land out in Sonoma and Oregon is pricey compared to Texas. If they're used to paying those kinds of dollars, then buying here will seem cheap to them. Who knows?"

"Okay," Johnny replied. "Let me know when they want to come down so we can get things organized."

Karen made a pouty mouth and batted her eyelashes. "I miss you, Johnny. It's been a while since you stopped by." She reached out and discreetly touched his arm. "Is there somewhere we could sneak off to here, maybe? And . . . talk . . . a little more privately?"

Johnny looked at her gorgeous green eyes and could imagine her nipples hardening under her blouse. Two places on the property immediately came to mind where they wouldn't be found.

Johnny didn't notice that from across the field, as she made her rounds, Mary had seen him walking and talking with Karen. Mary was up near the stage chatting up the local Ford dealer and his wife—and periodically glancing their way—when Pedro found her.

"Are you ready?" Pedro asked Mary loudly, to be heard over the music.

Every year, Nellie said a quick thank you to everyone for coming out to the barbecue. This year Mary was doing it. She'd written up something short and simple, just like her grandma used to do. She was up to speak after the band finished the song they were playing.

She smiled at Pedro and said, "I'm good." She pulled a crumpled piece of paper out of her pocket that contained her speech.

"Okay, then. Come on."

Mary made her excuses to the couple she'd been talking to, and she and Pedro headed toward the stage. "They're just about done with this song. When they finish, I'll introduce you," Pedro said.

Pedro walked up the steps to the stage. As he did, Mary looked back over towards Johnny and Karen, but they were gone. She scanned the crowd. Nothing. Back by the barbecue smoker. Nothing. Over by the beer kegs. Nothing. She re-scanned the entire area. Nothing.

She waited patiently for the song, a longish country ballad, to finish, and snapped out of her reverie as she heard the tail end of Pedro's introduction, ". . . the new owner of Crabapple Creek Vineyard, Nellie's own granddaughter, and my boss . . . Mary Miracle!"

Mary climbed up onto the stage and looked out over the crowd. She saw many familiar faces. Kids running around. Folks getting beer, smoking, eating, and playing horseshoes. Just like every other year. But with one major difference. Grandma Nellie was gone.

"When my grandma first started throwing these barbecues, I was just a little girl. And I loved the balloons, and the music, and the funnel cakes. It was always a great day.

"It was only when I got older that I understood why she started having these barbecues on Labor Day weekend. To celebrate all the hard work it takes to run a business, to make ends meet, to raise kids right so they grow up to be good people . . . so thanks to all you hardworking folks out there that give your all to make this country great!"

There was a round of applause.

"None of that, of course, would be possible without another kind of labor—much harder than what most of us do. So I also want to say 'thank you' to those men and women who put themselves through hell in basic training, wore our country's uniform, and took up arms to defend our nation so that we all can have the freedom and the security to have a barbecue like this here today.

"I'd like to ask that all our veterans and active or reserve military please raise their hands."

There was a bit of rustling and throat clearing while folks looked around as men and women around the grounds raised their hands. A spontaneous round of applause began, and Mary joined in.

"Thank you to all of you. And God bless us all!" As she said the words, she spotted Karen walking back onto the field where the barbecue was being held. She had just come out of the service garage—which housed the vineyard offices and a large bay for equipment and storage.

*What the hell was she doing in there?* Mary wondered. *That should all be locked.*

She scanned for Johnny and, a moment later, spotted him coming out of the warehouse door on the other side of the same building.

*That bastard . . .* she thought. *And Karen . . .*

Mary felt the back of her neck tighten. She was furious. That Johnny was cheating. That Karen had lied to her.

*How did I not see that?*

*Stupid Mary! Stupid! Stupid! Stupid!*

Mary's remarks were finished, and she was about to turn to hand the mic back to the band, but as she watched her husband making his way closer, smiling and waving at her, she had an idea.

*Channel the rage, girl.*

"You know, the one big thing that's different this year is that my Grandma Nellie passed away last month." There were some "awws," and a few folks clapped lightly. "I'd like to take just a short moment of silence to remember her, if that's all right with y'all."

There was a brief hush, followed by silence. Mary held her head bowed, counting slowly to twenty.

"Thank you," she said. There was a round of applause. Mary nodded, raising her hand to quiet the crowd.

"Losing Nellie was hard. It was a difficult time for all of us here. But we got through it. And I want to say thank you, personally. Because I couldn't have gotten through it without support from so many of you."

Applause.

"But in particular, there's one man without whose help and love and support . . . well, it would've been a helluva lot harder."

There was chatter and a bit of scattered applause.

"He's someone special . . . to me, obviously. But also to our community. Someone you can always count on. To lend a hand. Or for a kind word."

Mary paused, letting expectations build.

"I know I wouldn't be the woman I am today, and this vineyard wouldn't be either . . . if it wasn't for him." She watched Johnny draw closer. "So, I want to recognize and say a big Texas thank you," Mary smiled, ". . . to Pedro Gomez." Mary turned toward Pedro with arms wide open.

There was a short pause, then applause broke out.

Pedro crossed the stage, hugged Mary, and said to her, "Not nice, Mary . . . why do you want to put me in the middle of your mess with Johnny?"

Mary laughed for a moment as she hugged him. Then as she stepped back, seeing that he was serious and a bit bothered, she looked Pedro hard in the eyes, and answered. "Because it's true. Thank you," she added, and gave him a gentle kiss on the cheek.

Pedro smiled at her and nodded softly. "You're welcome."

Then she turned to face the crowd, holding Pedro's hand, and said, "Y'all have a great Labor Day!"

# CHAPTER THIRTY-SEVEN

"Well, that was kind of awkward, wasn't it?" Rio asked David.

They had arrived at the barbecue a bit earlier. And after grabbing beers, they'd spotted Mary and had been making their way over to say hello just before she went on stage. So, they'd stood to the left of the stage to hear her speech.

"How do you mean?" David asked.

"Well, I kind of assumed she was talking about her husband. At least that's the direction it sounded like she was heading."

"Nah," David replied. "Pedro's been around here forever. He was like an uncle to Mary growing up." David agreed but didn't want to go down that conversation's path. He hadn't told Rio—or anyone—about Mary's divorce plans.

Rio was going to press the matter further, but David turned away smiling, and she followed his gaze to see Mary coming off the stage steps to greet them.

"Y'all having a good time so far?" Mary asked as she hugged one and then the other.

"This place is incredible!" Rio smiled broadly. "You must get the most amazing sunsets out here."

"Well, tonight, you're gonna see for yourself!" Mary looked at her watch. "We've still got a few more hours until this starts to wind down. We like to get everyone off the property before dark. Then, we're gonna get the firepit going, and then we can watch the sun go down."

"Mary," Pedro inserted himself, "someone needs to speak with you for a moment."

"Sorry." Mary excused herself, then added as she began to step away, "Oh, David, you guys are gonna be staying in the green guest room. With the canopy bed."

"Got it," he confirmed.

"Right. So, if you get tired of all this and want to chill, you can go up to the main house, put your bags in there, and just hang out. Hey!" Mary added, recalling Rio's interest. "You can show her the Monet."

"Ohh! I'd love that! Thank you, Mary!" Rio effused.

"See y'all in a bit!" Mary began to walk away, then suddenly paused. "Hold on," she reached into her pocket. "Keys." She tossed a small key chain to David. "Just make sure you keep the place locked. Don't want anyone from the barbecue wandering into the house."

"Sure. Thanks," David replied.

Mary left David and Rio and followed Pedro behind the stage, where the Rhinestone Realtor, Kitty Clark, was waiting.

# CHAPTER THIRTY-EIGHT

Johnny Miracle was fuming. He had supported Mary for years, worked tirelessly on the vineyard, and been right by Mary's side after Nellie's death—*and through Mary's ridiculous depression.*

*He'd* been there for her, helping with the vineyard since they'd married.

*I should've been up on that stage with her. Not that faggot, Pedro. She should have told everyone what a great guy I am! Everyone already knows . . . but still. I'm entitled to some affirmation.*

It was because of this kind of shit that Mary deserved what she got. It was because of this kind of shit that he'd just fucked Karen . . . in Pedro's office . . . on his desk.

*Mary doesn't deserve me—hell, she doesn't deserve the name "Miracle."*

He'd see to it that she got what she deserved once he got his ducks in a row.

"That's gotta sting a little, huh, cowboy?" Clive Connard rumbled as he double-slapped Johnny on the shoulder in greeting.

Johnny turned and forced a smile. "Whaddya mean, Clive?"

"I sure thought she was talkin' about you, Johnny. Gonna call you up on stage—"

"You know, Clive," Johnny interrupted, "for someone who needs my help to buy this place, you seem to be doin' your damnedest to piss me off."

Clive laughed good-naturedly. "Now, Johnny, it's all in good fun. Speakin' of buyin' . . . have you made any progress? See, I was thinkin' . . . we need to make the deal more real to Mary." Clive had been listening to his negotiation books again. "So, I brought the paperwork, the contract all signed and everything. I even brought a signed check for the down payment. Increases the sense of urgency, you know. Maybe it'll push her over the edge if you show her that?"

Johnny smirked smugly. “Well, my friend, things ain’t that simple. It looks like we’ve got another player at the table.”

Clive’s face fell. “What?”

“Yep. Some group outta Oregon or somethin’. Karen’s getting me the details. I’ve never heard of ‘em. But they own a bunch of vineyards, and they’re looking at expanding into Texas. So, buddy, you may be in a biddin’ war soon.” Johnny flashed an exaggerated smile imitating Clive’s and double-slapped his shoulder in return.

“Goddamnit, Johnny!” Clive shook his head. “Shit!”

“I told you your offer was too low.”

Clive eyed Johnny. “Well, I can always up it by the amount of your little commission.”

Johnny glared back at the man.

Then Clive smiled broadly. “Where there’s a will, there’s a way, Johnny boy. Why don’t you take the paperwork, show it to her. In the meantime, we’ll see what happens with these other folks. Lotsa looky-loos out there, you know?”

“All right, Clive. Let’s do that,” Johnny said absently as he watched Mary walk behind the stage with Pedro. Behind the musicians, the drum set, and all the equipment, he could make out three heads standing together. Mary was talking with someone, and from the sparkles, he thought it might be the Rhinestone Realtor.

*That’s odd. I didn’t know they knew each other.*

“Come on, Johnny!” Clive insisted. “The paperwork’s in my truck.”

# CHAPTER THIRTY-NINE

"What a cool place!" Rio was standing next to David in the entryway to the main house. Although the exterior was classic Texas, the interior was surprisingly contemporary.

"Yeah," David replied. "When Mary's grandmother bought the place, she completely gutted it. She just hated all the shiny old wood. It was a lot of pine . . . or cedar, I forget which, but real knotty wood. So, she put in tile everywhere instead. It's so hot most of the time in this part of Texas that the tile's nice. Stays cooler in the summer, you know?" David spoke while they walked down a hallway toward their bedroom. Rio followed him.

As they entered the room, Rio said, "So, she wasn't kidding when she said green." The room's walls were painted in a deep mint green—medicinal green. David placed his overnight bag on the bed, unzipped it, and began to unpack.

"Why don't you show me the painting first? We can unpack later," Rio suggested.

David led Rio back up the hallway and turned right, passing through a large opening into the family room. At the other end was a semi-open kitchen, separated from the family room by an island/bar. David headed towards the kitchen. To the left was a wall of multiple French doors leading out to a patio with chairs, a table, a firepit, and more. To the right was a set of double doors.

"This," David said, "is the study." Bookshelves were on all four walls, and two oversized leather chairs sat atop a Persian rug in front of a fireplace. The shelves were mostly filled with books and some photos, though one of them held liquor bottles and crystal glassware. And there above the fireplace hung the painting.

"Hooo-ly shit!" Rio whispered. She slowly walked closer, studying the piece. David stood back, watching her. "Dude . . . that," she pointed, "is a masterpiece! How the heck did it end up here?" Rio held up her hands. "Wait, that came out wrong. What I mean is, why does Mary own a Monet? I mean, from what I understood, she's selling this place because she can't afford to pay the taxes, but that painting's probably worth more than . . ." Rio spread her arms, indicating the house and vineyard and everything, "all of this."

"Yeah, I hear you. Here's what I know. This painting belonged to Mary's family way back. They were super-rich back in, like, the 1930s and '40s or something; I've never really gotten all of the deets. Hell, I don't know if Mary even knows everything. But, at some point, Nellie's dad screwed up royally. Like, *real bad* investments. I always imagined that he got over-leveraged in the stock market or something, but I don't really know. Anyway. It's a riches-to-rags story. They lost everything. This painting used to hang in their house when Nellie was growing up. And her mother had promised her that one day she could have it. But it ended up getting sold to pay debts or whatever. So, later, somehow, Nellie brought it back into the family."

"No. Shit," Rio said. "Look." She held her arm out towards David. "I've got goosebumps. That's so beautiful. Great paintings always have great stories behind them, you know?" She turned back to admire the Monet again.

"Of course, if it gave *you* goosebumps, imagine Mary. She sort of holds the family legacy. She can't imagine selling it, much less to pay taxes." David sighed.

"What a shitty situation. Sell the home you grew up in, or your one and only family heirloom . . . Damn . . ." Rio shook her head. "Poor Mary."

"Yeah," David agreed. "Poor Mary."

Rio stepped closer to David. "You know, stories like that, romantic stories, make me kinda horny . . ." she said, reaching up and kissing him softly. He responded, their kisses more passionate.

"You know, David . . . When they redecorated, I think they missed a piece of knotty wood," Rio giggled, pushing her hips up against David's.

David laughed and said in a British accent, "You're a knotty girl; that's what you are . . ."

The two went back to their mint green room and made love. Afterward, they both dozed off. Well, David did.

Rio didn't.

When she was sure he was asleep and she wouldn't disturb him, she slipped from the bed and quietly padded out of the room.

# CHAPTER FORTY

Later that afternoon, Art and Abby drove onto the vineyard property, passing several vehicles already leaving the barbecue. They had told Mary they would pass on the barbecue itself because of the heat. But they wouldn't dream of missing the sleepover.

It was a bittersweet moment for Abby, knowing that Mary was selling the vineyard. She had spent a lot of time hanging out with Mary and Karen while growing up, and much of that time right here on Grandma Nellie's, now Mary's, property. The vineyard had created an environment where the three could be friends, but Abby knew she was the glue that made the threesome work.

Karen's situation growing up had been the least stable. The one thing she'd had going for her was that she had always been mature for her age—physically—and drop-dead gorgeous. This was her greatest asset, but sometimes, it was a liability. Karen was relatively bright; yet early on, she'd found it easier to rely on her looks to get what she wanted. As a result, her academics had suffered—at least, this was Abby's opinion.

Mary was more outdoorsy, more of a tomboy, especially when they'd been younger. By high school, she had come into her own as a young woman. Still, she never got excessively into make-up and high heels; she was much more comfortable in jeans, ropers, and a baseball cap. She'd also been much slower getting into the whole dating scene.

Karen had been way ahead of them both on that count. Abby shook her head, wondering how much of that may have had to do with something abusive going on at home. She'd touched on that subject once with Karen.

* * *

*It was their junior year, just a week before prom. Karen corralled Abby in the parking lot after school. She said she needed a favor, so they'd gotten into Abby's car to chat.*

*"I've got a little problem, and I wanted to see if you could help me out," Karen began.*

*Abby nodded. "Sure, girl. What's up?"*

*"But you have to promise not to tell anyone, especially Mary."*

*"Okay." Abby rolled her eyes and held up her hand as if taking an oath, "I promise."*

*"I need a ride, well, company." Karen's eyes watered slightly, but she took a deep breath, steeling herself. The tears evaporated. "I'm getting an abortion, and I could use . . . well, could you come with me?"*

*"Oh God! Honey . . ." Abby immediately took her friend's hand in both of her own. "Shoot. That's . . . Wow, that's a big one. Who, well . . . I . . . I guess your folks don't know?"*

*Karen scoffed and shook her head. "Are you kidding? No way."*

*Abby had wanted ask the obvious: Who's the father? Karen had never really had a steady boyfriend; she just sort of went out with different guys, usually older, on and off. But Abby decided that if Karen wanted her to know who the father was, she would tell her. The fact that Karen was asking for help meant that the other responsible party either didn't know or didn't want to be involved. Still, Abby was concerned that maybe something abusive was involved.*

*"Should we," Abby struggled to find the best way to word what she wanted to say, "is there maybe any reason that the cops should know?"*

*"What?" Karen pulled her hand away. "Like, was I raped or something? What the fuck, Abby? You think I'd keep something like that quiet?"*

*"No, no," Abby spoke calmly in a low voice. "I just mean that . . . well, you're not eighteen, so technically . . ."*

*"Oh, fuck you! So, you think poor white trash Karen from the shitty side of town got fucked by her uncle or something and doesn't know enough to go to the police?"*

*"Karen! Stop!" Abby shouted. She always knew how to get through to Karen. Her friend responded to the shout, visibly backing down. "All I'm saying is . . . well, this is a big deal, and if there's anyone that needs to be dealt with . . . Let me start over," Abby took a breath. "If this was in any way not consensual . . ."*

*They looked at each other, and Karen shook her head slowly. "It's nothing like that."*

*"And," it was an awkward question, a complicated subject, "I don't suppose you'd consider keepin' it?" Abby asked.*

*Karen glared at Abby in reply.*

*"Well, that's your decision. And . . . yeah. I'll take you. Sure."*

*"Thanks."*

*"Oh, come here." Abby said, and hugged Karen, who cried into her shoulder.*

*Three days later, Abby accompanied Karen to the Bluebonnet Women's Center. While she waited for Karen in the lobby, she flipped idly through a magazine. She'd been waiting about fifteen minutes when she heard it.*

*"LIFE BEGINS," one voice shouted.*

*"AT CONCEPTION," multiple voices shouted in response.*

*And it repeated.*

*Abby turned and looked out the window. The parking lot was full of cars, and protestors were carrying signs.*

*"There's some sort of anti-choice protest going on," she overheard the receptionist tell someone on the phone. Another attendant walked past Abby and closed the blinds on all the windows. Abby turned back to her magazine. About ten minutes later, the chanting stopped.*

*When Karen returned to the reception area, she looked pale and frightened. Abby went to her friend.*

*"You okay, hon?"*

*"Let's just go," she nodded.*

*"Hold on a sec, ladies," said the receptionist. She got up and looked through the blinds in front of the one of the windows. "Okay . . . They're gone. It's just the cops out there now."*

*Several officers were at the far end of the parking lot talking to two protestors. One was still holding a sign. As Abby and Karen pulled out of the parking lot and onto the road, they drove right past them. The one holding the sign was Mrs. Shoe, their high school history teacher. Karen turned her head away, and Abby gunned it.*

*"Don't worry. She didn't see us. She was too busy yellin' at the cops," Abby said.*

* * *

Abby never told anyone about Karen's abortion. It was the one big secret among the girlfriends that she had kept from Mary. But then, it wasn't any of her business.

Throughout college, Abby had been the one that kept the group together. She didn't know if they realized it, but she was always the one coming up with excuses to get together, reaching out to include Mary when Karen called Abby to do something, and vice versa.

In the years since college, their get-togethers had become fewer and farther between. And lately, she'd picked up tension between the two; it seemed to be coming from Karen. Abby wondered whether maybe a girls' night out, just the three of them, might set things right.

*I'll keep an eye on them tonight. See how they're gettin' on . . .*

# CHAPTER FORTY-ONE

The barbecue had ended at 4:00 p.m. Although Pedro was still working with a couple of guys putting away chairs and tables, most of the clean-up was done by 5:30 p.m., the time at which Mary had asked all the friends to gather up at the vineyard's main house.

As the barbecue wound down, Karen made her way up to the main house and decided to take a hot bath in one of the guest rooms. She was in a pensive mood and took her time getting ready. She could hear noises, conversation in the house. When she finally decided to join the party, everyone else had arrived. She made her way to the kitchen and saw that, as sometimes happens at these sorts of gatherings, the guests had naturally divided up by gender. The guys had congregated out on the patio where Johnny was putting wood on the firepit. So, Karen joined the women in the kitchen organizing the food, setting out plates, chopping, and preparing. Although there was plenty of barbecue left, they also wanted to put out some lighter fare.

The four ladies—Mary, Abby, Rio, and Karen—talked across the kitchen.

"Do you want to serve the hummus in the container . . . or should I put it in a bowl?"

"Container's fine, don't you think?"

"Oh, hon, the less clean-up, the better. Leave it in the container."

"I agree."

"Where do you keep the napkins?"

"They're in the pantry; use the paper napkins, since we're going with the container."

"Keep it casual, sweetie. It's just us."

"Do you want me to make two platters, separate the cheese and the meat, or mix them up?"

"Mix it up, I think, no?"

"Definitely."

"I agree."

"That way, you can get whichever you want, meat or cheese, from the platter that's close to you."

"That's smart. Mix it up."

"Oh, this hummus is amazing."

"Trader Joe's."

"Oh, I *love* Trader Joe's!"

"I shop there *all the time.*"

"They have the best plantain chips. Have you tried them?"

"I think we have some—of the plantain chips, I mean. Do you think they'd work with the hummus?"

"Oh, definitely."

"*Yes!*"

"Check the pantry . . ."

"Found themmm!"

"Do you want some more wine?"

"Actually, I would love a G&T . . ."

"Tonic's in the fridge. Gin's in the study."

"Got it. Anyone else?"

"I'll take one, light on the gin."

"So, what's the latest on the dating front?" Abby asked Karen.

"Oh, it's pretty slim pickings out there."

"No one special right now?"

"Well, there is one guy that's . . . a possibility. But, well, I don't wanna jinx it."

"Oh, you should have asked him to come tonight, Karen," Mary added. "We'd *love* to meet him."

"I think that would've been . . . *awkward* . . . So many close friends all of a sudden, I mean. You know. I don't want to scare him off."

"It's hard to keep a *good* man, isn't it?" Mary eyed Karen.

"Anyone gonna want red wine, or should we stick to white?"

"I'll do either."

"Me too."

"What about the guys?"

"Johnny's a beer man."

"Art'll probably have a glass. And I'll join you, too."

"I'm gonna stick to gin and tonic, thanks."

As Karen watched, she reflected: there was something about women that is communal, organized, and cooperative. It wasn't the first time she'd noticed. Maybe it was something evolutionary, coming down from centuries spent together gathering and preparing—versus the hunting that the men did?

But there was more to it. At least to Karen. There was a rhythm, a camaraderie. Karen understood it. She knew how to fake it. But she didn't share it. As the women in Mary's kitchen chatted while organizing platters, napkins, and plantain chips, Karen Kline sat at the island, sipping her gin and tonic, wondering why she didn't fit in. Why she had never fit in . . .

# CHAPTER FORTY-TWO

Meanwhile, the men were out on the patio. Art and David were standing, holding their drinks, watching Johnny lay wood in the firepit. Contrary to the communal atmosphere in the kitchen, the vibe outdoors was different; a certain alpha male competitiveness was evident.

"You sure you don't need a hand?"

"Nah, I got this . . . I do it all the time."

"You'll wanna stand that wood more upright, teepee-like, and leave a bit more space, so the air can circulate, Johnny."

"Don't worry. This'll work. This wood's drier than a witch's pussy."

"Ugh, dude. Not a mental image I wanna take home with me . . ."

"I dunno, man . . . Are you sure that's gonna light up? Dry or not, it needs ventilation. You got any smaller pieces, like little branches, for tinder?"

"Leave Johnny alone; he's doing fine. Besides, small branches aren't tinder. That'd be kindling. Tinder's like paper or dried leaves—something that'll light right up quick. The tinder is what gets the kindling burning. Kindling's the little branches you're talking about."

"What're you? A fuckin' Eagle Scout?"

"Actually, yes. But also, a bit of a pyromaniac . . . When I was a kid, I loved burning shit, but hey, the difference between tinder and kindling . . . that's basic stuff any man should know."

"Oh, so now *tinder* is a life skill?"

Laughter.

"Knowing how to build a fire, I'd agree, is a life skill. But, knowing the technical names of each part of the process, no way."

"You sure you've done this before, Johnny?"

"What, Tinder?"

Laughter.

"Did you know that the average Tinder message sent by guys is twelve characters long? While women's average messages are 122 characters long?"

Laughter.

"You're surprised?"

"What I don't get is . . . what're those guys writing that's so complicated that they need twelve characters?!"

Laughter.

"I know . . . an eggplant emoji . . . twelve times!"

Laughter.

"You're gonna need some starter fluid, buddy. The way you've built that thing, there's no way it's gonna light up."

"I'm telling you, *it's fine!* I do this all the time. And this wood's dry as hell. Just watch . . . Oh, shit . . ."

"Ha! The great outdoorsman caught without his trusty lighter?"

"Fuck off. Hey, Art, can you get me a lighter? In the study, the drawer under the liquor bottles."

"Sure."

Johnny grabbed himself a beer out of the cooler. A moment later, Art returned with a small red plastic lighter and a glass of wine. And five minutes later, the large pieces of wood in the firepit were catching flame.

"Gentlemen," Abby shouted out to the patio. "Come on in. We got appetizers. And leftover barbecue for those who are extra-hungry."

The men responded, grabbing their drinks and making their way indoors. Places were set for everyone around the dining table. Mary watched as all her guests took a seat. She couldn't help but notice that Johnny took the seat at the table where Grandma Nellie would usually sit.

As everyone conversed, Mary made her way to her own chair. So many memories were flooding back. The fact that this might be the last gathering of friends she ever had in the only home she'd ever known weighed on her. She felt a sharp tug of nostalgia. So many years in this space. Her whole childhood, her life. Soon, it wouldn't be hers anymore.

What Mary didn't know is that things were about to get even worse.

# CHAPTER FORTY-THREE

All of the party sounds faded away. The conversation. The music. The laughter. All Mary could hear was a high-pitched tone buzzing in her ears. Her first reaction was confusion.

She was standing in the study. Wooden shelves. Photos. Comfy leather chairs. Soft rug in front of the fireplace. She was holding a rocks glass in her hand. Karen had spilled her gin and tonic and broken hers. While she cleaned up the mess, Mary had gone into the study to get her another from the bar. As she'd gotten it from the bar, she'd noted—almost subconsciously—that something felt amiss. Wrong. She looked around. Everything seemed to be in order.

Then . . .

That was when she saw that the space above the fireplace was empty, save for a nail supporting a little brass picture hook.

*Where is the Monet?*

*Gone . . .*

*Stolen?*

*Stolen.*

Her first thought was of Nellie, who had died not ten feet from where she was standing. Her first emotion—anger—at herself. Her heart was pounding. She realized that she was holding her breath and exhaled.

Her mind raced. The barbecue. All those people on the property. Pedro. The loose cord. David and Rio still had her keys.

*Did I come in here earlier today?*

*Would I have noticed it was gone? So much going on . . .*

She couldn't remember.

Johnny?

*Would he?*

Mary's stomach clenched. She had slight tunnel vision and felt as though the ground was moving from under her, and she was starting to fall, that feeling you get in your head when you're on a roller coaster that's just crested to the top of the first big climb, crosses the apex, and starts to drop.

"Johnny . . ." she tried to call out, but the name came out in a hoarse whisper. She could hear his voice in conversation in the next room. She licked her lips, cleared her throat, and succeeded in calling out loudly, "Johnny!"

The voices in the next room stopped for a second, then continued. She heard his footsteps. Felt his presence as he came up next to her.

"What's up?"

She looked at him, then looked back towards the fireplace, then looked back at him.

"What the hell?!" he exclaimed.

She studied his reaction, analyzing the lines around his eyes, his mouth. She knew that face so well. Every millimeter of it. She was looking for any hint, *any sign*, of betrayal, of guilt, any indication that he was feigning surprise. His eyes grew wide, mouth hung half-open. He swallowed hard and looked her right in the eye. "What happened?"

*Oh my God . . . is he really that good? Or maybe it wasn't him . . . ?*

"You'd better call the police," she replied. "We've been robbed."

# CHAPTER FORTY-FOUR

Nothing puts a damper on a party quite like the cops.

An officer arrived at the house about thirty minutes after Johnny called the police. Mary recognized him immediately. He was the same officer who had come to the house the day Nellie died.

After Mary explained that the Monet was gone, the officer questioned everyone to get basic information. He stood at the kitchen island, taking notes. Mary and Johnny were there with him. Their guests were sitting at the dining table or standing nearby.

"I wanna try and establish a timeline as best we can. When did you see it last? The painting?" he asked.

"Me?" Mary responded. "I dunno. This morning maybe? Yesterday? It was a busy day."

"We had the Labor Day barbecue," Johnny chimed in.

"I know," the officer said. "I came before my shift, with the wife and kids. Real nice event."

"We saw it," David added, looking at his date.

"Better than that," Rio rose and walked over, tapping her phone screen. "Yep. Here it is. I took a selfie with it around two forty-five."

The officer looked, nodding. "Can you email me all the photos you took of the painting?" He handed Rio a card with his contact information.

"Doing it right now," she replied.

Rio sat down, and David looked at her, not recalling her having taken a selfie.

"I snuck out of our room . . . after . . ." she whispered to him, shrugging.

"What about after that?" the officer asked the room. "Anyone else?"

"I went in there to get the gin, but honestly, I didn't really notice the painting," Karen said.

"Okay. That's good. Around what time?" the officer asked as he scribbled notes.

Karen shrugged, looking at the other women. "Five thirty? Five forty-five?"

"Around then," Abby nodded.

"Anyone else?" the officer asked.

Art raised his hand. "I got a lighter from the drawer. For the firepit."

"That was earlier. Before me," Karen added. "I remember you coming in."

"Did you notice if the painting was there?" the officer asked.

Art shook his head. "I *think* I would have noticed if it was missing. I mean, now that I look in there, it seems obvious that something should be hanging over the fireplace. But I was focused on finding the lighter. So, I didn't really look . . ."

"So, you don't specifically remember seeing it; you just think you would have noticed if it wasn't there?" the officer asked.

"That's not very helpful, I guess," Art said.

"Okay. Anyone else?"

Silence.

"And then," the officer turned to Mary, "at what time did you notice it was missing?"

"What time did you call them?" Mary asked Johnny.

He looked at his phone. "6:12 p.m."

"Just before that. I went into the study," she sighed. "I went to get another rocks glass."

"I dropped mine. Shattered," Karen added.

Mary nodded in agreement.

The officer nodded, reviewing his notes. "Well, you had a ton of folks on property for the barbecue . . ."

"We have security cameras all over," Johnny added.

"Mind if we have a look? At the footage?"

Johnny shrugged and turned to Mary. "You tell him."

"We had a slight problem, earlier. My key broke off in the lock to the security office," Mary said.

"When did that happen?"

"Earlier. I was locking it—since we were having the barbecue. For security. And I twisted too hard. We'll need to get a locksmith to come out."

"Isn't there an app or something?" the officer asked.

"The app can show you the video in real time. But it doesn't let you rewind," Mary shrugged. "It's an old system. Very basic."

"Okay. Well, make sure to save the footage. We'll need to get a copy. And your insurance company will probably want to see it too," the officer said. "For tonight, I've got enough for the police report," he concluded, looking around the room. "But now, I have to ask a sort of awkward question . . ."

Everyone looked at him expectantly.

"So, based on your photo," he looked at Rio, "the painting was last seen around two forty-five today. And the barbecue ended at four. So, someone from the barbecue could have gotten into the house and taken it, of course. But I can't discount the fact that someone here right now is . . . maybe the thief." He looked around the room. "No offense, but I don't know you folks, and I gotta call it like I see it. Just doing my job. So, ma'am," he turned to Mary, "the only way to secure the scene here is for me to ask your guests to leave and check them on the way out. That way, at least, we know that no one here right now is leaving with the painting. It's up to you. But that's what I'd recommend. Then I can put in the report that everyone present was searched, and so on . . ."

"Oh." Mary looked around anxiously.

*No, no, no . . . not yet. Let me think . . . what am I missing?* It was useless; her brain was on overload from the barbecue, the shock, and now the thought of agreeing to have her friends searched . . . "I don't think . . ."

"Now, hold on, Mary," Art said. "This is a big deal. And it's not just going to be the police that investigate this. You're going to have to deal with your insurance company too. So, I think it's best to do what the officer says. We can call it a night. Let him check everyone on the way out. Then we're all in the clear. And then they can focus their energy where it needs to focus."

"I think Art's right, Mary," Karen added. "The more they can narrow the possibilities, the better."

"And really, hon," Abby contributed, "this kinda takes the steam out . . . well, we're just not going to have fun now, after this . . . you know?" She looked at everyone else for approval. "Kinda like a turd in the swimming pool . . . Why don't we just wrap things up and head home, guys?"

Everyone agreed. The friends helped bring the appetizer platters and drink glasses into the kitchen, leaving everything on the island. Then they all went to their respective rooms and packed. One by one, the officer checked their luggage and vehicles as they left.

"Here's my card, ma'am. You can get a copy of the police report prob'ly by Tuesday. Admin's closed Monday for the holiday." The officer was the last to leave.

Johnny and Mary picked up in the kitchen in silence. As Johnny loaded the dishwasher, he looked around and saw that Mary was gone. He walked to the study door and saw her standing in front of the fireplace, facing the empty spot on the wall where the Monet should have been.

Crying.

# RUBY YI – 1983

Old man Cho's disappearance was never resolved. His body was never found, but it was widely accepted that the Chinese Mafia had him killed. In his absence, his son Arvin Cho ostensibly took over managing the family business. However, everyone close to the business knew that Ruby Yi ran things. She not only succeeded in eliminating drugs and prostitution from the Cho Family's business portfolio but, over the next ten years, became an integral part of purging the remaining questionable aspects of their business, focusing all of their investments on real estate.

With this shift, Ruby Yi learned to conduct a new kind of warfare.

Tom Bradly was not accustomed to being kept waiting. He scowled, checking his watch for the fifth time, then looked around the restaurant. The only people standing or moving about were staff. Everyone else was seated, dining.

"Enough's enough," he said out loud to himself.

Just as he stood up to leave, he spied a petite Asian woman waving off the hostess and weaving her way in his direction. She wore a black Chanel dress, bright red pumps, and carried a matching purse. Her only jewelry was two large pearl earrings and a matching choker. As she approached, he guessed her age to be . . . well, he couldn't tell. She looked mid-to-late twenties but carried herself with much more maturity. Confidence.

"I'm so sorry I'm late, Mr. Mayor," she said, holding out her hand.

The mayor's tight lips softened slightly. He shook her hand and replied, "Mrs. Cho—"

"Please," she interrupted, beaming, "call me Ruby." She held on to his hand, and gave it a second, gentle squeeze pulling it just slightly towards her.

"I was expecting Mr. Cho," he added, a slight gleam in his eye.

"Well then," Ruby leaned in, still holding his hand, and stage whispered, "today is your lucky day, isn't it?"

He laughed. "I *am* pleasantly surprised."

The table was set for two with a white linen tablecloth, napkins, fine china, and silverware. Ruby moved to her chair and stood next to it. She waited, smiling, holding her purse handle in both hands. The mayor was about to take his seat, then jumped and scrambled to pull her chair out for her just a maître d' approached to do the same.

"You *are* too kind." She smiled, sitting down. Then to the maître d', she said, "A black napkin, please."

The mayor ordered clam chowder to start, followed by a ribeye with mashed potatoes. Ruby ordered a salad, which she did not touch, except to place her fork and knife on the plate when the mayor was done with his second course.

During the meal, Ruby and the mayor shared gossip about local and national politicians. Ruby gave him the scoop on President Reagan's Inaugural Ball, which she had attended with her husband, Arvin, but to which the mayor had not been invited—*wrong political party.* For dessert, the mayor had peach pie, Ruby chamomile tea with lime on the side.

She got what she came for: the mayor's support for zoning concessions for a real estate development she and her husband had in the works.

As soon as the back door to her Cadillac limousine closed, Ruby slipped off her shoes and rubbed her feet. She picked up the bulky car phone she'd had installed between the two back seats and began dialing, then paused to ask the driver, "Any idea why my idiot husband missed this lunch? With the *mayor*? It was important!" She spat out the words.

There was silence as the driver eased the car out into traffic.

"Well?!"

"Apparently," sighed Kong, "he was with the blonde woman again." He gazed into the rearview mirror, leaning slightly left to see Ruby's reaction. She looked back at him in the mirror, pensive. He could see her nostrils flaring. She turned and looked out the window for several beats.

"You have that on good authority?" she asked, the edge in her voice gone. She sounded tired.

Kong nodded.

"Take me," Ruby said, shaking her head, gently replacing the phone in its cradle.

Fifteen minutes later, they were driving past an address all too familiar to her. Her husband's red BMW 5 Series was parked on the curb.

"Keep going, then turn around and let's park, there," she indicated about half a block from the BMW.

An hour later, Arvin Cho appeared through the front doors to the building, glanced quickly up and down the street, then made a beeline for his car and pulled into traffic.

"Should I follow?" Kong asked.

Ruby sat, watching as the car turned left, then kept staring at the last spot the BMW had been visible before disappearing around the corner. She briefly looked up at the building, considered paying the blonde a visit. But that was pointless. The problem wasn't her; she'd be replaced soon by another blonde, brunette, or redhead.

"No, don't follow," she replied. "Take me home."

"I'm sorry, Ruby Yi," Kong said, his eyes fixed on the road.

Kong had always called her by her full name until she married and became Madame Cho. But he still called her Ruby Yi when they were alone.

Ruby half-smiled. "Don't be sorry, Kong," she said. "You've done nothing wrong."

Ruby sat back, looking out the window, and sighed.

*Arvin swore. Never again . . .*

Ruby didn't care about the woman or the infidelity. Arvin could screw whoever he wanted as long as he didn't expect sex from her; he was a repugnant little man. But his extracurricular activities were one thing. Business was another. Ruby had fought too hard to get where she was to let some coked-up bimbo—or a series of them—ruin everything.

*When we first met, he was a papa's boy running a two-bit pawn shop. Now, we've built a legitimate real estate business. And, thanks to our lunch today . . . my lunch . . . with the mayor . . .*

She slowly shook her head from side to side, like a mother with a problem child. "Stupid bastard . . ." she said under her breath, shaking her head. She'd been very clear about it.

*No more drugs. No more whores. Business first.*

He'd cried. He'd pled. But most importantly, he'd sworn to her—on his father's grave, on his love for her, on his life.

*Well, so be it,* she thought. She didn't relish what needed to be done. But it was business. Knowing her husband, he'd be home sometime after six. Ruby glanced at her watch. Accounting for traffic, she had four hours to prepare.

"Please stop by the bank on the way, Kong."

Ruby had opened a personal safety deposit box more than a year prior, in her name. She visited it periodically, leaving and retrieving various items of jewelry. The Chos had a small home safe in their condominium where she kept items for daily wear. The safety deposit box was unnecessary.

The box, and her regular visits to it, were all part of the plan she had devised more than a year before in the event that she decided to kill her husband. She had hoped it wouldn't be necessary—mainly due to the hassle. She'd hoped her killing days were done. But he'd left her with no choice.

*He's a liability. We're now worth ten times what old Cho had and he's putting it all at risk. And I'll be damned if I let him take half of everything I've built in a divorce.*

The security cameras at Wells Fargo registered Ruby Cho's arrival that day at 2:17 p.m. She was inside the bank for twenty minutes. When she entered, she was clearly wearing a pearl choker, which was gone when she departed. As she later explained to the police, she had dropped off her pearls, choker and earrings, at the bank and retrieved her rubies.

What she didn't tell the police was that, in addition to the rubies, she removed two other items: an envelope and a small vial.

At 3:07 p.m., after a brief stop at an upscale liquor store, Kong delivered Ruby to her front door. He looked her in the eyes knowingly and said, "Be careful, Ruby Yi."

Ruby nodded.

The giant knew that if she needed his help, she would ask.

The Chos' high-rise condominium was new, just built the previous year. It was this building that had inspired Ruby to move into commercial real estate. She loved the idea of leaving a mark on the skyline. And the land. Something permanent. Something that would last.

She changed into comfortable clothes—acid-washed jeans, a neon yellow off-the-shoulder sweatshirt, and no shoes. She preferred going barefoot around the house.

Ruby headed into the kitchen. After thirty minutes of chopping and preparation, she had a pot of kimchee stew simmering on the stove and started the white rice. By 5:00 p.m., dinner was ready. She set the table for one, then poured herself a glass of white wine. The last thing she did before sitting down was pull the curtains over the sliding glass doors that led to the balcony.

When her husband came home that evening, she was sitting at the bar, sipping her white wine. As soon as he saw her, he began, "Ruby, I'm so sorry I missed lunch—"

She enthusiastically popped off her chair, "It couldn't have gone better! We are *in*, Arvin. The deal is done!" She ran up and gave him a big hug.

Ruby could be effusive, particularly when things went well. But she could sense Arvin was suspicious as he held her tentatively. So, she adjusted course slightly.

"Of course," she pulled back and poked him in the chest with her finger, doing naughty child, "*you* could have let me know you weren't going to make it! I waited for you until I couldn't anymore. What happened?" she asked, turning and heading back to the bar. "Drink?"

"Sure. Scotch," Arvin removed his jacket and loosened his tie, then flopped on the sofa. "I got tied up. You know Ed . . . he never gives you solutions. Just options, so it's always back and forth, back and forth . . ."

Her husband sat down on the sofa, one leg crossed, hands behind his head. While he yammered on, she prepared his drink. She had already added the contents of the vial to the rocks glass. She added scotch, water, and two cubes of ice, just the way he liked it.

". . . finally put everything in writing, so we don't have to go through it all again."

As he finished his rambling lie, Ruby brought him his drink. She held it in her left hand. Her right hand was hidden behind her back.

"I have a surprise for you," she said.

He took the glass, his eyes narrowing slightly, and said, "Okay. Show me."

"To celebrate our win . . ."

As he took a sip, she presented to him the scotch bottle, a twenty-year-old Glenfarclas.

"Oh wow!" he exclaimed, admiring the color of the scotch in his rocks glass. "This is *really* good stuff."

She handed him the bottle, retrieved her wineglass, and sat next to him on the sofa.

"A toast," she said, "to the first of many Cho-Yi Enterprises high-rise buildings!" They clinked glasses and drank. Ruby took a sip and saw that her husband swallowed almost half of his drink in one gulp.

"Damn, that's good," he said as he picked up the bottle and poured himself three more fingers.

"Why don't you put on some music?" she asked, rising from the sofa. "I'll be right back."

He gave her an inquisitive look. She frowned and gestured with both hands at her belly. "That time of the month . . ."

When Ruby closed the door to the bathroom, it was 6:18 p.m. She checked herself in the mirror. She adjusted her hair. Checked her teeth. A moment later, she heard music.

Journey.

*Here we stand. Worlds apart, hearts broken in two . . . two . . . two-ooo*

Ruby laughed out loud. The irony . . . She marveled at how the universe often offered you clues to the future, if you were paying attention.

*I'll bet Arvin isn't paying attention . . .* She pulled a nail file from the drawer and sat down on the toilet. She had chipped her left pinkie nail chopping the onions for dinner. Seven minutes later, halfway through "Send Her My Love," she heard, "Rubyyyy? Why is the table set for one?"

She shouted, "I'll be right the-ere!"

Thirteen minutes later, she heard a loud thump followed by what she assumed was her husband's rocks glass bouncing and rolling across the wood floor. She popped up off the toilet and returned to the living room. There, laying on his side in the middle of the floor, was Arvin Cho, eyes wide, expression blank.

"How appropriate." She'd seen that look on his face a thousand times. "As in life, so in death . . ." She nudged him with her bare foot once. Then again. No reaction.

She took a sip of wine, went into the kitchen, and returned with a pair of latex gloves. She picked up the unbroken scotch glass, cleaned it thoroughly, and then put it in the dishwasher. As she did, she sang along with the music.

*Circus life*
*Under the big top wo-ooorld*
*We all need the clowns*
*To make us smile*

Next, she turned to the task of dealing with the body. She rolled her dead husband onto his back.

"Well, at least you had the decency to die with an empty bladder."

She went to their bedroom and returned with his pajamas. After ten minutes of pulling and pushing, she had changed him into the jammies, hung his suit in the closet, and put his shirt, socks, and underwear in the dirty clothes bin. She returned and carefully brushed and flossed his teeth. As she did, she noticed that one of his molars had a tiny black mark on it. "Hmmm. That might be the beginnings of a cavity, my love. Oh, how you hated the dentist." She patted him lightly on the chest when she finished, then stood and appraised her work. Arvin Cho appeared to be sleeping peacefully on his back on the living room floor. Except that his eyes were wide open.

Ruby looked towards the windows. It was dark out. Not having eaten anything at lunch, she was famished. She served herself kimchee stew and rice and refreshed her glass of wine. She sat at the one place setting in the dining room to have dinner. Delicious. While she ate, she read *Cosmo*. Every fifteen minutes, she got up and rolled Arvin over to keep the blood from pooling in any one part of his body. If the police asked, she would tell them that Arvin was not hungry and had not eaten dinner. If they did an autopsy and checked his stomach, the contents would be consistent with her story.

Done with dinner, she decided to treat herself to a pint of ice cream while watching Johnny Carson—still turning Arvin's body every fifteen minutes. After Carson, she got ready for bed and then went around turning out lights. She stopped at his body on the way to the bedroom. "I should have waited to kill you later in the evening," she said out loud as she turned him over once more before going to bed; as the body came to rest on its back, it farted.

Before getting into bed, she mussed her husband's side to make it appear that both had been in bed. She placed the envelope containing his suicide note on his pillow—a note she had forged almost a year prior. She read a book by lamplight, continuing her fifteen-minute ritual. From 1:00 a.m. onwards, every time she turned the body, she peeked out the curtains to the balcony in the dining room. Each time there were fewer lights on in the building across the street.

By 1:45 a.m., all the neighboring lights were out. Finally, at 2:15 a.m., she felt certain that the neighbors were all sleeping. Ruby pulled the curtains just enough to fit between them and opened the sliding glass door using a paper towel. She then dragged her dead husband from the living room, through the dining room, and out to the balcony door. She sat Arvin up and manipulated his right hand, getting his fingerprints first on the latch to the balcony door, and then on the door handle. She then dragged him out onto the balcony and, with a great deal of effort, got the corpse up onto the rail and gave a little push, letting gravity do the rest. She heard a crash and a car alarm go off as she re-entered the apartment, leaving the sliding glass door open. Ruby Cho—now Yi again—went back to bed. She closed her eyes and waited. About twenty-five minutes later, the doorbell rang. She opened the door to a man and a woman in police uniforms.

"Oh. Hello. Can I help you?"

"Mrs. Cho?" said the woman.

"Yes . . ."

"May we come in?"

"Is there a problem?"

"We'd prefer to speak inside, if that's okay."

"Um, well . . . yes. Of course." She stepped to the side, letting them pass. "Please have a seat in the living room. I should get my husband." Ruby started towards the bedroom.

"Ma'am," the female officer called out. Ruby stopped. "When did you last see your husband?"

She looked towards her bedroom, then at the officer, eyebrows raised. "Right now. He's in bed."

The two officers looked at one another. Ruby headed for the bedroom, already working up tears. She turned on the lights, and opened the envelope with Arvin's suicide note, dropping the envelope on the floor. She paused, listening to make sure the police were not coming to the bedroom. When she felt the first teardrop leave her eye, she screamed.

# PART FOUR

## MARY SCORES SOME POINTS

# CHAPTER FORTY-FIVE

As Mary walked toward the kitchen Sunday morning, she saw to her right through the study doors the empty space above the fireplace, and Johnny working on his laptop at the kitchen island, a coffee cup sitting next to him. He was wearing earbuds attached to his phone.

Mary clenched her jaw when she saw her husband. She'd tossed and turned all night, thinking through the events of the prior evening.

*Who has a better motive and better access? Bastard.*

"More coffee?" she asked.

"That would be—" Johnny held up a finger and spoke to the air. "Hello, yes, I'm still here."

Mary popped another capsule into the machine, made him a refill, and listened to his end of the conversation, curious about who he might be talking to on a Sunday morning.

"No. The police report won't be ready for a couple of days. That's what the officer said."

*It's about the Monet.*

"Whenever is convenient," Johnny continued. "The sooner, the better, I would imagine. I assume y'all don't work Labor Day." A pause. "So day-after-tomorrow, Tuesday?" Johnny typed on his laptop keyboard. "That would be fine with us." He took a sip of coffee and gave Mary a thumbs-up. "Okay. We'll wait to hear from him." Silence. "No, no. Thank you." Johnny ended the call.

"What was that all about?" Mary asked.

"Well, there's good news and bad news, Mary."

"Please start with the good news," she replied, leaning against the kitchen counter. *What could possibly be positive about this situation?*

"Well . . . I probably should have told you, but after Nellie passed and we got hit with the tax bill, I kind of freaked out—about the life insurance. I mean, it just seemed horrible that we got hit with all those taxes, and there was no insurance to cover it, you know? Well, that got me thinking about our insurance in general.

"So, I called our agent and went through everything, all the other insurance. Everything was okay . . . although it turns out that there was a cap on the homeowner's policy of $2,500 maximum for artwork."

"Oh, no," Mary's face dropped, but her expression quickly changed to confusion. "But, that's *bad* news . . ."

"Yes—but the good news is Nellie had the Monet insured *separately* for five million dollars."

"Okay," Mary nodded. *This is all starting to make sense now. I won't sell the painting, so you steal it.* Mary felt queasy. *Or destroy it . . . ?* "So, it's insured for five million?"

"Well, I know that money won't solve the problem; I know the painting means more to you than just money. But the real good news is that, for sure, the insurance company will be more on top of things than the cops . . . I mean, I bet they don't want to have to pay five million if they can avoid it," Johnny shrugged. "I was just submitting a claim to the carrier. Because of the size of the loss, they're going to send an investigator first thing Tuesday morning."

Having an insurance investigator involved *would* be a good thing. They'd have to be more competent—and definitely more motivated to find it—than the local cops.

"That was good thinking, Johnny. It hadn't occurred to me to check the insurance policies before now."

"Do you want to hear more good news?" he asked.

"Sure."

"Well." With all the drama regarding the painting's disappearance, he hadn't told Mary about his conversation with Karen at the barbecue. "This Wednesday, we have a showing. Some folks from out west are coming to look at the vineyard. Karen's got it all set up."

Mary nodded. "So, we may have a buyer . . . or at the very least, they'll make Clive edgy; maybe he'll up his offer," she said. "That *is* good news, I guess."

# CHAPTER FORTY-SIX

Mary went to the vineyard office to catch up on paperwork; at least, that's what she told Johnny. When she was sure she was alone, she called Betsy Beavers, told her about the missing Monet, and what she had just learned from Johnny.

"I know we were going to serve him with divorce papers in a few days . . . but does this change anything?" Mary asked.

"Yes and no," Beavers said.

*Typical lawyer.*

"As far as the painting, I wouldn't be surprised if he stole it—or even destroyed it."

At the word "destroyed," Mary felt like she'd been kicked in the stomach. Again.

"On your inventory, you listed the Monet as yours, not community property. Can you prove that?"

"When we got married, Grandma Nellie gave it to me. She wrote on the back of the painting, 'To Mary. Love, Grandma Nellie,' just like her mom did for her."

"On the painting itself . . . Ugh. I see. Is there anything else, though? A card or something? Anything to prove she gave it to you and *only* you?"

Mary shook her head and was about to reply in the negative. She hesitated a moment, thinking. Then she lied to her lawyer . . . for the first time. "There *was* also a card. I'll have to dig around, but I'm sure I can find it."

"Good. That's important. Get it to me as soon as you can. And if it was handwritten, see if you can find another sample of your grandmother's handwriting. Since you wouldn't sell the painting, it wouldn't surprise me if he made it 'disappear,' and now there's insurance money. Insurance money *can* be split—divided in the divorce. And then he can still sell the painting somewhere and double-dip."

"There was a photo of it taken earlier that afternoon . . ." Mary stated. "So, he had a small window of time. I still need to check the security videos." Mary explained to Beavers about breaking her key off in the lock to the room where the security footage was stored.

"If I were you, I would have that locksmith come out when the insurance company's investigator is there. The room is inaccessible now, so the footage is safe." Beavers said. "Open it when the investigator is there and review the footage with him. That way, they can't claim you tampered with it in advance. And no one else will be able to either."

"Good point."

"As far as your question about the divorce, I don't think *the theft of the painting* affects the timing of the divorce, but the vineyard buyer . . ." Beavers paused for a moment. "Well, I know one thing for sure, Mary. Nothing scares off a buyer like a lawsuit. I guarantee you that once the divorce process starts, Johnny will try to claim some piece of the vineyard after all his 'years of hard work.' If you think you have a buyer for the property, it'd be better to wait a bit and see what happens. Go ahead and have your showing. Let's hold off on serving Johnny and see if your buyer is real or not. It's much easier to fight over money in hand than to try to sell something in the middle of a divorce."

Mary was sick of the strategizing and the waiting. She wanted Johnny out of her house and out of her life. But she knew she needed to be practical about the situation.

"Okay then," Mary concluded reluctantly. "Let's wait."

# CHAPTER FORTY-SEVEN

Tuesday morning, promptly at 9:00 a.m., the doorbell to the main house rang. Mary answered, with Johnny joining her moments later.

"Mornin', ma'am. I'm Carl Gandy. I spoke with your husband on the phone." He handed her his business card. His title: Investigator, Allied Insurance.

Mary had expected someone who looked more like an FBI agent or a banker. This guy looked like he worked at Whole Foods.

He was in cargo pants, a khaki Columbia hiking shirt, and carried a backpack slung over one shoulder. He looked to be in his late forties and wore his thinning salt and pepper hair (that matched his goatee) in a neat ponytail. He had a slight Texas accent. Gandy took notes for the next thirty minutes as Mary and Johnny explained what had happened. She also advised that a locksmith was on his way to open the door to where the security footage was stored.

"This is where the painting hung," Mary said. The three were standing in the study. Gandy carefully studied the wall, then removed a large 35mm-style camera from his backpack. "May I?" he asked before taking photos.

"Sure," Mary replied.

He spoke as he snapped photos.

"I saw online that the vineyard's for sale. You guys tired of the life of a vigneron?"

Mary chuckled. "Haven't heard that word in a while."

"I googled it before I came," Gandy replied.

"Taxes, actually," Mary said. "I inherited the vineyard from my grandmother. She passed recently. And the estate taxes are a killer. We just can't afford to pay them."

"I see," Gandy nodded. "Where does that door lead?" He pointed to a door to the right of the fireplace in the study.

Mary walked over and opened it. "A hallway that leads back to the foyer."

Gandy snapped a photo of the open door and said, "So, access to this room can be had via the sliding doors from the family room, from the foyer via the hallway, and then, of course, via the windows. Do they open?" he asked, approaching and inspecting the window to the right of the fireplace. "Not painted shut or anything?"

"They do open," Johnny said. "Nellie had the place redone when she bought the land. They're older now, but they're not original. They work." Johnny unlatched the window to the left side of the fireplace, raising and lowering it. It moved smoothly.

Gandy nodded, slid the latch on the window to the *right* of the fireplace, and then tried to open it. It didn't budge. He looked at Johnny, who came over and tried; he couldn't get it to move, either. Then he slid the latch in the other direction, and the window opened.

"You saw me slide the latch," Gandy said. "This window was *unlocked.* Did either of you unlock it recently?"

Johnny shook his head, and Mary replied, "No."

The investigator stood in front of the window on the right, then turned on the spot and faced the doorway to the family room. From there, he could see the French doors leading out to the patio. The kitchen was not visible. He snapped a photo.

Gandy paced slowly around the room, looking at the walls, ceiling, and shelves. He stopped and picked up a framed picture. "Is this your grandmother?" It was a photo of Grandma Nellie, Mary, and Johnny standing in front of the fireplace, from the first Christmas after Mary married.

"It is."

"She looks like a happy person . . . And that's the painting? The Monet?"

"Yes."

Gandy nodded, replacing the photo on the shelf. Then he stepped back and took several pictures of the photo at different angles. "You mentioned security cameras earlier. Do they cover these areas? I mean, the entry to the house, these windows, the access points to this room, basically?"

"They do," Mary replied. "There should be coverage of the exterior wall, here, where the windows are, and then of the entrances to the house. You can see one of the cameras from the window here." Mary pointed. "There aren't any interior cameras."

Gandy looked and nodded. "Okay. While we're waiting for the locksmith, I'd like your permission to search through the house. I know that the police searched your guests and all, but it could be that whoever took the painting didn't get it off the premises. They could have simply removed it from the wall, hiding it somewhere in the house, planning to return for it later."

Johnny made a face and shrugged, looking at Mary.

"I hadn't thought of that," she said. "Sure. Go ahead."

Gandy put on blue latex gloves, and for the next two hours, he thoroughly searched the home, opening closets, drawers, and cabinets, looking under sofas, beds . . . *everywhere.* He went through the kitchen, drawer by drawer. He lifted rugs. Using a flashlight, he spent almost twenty minutes looking up the chimney, then got a ladder and examined it from the roof as well. He thoroughly searched the garage, opening boxes and old suitcases and climbing up through the attic.

During the search, Johnny left to begin his normal day's work, and Mary stayed at the main house in case the investigator had any questions.

Gandy rejoined her in the kitchen once his search was finished.

"Okay. Nothing here," he said.

"There's a whole other building over where the vineyard offices are. You're welcome to search there as well," Mary told him.

Gandy nodded.

He told her, "You should know that when it comes to art theft, especially high-end art, there's not a big black market. The kind of people that appreciate art and have the money to pay for a Monet generally aren't interested in buying stolen goods. They want to be able to show off their art, and you can't do that if the police are looking for it. So, most thefts are either by amateurs that don't know what they're getting themselves into, or there are some that are orchestrated by owners who need cash."

Mary was about to interrupt, but Gandy raised his hands. "Please, please, Mrs. Miracle. I'm not saying that's the case here. In fact, it'd be kind of stupid as your Monet is probably worth at least twice what it's insured for. If you needed cash, you could just sell it. My point is that there is a third possibility, and one you need to be prepared for . . . art-knapping."

"You mean someone may call me and ask me to pay a ransom to get her back?"

"I do. It's a possibility. Just something you need to be prepared for. I assume you haven't gotten any calls or—"

Mary shook her head. "Nothing. No calls. No ransom note with glued-on letters."

They both laughed.

Mary's phone rang.

After a brief conversation, she hung up and said, "Good timing. The locksmith is pulling up now. We can head over."

As they left the main house to walk over to the vineyard offices, Mary asked, "What's the recovery rate for stolen art?"

Gandy frowned and replied, "Only about five percent of stolen artworks are recovered."

# CHAPTER FORTY-EIGHT

After five minutes, a locksmith in green coveralls and a baseball cap with a patch on it that said *Goldie's Locks* opened the door to the security room. Mary and Gandy crowded into the small office at a tiny desk upon which an old computer monitor rested. Gandy had opened his backpack and removed a small box. Mary saw that it was a brand-new portable external hard drive.

"So, we know the painting was in place at around two forty-five p.m. when the selfie was taken. I'd like to get a download of all the security footage from two o'clock on." Mary pointed at a desktop computer that rested on the floor between the desk and the wall.

As Gandy attached the disk to the CPU, Mary asked, "From two until what point?"

"Today."

"Really?" Mary asked.

"Well, I just searched the house, so I'm pretty confident the painting is not on the premises now. I'll do the same here in the offices in a bit. But we know it was hanging on the wall on Saturday at two forty-five. So, logically, it was removed sometime between then and now, right?"

"Makes sense." Mary typed on the keyboard and moved the mouse about. "Okay. Exporting and downloading."

"Have you reviewed the footage?" Gandy asked.

"Nope. Can't on the app. And no one has been in here since the key broke in the lock," Mary replied.

Gandy nodded. "Okay. Can you pull up the security footage from the camera that covers the windows to the study? The one you pointed out to me."

Mary clicked on an icon, then selected the camera in question. A window opened on the computer screen. At the top of the window were the words *Camera 4,* followed by the actual date and time. The image in the window was black.

"That's strange," Mary said. "It should show the side of the house." She clicked on another icon to show the view from *Camera 3*, which provided a view of the front of the main house. "See? That's working . . ."

"The camera covering the study windows isn't working?" asked Gandy.

"Seems not," Mary replied. "Hold on. I'm gonna scrub back and see."

As Mary clicked and dragged with the mouse, the clock next to the words *Camera 4* counted in reverse. The image stayed the same for a bit, then suddenly re-populated with an image of the side of the house. Mary stopped the scrub and moved forward in time until the point where the image disappeared again, then pinpointed the spot and played the footage at normal speed. They both watched. One moment the screen showed an image of the side of the house, then everything went black. Mary stopped the replay.

"It goes dark at 1:56 p.m. the day of the barbecue," Gandy said, pointing at the date and time on the screen. "Can we go and see that camera?"

They walked out of the offices, Gandy carrying an aluminum ladder to check on the non-functioning camera.

"Who all has access to the security room?" Gandy asked.

"Well, there's Pedro," Mary replied. "Our groundskeeper. He's the one that found the problem with the electrical cord and fixed it."

"Who else has access?"

"Just him, me, and Johnny."

Gandy nodded. They walked in silence toward the side of the house. When they reached the camera, Gandy set up the ladder and asked, "How long have y'all been married?"

It didn't sound like small talk to Mary.

"Five wonderful years," she replied.

The inspector turned, studying her. "Any kids?"

"No," she replied.

"Eighteen years. Me and the missus," he said. "Second time around . . . for both of us."

"Congrats. On the eighteen years, I mean."

Gandy smiled.

Mary noticed a change in the man's demeanor. He had suddenly grown quiet. Pensive.

"Were you and the mister together most of the time? At the barbecue?" Gandy asked clambering up the ladder.

"Off and on. He does the grillin'. I do the greetin'."

Standing near the top rung, Gandy inspected the camera briefly and took photos. "Someone spray-painted it," he said. "They knew enough to bring white spray paint, same color as the camera body, so that shows some pre-meditation. Planning."

From the ground looking up, it was not immediately apparent that the security camera had been tampered with.

"Did you see anyone go into the office area during the barbecue?"

Mary clearly recalled seeing Johnny and Karen *leave* the building from opposite sides, but she didn't want to open that can of worms—not yet. She didn't want to lie to Gandy either. So, she told the truth finely, answering his question as asked, "The only people I saw go into that building all day were Pedro and Johnny, and me, of course."

Gandy climbed down the ladder and studied the area near the two windows. There was grass and a steppingstone path that led back to the front of the house. He snapped photos. "They could have used the windows for access. Or, they could have already been inside and just put the painting outside, through the window, then came back for it later," he said, carefully studying the area around the window he had previously found unlocked. "Who has access to the house?" he asked.

"In terms of keys, just me, Johnny, and Pedro," Mary replied.

"How long has he been with you guys—Pedro?"

"Uff. Ever since I can remember. Grandma Nellie hired him way back."

"And how is he, financially? I mean, any money problems?"

"Not that I know of."

Gandy nodded, thinking. "Is he around? Maybe I could talk to him. See if he saw anything unusual."

"Sure," Mary said. "He should be out in the north hundred today. We can take a UTV."

# CHAPTER FORTY-NINE

All the activity associated with the Monet's disappearance distracted Mary from the vineyard's sale; she'd almost forgotten about the showing. On Wednesday at 11:00 a.m., Karen's Lexus pulled up in front of the vineyard offices. Johnny and Mary went down to meet the guests: Karen, the potential buyer, and his realtor.

"Hi there," a thirty-ish-looking man standing with Karen said. "I'm Nick Rosenbaum."

As Mary shook his hand, she felt a familiar tingle in her belly.

Rosenbaum was about Johnny's height, five-foot-ten or so, and just as good-looking as Johnny, but different. While Johnny looked like a farm boy, Rosenbaum had more international good looks. He had short dark hair, very well cut and styled, and seemed vaguely ethnic. He wore faded jeans, desert boots, a white shirt, and a bright blue blazer. If Johnny looked good shirtless in jeans leaning up against a tractor—which Mary could attest, *he did*—Rosenbaum was more of a swimsuit-on-a-yacht-in-Antibes kind of handsome.

*For God's sake, Mary. Focus . . .*

Greetings and introductions were made all around.

"So, I don't know where you would like to start, Mr. Rosenbaum," Karen began. "Is there anything in particular you want to see first?"

"Do you guys do tours?" Rosenbaum asked.

"We do," Johnny replied. "Fifty bucks for a tour and sampling."

"Then let's do that. Show me what you'd show anyone who was taking a tour."

They started out with the fields. The group hopped into a UTV, and as they drove through the acreage, Mary and Johnny took turns explaining the types of grapes they grew, irrigation, the typical harvest season, and approximate output per acre. After the fields, they toured the warehouse and business office. Rosenbaum asked for production logs, which he reviewed. Mary agreed to also send along a copy by email.

Last, they gave Rosenbaum a tour of the main house.

As they stood in the kitchen, having coffee, he remarked, "This is a great house. Did you guys buy it, or . . ."

"I grew up here, actually. My grandmother started the vineyard. The house is old, but she remodeled it after she bought it."

"It's really nice," Rosenbaum looked around the room. "Feels like a home, you know? So, why sell?"

"Well—" Mary sighed.

"We got an offer," Johnny interrupted. "I don't know if Karen told you?"

Karen shook her head. And Rosenbaum looked surprised. "No, she didn't."

"That's what started all this," Johnny continued. "We got an offer that seemed kind of low. So, before considering it seriously, we wanted to test the market, and that's why we listed the property."

"Well," Rosenbaum replied, "I'm not interested in getting into a bidding war—"

"Well—"

Mary interrupted Johnny. "No. No. No," she said. "This isn't an auction situation. I want to sell. It's just that since we got that one offer . . . Well, I didn't just want to take the first offer I got, you know?"

"They do say," Rosenbaum said, "that your first offer is almost always your best offer."

Karen nodded.

Johnny pursed his lips and shrugged.

Mary straightened up and said, "Look, Mr. Rosenbaum."

"Please, call me Nick," he insisted with a smile.

Mary felt her ears burn. "Look, Nick. I'm not trying to start a bidding war here. The reality is that I inherited the property, and I can't afford the estate taxes . . ."

Johnny's face flushed. *You're fucking killing the deal, Mary. This guy's gonna smell blood in the water.*

". . . so I *need* to sell the vineyard," Mary continued. "But I'm not going to sell to the first local schmuck that makes a lowball offer because he knows about my problem. I know what this place is worth, and I know what I'm willing to sell it for. I just want a fair market price. So, if you decide to make an offer, I won't be sharing it with anyone else to try and get them to one-up you. Is that okay?" she paused, then added, "That's fair, isn't it, Nick?"

Rosenbaum smiled and studied her, then replied, "Okay. Yeah. That's fair." He looked at his watch, then said, "I need to get to the airport, but let me sleep on it and take another look at your production numbers. And I'll get back to you."

# CHAPTER FIFTY

Late the next afternoon, Johnny was driving a four-wheeler back from the fields when his mobile phone rang. It was Karen.

He stopped so he could hear her, listened with interest, then disconnected the call and dialed Clive. Rosenbaum had called Karen, indicating he was prepared to make an offer. A *really good* one. While Johnny was disappointed that he probably wasn't getting his commission from selling to Clive, he was happy that at least he could rub in Clive's face that the vineyard was being sold to someone else.

"I just got off the phone with Karen, Clive," Johnny said, stepping out of the UTV and stretching his legs.

"And . . . ?" Clive prompted.

"The Jew's ready to make an offer," he paused for effect, ". . . six million dollars." He spoke the words quietly, letting them sink in.

"Six! Is he crazy?!" Clive shouted.

Johnny laughed. "That's what I said, Clive. Can you believe it?"

But Clive had thought through different scenarios in the event that a third-party offer came in and had a response ready.

"Now, hold on just a second, Johnny," Clive cleared his throat. "Does he know that I own fifteen percent of the vineyard? Is he aware that Mary can only sell him her eighty-five percent?"

Johnny swallowed hard; he hadn't thought of that. They hadn't discussed that little wrinkle with Rosenbaum, and he was struggling to find a good reply.

"I didn't think so," Clive added, then chuckled. "Six million is his price for the whole kit-and-kaboodle, Johnny. Not just for eighty-five percent . . ."

"Oh, he'll buy all right, Clive. And you'll just be his silent partner, same as now . . ." Johnny said, but the uncertainty in his voice was apparent.

"I don't think so," Clive retorted. "You can't do this deal without me, Johnny—not you and not Mary." Johnny heard Clive's office chair creak under the man's weight. "But now, before we get all tangled and twisted, let me throw a little idea your direction. One of my brilliant ideas." Johnny heard clacking at the other end of the line. Either a keyboard or a calculator. "Tell me this," Clive continued. "Does Mary know about this offer yet? Have they put anything in writing?"

Johnny's mind raced. *What the hell is Clive thinking?* He was trying to think ahead of the man, but nothing came to mind. "No," he replied honestly. "I haven't told Mary yet. The guy just now floated the number to Karen by phone. There's no written offer yet."

"Well then, Johnny," Clive chuckled. "You may be able to earn your commission after all."

"I'm listening."

"What we're gonna do, is . . . *I'm gonna sell* the Jew the vineyard—everything, lock, stock, and barrel for six million dollars."

Clive paused, knowing Johnny wouldn't get it.

"Go on . . ." Johnny prompted.

"See, *first,* I'm gonna increase my offer to Mary. I'll buy the vineyard from her for the four million she wanted," Clive paused to let that sink in. He knew Johnny was a bit slow sometimes. "*Then,* I'm gonna flip it to the Jew for six million. We'll net two million, and I'll pay you five hundred thousand."

Clive had just thrown a lot of numbers at Johnny. He wasn't the best when it came to math, but what was clear from what he'd just heard was that he would get five hundred thousand dollars out of two million; Clive's cut was bigger.

Johnny tried doing the math in his head but couldn't. So instead, he said, "The split needs to be fifty-fifty."

"Now hold on . . . I'm taking all the risk. I gotta put up the money to pay Mary. You're not putting anything in the deal."

"But you can't do it without me."

"But that ain't worth half."

"I can put in cash," Johnny spit out. "I'll get it back when we sell, right?"

"Yeah . . ." Clive replied. He knew country boy didn't have that kind of cash. He was flat out bluffing. "I tell you what, then. I'll give you credit for cutting Mary out of the deal, for not telling her about the Jew's offer. That's worth something; you're right. So, if you put in one million of the four we have to pay her, we'll split the profit fifty-fifty after we get our money back. One million dollars each."

"It's a deal."

Clive just about dropped his phone. He cleared his throat. "Uh . . . Alright, then."

"So, what needs to happen now?" Johnny asked.

"Well, don't tell Mary about the offer. If she asks, just say they never got back to you. Meanwhile, I'll send Karen all the paperwork—"

"Send it to me, Clive. I'll deal with Karen."

Clive paused, then said, "Okay. Sure. The contract will list me as seller, selling the vineyard to Rosenbaum for six million. Once they sign," Clive lowered his voice, imitating Marlon Brando, "I'll make Mary an offer she can't refuse." He laughed.

Johnny didn't laugh.

"Why don't you just make Mary the offer now? So we can speed this up?"

"Oh no, Johnny. Hold your horses there, pal . . . I'm not offering Mary four million dollars for the vineyard, and definitely not in writing, until I have a signed contract from your Jew for six million. Once that's done, and his escrow money is in the bank, then I know he's for real."

"But won't they check to see who owns the land? And see that it's not you?" Johnny asked.

"All that gets done by the title company, after the contract's signed, but before closing. If I don't own by then, they can walk away. But by then, I *will* own it. We'll schedule my closing—me buying the vineyard from Mary—as soon as possible. And we'll close the second deal thirty days from now. Just to be safe. Trust me Johnny. I know real estate."

"Okay, then," Johnny said. "Send me over that paperwork, quick. I need to explain this to Karen and then get it over to the buyer. I don't wanna waste any time and have him get cold feet."

"I can have it ready for you in an hour if you want," Clive replied.

As Johnny hung up, he heard Clive bellow, "Kitty!"

# CHAPTER FIFTY-ONE

Two hours later, Johnny was sitting in Karen's office. He'd explained the plan to her, and they were calling Nicholas Rosenbaum.

"Hi, Mr. Rosenbaum! I've got Johnny Miracle here with me. We've talked about your number, and I think we can get a deal done," Karen said.

"That's great news, Karen!" Rosenbaum replied.

"Fantastic. I've taken the liberty of preparing the documentation. I can send it to you, and all you need to do is confirm the numbers, sign it, and we're good to go."

"Perfect. Send it over," Rosenbaum said.

"I did have one question, Mr. Rosenbaum," Johnny chimed in.

"Please, call me Nick."

"Okay, Nick. So, I know you're an expert in wine and vineyards and all, but Texas, well, Texas is a whole 'nother animal. I'm thinking that maybe you could use some help, at least at the start?" Johnny paused.

"Go on," Rosenbaum said.

"Well, I'd be interested in stayin' on at Crabapple for a while, maybe a year or two, to help with the transition, make sure everything runs as smooth as it always has. Basically, I'd just wanna see to it that there's no interruption to operations and so forth. The place means a lot to us, and we just wanna do whatever we can to make sure that you're as happy with it as we've been," Johnny added.

"I think that is a great idea, Johnny! Just before you called, I was talking with my head of operations about who we would send down to Fredericksburg to take over. If we had some time to make that transition happen, and meanwhile, you could run things, that'd be a load off my mind," he replied. "Whaddya have in mind?"

"Well, I was thinkin' the same as I'm pullin' down right now—two hundred thousand in salary. And maybe a signing bonus upfront? If you want, we could reduce the purchase price by the bonus . . ."

There was silence on the line.

Johnny squinted, his hand on his forehead. Maybe he'd asked for too much.

"I think that's doable. A signing bonus payable at the closing, and you start immediately after. But let's make it one fifty a year. Two hundred's kinda pricey for Texas. And a fifty thousand dollar signing bonus—it doesn't need to come out of the purchase price. Fair is fair."

Johnny beamed at Karen and made a silent fist-pump. But he paused a few seconds, so he didn't sound too eager, before saying, "Sounds like we got a deal, Nick."

"Great. I'll have my lawyer draw that up!" Rosenbaum exclaimed. "Well, this is very exciting. I'm really looking forward to adding Crabapple Creek to our portfolio!"

Johnny took a deep breath and sat back, giving Karen a wink. Now, he just needed to get a million dollars to fund his part of the deal with Clive.

# CHAPTER FIFTY-TWO

Johnny had always had his eye on the Monet. He had done his homework. Although it was only insured for five million dollars, he'd checked around online and figured that the fair market value of the painting was significantly higher. He suspected that a stolen artwork would be subject to a deep discount versus its actual value. He hoped to get around a million dollars when he got around to selling it.

But, for now, he needed cash to fund his part of the vineyard deal with Clive. Johnny knew who to go to for quick money. He'd also read an article online about how criminals sometimes used stolen artworks as collateral. With the Monet as collateral, he felt confident he could get the million dollars.

Johnny parked in the rear lot of Cherries Gentlemen's Club. He'd driven through the lot once, making sure he didn't see Summer's car; the last thing he needed was his ex-stripper booty call making a scene while he was trying to do business. Satisfied that she wasn't there, he made his way to the door. Although it was 1:00 in the afternoon, once inside the vestibule, the club was dark as night.

"I have an appointment with Sick Eddie," Johnny told the big guy at the host stand. "Johnny Miracle."

"You mean Mr. de la Rosa?"

"Oh. Yeah. Right."

The man spoke into a small hand-held radio, then nodded and pointed, "All the way in the back, to the left."

Johnny nodded. He knew the way. He opened the door leading from the vestibule into the club and walked through a wall of conditioned air and throbbing music that smelled of alcohol, cheap perfume, and lost hope. There were several stages, each occupied by a topless dancer wearing a neon-colored thong. Johnny appraised the ladies, scanning tits to ass, tits to ass, before reminding himself that he was here on business. There was a decent crowd for the time of day, and a few men were hovering around a buffet. He reached the back left of the building and found another big guy standing by a black door.

"Miracle?" the man queried.

Johnny nodded.

The man opened the door, and Johnny passed through into a hallway about twenty feet long, leading to another black door with a security camera perched above. As he walked, the door behind him closed, and the sound of the music dropped significantly. Almost reaching the second door, he heard a soft electric buzz as it opened inward to an office. There was a large desk with several chairs in front of it.

Sick Eddie was seated behind the desk. The man was not what one would expect of a strip club owner. He looked to be in his late twenties and more like the lead singer in an indie rock band than a loan shark. He had short, well-groomed hair and a tight goatee.

"So, Johnny," the guy said. "Johnny Miracle. You know what would be miraculous? A real miracle?" He raised his arms. "Making my money appear . . . *right now*!"

Johnny heard someone laugh behind him and looked to see yet another refrigerator-of-a-man standing a few feet over in the corner. Shaved head. One earring. And a tattoo that crawled up his neck and onto the left side of his face.

"Look, Eddie, I know I'm late."

"Late?!" Sick Eddie scoffed. "Your delinquency is like *a rock in my gut*! You know, I oughta let Javier discuss punctuality with you, that's what I oughta do." Sick Eddie nodded at the man standing behind Johnny.

"Wait, wait!" Johnny said frantically, cringing protectively. "I have a deal . . . a proposition. You can make a *ton more*. It's a real estate deal."

Sick Eddie held up a hand, studying Johnny. "A ton? Real estate?" Then nodded, "Go on."

"I need a real short short-term loan."

"How much? How long? What's my cut?"

"I'm basically buying some land, then flipping it. So, I'll only need the money for thirty days, max," Johnny replied.

Sick Eddie stared at Johnny. He either feigned disgust really well or actually found Johnny repugnant.

"Go on."

Johnny started to sit in one of the two chairs in front of the desk.

"*NO!*" Sick Eddie screamed. "*Delinquents* do not have sitting privileges!"

Johnny froze.

"Talk, man! Out with it!"

"It's land—in Fredericksburg," Johnny replied. Sick Eddie said nothing. "It's farmland."

"How big is the deal?"

"Four million."

Sick Eddie's eyes grew wide. "You owe me what has now become sixty large, and you have the balls to come and ask to borrow four million?"

"No. No. I only need one million."

Sick Eddie's eyebrows rose, eyes narrowed, ever so slightly. "So, where's the other three coming from? A bank?"

"No. No banks," Johnny replied. "It's cash too. From my partner."

"Three million." Sick Eddie tilted his head to the side. "Cash." He waited. Silence. He prompted, "From. . . ?"

"Clive, Clive Connard. He's a rancher."

"And what's my cut?"

"A hundred thousand dollars," Johnny said confidently.

Sicked Eddie grinned. "So, let me get this straight. You owe me sixty thousand. You want to borrow a million for thirty days. And then you're going to pay me back my million plus a hundred grand? So, I'm making forty-K on a million-dollar loan? What're you, fuckin' stupid?"

Sick Eddie shook his head, frowning. But his belly was tingling. Real estate was one of the safer investments he dabbled in. If the property was worth four million, and Connard was putting in three million cash, he knew that once he got his claws into the deal, he could *persuade* himself into a larger cut. Eddie didn't make his money by taking big risks. He was a conservative businessman. He was thinking that he'd need to get more details on the land to be sure it was worth somewhere near the four million.

Johnny took his hesitation for reluctance to loan the money.

"I have collateral also," Johnny added. "A painting."

Sick Eddie frowned for a moment, then laughed, and the man behind Johnny joined in immediately. When Sick Eddie stopped laughing, so did Javier.

"A painting?" he asked.

"Yep. By Monet."

"Oh! By Monet! That's great! Do you own it?"

"How do you mean?"

"It's a simple question. Is it yours? Do—you—own—it? Legally?"

Johnny hesitated, looking over his shoulder at the man behind him.

"Okay," Sick Eddie held up his hand. "Don't answer that. I tell you what. Keep your fucking painting. Here's what I *can* do." Sick Eddie flipped a business card at Johnny like he was throwing a playing card. Johnny managed to catch it after it bounced off his chest. "Email me the details on the property flip. Your partner's info, title company, details on the land and where the money I'm loaning you is going—what *exactly* it's buying. I'll get back to you if my lawyer's okay with it. And . . . *if I get back to you*, and we do this thing, then it's five points per week."

Johnny stared back at the man.

*Was that five thousand or fifty thousand? It couldn't be five hundred thousand dollars, could it?*

Sick Eddie hadn't gotten as far as he had in life without strong people skills. He saw the vacant cow look in Johnny's eyes. "That means that each week you have the money, your debt grows by five percent interest on the million and the sixty. Each week. Every seven days. Understand?"

Johnny nodded.

"Since you said this is a quick deal, in and out, I'll give you forty days to repay in full. After that, I undertake to collect on the debt."

In Sick Eddie's experience, there were always delays, hence the extra ten days. And, if the deal was well-collateralized, and his money was safe, five points a week was good money.

Johnny nodded. He wanted to understand, so took a guess on the percentage. "So, just to be clear, after a week, I owe you a million and fifty thousand?"

Sick Eddie shook his head. "You're forgetting the sixty you owe me, which will also continue to accrue interest," Sick Eddie replied. "If you repay in week one, you pay me my million sixty *plus* five points on a million sixty, that's fifty-*three* thousand. Week two, you pay me my million sixty *plus* five points on my million sixty *and five points on the fifty-three from week one*. Week three, you pay—"

Johnny was utterly lost. He would need a calculator. Despite that, he nodded.

"Okay. Yeah, I get it. That won't be a problem. It'll only take thirty days, max."

"Again, assuming we do this thing, the funds will be wired to the title company at the sale's closing. My name will not appear anywhere on the documents. But you *and your partner* must understand that my money comes out of the deal first. Is that all clear?"

"Crystal clear," Johnny replied.

Sick Eddie smiled to himself. For one million dollars, he'd control four million dollars' worth of real estate. Not a bad day's work, assuming his lawyer said everything was legit.

# CHAPTER FIFTY-THREE

The next day, Johnny received a call from Sick Eddie. "My lawyer says the deal looks good. So, once you get the contract over to him, we'll get everything organized, and we'll be set to wire the funds to the title company for closing."

Johnny was ecstatic. He'd told Clive nothing about the loan from Sick Eddie and had been acting as though everything was fine. But he'd been on pins and needles, worried that he wouldn't be able to come up with the cash. Thankfully, Sick Eddie had come through just in time.

Meanwhile, Rosenbaum's lawyer had been reviewing the paperwork for his purchase of the vineyard for six million dollars. Earlier that day he'd confirmed that with a couple of minor changes—mostly spelling corrections—everything looked good. Two days later, all the pieces were in place. Rosenbaum signed the contract to buy the vineyard from Clive and put up a deposit of $200,000. That same afternoon, Johnny, Karen, and Clive all went to the vineyard together with Clive's contract to buy for four million dollars, prepared for Mary to sign.

They met in the vineyard's business office.

Mary sat at the desk with the documents in front of her, pen in hand. "So, why the change of heart, Clive?" she asked. She'd received the contract from Karen the day before via email and, unbeknownst to Johnny, she'd cleared it with Betsy Beavers.

"How do you mean?" Clive asked.

"From two million dollars to four million . . . That's not really a *change* of heart even; it's a heart transplant," she added.

"It's just one of those things, I guess. I was originally focused on how the vineyard had performed financially. In the past, it hadn't really made much money, you know. But then I started to think about what it could become, and I think that looking at it from that perspective, this price makes sense."

Mary nodded along with Clive as she initialed the bottom of each page.

"Well," she looked up at Clive, "lucky for me you changed your perspective then, I guess?"

Clive smiled, licking his lips as Mary initialed the last few pages and—finally—signed the last page of the agreement.

"The deposit check for the escrow?" Mary asked.

"That's already at the title company," Karen said, passing a sheet of paper to Mary. "Here is confirmation as well as a copy of the check."

Mary looked and saw that Clive had deposited $100,000 in connection with his purchase of the vineyard from her for four million dollars.

Karen looked through the papers, making sure that Mary and Clive had signed in all the right places. Then she looked up, smiling, and said, "That's all of it. So, we can close as soon as Wednesday."

Mary raised her eyebrows. "Wow. That's fast."

"I already know what I'm buyin', Mary," Clive replied.

"Okay," Mary nodded.

"We can do it at the title company or at Clive's office," Karen offered.

Johnny and Clive shrugged. They all looked at Mary.

"Clive's office is fine. After all, he's going to be the owner. Seems right somehow," Mary replied.

# CHAPTER FIFTY-FOUR

On Wednesday, Johnny cheerfully announced, "Good morning, Kitty," as he entered Clive's office.

"Mornin', Mr. Miracle!" she replied, coming around from behind her reception desk. "Closing's gonna be in the upstairs conference room. Mr. Connard's in his office getting some last-minute documents done."

Johnny nodded, "I'm gonna hang out here for a minute until the missus— " he turned to look towards street. "Well, here she comes."

Mary entered the offices.

"Good morning!" said the receptionist as she extended her hand. "I'm Kitty Clark."

Mary moved her purse to her other arm and shook Kitty's hand, "Mary Miracle, nice to meet you."

Johnny's lips pursed. *Weren't they chatting at the barbecue?*

"Y'all come with me," Kitty added. "Coffee? Water? Mr. Connard should be ready in a few minutes—oh, hold on!" Kitty paused as a professionally dressed woman entered the offices. "May I help you?"

"She's with me," Mary said. "My lawyer."

Johnny gave Mary a look, to which she responded with a shrug and a smile, saying in a low voice, "Just wanna make sure all the t's are crossed. You know Clive . . ."

"Betsy Beavers," the woman shook Johnny's hand.

Their introductions were interrupted by the moving earthquake that was Clive Connard stepping out into the lobby carrying a legal-sized Manila folder in his arms, from which protruded a mess of papers with dozens of red "sign here" stickers on their edges.

"Mornin', everyone!" he roared. "Let's get this puppy closed!" As the four turned towards the stairs, Karen Kline arrived and joined them.

Minutes later, the group sat quietly around the conference table while Mary's lawyer carefully read through every document in Clive's folder. Johnny leaned over to Mary and asked, "When did we get a lawyer?"

Mary *shushed* him, and Beavers looked up with a half-smile, clearly indicating that the noise was disturbing her review of the documents. After that, they remained silent, save for Clive's panting at the exertion from having climbed the stairs, which slowly subsided.

"It seems everything is in order," concluded the attorney, sliding the pile of paper back over to Clive. Karen had been through the documents earlier and let Clive run the show. He clambered to his feet and positioned the documents in front of Mary. Then, very delicately for such a big man, he handed her a pen and assisted her by turning pages to all the "sign here" tags by which Mary put her signature or initials. When the last page was signed, Clive picked up the stack and handed it to Kitty, who'd been standing by in the corner. She took them all downstairs to make copies.

"So, y'all gonna be okay movin' out by the end of the month? I know it's a big house—"

"We should—"

"That—"

Both Johnny and Mary began to respond, but Mary spoke over her husband.

"That won't be a problem, Clive. The end of the month is fine," Mary said. She was lying. She planned to take her sweet time getting out.

Clive nodded, then removed the only remaining item in the Manila folder. He handed her a letter-size envelope, "Then, here is a cashier's check for the full amount."

Mary opened the envelope and peeked in at the check, made out to Mary Miracle, drawn on a national bank. Grandma Nellie's vineyard was officially sold to Clive Connard. After closing costs, the net to Mary was $3,680,022.56. She handed the check to Beavers, who looked at it, nodded, and returned it to her. Mary closed the envelope and placed it in her purse.

"I've gotta run an errand real quick," Mary said, standing abruptly.

Johnny looked at her, surprised.

"No problem," said her lawyer to the room. "I'll wait for the copies. I also need to have a word with Mr. Miracle." She smiled at Johnny.

"What about?" he asked.

"Better in private," she indicated with her head at Clive, smiling conspiratorially.

"Should I—" Clive began.

"Well, I gotta run," Mary said.

"See you at the house, babe," Johnny replied. He leaned over to kiss her, but Mary was already on her feet and headed out of the conference room.

"Kitty should be about done," Clive said. "We can head on down if you like?" The remaining four nodded at one another in consensus, and the attorney led the way slowly down the stairs behind Mary, who had already reached the bottom. While they descended the stairs, Karen placed her hand gently on Johnny's shoulder and squeezed.

As Mary passed through the foyer on her way out, she gave Kitty, who had just finished copying, a small wave. Kitty waved back and winked. Once the rest of the group reached the foyer, Mary's lawyer stepped forward and said, "I'll take those." Kitty handed the copies of the closing documents to Beavers, who carefully slipped the stack into her briefcase.

There were handshakes all around, and Johnny and the lawyer headed out onto the street.

# CHAPTER FIFTY-FIVE

"Can I help you with that?" Johnny asked as he and Beavers walked out of Clive's office. Johnny was doing his best to channel Ryan Gosling. This lawyer was an attractive woman.

She let him take the briefcase. "I'm right here," she indicated, walking towards a red Benz. As she popped the trunk and opened it so that Johnny could put the briefcase in it, he took a good long look.

*That is one very nice pear-shaped ass. I wonder if she does yoga? How far can she bend over?* "So," Johnny assessed her, looking at her neck and breasts while he spoke. "What can I do you for?"

"Smoke?" she offered.

Johnny looked up and down the street, then shrugged. "Sure. Why not?"

She lit up a cigarette, then handed him the pack and lighter.

"Filthy habit," she said. She walked around and opened the back door to her car.

Johnny lit up his smoke. "So, you're a real estate lawyer. From Austin?"

"Originally from further south. Corpus Christi, but now I live in Austin. I do a little bit of everything and work kinda all over central Texas. Real estate's not really my specialty. But it comes with the territory."

As she leaned into the car, Johnny angled to try and get a better view of her around the car door.

"You enjoy law?"

She emerged with an 8.5 x 11 brown envelope in her hand and closed the door. "Some days are better than others, I suppose. Of course, you get to meet all kinds. It's never dull."

Johnny slipped the plastic lighter into the cigarette pack and offered it back to her. Betsy's hands were full with her purse, the envelope, and her cigarette; she put her cigarette in her mouth and said through clenched teeth, “Hold this.”

Johnny took the envelope. Betsy took the cigarette pack from him, put it in her purse while she inhaled deeply, and then took the cigarette out of her mouth.

“Goddamn,” she said. “It’s like a metaphor for life, right? Constantly juggling. Trying to keep from dropping the ball . . .” She laughed.

Johnny laughed too.

“So, you wanted to talk?” Johnny put on his best country-boy smile. “Let’s talk,” he purred.

“Oh yeah,” she said. “That. It’s kind of my favorite part of the job.” She indicated with her cigarette at the envelope Johnny was holding.

“You’ve been served.”

# CHAPTER FIFTY-SIX

As Karen drove back to her office, she passed by the high school, and for once, rather than anger, she felt satisfaction. She'd struggled to come out from under Mary's shadow for most of her life.

*Mary's grandma owns a vineyard.*

*Mary always gets top grades.*

*Mary knows how to eat at a table. See, no elbows.*

*Mary doesn't chew like a cow.*

*Mary's going to prom with David.*

*Mary's so pretty, elegant. Not slutty-looking like you.*

*Mary got into UT.*

*Mary's marrying Johnny.*

"Everything is always about fucking Mary," she hissed out loud. But finally, Karen was getting her revenge. She'd tried once long ago with David, and that had backfired horribly. It had turned into a daisy chain of shit. Not only had he not asked her to prom, but he'd ignored her after having sex with her. Then she'd ended up pregnant. Then came the abortion. And finally . . . what should have been a high point for Karen ended up being one of her worst memories.

* * *

*Prom night. A few days after her abortion. Karen was radiant in a beautiful blue gown. Even her mother, for once, had said so. "Not just pretty, honey—you reek of class. Like Princess Grace from Morocco," she'd said, beaming at her daughter.*

*The high school gym décor was in keeping with the prom theme: Arabian Nights. And, although Karen's date was a complete douche, he was tall and made for a good prom picture. As the evening progressed, she danced some with her date, and even more with different groups of girls.*

*Abby was there with some band nerd. She really needed to do something about her weight. It was getting out of control. She was fat, but she was a friend. Karen tried her best to overlook Abby's obesity, but fat people grossed her out.*

*As a slow dance song faded out, the lights came up, and the student council president took the mic. "I hope everyone's having a great time. Now comes the part where we announce the Prom King and Queen and their Court."*

*The students who had been nominated were all asked to come up backstage. Karen made her way with her head held high. This was a huge moment for her; she didn't know the results, but just being in the mix made her feel special.*

*She waited with several other students as they announced the court, building up to the announcement of King and Queen. As the moment approached, Karen's heart skipped a beat when she spotted her history teacher walking up to her. "Here, let me adjust your corsage, dear," Mrs. Shoe said with a smile.*

*After a few seconds, Karen released the breath she was holding. The woman was being pleasant enough. Friendly. Karen was sure she hadn't seen her leaving the abortion clinic with Abby.*

*"There you go, honey. Good luck!" Then she leaned in and added, "And remember. You'll always be trash, dear. Mary won Prom Queen. She got the most votes. But she's not here tonight. So, even though you'll be crowned, you'll always know, and I'll always know. You're a loser . . . and a baby killer." Mrs. Shoe stepped back. Still smiling ear to ear, she patted Karen on the shoulder and added more audibly, "Oh . . . bless your heart . . ."*

*Moments later, Karen heard her name called, "Our Prom Queen, Karen Kline!"*

*As she walked on stage, everyone assumed she was crying tears of joy.*

* * *

"Fuck you, Mary!" Karen screamed as she drove. "I win! I finally win!" Johnny and Clive had just bought Mary's precious vineyard out from under her, and they'd be flipping it for an extra two million dollars.

And Karen was the realtor on both deals (one for buyer, one for seller), earning her a commission of three hundred thousand dollars, although she had to split some of that with Johnny.

And Karen was screwing Johnny.

And Johnny was going to leave Mary for her, for Karen Kline.

Karen pulled into her real estate office and quickly checked her face in the rearview mirror before going in.

Everything was finally going her way.

# CHAPTER FIFTY-SEVEN

Johnny called Mary's mobile phone as he raced back to the vineyard, with no luck. After the sixth call that went to voicemail, he finally left a message, confused and apologetic. He wanted to set the tone before he spoke with her in person.

"Mary, babe. I don't know what this is all about . . . I'm . . . I'm shocked. I don't know what to say except that I love you, and I know we can work this out. I know losing Grandma Nellie's been hard on you, and maybe you're not thinking straight. But I know we can figure this out, the two of us. I'll be home in a bit. I love you forever, babe."

Johnny hit END and screamed at the top of his lungs, "*FUUCKIN' CUUUNTT!!!*"

Five minutes later, he pulled into the drive to the vineyard, and his heart fell as he approached the gate.

"Shit . . ."

One of the vineyard's pick-up trucks was backed up against the inside of the gate. And there, standing in the cargo bed, holding a shotgun, was Pedro.

Johnny pressed the button on his opener. The gate didn't move. Neither did Pedro. He just stood there, smiling.

Johnny got out and shouted, "Open up, man. I need to see Mary."

Pedro took a few slow steps to the back edge of the bed and said, "But she doesn't want to see you, Johnny. She just needs for you to take your stuff and go." Pedro indicated to the right with the butt of his shotgun, and there, outside the fence, were several large boxes and three suitcases.

"Come on, Pedro. Do me a solid, man. Let me in . . ."

Pedro turned and took a few steps back, then turned to face Johnny again, leaning against the cab. "Can't do that, Johnny. Boss's orders."

"Fuck you, then!"

Johnny took out his mobile phone and texted Mary.

> *Hey babe. I'm here. Out front. Come out and let me in. We can fix this. I love you.*

Johnny waited a few minutes. No reply. He called Mary's mobile phone. Voicemail again.

"Fuck!"

Johnny stalked over and carried the boxes and suitcases to his pick-up, placed them in the bed, climbed in, and started the engine. He rolled down his window and stuck his left arm out, raising it up high and giving Pedro the bird. "Fuck you, you fuckin' faggot!" he shouted, then slammed his Chevy in reverse, kicking up gravel and dirt as he pulled out and left.

As Johnny drove away, it dawned on him that he had nowhere to go. He called Karen.

Voicemail.

He called three more times. Same result.

"*FUUUCCCK!!!*" he yelled.

Suddenly, his phone chirped.

*Mary?*

No. It was Karen.

"Hey, sweetie," she said. "What did that lawyer want? Any hiccups?"

*Hiccups?! Fuck me . . . hiccups!*

"Hey, babe. Naaaw. No hiccups. Everything's perfect. Smooth as can be."

Johnny didn't want to show any signs of weakness. They still needed to close the deal with Rosenbaum.

"Well, good. When I got back to the office, I had an email waiting for me from Rosenbaum's lawyer . . ."

*Shit! What now?*

". . . they sent me the final draft of your contract as vineyard manager. You'll need to take a look and make sure you're good with it," she said.

Johnny breathed a sigh of relief. Everything was still going according to plan. In fact, now that he thought about it, Mary filing for divorce saved him the hassle of doing it himself later.

*Stupid bitch! One less headache for me.*

"That's great, babe," he replied. "How about I swing by now and take a look. And maybe after, we can spend a little . . . *quality time* together?"

# CHAPTER FIFTY-EIGHT

Johnny and Karen had just finished having sex.

"So, I got a surprise for you," Johnny said.

"Ooh," Karen cuddled up against him. "I love surprises."

"What if I told you I'm done with her?"

A part of Karen had doubted that Johnny would ever leave Mary for her. While the narcissist in her screamed that she was better than Mary, deep inside, as with most narcissists, there was an insecure child. Beneath all the bravado, Karen felt cheap and unworthy.

"I thought you were going to wait until after you flipped the vineyard?" she asked.

"I was, but I've been thinking . . . she's out of the picture, and everything is on track with Rosenbaum . . . so why not now?"

"Oh, Johnny! Really!?" Karen sat up in bed, the sheets falling away from her breasts.

"Yep. I packed up this morning while Mary was out. Got all my stuff in the truck . . ."

Karen leaned forward and kissed him passionately.

Johnny returned the kiss for a bit, then pulled away, saying, "I'm gonna go unload my stuff before someone steals something!" He dressed quickly and began bringing suitcases and boxes into the house. Karen pulled on a pair of jeans and a t-shirt and helped him.

Once they were done unloading the back, he opened the crew cab and removed a toolbox to get at a folded blue furniture pad that had been resting behind it. The pad was wrapped around something that looked about the size of half a movie poster.

"Here," he told Karen, handing her the package. "Take this."

As she carried it, she felt that the edges were hard, but not flat, irregular. Back in the house, Karen put the blue pad on her sofa and asked, "Is this what I think it is?"

"Open it up," Johnny replied, placing his toolbox in the hall closet.

"Hoooly shit!"

There on Karen Kline's sofa sat Mary's Monet.

"So, how did you do it?" she asked. She didn't care much for art but studied the piece closely, wondering exactly what made it worth so much money.

"Easy as pie," he replied. "I unplugged the security system before the barbecue began, but when I checked the app later, it was up and running again. Someone had plugged it back in. Prob'ly that queer, Pedro. So, I decided, plan B, to spray-paint the security camera that covers that side of the house. Then, before the barbecue started winding down, when I was sure the place was empty, I ran up to the house, opened the window, and put the Monet outside. Later, first trip out to the firepit, I ran around real quick and stashed it in my truck. Cops didn't check it 'cause I wasn't leaving the property. And the insurance guy didn't check it 'cause I took off when he started searching the property, and I didn't come back until he was gone."

"And you've just been driving around with it?" Karen couldn't believe that he'd been so stupid as to keep a multi-million-dollar artwork in his truck. *Fucking moron . . .*

Johnny shrugged. "Yeah."

"Well, we should put it somewhere safe, now," Karen said aloud, but more to herself than to Johnny. "I know just where. Come here."

Karen opened a door next to the staircase to what looked like a coat closet. After removing several winter coats and laying them over the back of the sofa, she unfastened two latches at the back of the closet, removing a wood panel about half the size of a standard door.

"You have a secret compartment?" Johnny asked.

"It was for access to the old water heater. Before I moved in, I convinced the landlord to replace it with an Insta-Hot unit."

Johnny looked in and saw that the closet went deeper, turning under the staircase. Karen wrapped the Monet in the furniture pad, leaned it against the wall inside the hidden space, and replaced the panel.

"No one will ever find it there," she smiled as she hung the coats back in the closet. "Now, let's get your stuff organized."

# CHAPTER FIFTY-NINE

Carl Gandy had been through the police report, the photos, and his notes, puzzling through the clues. And finally, he'd figured it out. He knew how the theft of the Monet had been committed. He set a follow-up meeting with Johnny and Mary Miracle to present his findings but when he arrived at the vineyard, he found only Mary at home.

"We're getting a divorce," Mary told Gandy after initial pleasantries. "And I wouldn't put it past Johnny to have stolen the Monet."

Gandy paused for a moment, then looked at her askance, "You two seemed fine when I was here last."

"It's been a while in the making, but things came to a head since your last visit."

"I see," he nodded.

They were standing in the study in front of the fireplace where the painting had once hung. He was carrying the same backpack as before and removed a folder. "Well," he began. "Let's discuss the *how* first, then we can explore the *who.* We know that the painting was still in place at approximately 2:45 p.m. on Saturday when the selfie was taken. So, someone took it sometime between 2:45 and the time you discovered it missing."

Mary nodded. "That makes sense."

"But I believe we are dealing with two crimes. Not just one."

"Okay . . ." Mary raised her eyebrows.

"The second crime is pretty straightforward," Gandy continued. "We know that this window on the right was unlocked. Standing here . . ." he positioned himself in front of the window, "I can't be seen from the kitchen or the dining room. A person could easily open the window, step in, take the painting, and leave."

Mary nodded.

"And, because the camera outside was rendered inoperable, they could have walked off with the painting and done with it what they pleased, again without being seen."

"Makes sense," Mary agreed again.

"That is the second crime," Gandy added. "But here is the critical clue to the first crime. Take a look here." Gandy pointed above the fireplace. A single nail holding a brass picture hanging hook was on the wall where the painting had hung.

Mary scanned the wall, then looked back at Gandy. She shrugged. "I don't get it."

"If you look closely, you will see that there is just the one hook here. And no other nail holes. But," Gandy removed two large sheets from a folder he had left on one of the leather chairs, "look here." One was a blow-up of the selfie photo taken by Rio. The second was a blow-up of the picture of Johnny, Mary, and Grandma Nellie in front of the fireplace. On both, red lines had been drawn around the Monet, between it and the fireplace mantle, and measurements were neatly written in the same red ink.

"You can see here that in the photo from Christmas—you said this was five years ago, correct?"

Mary nodded. "Yes."

"In the Christmas photo, look there," Gandy pointed at the line running along the bottom of the Monet. "When you scale the two photos by using the size of the painting—so that the dimensions match—you can see that the painting in the selfie is hanging lower than the painting in the Christmas photo. If you zoom it way in, it's about an 11/16" difference. Almost three quarters of an inch. Small, but significant."

"What?" Mary exclaimed. She studied the two photos and saw that in photo one, the distance from the bottom of the painting to the fireplace mantle read seven inches, and in the other, it read seven point six eight inches. The same discrepancy existed at the top of the painting.

"What does that mean?" she asked. Gandy paused, studying her.

"You tell me," Gandy replied.

She looked at the two photos, then back at Gandy, then asked, "The painting was rehung?"

Gandy shook his head. "Or they aren't the same painting."

"Wait . . . two Monets?"

Gandy nodded. "I am guessing that the Monet was hanging by a wire, attached to screw eyes on each side . . . or D-rings, correct?"

She nodded. "When my grandma gave it to me, she showed me the back so I could see the note that she wrote to me, and the one from when her mother gave it to her. And, yeah, I remember it had these little metal loops screwed into the frame that the wire ran through."

"Those would be screw eyes. So, sometime between that photo from Christmas five years ago and the selfie last week, someone took the original Monet off the wall and hung a fake. And when they were switched, they didn't get the placement of the wire exactly right, hence the discrepancy in the height."

Mary looked at Gandy, the photos, and then the wall. "So, the actual theft . . ."

Gandy nodded. "You've been robbed, all right. Twice. At some point after that Christmas photo, someone stole the original and put a fake in its place. And on Labor Day, someone stole the fake."

"Couldn't it have just been re-hung? I mean, I'm not saying I saw her do it because I didn't, but couldn't my grandmother have rewired it?" Mary asked.

"Did she ever tell you she rewired it? Or mention any reason why she would have?"

"Well, no . . ." Mary shook her head.

"Occam's razor, Mrs. Miracle. The simplest explanation is usually the correct one. If you want to change the height that a painting hangs, you move the nail, not the wire." He pointed at the nail above the fireplace.

"So . . . when—"

He anticipated her question. "Unless you have a more recent photo, there's no way to know when the switch happened. All we know is that Christmas five years ago, there was one Monet on this wall, and last week there was another." Gandy replied. "And . . . you don't have any other recent photos?"

"No, not that I can think of. But I still can't wrap my head around how—if the thief already had the painting, then why steal it again?"

"What makes you think it was the same person?" Gandy replied.

Mary shrugged, baffled.

"I think you've been robbed by two different people. The first one got the Monet, the second . . . didn't." Gandy stated, taking back the photos and replacing them in the folder.

Mary stared in disbelief at the nail above the fireplace.

Gandy walked slowly away from the fireplace, uncrossing his arms. "Now, as to *who* stole it . . ."

# CHAPTER SIXTY

Gandy's voice softened. He'd been speaking very matter-of-factly. Suddenly, his speech and posture seemed to take on a more personal tone. "In your divorce proceeding, as far as marital assets, do you think there will be any dispute?" He pursed his lips.

"Do you mean, is Johnny after money?" Mary asked.

Gandy shrugged and nodded.

Mary's shoulders lifted slightly. "*He* wanted me to sell the painting. I told him, 'No way in hell.' A month later, it's gone, and I find out Johnny's been checking on the insurance—how much the Monet was insured for, I mean. I had no idea there even was insurance on it . . . As far as the divorce goes, we just recently served him, so his lawyer—I'm assuming he'll get one—hasn't filed any response. So, I don't know if he wants money, but it wouldn't surprise me."

Her words hung in the air. Both looked back at the empty space above the fireplace.

Then, Gandy added, "I read about the divorce."

"What? Where?" Mary asked.

"Our division subscribes to a bunch of services. It came through, like on a Google Alert, but not Google. Public document filings."

"Oh." Mary rolled her eyes in relief. "I thought you meant like in the news or something."

"Does he still live here?"

Mary shook her head. Then she scrunched her nose, smiling sheepishly. "No. I sort of kicked him out. Don't know where he's living."

Gandy nodded.

"The loose security system cord, that points to an inside job. It could have been the thief's original plan to simply disconnect the system and steal the painting. But, when that failed, he or she found another way to disable the camera."

"That makes sense," Mary said.

"Well, the insurance will pay. But five million dollars is a lot of money. We may need to do some more . . . poking around. We'll be putting the word out, in the art world. To dealers and such, though no one legitimate will buy it without solid provenance. Could you . . . once the divorce proceeding . . . evolves . . . would you mind if I call you, just to find out what your husband's posture is with regards to the insurance proceeds?"

Mary thought for a moment, then replied, "No, that's fine."

As she watched Gandy drive off, Mary tried to stay upbeat. But it wasn't easy. So much had happened in so little time.

Grandma Nellie was gone. The vineyard was gone. The Monet was gone. And from the sound of it, it was unlikely that she'd ever see it again. And on top of it, she was sure she had a fight ahead of her with Johnny over the insurance money.

"Something's gotta break my way at some point," she said out loud to no one. She looked at her phone, checking the date, and her eyes sparkled. Johnny would soon be getting a taste of his own medicine.

# CHAPTER SIXTY-ONE

For the next few weeks, Johnny settled into living with Karen Kline. Initially, he missed being at the vineyard. While he used to hate getting out of bed to go out and work the fields, he found that having nothing to do was even worse. The second thing he noticed—much to his chagrin—was that screwing Karen and living with her were two very different things.

The first week, he drove by the vineyard every day.

*Just to see what's going on . . .*

Soon, he settled into a routine of waking early, and getting out of the house before Karen was up. He made up excuses—"going to check on my dad in Buda; looking at a real estate deal in Burnet." Then, he'd come back home and binge Netflix once he was sure she'd left for work.

Johnny hadn't told Clive about the divorce. He thought Johnny was still keeping things going at the vineyard. Johnny pretended that everything was fine, not wanting to show any weakness until they closed the vineyard flip and he had his cash in hand. He also used the time to hire a lawyer to deal with the divorce.

Finally, the day of the closing with Rosenbaum arrived. Johnny got to Clive's office thirty minutes before the scheduled closing time. He'd swung by to pick up Karen on the way. When they arrived, they went up to the conference room, where Clive was waiting for them. Karen sat down and reviewed the closing statement one last time. While she did, Clive pulled Johnny aside.

"What the hell is going on between you and Mary?" he hissed.

"What are you talkin' about?" Johnny frowned.

"I swung by the property this morning, just to check on things. Mary said you moved out? There's boxes and stuff. She's packing. But she's still there. She promised me she'd be out in a week or two. Said she's got an apartment lined up. And that if I had any other questions to ask you . . .?"

"Don't worry about it, Clive. It's all under control," Johnny replied unconvincingly. *What is Mary playing at? Why hasn't she moved out?*

Clive was about to press the issue when they heard a knock on the door frame to the conference room.

"Right this way," Kitty said, entering the conference room. "This is Mr. Gross."

"Hello, everyone," said a gentleman in a blue suit and gold tie. "I'm Saul Gross, attorney for Nick Rosenbaum."

Clive's demeanor shifted into good ole boy mode. Smiling broadly, he almost shouted, "Welcome! Great to meet'cha! I'm Clive, sir, Clive Connard. I've seen your name on emails and such. Great to finally put a face to the name."

Introductions were made all around, Clive gestured broadly to the chairs, and everyone took their seats.

As they did, Johnny pulled out a crumpled receipt on the back of which he'd scribbled out the basics of the pay day. The total deal was six million dollars.

Clive would get four million: the three million he had used to buy out Mary, along with another million in profit.

Johnny would get two million: one million to pay back to Sick Eddie, plus one million in profit. He also had to pay Sick Eddie interest but hadn't been able to do that math.

*I need to buy that damned calculator.*

He was also getting half of the real estate commission based on the deal he'd cut with Karen. And he had his deal with Rosenbaum to run the vineyard for them.

It was a great day for Johnny Miracle.

"Well, you've seen all the documentation, so I guess we're all good there," Karen said. "Is Mr. Rosenbaum coming, or have you brought signed copies?"

"Yes," Mr. Gross said, "about that." He cleared his throat. "There has been a complication."

The three looked at one another uncomfortably as the attorney opened his briefcase. He dug around for a few moments, then finally extracted a folder and placed it on the table in front of him.

"Let me begin by saying that . . . well, this is somewhat embarrassing. And, I have to say, both on behalf of myself as well as Mr. Rosenbaum, that this has never happened before. I have been working with the family for over a decade, and—well, you know that the family's land holdings are significant. This is not our first rodeo, so to speak. So, that said, I apologize. And Mr. Rosenbaum also offers his sincerest apologies. But," the lawyer opened the folder and passed a sheet of paper across to Karen, "for reasons that I am afraid I cannot share, the family has decided not to proceed with the transaction."

It was as if the air had been sucked from the room. Johnny's belly flipped.

Gross droned on, "I know this is disappointing, but the letter before you speaks for itself . . ."

Johnny didn't hear the rest of what the lawyer had to say. He felt the back of his neck getting hot. He began to stand, then, feeling woozy, thought better of it, and sank back in his chair, blankly gawking across at Clive and Karen, who had huddled their heads together so they could read the letter simultaneously. When they finished, Johnny reached over and pulled the letter toward him, flipping it around.

*Dear Mr. Connard,*

*My client, Bella Dona Holdings, Inc., is unable to close on the purchase of the Crabapple Creek Vineyard.*

*This decision is not taken lightly, but in good faith. And in similar good faith, my clients request the return of their escrow deposit of $200,000.00 (TWO HUNDRED THOUSAND DOLLARS).*

*Warm regards,*
*Saul Gross, Esquire*

Clive shook his head. Karen released the breath she'd been holding as she looked at him and then at Johnny, whose face had turned red. Suddenly, Johnny slammed a fist on the table. "*WHAT THE FUCK! YOU CAN'T DO THIS! YOU CANNOT FUCKIN' DO THIS!*"

Clive sat in silence, hands pressed to either temple, staring at the table, slowly rocking back and forth.

"I'm so very sorry," Gross said again.

"*WE'LL FUCKIN' SUE!*" Johnny shouted, looking to Karen for support in his threat.

She sat with her lips pursed. Expressionless.

"I'm afraid there's nothing to sue for, Mr. Miracle," Gross said. "If you sue, you will lose. It's all in the contract. You get to keep the escrow money if my client fails to perform. And that's it. We had hoped you might, in good faith, see fit to return the funds. But I gather from your reaction that that's not likely." He pursed his lips and shrugged. "I know this must be a blow. But," the lawyer stood, "it's a beautiful property. I passed it on the way in. And I am sure you will find another buyer. And when you do, you'll look back on all this as a small bump in the road. But one for which you were paid the handsome sum of two hundred thousand dollars." He nodded, looked each person in the eyes, then added, "I'll show myself out."

"He can't just leave!" Johnny shouted, standing and pointing at Gross's back, looking at Clive and Karen for support.

"Shut up, Johnny," Clive almost whispered. His quick million-dollar profit had evaporated right before his eyes. "He's right. We're fucked."

# CHAPTER SIXTY-TWO

About an hour later, Mary's phone rang.

"Well, you're not gonna believe this!"

Mary smiled. She'd been expecting a call about the closing, but not from the Rhinestone Realtor. "What happened, Kitty? Is everything okay?"

In hushed tones, Kitty conveyed to Mary what she'd overheard through the vent from her hiding spot below the stairs.

Mary laughed inside, though outwardly, she feigned surprise.

"I owe you a big one, Kitty," Mary said. "If you hadn't given me a heads up on Johnny's plan with Clive . . ."

"Well, it's just a good thing you took the deal from Clive and didn't call 'im out on it. If you'd done the deal with Rosenbaum instead, you'd be the one screwed right now instead of them."

Mary thought about whether to fill Kitty in on all the details of how she'd conned Johnny and Clive but decided against it. She replied, "Four million dollars was a fair price for the vineyard, Kitty. It doesn't pay to be greedy. Grandma Nellie always used to say, 'Pigs get fat—'"

"—hogs get slaughtered," Kitty finished, giggling. "Well, there were some really pissed-off hogs up there today. You should've heard Johnny yellin'!"

As they ended the call, Mary smiled, satisfied. *At least I'm getting my financial world under control.*

The vineyard was property Mary had inherited from her grandmother; under Texas law, Johnny couldn't touch the money she'd gotten when she sold it to Clive. Her plan to get Clive to pay more for the property had worked, though Mary had never anticipated that Clive and Johnny would try to screw her and flip the property.

*Just desserts.*

About an hour later, Mary's phone rang again—the call she'd been expecting.

Mary answered, saying, "I heard everything went according to plan."

"Your little spy updated you?"

"Uh huh," Mary replied.

"Well, yes, it all did. And it seems that Johnny was not a happy camper, as well he shouldn't be. He said he was going to sue and . . . a lot of other nonsense."

"But he can't sue. The contract—"

"Anyone can sue anyone for anything. Don't ever forget that. But the contract *is* crystal clear. All they're entitled to is to keep the earnest money. Suing would be a waste of time."

"You're right," Mary paused. "I'm still amazed that they tried to pull this stunt. When I think about it . . ." she sighed.

"Well. I'm just glad that everything worked out."

"So, we still need to settle up. What do I—"

"If it's all right, Mary, why don't we get together? We can settle up then. There's also one other loose end that I need to discuss with you. But that would be best dealt with face to face."

Mary was intrigued. "That sounds fine."

"But let's find a discreet place to meet. Far from prying eyes."

The two discussed dates and times, and Mary ended the call by saying, "Thanks again for everything. I don't know how I would have handled this without your advice."

"You'd have done fine, with or without me. After all, you are a *highly* motivated woman . . ."

# RUBY YI – 1983

In the weeks after Arvin Cho's 'suicide,' Ruby Yi's time was consumed with legal matters, primarily transitioning ownership of the Chos' businesses into solely her name based upon her husband's last will and testament. She was also interviewed several times by the police in connection with her husband's death. Her story never wavered.

She had lunched with the mayor. Arvin had come home tired. As was his habit, he'd had a couple of drinks, then gone to bed early. Ruby had eaten alone, then went to sleep by his side. And next thing she knew, the police were at her door, and her dear husband was gone.

Arvin had been an only child, and his mother had died in the same car accident that had left old Cho crippled. Ruby Yi was Arvin's sole heir. This made her a wealthy woman, and it also meant that no family members existed to question her story.

Life went on for Ruby Yi as usual until a surprise phone call drew her attention away from her day-to-day responsibilities, leading her to a city she'd never been to.

"Is this Ruby Yi, daughter of Beverly Yi?"

Ruby had not heard her mother's name in years. Curiosity getting the better of her, she'd responded in the affirmative.

"I'm calling from St. Joan's Hospital in Los Angeles. I'm sorry to have to tell you that your mother passed away this morning. She listed you as next of kin."

Her mother had apparently been done in by her fourth heart attack. She'd lived alone in a small government housing project. She'd had no family other than Ruby.

Ruby took care of the arrangements. She had her mother cremated because it was cheap. She didn't bother with a funeral. The hospital mailed Beverly Yi's personal effects, her clothing and purse, to Ruby. In her mother's pocketbook, she found a photo she hadn't seen in years; it was creased and bent, but the image was still clear: her mother and father. It was the only image Ruby had ever seen of him.

All she'd ever known about her father was that his name was Tony and the likeness from that photo. Nothing more, not even a last name. As a child, she'd often fantasized that he came back to California . . . and that he came back for her. She'd imagined he was a diplomat, a spy, an astronaut, always jobs that kept him away from her and from living a normal family life. Over the years, her feelings towards him had oscillated between sadness at missing out on a father, anger at him for abandoning her, indifference towards the man who had never cared enough to seek her out, and hating him for what she'd had to suffer through for not having a father or, eventually, a mother.

She had long ago resigned herself to never meeting him or knowing him.

That changed when she turned over the photo. On the back, as she remembered, was written *Tony and Beverly, 1949.* But *now*, just below that, there was a phone number in her mother's handwriting in different ink. After a week of indecision, Ruby hired a private investigator to look into Tony and the phone number. And three days later, she learned her father's name: Tony Lombardi. And so much more.

The private investigator prepared a small dossier with a few news articles suggesting that Little Tony was involved in organized crime. She had background information—social security number, driver's license, credit history, marriages, children, list of residences and vehicles owned, past and present. And lastly, the investigator provided Ruby with Tony Lombardi's current address and phone number at the Autumn Winds Retirement Home. Suddenly, he was real, at least on paper. Ruby was overwhelmed with information about the man that had never been in her life yet formed a significant part of her childhood, though only through his absence. She called the retirement home in Chicago to speak to him but was told that he was lucid only at times. She decided to pay a visit.

She'd flown into the Windy City that morning with Kong.

As she walked down the hall and into the common room, Ruby Yi felt something akin to fear for the first time in decades. Her belly tightened when the nurse pointed her to a man in a wheelchair positioned in front of a large window that overlooked a terrace, yard, and garden beyond.

Ruby took a deep breath, raised her chin, and approached slowly, studying what she could see of the man. He wore a plaid long-sleeved shirt over a dingy white t-shirt and beige pants. His wool stocking feet were in cheap brown corduroy slippers, one of which was falling off. His hair was thin, mottled grey and brown, and looked greasy, as though he hadn't showered in days. As she got close, she smelled body odor and something acrid; urine?

"Mr. Lombardi?"

The man slowly turned, his head slightly quivering. He had sharp features, an aquiline nose, and bushy gray eyebrows. His rheumy eyes were faded brown with grey flecks. He looked to have the beginnings of cataracts. Her father stared at her but said nothing. And after a moment, he turned again to look back out the window.

Ruby pulled up a chair and sat down next to him. "My name is Ruby. Ruby Yi." Lombardi didn't react. "I think you knew my mother, Beverly?" Still nothing. She carefully removed the photo from her purse and held it out in front of the man. After a few moments, he looked down at it. Slowly, his trembling hand moved. He held the photo up at arm's length and studied it.

"Are you family?" a raspy voice asked.

Ruby turned to see an older woman in a tattered dressing gown standing a few feet away. She had purplish gray hair and quick dark eyes that studied Ruby through horn-rimmed glasses. Her nicotine-stained fingers gripped an aluminum walker.

"Um . . . sort of," Ruby answered.

"Well, it's high time," the woman replied. "I been here two years. And you're the first one to visit Tony in all that time. Used to bug him to no end when I first got here." She looked at Lombardi. "Ain't that right, Tony?" she added loudly, though Lombardi seemed not to notice. "He don't hear so good. Ya gotta shout!" Which she did, and the old man jumped, turning to look at her. "Heh, heh, heh. . ." she chuckled.

The woman reached into her pocket, and took out an extra-long cigarette, putting it in her mouth. "He was always asking when his family was coming to see him. His kids 'specially." As she spoke, the cigarette bobbed up and down. "But then, well, he was better then. Up here, I mean," she said, tapping her temple.

Ruby tilted her head slightly.

"He had a stroke a few months back," the lady explained. "A mild one, so *they* claim . . ." she glared back over her shoulder when she said *they*, ". . . but he ain't said a word since." The old woman moved the walker forward. "Doctors say he's fine, 'cept for the Alzheimer's. But he don't talk no more. Not like he used to." The woman looked at Lombardi holding the photo. "Who's in the picture?" she asked.

Ruby reached out and took the photo back from Lombardi. As she did, he glanced at her, startled—as if she had just appeared out of nowhere. A rivulet of drool was running along his unshaven chin and down his neck. Ruby thought he might be having a moment of lucidity. But then he slowly looked away.

"It's of him and my mother. A long time ago," Ruby replied. "So, nobody visits him?"

"Not in the two years I been here." She removed the unlit cigarette and held it between her index and middle fingers, unconsciously tapping it, ashing it out of habit.

Ruby knew from her file that Lombardi was twice divorced and currently married. And that he had nine children.

"And he hasn't spoken since the stroke?"

"Not a peep, missy. Before then, he'd complain some. Asked about Judith, I think it was. But since then, nothing," the old woman said.

Judith was Lombardi's current wife, per the file. Ruby took a half breath and sighed.

"He's your pappy, ain't he?"

Ruby started; she looked nothing like the man—her features were decidedly Asian. Her first instinct was to lie, to answer in the negative. But something inside her was drawn to the idea of claiming him as her own, as her father. At least once, out loud. She looked around. There was no one within earshot. And this place was so foreign to Ruby that she felt as though she'd entered some sort of an alternate reality where, at least with this old woman, she could be completely honest.

"Yes. He is my father. I . . ." she hesitated. Those words, claiming a father. For the first time, Ruby felt a sense of completeness, a sense of warmth, family, home, and love. But the man before her was present only physically; his mind was gone. And in the same way, all those feelings were just as fleeting, and in a moment, they were gone to the same place as her father's mind.

The old woman's face registered no emotion. If it had, Ruby would have stopped. But to the stranger, this was just small talk, a distraction, one more little thing to pass the time before dying.

"I'd never met him. I just recently found out he was here."

The old woman studied Ruby with pursed lips. She put the cigarette back in her mouth and said, "Well, hon, you look like life's treated you pretty good. If you're just meeting Tony now—my advice—you go on and get outta here. This place is a dead end.

"We're all here 'cuz we can't take care of ourselves, and no one loves us enough to be bothered. Easier to pay someone to feed us and clean us. Then they check in around the holidays, like visiting a dog at the kennel, on account of the guilt. My boys," she scoffed. "Two entitled little pricks. Ed's a doctor. Nicky's a teacher at the university. But them and their wives can't be bothered with me, no ma'am. After birthing 'em, feeding 'em, educatin' 'em . . . They don't wanna have nothin' to do with me." She shrugged and looked down at Lombardi. "They call me for my birthday, holidays. Bring the grandkids by once a year if I'm lucky." She shook her head and looked around her. "But then, this place stinks of piss and death. I don't blame the little ones for bein' scared of me, poor things," she sighed, taking a pull on her unlit cigarette. "I took good care of my boys when it was my turn. Ungrateful shits. I deserve better."

The old woman looked back at Ruby as if remembering she was there. "But, hon . . . If you're just meeting your pappy here, for the first time . . . well then, honey, you don't owe him shit. Blood only flows in one direction."

Ruby raised an eyebrow.

"That means *he* made a choice, at some point, to screw your momma and here you are. That wasn't your choice, that was his. His blood flowed to you. One way. Means you're relatives. Don't mean you're family. Family's earned. Family's a two-way street. And it sounds like Tony didn't earn your love. He don't deserve you." The old lady shook her head, scowling at Lombardi. "I'd get outta here if I was you. And don't look back." She raised her voice, then shouted, "Ain't that right, Tony?" Lombardi's head jerked at the sound of his name. "Heh. Heh. Heh," she cackled. "Lousy sonofabitch . . ." she mumbled.

Satisfied with her speech, the old woman nodded at Ruby, then turned her walker and loped off like some sort of half-metal, half-human geriatric creature.

Ruby took a last long look at Tony Lombardi, then stood and left the common room. As she exited the building into the cool air, she inhaled deeply, trying to cleanse her lungs of the grime and depression she'd been breathing inside.

Kong saw Ruby exit the building, pulled the Escalade up, then climbed out and opened the rear passenger door for her. As they drove back to the airport, Ruby contemplated that she had lived most of her life alone. With the exception of Kong, everyone in her life was a means to an end. As the old woman had pointed out, this had worked well for Ruby. All in all, life had been good to her. Still, she shivered as she thought of her father alone in his wheelchair, drooling his days away.

Since she'd been a teen and her mother had abandoned her, it had simply been a fact of life for Ruby that she was by herself. She'd grown accustomed to it. She was comfortable living alone. Happy, even. But, as she thought of the two images she would now carry of her father for the rest of her life—one of him smiling with her mother in the photo, the other of him in a wheelchair smelling of abandonment—she learned something new about herself.

Ruby Yi did not want to die alone.

# PART FIVE

## JOHNNY STRIKES BACK

# CHAPTER SIXTY-THREE

Johnny Miracle still had two cards up his sleeve. Sure, the vineyard deal didn't go exactly as planned. Fine. But there was still five million dollars coming from the insurance settlement on the Monet, and his lawyer had told him that he was entitled to at least half. And then, there was the painting itself. *There's plenty of money to pay Sick Eddie. Late maybe, but he'll get his money back. Unless maybe I just skip town . . .*

He was sitting in Karen's kitchen in boxers, a half-eaten bowl of Cap'n Crunch on the table in front of him. She'd left for work earlier, and he was killing time on Tinder while he weighed his options.

*Swipe left.*

*Swipe right.*

*Swipe left.*

*Swipe left.*

Johnny had received a phone call from Sick Eddie on the fortieth day after his one million dollars had been wired to the title company. He had let it go to voicemail, and when he checked the message, there was silence for almost fifteen seconds, and then the caller hung up. That had been over a week ago. There had been no other calls from the man.

*He'll just have to wait until I settle up with the bitch.*

Johnny's heart leaped when his phone lit up with Clive Connard's name.

*Maybe Rosenbaum changed his mind!*

He answered.

"Johnny, who the hell is Edward de la Rosa?" Clive growled.

"Who?" Johnny's mind raced. *Shit . . . Sick Eddie.*

"Edward de la Rosa," Clive fumed. "His lawyer called to *introduce* himself. Says de la Rosa's *my partner* and just emailed me paperwork to transfer the vineyard to De La Rosa Winery, Inc. The whole vineyard, Johnny! He claims you borrowed your million dollars from him, and you haven't paid it back?"

"Look, Clive . . ." Johnny stammered. He was at a loss for words and sat looking at the soggy cereal in his bowl.

"Look what?"

Silence.

"Johnny! Say something! I got three million sunk into that place, and I'll be goddamned if I'm signin' it away to save your ass."

More silence.

"You fix this Johnny! That's a warnin', that's what that is!"

Clive hung up.

Johnny took a deep breath, then dialed Sick Eddie. The phone rang and rang, then went to voicemail. He called again. After the fifth attempt, he took a deep breath and swallowed hard.

*Shit!*

# CHAPTER SIXTY-FOUR

Johnny sat in his truck in the Cherries Gentlemen's Club parking lot. He'd brought a handgun but wasn't sure whether to bring it in with him or not. For one thing, it was a felony to carry a gun onto the property, as they served liquor. There was a huge sign by the front door as a reminder. And, having a weapon on him might not send the right signal, especially if he got patted down and they found it.

Johnny decided against the gun. After all, the guy had a lawyer. And he'd already called Clive to settle up by transferring the vineyard. This wasn't some mobster movie. Sick Eddie was civilized. Johnny felt confident he could negotiate a resolution. He entered the building and was glad of his decision. When he gave his name to the gorilla at the door, he patted him down, then pointed towards the back. Johnny found himself standing in front of the door to the office. It buzzed, and he entered.

"Hey, Johnny! How you doin', my man?" asked Sick Eddie, seated at his desk.

"Good, Eddie. I'm good." Johnny smiled. Relieved. Everything was cool. Sick Eddie was a businessman. "I wanted to talk to you about the money."

"The money?" Sick Eddie laughed. "What money?" Sick Eddie directed himself to the refrigerator-of-a-man standing in the corner, same as he'd been when Johnny last visited. "Javier, do you remember any money?" Sick Eddie shook his head, "'cuz I don't . . . Oh . . . Wait," he raised a finger, "the moooney!" and pointed at Johnny. "Oh yeaaah, the million dollars you were going to pay back," he raised his voice an octave, mimicking Johnny, making sarcastic jazz hands, "'*in thirty days, max!*'"

"Look, it's just that—" Johnny moved to take a seat.

"*DON'T!*" Sick Eddie screamed, jumping to his feet with both hands in the air. Johnny stopped dead.

Dead silence, save for the muffled *boom* of music from the strip club.

"I—"

Sick Eddie screamed again, punching at Johnny in the air with a pointed index finger, "*I DIDN'T SAY YOU COULD TALK, YOU FUCKIN' FUCKFACED MOTHERFUCKER!*"

Johnny froze.

Sick Eddie leaned, resting his hands on his desk, panting heavily. He wiped spittle from his face with the back of his sleeve. Then, he sat down, ran his hand through his hair, and after taking a deep breath, spoke again in a normal voice, though his face was flushed bright red. "Javier, did I tell Mr. Miracle he could talk?"

"No, sir. You did not."

"No. I did not. So . . ." Sick Eddie sat back in his chair, put his feet up on his desk, and cleared his throat, "where is my one million dollars that you were going to repay 'in thirty days, max'?" Sick Eddie waved his hand, indicating that Johnny could now speak.

"I have it. I mean, I will . . . in a few weeks. It's just that I'm getting divorced, so everything got tied up with the lawyers, but we have a mediation set, and it'll get resolved then, and then I'll pay you. With all the interest. I swear . . ."

Sick Eddie nodded along as Johnny spoke, his eyes shut tight. He sat, thinking for a few moments. Then, he picked up his phone and sent a text message.

"If you—" Johnny began.

"Quiet," Sick Eddie said, almost whispering, raising his index finger to his lips.

Johnny stood, waiting.

Sick Eddie opened his laptop and began mousing, typing, and reading. After about ten minutes, his phone pinged. He picked it up and studied it for a moment. "My lawyer says that it's true. Your wife filed for divorce, and court-ordered mediation is scheduled for early November. Meanwhile, the interest continues to accumulate on your debt, and I am now the owner of a beautiful vineyard. So, here's what's gonna happen." He raised one finger. "You're gonna talk to your buddy Connard and get him to sign the papers, as collateral." He raised a second finger. "And I will wait until your meditation to collect, with interest. You pay me on time, and you guys can keep your vineyard. Deal?"

"Oh, yeah. Deal. Definitely."

Johnny felt a weight come off his chest. He'd bought more time. He'd heard stories about what happened to people who didn't repay Sick Eddie on time. Clearly, they were exaggerations. The man was reasonable. A businessman. Johnny closed his eyes and sighed with relief. As a result, he didn't see Sick Eddie nod at

Javier. Suddenly, Johnny heard a *THUMP!* and his right side went numb. He found himself on the floor, looking up at Javier, who was holding a tire iron like a baseball bat.

Johnny slowly realized what had happened. His right side was on fire, where Javier had hit him with the tire iron. On reflex, he had folded his arm in, stifling a sob as pain burned through him with every breath.

"What the hell?" he whimpered, cowering.

"Help him up," Sick Eddie said.

"Why?" he whimpered again.

Javier helped him to his feet, and Johnny looked over at Sick Eddie through watery eyes.

"It's just a few ribs, Johnny. They'll heal." Sick Eddie smiled. "That wasn't about the money, by the way. A deal is a deal. The interest will simply continue to accumulate. And you *will* pay me everything, principal and interest, after the mediation. But you need to understand that this is your *very very very* last chance. The ribs . . . that's a question of respect. I call you repeatedly. You don't answer. That's very disrespectful. Childish, really. Normally, that would be a big strike in our relationship. For you, it would be strike number two. But Johnny . . . *nobody* gets two strikes. So, the ribs are my compensation. You should thank me." He paused.

Johnny stood, eyes wide, breathing slowly through his mouth.

Javier gave him a shove, jarring his broken ribs and unleashing another surge of searing pain.

"You're serious?!" Johnny tried to scream, but the sound came out in a strange hiss.

"Johnny . . . ?" Sick Eddie prompted.

"Okay. Okay," Johnny said. "Thank you."

"For . . . ?"

". . . for breaking my ribs?"

"Hmmm. That sounded like a question. The inflection was kind of upwards at the end," Sick Eddie imitated Johnny. "Try again."

"Thank you," Johnny took a shallow breath, wincing, "for breaking my ribs."

"Much better. You are welcome." Sick Eddie smiled. "And the next time I call you, you will answer the phone, right?"

Johnny nodded.

"Javier, help Mr. Miracle to his truck."

They started to leave, but Sick Eddie called after them. "And Johnny." Johnny turned slowly and painfully. "If you try *in any way* to screw me over—skip town, steal my money, anything your teeny redneck brain might concoct—you will find out firsthand why everyone calls me 'Sick Eddie.'"

Johnny walked slowly back to his truck, pain in every step. Climbing up into the cab was excruciating. He was drenched with sweat by the time he got behind the wheel and drove himself to the ER.

# CHAPTER SIXTY-FIVE

Karen arrived home early and saw Johnny's pickup truck parked in her driveway.

*Odd.*

She had texted him late that morning to see about getting lunch together, but he hadn't replied. Karen found the front door unlocked and quietly entered the house. Listening. She heard a muffled *"Fuuuck!"* echo through the rooms and into the kitchen. As she entered the living room, she found Johnny lying across the sofa.

"What's wrong with you?" Karen asked with genuine concern.

"I tripped and fell in the bed of my truck. Bruised a couple of ribs," he replied.

"Oh God, Johnny," Karen said, coming closer. "Shouldn't you see a doctor? Get a cast or something?"

"*I went*," Johnny had started to raise his voice, but the pain in his chest stopped him. "Aaaahh . . . Oh man . . . I went to the ER," he said more slowly. "No cast. It's just a bruise. Just ice and pain meds."

"Are you sure this was just . . . an accident?" Karen walked past Johnny and looked up and down the street out the front windows to her apartment.

A few days back, Johnny had told Karen about his deal with Sick Eddie. She had been stunned at the man's stupidity. That same night, while he slept, she'd moved the Monet, hiding it somewhere that he'd never find it, just in case.

Johnny was embarrassed about his ribs. He saw it as a sign of weakness. No way was he going to tell Karen the truth.

He nodded. "Just clumsy. That's all. The meeting with Sick Eddie went fine. Not a problem. But I gotta make sure I get enough out of the divorce to pay him off and still leave plenty for us."

"Well, the vineyard money's out of play, and your lawyer said you're only entitled to half of the insurance money. That doesn't leave much."

Johnny needed to pull out all the stops. The mediation *had* to go his way. He just wasn't sure how best to use the ammunition at his disposal.

"Yeah . . . argh!" Johnny moaned as he sat up. He breathed in and out slowly a few times, waiting for the pain to pass. "But I had an idea. I wanted to run it by you. There was this cop at the barbecue. Don't know if you saw him . . . only guy there in uniform . . . ?"

"Older guy? Ray Bans? I thought he was there for security."

"Nope. Not security. But yeah, that's him. Well, he's investigating an old case, this guy Zeke that disappeared—"

"Sure. I remember that. Back when I was in high school," Karen said.

"What do you know about it?" Johnny asked, eyeing Karen.

"That's about it. He was a local guy. Older than us . . . Maybe in his twenties back then. The guy just disappeared."

"Well, I don't have all the details, but I think what I do know is enough that Mary'll wanna pay to keep me quiet."

Johnny explained to Karen what Mary had confided in him, Pedro digging a hole, the body.

And together, they came up with a game plan.

# CHAPTER SIXTY-SIX

On Monday a week before the court-ordered mediation, Mary met with her lawyer at her office. She was escorted by a receptionist down a short hallway to a conference room. Betsy Beavers's offices were posh.

*She must be doing well for herself.*

Mary couldn't help but wonder if, had she not married Johnny, had she finished law school instead, where would her career have taken her? Giving clients legal advice in a snazzy downtown office of her own? Instead of being 'the client' dealing with a nasty divorce? She'd be resuming law school in a couple of months, just after the Christmas holidays. She was so looking forward to it. A new chapter in her life.

"Good morning, Mary," Beavers said as she entered the conference room.

She sat at the head of the table, kitty-corner to Mary, and placed a thin Redweld folder on the table. Mary could smell a very expensive perfume, almost masking the scent of a recently smoked cigarette.

"Any attempts at communication? Phone calls? Text messages?" From the outset, Beavers had been adamant that, once they served Johnny with the divorce papers, Mary should avoid direct communication with him.

*Anything we need to communicate should be done through lawyers so that there are no misunderstandings, no "he said, she said" later.*

"Nothing after the first few days. Though Pedro said he was driving by the vineyard every now and then."

Beavers nodded. "Good."

"I still don't see the point of this mediation. Seems like a waste of time. There's no way in hell I'm going to agree to give him anything," Mary said.

Beavers nodded along in agreement.

"Look, the courts are crowded. Judges are swamped," she pointed out. "So, everything, every single case, gets sent to mediation. And for what it's worth, it makes sense. Something like ninety-eight percent of all cases settle without a trial. The judges just don't know which ones will and won't." She shrugged. "In our case, once Johnny's lawyer sees what we've got, he may tell him to walk away." She half-smiled. "Joe," she continued, referring to Joe Graves, Johnny's lawyer, "ain't the sharpest tool, but he doesn't want to waste his time, either. I'm sure he took Johnny's case on a contingency because Johnny told him there's a big fat insurance check sitting out there ripe for the taking. So he only gets paid if he gets money from you."

Mary nodded.

"Now, the vineyard's sold. And you inherited *that* directly from your grandmother. So it's your separate property. Johnny can't touch it. All that's left of any significant value is the Monet, well, '*was*'—now it's the insurance proceeds related to the painting. So, we have our expert report back . . . and it's really solid." She smiled as she removed several documents from the Redweld and placed them on the table. "Here," she turned a document towards Mary, "is the excerpt from Nellie's journal you found, with some words highlighted for the mediator. We'd show this to the jury if we have to."

Mary looked at the document. The journal she *had* found while packing up the house on Crabapple Creek Vineyard.

> **We celebrated Mary's sixteenth birthday this past sat. Technically, her birthday was on friday. but Seeing as how sixteen is a special occasion, I wanted to do something extra for her. But she wouldn't have any of that, just wanted to have some friends over for a slumber party. She is an amazing soul, and I am truly blessed to have her for a grandaughter.**

"Of all the highlights, you will note," she added, "that 'granddaughter' is misspelled, as the correct spelling contains two d's."

"And here," Beavers placed the second document alongside the first, "is a copy of the card you gave me." *This* document was the one Mary had forged, using Nellie's journal as a reference. She'd made almost twenty versions before coming up with one that she felt looked 'right.' She hoped it was good enough . . .

> **To my grandaughter Mary,**
>
> **On the occasion of your wedding, I hope this painting brings you the same joy it has brought me, and that someday you can pass it down to your kids.**

**Love, Grandma Nellie**

"Go ahead and compare them. The highlights. You'll see that the handwriting on both documents is the same, and the word 'granddaughter' is misspelled here as well."

Mary nodded as she pretended to study the highlighted portions. "And what does the expert think?" she asked nonchalantly.

Beavers's eyes narrowed slightly, and she almost succeeded in suppressing a smile. She placed a third document in front of Mary, "This is our expert's affidavit, stating that, in her expert opinion, the card is genuine and in your grandmother's handwriting. It meets all the requirements. She can testify at trial if necessary."

Mary involuntarily sighed with relief as she picked up the affidavit. It was six pages long. But only the first two pages, four paragraphs, were the actual affidavit. The last four pages were the expert's resume. "It's very short. This is all it takes?"

"Well," Beavers replied, "it just contains the essential facts to qualify the expert and meet the legal requirements to present the opinion. If she testifies, she'll add lots more detail."

Mary nodded, skimming the resume, which detailed numerous articles, books, and other relevant work done by the expert.

"The bottom line is that this proves that your grandmother gave you that painting as a gift. The note clearly says, 'To my granddaughter Mary . . .'" Beavers quoted. "It doesn't say 'to my son-in-law' or 'to Mary and Johnny' or 'to the happy couple.' So, the insurance funds, or hopefully the painting if someday it's recovered, belong solely to you as your separate property. End of story."

Beavers sat back in her chair, studying Mary. "You know, if your grandmother had written this note with our case in mind, it couldn't be any better . . ."

Mary nodded, ignoring the implication.

"So you think this'll do it?" Mary asked. She knew the legal requirements; she just wanted reassurance.

Beavers shrugged. "I can't tell you what Johnny will ultimately decide. He may want to take his chances with a jury. What's he got to lose? But now," Beavers tapped with her index finger on the affidavit, "his odds are very, very low. And his lawyer probably won't want to waste the time."

# CHAPTER SIXTY-SEVEN

After her meeting with Beavers, Mary went straight home. She still needed to finish packing up the house but just wasn't up to it. Instead, she opened a bottle of red wine and found a movie to watch. Something mindless that went well with merlot. She had one glass. Then another. Then opened a second bottle.

Mary startled awake, her mouth pasty and dry, and her neck aching. She was disoriented for a moment, finding herself surrounded by boxes. The TV was off. Slowly, she realized that she was in the study. She saw on the coffee table in front of her a wine bottle . . . and her glass. She sat up quickly, wiping sleep from her eyes and inhaling sharply.

"Nice nap, babe?" Johnny asked.

Mary jumped. Johnny was standing by the fireplace.

In his left hand, he held a half-filled wineglass. A handgun was in his right hand, which hung casually by his right thigh. His Smith and Wesson six-shooter, from the looks of it.

At the sight of the gun, Mary stifled her anger and, in a more measured tone than she would otherwise have used, asked, "What do you want?"

Johnny took a sip of wine and smiled. "I just came for a little pre-mediation chat. You always said I didn't talk enough, so I'm here to do just that."

"How'd you get in?" she asked. "I changed the locks."

Johnny shook his head. "Objection. Irrelevant." He placed the wineglass on the coffee table and stood . . . slowly.

He seemed stiff to Mary. Like he was in some kind of pain.

"Look, this is gonna be real simple, Mary. We had a nice run. Which you," he pointed at her with the gun, "decided to end.

"*You* filed for divorce, babe, not me. And you know what?" Johnny began to pace slowly in front of the fireplace, gun hanging loosely at his side, eyes on Mary. "I think you did me a favor. I would've stuck it out longer. But *this time*," he emphasized, "I think you were right. Dead on." He pointed at her with the gun again, smiling. "So, here's what's gonna happen. You're gonna tell your lawyer what I just said, that we had a good run, and that you want to be fair about things. That I worked here for years without a salary. And that you're gonna keep the vineyard money, and you're gonna *give me all* of the insurance money."

Mary scoffed loudly, "Why would I do that?"

"Because you've got a *BIG MOUTH*, Mary!" Johnny yelled. "And . . ." he lowered his voice to conversational levels, "a short memory, it would appear. Don't you remember us *sharing* all our hopes and all our fears? Remember your deep, dark secret?"

Mary felt the room closing in on her.

"I'm not stupid. Deputy Gripke's just dyin' to find someone to point him in the right direction. You don't really want me to do that, do you?"

Mary had been dreading this moment, but she had prepared.

"You can't say anything, Johnny. I told you about that when we were married. The law says—"

"Oh, shut up!" Johnny commanded. "*The law says, the law says*," he mimicked. "You don't have a monopoly on Google, Mary." Johnny reached into the back pocket of his blue jeans and unfolded a sheet of paper. "Spousal Privilege," he shouted. "*IS THIS*," he held the paper out toward her, "*WHAT YOU WERE COUNTING ON?*"

Johnny laughed.

"I can and will testify against you, wifey!"

Mary stared at him, raging.

"If you read closely, there are exceptions to the rule, Mary. And it states specifically that," Johnny paused, scanning the document, "here . . . 'This privilege does not apply . . . in a civil proceeding brought by or on behalf of one spouse against the other.'

"So, Mary, if you don't do what I say, I *will not* agree to settle this case, I *will* go to court, and *when* I get up in front of that jury, I am going to talk all about *how I suffered*, having to sleep next to a murderer for years. I'll tell the jury and the judge all about how hard it was to work for you and your grandmother, knowing that there's *A DEAD MAN BURIED OUT THERE!*" he said, pointing at the window with his gun. "And not only that, I'll tell them that *YOU FIRED THE GUN!*" He winced, hand involuntarily rising to his ribs. He was panting. Fighting to control his breath, then he swallowed and added, "Once they find the body where I tell them to dig, they won't believe anything you and Pedro have to say. If I don't get my money," he hissed, "you'll go to prison for a long, long time. You *and* your pansy-assed Pedro."

He walked slowly toward the door to the study, watching his wife. He stopped, gun at his side. "Don't be stupid, Mare. Let's not end *this*," he waved his hands generally in the air, "on a sour note. Give me the insurance money. You keep the money from the vineyard." He chuckled. "You got a really good deal from Clive, by the way." He shook his head. "Oh, if you only knew . . ."

Suddenly he raised the gun and pointed it at his wife. She instinctively flinched.

He grinned. "I'm not going to shoot you, silly rabbit. You're worth five million to me." He mimed a set of scales, raising and lowering his hands. "Insurance money. Prison. Insurance money. Lethal injection. Insurance money. Prison." He lowered both hands. "You were never *that* stupid, Mary," he said. "I know you'll do the smart thing. See ya Monday."

# CHAPTER SIXTY-EIGHT

The following day, Mary awoke with a splitting headache. The wine bottle stared back at her accusatorily from the coffee table, witness to the fact that she'd ultimately finished off the second bottle of red before she passed out. She dragged herself from the study and went into the kitchen to make herself a cup of tea. As she poured hot water from the kettle, she spied the coffee maker Johnny had recently purchased. The coffee machine brought Johnny top of mind; she ran through his performance from the night before. And his threat. She didn't see any simple way out. If the police started digging up the fields, they'd eventually find Zeke Fulton's remains.

*Shit . . . Why even bother with mediation?*

Mary turned on the TV to a news channel and sat while her mind wandered. She was sick of everything. Looking at the half-filled boxes around her, she regretted agreeing to sell the vineyard. Just weeks before, she'd thought things couldn't get any worse, and last night they had. Mary's main concern wasn't the idea of giving Johnny the insurance money; she could live very, very well on the money she'd made from selling the vineyard. Her problem was that the insurance money wouldn't be enough.

*Will he stop there? Of course not . . . What happens when that money runs out? He'll be back.*

Mary had read about never giving in to blackmail because the blackmailer will always come back for more.

*He'll always hold this over me.*

But what other choice did she have?

Well, at least there was one thing she could control.

*I'm going to end this shit show now . . .*

Mary picked up her phone and called Betsy Beavers's office.

"This is Betsy," a familiar voice answered on the first ring.

"Oh. Hi. It's Mary. I didn't expect you to answer."

"I was just thinking about you, and when I saw your number on the screen . . . synchronicity, you know?" Beavers was excited. "Listen, I'm thinking, for the mediation, that I'm going to do the presentation much like I would at trial. I'm going to enlarge the card and the page from your grandmother's journal, put them on a poster board, blown up with the highlighting in bright yellow, right there in your face. I want the mediator to get the full effect. I think that'll go a long way to getting the point across."

It sounded as though Beavers was pacing as she spoke.

"I just don't see Graves letting Johnny take this to a jury. It'll be a three-to-four-day trial, and all of that will be time wasted for Joe. I want to be sure the mediator is as forceful as possible about how this will look at trial. After all, *when* we win," Beavers emphasized the 'when,' "Graves won't get paid any fees. Zippo . . ."

Mary's stomach turned. But she felt that she had to give in. He was going to win. He was going to get his way after all.

"I can't wait to see the look on Graves's face." Beavers chuckled. "And Johnny's. Hope he doesn't stroke out when he sees that card—" Beavers interrupted her own train of thought. "But, hey . . . you called me. What's up?"

Mary took a deep breath, then said, "Maybe we should just pay him to go away?" Her statement, in the form of a question, was met with several beats of silence at Beavers's end.

"Look," Beavers replied, "this ain't my first rodeo. And you aren't the first client to call before mediation or trial, just wanting everything to be over. I get it—"

"It's just that . . ." Mary was at a loss.

After a few moments, Beavers began, "If it's the card . . . your Grandma's card . . . our expert is super-solid, and she's prepared to testify that *it is* your grandmother's handwriting—"

"No. It's not *that.* I just . . ." Mary choked up, stifling a sob. She couldn't tell Beavers the truth. Johnny had her over a barrel.

Beavers sighed. "I think I understand. I've seen this a hundred times if I've seen it once. Call it the yips, pre-game jitters, performance anxiety if you want to get more technical or psychological. Listen to me, Mary. It's normal. Wishing this was all over and done with is normal. Wanting to go back to your regular life is normal. All this tension and conflict is draining, I know. Believe me, I do this for a living. But, honey, this is a marathon. And right now, you're just hitting the wall at mile twenty. Which. Is. Perfectly. Normal. It happens to everyone.

"So, here's the plan. I promise you, we are going to do whatever you want. Okay? *I promise you that.* But first, you have to do something for me. 'Cause if you don't, you'll regret it, and you'll regret it for a long time. Here's what you're gonna do for me. You . . . are going to take a deep breath, and you're going to say, 'Goodbye, Betsy,' and you're gonna hang up the phone. And then you're gonna go do something unrelated to your divorce. Even if it's busy work. Don't you have to get packed and out of that house? Do that. And this whole decision you're trying to make right now . . . don't. Just sleep on it. Okay?

"Then tomorrow morning, same time. We'll get together, and we'll talk. And then *I will do whatever* you say you want to do, okay? Is that a deal?"

Mary sat staring at the TV, *through it,* really . . . into the distance. Given his threat, she couldn't imagine any scenario under which she would refuse Johnny's demand. But Beavers was persuasive. And Mary had no fight left in her.

She decided to do as told.

"Goodbye, Betsy," Mary said, pressing the red *end call* button on her phone screen.

# CHAPTER SIXTY-NINE

Mary dragged herself from the kitchen with an empty box to begin a dreaded task, one she had been postponing with every possible excuse: packing up Grandma Nellie's room.

Since Nellie died, Mary had hardly been in that part of the house. She'd preferred to leave things as they were. As she entered, she could still smell her grandmother. It was hard to believe she was gone. All of her things were where they'd always been. The pillows and bedspread, the photos on her nightstand, the clothes in her closet.

Mary started with the closet, putting items for donation in trash bags and boxing the few items she came across that had any sentimental value. She went through the trunk at the foot of Nellie's bed. Last, she went through the bathroom.

A lot of what was in there was just trash. Old hairbrushes, bobby pins, a broken nail file, almost empty tubes of cream, two pennies and a sticky nickel at the back of one drawer, the usual items that accumulate in a bathroom. A lot of expired medicines, too: a bottle of aspirin with two capsules in it that had to be over ten years old, and a crusty vial of mercurochrome.

Mary opened the last drawer on the right. She removed the first item from the drawer, a small, orange-brown prescription medicine vial, and read the label. She was about to throw it in the trash bag—diltiazem, Grandma Nellie's blood pressure medicine—when she froze.

For some time now, Mary's subconscious had been collecting data without her realizing it, and it had been putting pieces into place. And now, a chill ran down Mary's spine as her subconscious pushed through and forced a horrible conclusion into her conscious mind—like the answer to some sort of macabre math problem.

Mary swallowed hard and began mentally processing the pieces.

An insignificant comment by Grandma Nellie.

Plus.

An incongruent datapoint.

Plus.

Strangely timed behavior by Johnny.

Plus.

Something odd that Betsy Beavers had said just an hour ago.

All these inputs, taken alone, meant nothing.

But if she *combined* them all and then imagined the most horrible solution to the problem . . .

Mary felt dizzy. She grabbed the vanity countertop for balance with both hands, dropping the vial on the floor.

*It's not possible. There's no way . . .*

Her legs turned to jelly, and she slowly slid down onto the bathroom floor, fighting not to pass out. She sat for a few moments, panting. Hoping she was wrong. Willing it . . .

She slipped her phone out of her back pocket. There, on the bathroom floor, she dialed and reached for the vial.

The phone rang.

Once.

Twice.

Thrice.

"I thought we agreed you would sleep on it," Betsy Beavers said in answer to Mary's call.

"I am. I mean, I will." Mary stifled a sob. *This can't be true. IT CAN'T BE TRUE!*

"Mary? What's wrong?"

"I just . . . it's something you said . . . before. When we talked. I just had a question . . ." she sputtered.

"Are you okay?" Beavers asked, concerned. "You sound—"

"I'M FINE!" Mary paused, fighting not to yell. "I'm fine. But . . . when you were talking about the mediation, about the card, you said 'stroke out' . . . about Johnny. Why?"

"Well, yeah. I mean, from the surprise, you know, when we show him the card."

"NO! I get that!" she shouted again, paused again. Calmly, "But why 'stroke'?"

"Okaaayy," Beavers's tone changed. "You're right. It probably wasn't the *most appropriate* thing to say, mocking someone's health issues . . ."

"No! Not . . ." Mary sat up straighter, her voice clearer. She felt more in control. "I don't care about him . . . No, it's *that. That's* it . . . explain to me what you mean by 'health issues.'"

"Well, yeah, okay. It's just when we were going through all your financial stuff, yours and Johnny's, there was a credit card charge to a company called UBER-ALL. I almost glossed over it at first, because I figured it was just Uber. But the address was in Canada. I chased it down. Turns out it's a pharmacy in Canada. That's usually for gray market stuff, you know, drugs that are hard to come by in the U.S., or something you need a prescription for, but don't have one . . . like Viagra, for example, that kind of thing. So, I thought we might have found some dirt on him. But I chased it down, and it turned out to be nothing. Just his blood pressure meds."

Mary's throat went dry.

"Blood pressure? Johnny?" Mary squeezed her eyes shut, pinching the bridge of her nose with her free hand. She took a deep breath, then asked, "Which drug?"

"Hold on." Mary heard some key tapping. "It's in my notes . . . Here it is. Diltiazem oral suspension. And some syringes."

Silence.

"When? When did he buy it?"

"Umm . . . Here it is. August third. This year."

Silence.

"Are you there, Mary?"

"Liquid diltiazem. August third. Got it."

"Is there a problem?"

"No. No. All good. I gotta go. Thanks."

Mary slowly slumped onto her side on the floor, laying her head on the cool tile, empty. Her mind blank. She wasn't sure how long she lay there in a fog of incredulity and numbness. Time ticked by. Through that haze of detachment, Mary realized that only one emotion remained when she thought of Johnny. Revulsion. As she slowly regained her composure, she became aware of the growing darkness outside.

With a deep breath, she pushed herself up onto all fours, then grabbed onto the vanity for support and rose unsteadily to her feet. The dizziness was passing, and out of the revulsion she felt for her husband grew a fierce determination that burned within her. She straightened up, hands gripping the countertop as she stared at her reflection in the mirror.

She was furious, fueled by a righteous anger that she had never known before. She was determined to right the wrongs that had been done to her, to take control of her life once and for all. And above all, she was motivated, driven by a fierce desire to honor her grandmother's memory.

"Who am I if I don't fix this for you, Grandma?" she whispered to her reflection.

And in that moment, with her eyes blazing and her fists clenched, she made a decision that would change her life forever. That was the moment when Mary Miracle decided to kill her husband.

# CHAPTER SEVENTY

Mary spent the rest of her week planning how to kill Johnny.

Once she had a plan, she texted Abby to set up dinner at her house Friday. She then rehearsed what she would tell her and how she would get her to help. Art was out with his daughter for dinner, so the two friends were alone on Abby's back porch when Friday rolled around.

Mary followed her plan, stating her intention with brutal clarity.

"I'm going to kill Johnny," she told Abby.

The way she spoke the words left no room for doubt. She was declaring her intent to commit murder.

Abby sat for a good while studying her friend. Mary had been through so much. Losing Nellie. Learning about Johnny's infidelities. Filing for divorce. Selling the vineyard. The Monet being stolen. Abby decided that getting Mary talking was the best thing she could do. Let her get it all off her chest. Vent. Mary was nothing if not sensible. She was just upset, that was all.

"Why?" Abby asked.

"He killed Nellie."

Again, brutal clarity.

Abby's face fell. She knew that Mary wouldn't make such a claim lightly. She sat for almost a minute digesting this bitter morsel.

Finally, she said exactly what Mary expected, "How do you know?"

"Let me lay it out for you.

"First, motive. Money. He tried to screw me on selling the vineyard. Then, shortly after I decide to sell the vineyard to pay the taxes, the Monet is stolen . . . which Johnny—being his 'usual responsible self'—confirmed beforehand was insured for five million dollars."

Mary paused there. Things had gotten even worse, with Johnny outright blackmailing her, threatening to go to expose what he knew about Zeke Fulton if she didn't settle the divorce with him . . . but Abby didn't know what had happened to Zeke. And Mary thought it best to keep that circle of knowledge small. She'd already made the mistake of oversharing once.

"That's a lot of bad shit, I agree. Worse than I ever thought he was capable of. But none of that has anything to do with Nellie," Abby said.

"True. All of that just establishes a pattern of behavior. Namely, that ever since Nellie died, Johnny's been focused on screwing me out of money. He's shown he's willing to lie, steal, do whatever it takes to get what he wants. So, who's to say he wasn't already in that mode before Nellie died? And who's to say he wouldn't kill to get what he wants? This whole shitstorm that's rained down on me, all of it started with Nellie dying."

When put in that context, Johnny did seem capable of very bad acts. "Okay. I'll give you motive. But murder?" Abby inquired.

"So, here's my proof that he did it. First, the day Nellie died, she was a bit hungover. So was I, to be honest. We'd had too much to drink the night before. When I came into the kitchen, I remember she was on her third cup of coffee. That morning, she complained that she wanted to get a new coffee machine. That the coffee 'tasted like crap.' It was the second time she'd complained about it. The first time was only a few days before. I remember because Johnny was there . . . we were talking about his trip to California. And *he said* he thought it tasted fine."

Abby nodded.

"Then, Nellie dies. Johnny comes back from California, and while we're getting the funeral organized, and meeting with the lawyers, all that mess . . . in the middle of *all of that SHIT*, he takes the time to buy a *new* coffee machine—another brand, the one with the *bigger* coffee pods, so the old ones were useless—saying *Nellie was right* about the bad taste. And then he throws out the old machine and all the old, smaller pods."

Abby's eyes narrowed a bit, and she pursed her lips. "That's weird. Strange timing. *And* inconsistent with his prior opinion about the taste of the coffee . . . but people do odd things under stress . . . *or* he was destroying evidence . . . of something . . ."

"Yes! According to the autopsy, Nellie died of heart failure. The only anomaly they found was that she had a higher level of blood pressure medicine in her system than she should have —diltiazem. The doctor said she was probably feeling unwell and took more, thinking it might help."

"You never told me that!" Abby said. "And the M.E. didn't explore it any further? Or the police?" She shook her head with surprise.

"They chalked it up to an old lady overmedicating."

"But low blood pressure—if it gets too low, that can cause a heart attack!" Abby said.

"And Grandma Nellie had a weak heart. She'd already had two heart attacks before."

Abby placed her wineglass on the side table and stood, pacing. "But Johnny was out of town . . ." She crossed her arms over her chest. "So," she continued, "you think he somehow spiked her coffee—the capsules, I guess—with the blood pressure medicine?"

Mary nodded.

Abby quietly thought through the facts. Mary could see her processing what she'd told her. Abby shook her head, "But any evidence that might prove that is gone. The pods, the machine. Still, it's extremely suspicious." She paused. Thinking. "The cops can't do jack shit. They won't. There's nothing to investigate. But he'd have to have ground up her pills and inserted them in the capsules somehow. So there would be missing pills or something," Abby looked toward her kitchen. "We should get some pills, aspirin or something, and coffee capsules and see if we can . . ." she waved her hands, ". . . figure out how he could have done it."

Mary held up a hand to get Abby's attention.

"What if I told you that a week before Nellie died, days before the coffee started tasting like crap, Johnny bought a bottle of liquid diltiazem from a Canadian mail-order pharmacy? And a pack of syringes."

Mary watched as Abby's eyes grew wide, then filled with tears. Her hands rose to cover her nose and mouth. She sat down.

After a few moments, she wiped the tears away, and sniffling, she said, almost to herself, "That sonofabitch." She shook her head. "Sonofabitch. Sonofabitch. Sonofabitch."

Then, looking at Mary, she asked, "I don't suppose Johnny has high blood pressure?" Mary could tell by her tone that Abby was now a believer. She was just ticking boxes.

"Fit as a damned fiddle," Mary replied.

Abby nodded. "Just had to ask." She sniffled again.

"In fact, beyond all that, I'm pretty sure he stole the Monet. And, I'm pretty sure he's been screwing Karen, though I don't know how much she knows about all of this." Mary shook her head, as if to shake those additional issues away.

"That doesn't matter . . . the point is . . . still the point. He's responsible for my grandma dying."

"Karen?" Abby responded. "Are you sure?"

"It doesn't matter, Abby. That's just piling on. . . What's important is, I'm gonna kill him. And I need your help."

"Well, shit, girl. But . . . are you sure? I mean, he deserves it, but if you get caught—"

"Abby." Mary's eyes teared up. "He *killed* Grandma Nellie."

"You need to think this through, Mary," Abby looked Mary hard in the eyes, "and be real careful. Real, real careful."

Mary nodded. "I will be. I have a plan."

# CHAPTER SEVENTY-ONE

Johnny and his lawyer, Joe Graves, arrived for the divorce mediation to find Mary and her lawyer already in the waiting room. The lawyers shook hands. Johnny nodded at Mary, who looked at him with disgust and shook her head.

Johnny was still moving stiffly.

Ten minutes later, they were in a large conference room. At the head of the table sat the mediator, a retired judge.

"So, good to meet you all. Again, I'm Judge Curry. And the ground rules here are very simple," said the mediator. "We are going to try to reach an agreement today so that you folks can stop fighting in court and go on with your lives. You both have good lawyers, and that's important. Because a good lawyer understands when they can win in court and when they can't. That makes this process a lot simpler.

"So, we're all starting out here in this room where I can explain the ground rules. Once I'm done, each of your lawyers will get as much time as they want—please try to keep it short—to explain the issues in this case as they see them. Please be respectful of one another." He looked down at his file. "I see there are no children involved, so once this is done, if you don't want to, you never have to see each other again. But, in my experience, leaving emotion and anger out of the equation for today always leads to a better result. You'll thank yourself later, trust me.

"Once your lawyers explain your cases to me in this room, I'm going to move Mary and her lawyer into another conference room. And then, it'll be my job to listen to each of your positions privately and see if I can get you to reach an agreement.

"But—and this is very important—anything you tell me once we divide up is one hundred percent confidential. I won't tell you," he pointed at Johnny, "anything she tells me, and vice versa, unless you give me permission. And anything at all that happens here is not admissible in court. I can't be called as a witness, and anything you say is off-limits too.

"Finally," the judge pointed at himself, "I'm not making any decisions today. I can't make you do anything you don't want to. After being on the bench for forty years, I am here to provide my perspective on what your case may sound like to a judge and jury. It's up to you to decide if you want to reach an agreement. Is that clear?"

Everyone nodded.

"Very well." The judge clapped his hands together. "So, who would like to begin?"

# CHAPTER SEVENTY-TWO

The lawyers looked at each other, and Johnny's attorney Joe Graves said, "Ladies first?"

To which Mary's lawyer, Betsy Beavers, replied, "Sure. Go ahead, Joe."

Joe Graves turned a bright shade of red, and before he could reply, Judge Curry jumped in, "Now, now, now. Hold on. Let's please save the posturing for the courtroom. We all know how tough you both are. No need to showboat, please." The judge reached into his pocket and removed a coin, "Heads is Mr. Graves. Tails is Ms. Beavers." He flipped the coin and said, "Okay, Mr. Graves. Please proceed."

Graves stood and cleared his throat while placing a sizeable blank poster board on the easel at the end of the room.

"This case, Your Honor, is a case of premeditated theft." He paused, letting the words sink in. "Mary Miracle is trying to cheat my client out of his half of their marital estate.

"When it comes down to it, there is only one item of community property of any significant value in this divorce. And this," he reached out, flipping over the poster board sheet, "is that item." On the flip side, now revealed for all to see, was a picture of the Monet. "This painting was a wedding gift to the couple from Mrs. Miracle's grandmother."

Mary shook her head, and Johnny smiled.

Johnny's lawyer droned on. "The painting is a valuable work of art and is the only asset of value in this divorce. Well, that is, it would have been . . .

"The timeline here is very simple. The Monet was last seen at 2:45 p.m. Saturday on Labor Day weekend." Graves placed a photo on the table. It was a printout of the selfie taken by Rio in front of the Monet.

"At that time, unbeknownst to my client, Johnny Miracle, his wife Mary was already planning to divorce him. How do we know this? Well, for starters, the divorce papers were filed at the courthouse less than two weeks later. And we also have Ms. Beavers's fee agreement," Graves passed a copy to the judge, "obtained through discovery, that was signed by Mary Miracle *before* the theft of the Monet.

"The police have thoroughly investigated the theft, and they believe that it was an inside job. You see, the house is located on a business property, a vineyard. And as a result, there are security cameras all over. The police and I have scoured every second of the footage on those cameras. And it's clear that in the three hours between the time of that photo," he pointed at the table, "and the time that *Mrs. Miracle discovered the painting missing*, no one left the house carrying anything even remotely close to the size of the painting.

"What can we therefore conclude? The same thing the police concluded. The painting never left the property. But a thorough search has yielded nothing, and the Monet has not been recovered."

Graves looked at the judge, who was taking notes, and waited for him to look up. "So, we know that Mrs. Miracle was planning to divorce my client. We know that she had already met with a divorce lawyer, presumably to better understand her rights. And any lawyer worth their salt—like Ms. Beavers—would have told her that anything the couple owned of value would have to be divided up in a divorce. And we all know, sitting here today, that the only thing of value they owned is that masterpiece." He pointed at the easel. "Then, mysteriously, that one asset, the only piece of property of any value to this couple, disappears.

"But what didn't Mrs. Miracle know? She didn't know that the painting was insured for five million dollars. So, while Mrs. Miracle stole the painting and has it hidden away somewhere —or even if we give her the benefit of the doubt and say the painting just magically disappeared, the insurance money did not.

"My client worked at Mrs. Miracle's family vineyard for years without pay. Mrs. Miracle has now sold that vineyard for four million dollars. We believe my client is entitled to all the proceeds from the insurance based on his hard work and Mrs. Miracle's bad faith in stealing the most significant community asset—the Monet. Thank you."

# CHAPTER SEVENTY-THREE

"Thank you, Mr. Graves," said Judge Curry. "So, before I turn the floor over to Ms. Beavers, it is your position that your client is entitled to *all of the proceeds* of the insurance policy?"

Johnny leaned over and whispered in his lawyer's ear.

Graves nodded. "That is our position."

The judge raised his eyebrows and pursed his lips. "Very well," Judge Curry said. "You can go ahead and present your side of the story, Ms. Beavers."

"Thank you, Judge." Beavers was about to stand when Mary placed her hand on her arm. "One moment," Beavers said.

Mary and Beavers whispered back and forth several times, then Beavers said, "Can I have a few minutes with my client?"

Mary and Beavers moved to a conference room down the hall for privacy.

"Why in God's name would you agree?!" Beavers was beside herself. "If he takes this case to trial, and *if* the jury refuses to believe that the card is legit, the *most* he could get would be half!"

Mary sighed. "I know you've got my best interests at heart, Betsy, but fair is fair. He worked a lot of years at the vineyard for no salary. I don't want to have any regrets about this later. And I think this is the best way to resolve things."

"This is bullshit!" Beavers exclaimed. She studied Mary's reaction closely as she asked, "Did he threaten you?"

Mary shook her head. "It's nothing like that. Please, just make the offer, and let's get this over with."

Beavers paced back and forth. Furious. She tried logic. She tried emotion.

She reminded Mary of the infidelities, of the stripper in the private investigator's report, of the likelihood that Johnny was the one who stole the Monet.

Nothing would make Mary budge.

Finally, Beavers flopped down in one of the conference chairs, legs extended straight in front of her. Exhausted. Defeated. She threw her arms up in the air in exasperation, shaking her head.

She studied Mary, who did her best to hold her gaze. But she blinked.

"Look, I know you're not telling me something, Mary," she said, pointing at her. "And I think ultimately you're going to regret this. But you *are* the client. If this is what you want, then this is what we'll do."

Johnny, Joe Graves, and the judge waited for thirty-five minutes while Mary conferred with her lawyer in another conference room. When they returned, Beavers was red-faced. She sat down, cleared her throat, and stated, "Your Honor, contrary to my advice, my client agrees to surrender all of the proceeds from the insurance policy to Mr. Miracle."

Mary sat, looking down at her hands.

Johnny smiled broadly at his attorney, who looked smugly at the mediator and said, "Well, I think we have a deal, then."

The judge shook his head once to the side, then said, "Okay, then. I will draw up the paperwork . . . if that's okay with everyone?" The mediator looked at Beavers and Mary.

Beavers glared at Mary, who nodded, eyes downcast.

"Just be sure to state that Mrs. Miracle is acting against the advice of counsel," Beavers repeated. "Once we have the agreement, we can go down to the presiding court and get the decree entered."

Graves was looking at his phone and said, "Sixty days from filing . . . that's next Thursday. I could do the following Monday."

Beavers was about to reply when Johnny interjected, "Make it Tuesday. Hunting season opens that weekend, and I'll be out of town until late Monday."

Graves nodded. "Tuesday works for me."

"Fine," Beavers said.

Johnny rose from his seat, smiling, and shook the mediator's hand. Then he waved at Beavers and Mary. "See you soon, ladies."

*Not if I see you first,* Mary thought.

* * *

"So, when do I get the money?" Johnny asked Graves as they walked towards their cars. "Do you need my bank information?"

Graves chuckled. "Not so fast, Speed Racer. The mediator is emailing us the agreement. Then, we go to court and get the divorce decree entered. Once we have that, we'll send it over to Pringle—he's handling Mary's grandmother's estate, right?"

"Yeah," Johnny replied, his belly sinking.

"So once the decree's submitted to Pringle, we'll have to see exactly how the funds get distributed. Since the insurance was in Nellie's name, if the insurance company pays, they'll probably submit the funds to the Court Registry. Then it'll be up to the judge to decide whether the estate just pays you directly. In my experience, that's *probably* what will happen."

"But, Joe," Johnny stopped, grabbing his attorney's arm. "That sounds like a lot of . . . steps. How long is this gonna take?"

"Don't worry. It sounds much more complicated than it is. Us lawyers do this all the time," he smiled. "You'll most likely have your money by spring, April or May at the latest."

"Spring . . . or May?" Johnny's ribs were starting to throb. Counting on his fingers, he clamored, "That's six to eight months, man! I need this cash now!"

"Whoa, buddy! What we just accomplished in there was incredible." Graves actually believed Mary had caved in because of his brilliant argument. "The wheels of justice grind slow, but fine. It's all good! We'll get our cash." Graves smiled. "This is me," he said, pointing at a silver BMW 7 Series. "I gotta go, man." He shook Johnny's hand. "Take care! And happy hunting!"

"Hold on, Joe," Johnny called after his lawyer. "What did you mean 'if' the insurance company pays?"

"Don't worry," his lawyer shouted back as he slipped into his BMW. "It's all good!"

# RUBY YI – 1985

By 1985, Ruby Yi was recognized as one of the most eligible divorcees—well, *widows*—in San Francisco. Once enough time had passed, her company, which she discreetly renamed Crown Enterprises, developed numerous high-rises and strip centers in the area. She'd also taken advantage of her strength in the real estate sector to establish Crown Construction and Crown Realty, to keep a toe in the residential real estate market. Life could not have been better.

Ruby lay on a lounge chair overlooking a swimming pool, a half-empty bottle of water on the small table next to her. She'd been forcing liquids all morning. She wore a small black bikini, large black Givenchy sunglasses, and was sweating off a medium-sized hangover. It was her first time in Cabo San Lucas. She'd come at the invitation of a friend and real estate client—she'd sold him his house in California—Sammy Hagar. He'd been visiting the small resort town in Mexico for several years and was trying to convince Ruby to invest in a nightclub he wanted to open there that he was going to call Cabo Wabo. She had spent the night before partying with him and Van Halen, the rock band he'd recently joined. Although Sammy was several years older than Ruby, she was amazed that she just could not keep up with him and his friends.

"You better flip over, or you'll burn." Ruby looked to her right and saw a woman about her age settling into the lounge chair next to her. "The sun down here is a real sonofabitch . . . so close to the equator."

Ruby was not in a conversational mood, but the woman had a point. She flipped over onto her belly, her face now turned left towards her new neighbor, who was lying on her back.

"Thanks," Ruby said. Through her sunglasses, she studied the woman. She had medium-length dark hair. Freckles splashed across her cheeks and shoulders. She wore a turquoise one-piece swimsuit and aviator sunglasses. Her body was toned, not overly muscular. She looked fit. Next to her lounge chair sat a bright red tote bag with the logo *Virginia is for Lovers* emblazoned on the side.

The woman reminded Ruby of someone from back home. She tried to remember who.

The sun was hot . . . pounding down . . .

A lovely breeze blew in off the ocean and across the pool . . . It carried with it the scent of the sea . . .

. . . and made a wonderful sound as it rustled through the palm fronds . . .

Ruby felt a cool hand on her shoulder, shaking her gently.

"Honey. You've been on your belly for almost an hour. You're gonna fry," said the woman in the turquoise swimsuit.

"Oh shit!" Ruby had drifted off to sleep. She sat up and, as she did, felt that telltale tightness on her back that told her she may not have burned yet, but she was well on her way. "Thanks . . . again," she said. Then, she beckoned a passing waiter, "Young man!" Turning to her neighbor, she asked, "What's your name?"

"Penelope."

"From Virginia, right?"

"How'd you . . ." Penelope smiled. "Oh yeah, right. The bag. Yep. From Richmond."

"Well, Penelope from Richmond, would you like a margarita?"

It was very hot by the pool, so the two women found a table in the shade where they chatted over their drinks. Small talk at first. The weather. The resort. Over their second margarita they began to share their stories.

"So," Penelope summarized, "let me see if I got this straight. A widow—" she put her hand on her heart, "again, so sorry for your loss—a businesswoman, with rock star friends, slummin' it in Cabo because she didn't want to disappoint Sammy Hagar?"

*When you put it that way*, Ruby thought, *I sound pretty . . . cool?*

She was feeling much better, the hair of the dog no doubt, and said, "You make it sound very glamorous. It's really not. But you're quite the little private investigator. I don't know if it's the hangover or what, but *I am off my game*. You haven't told me anything about you."

"Not much to tell," said Penelope. "From Virginia. Married." She held up her hand while shrugging and holding out her ring finger, on which she wore a mid-sized diamond and a wedding band. "We have a daughter, Chloe. My husband, Jerry, sells life insurance. That's why we're here—company retreat. And . . . yeah . . . that's me," she shrugged again.

"Oh, come on now," Ruby said. "There is so much more to you. I can see that just by looking in your eyes." They were pretty eyes. Blue, turned up slightly, intelligent, with short eyelashes.

"Really, that's me . . . I . . . I don't know. With a kid, it's . . . and don't get me wrong, I love mine. I couldn't imagine my life without Chloe. But," Penelope paused, looking up, thinking, "she doesn't leave a lot of time for much else. It's sort of like . . . like a black hole . . . of joy. Kids suck the life out of you and leave you drained, empty, with nothing. But you're happy about it at the same time. Like someone took everything from you, *killed you* . . . the real you . . . and you're happy that they did. I dunno, it must sound stupid . . ."

"No," Ruby replied. "It sounds . . . nice. Like having a plant that you care for and watch grow, and then you start to realize that you can't travel because you don't trust anyone to take care of it properly . . . but you don't mind." *Shit . . . Did I just compare her kid to a plant?* Inside Ruby's head, that little voice that protected her said, *Careful, Yi. You're getting drunk.*

"Yes!" Penelope exclaimed. "Exactly like that. Only, the plant needs a car and has to go to college!"

They laughed.

Ruby said, "So, I get that kids are all-absorbing—"

"And I hope that's not a sore spot or something. I don't know if—"

"Not at all," Ruby replied. "No, please. I'm fine. It's a choice in my case. But I guess my question is, so far, I've defined my life with certain . . . business things. But," Ruby signaled the waiter with a swirl of her hand to bring another round, "I am at a point where I realize that those business things are . . . well, *that*. Just things. I want . . . no, *need* more. Is it like that with kids?" Ruby asked.

Her new friend nodded. "Definitely, but then there's also *him*. The husband. And he's a wonderful man, the love of my life, don't get me wrong. But you try to balance everything and dream a little . . . I guess."

The waiter put the drinks on the table and took away their empties. They were starting their third round.

"*You* have a dream . . . something specific . . . I can tell," Ruby pointed at Penelope.

"I do, I do. But it's just that, a dream."

"Peneloply," Ruby noticed that she slurred slightly when she said it, and goddamned if it wasn't hot, even in the shade, "if you will it, it is no dream."

"Awww . . . that's byoootiful," Penelope replied. "Is that some Eastern thing, like Confucius?"

Ruby broke out in contagious laughter that soon had Penelope laughing as well. "Or Bruce Lee?" Penelope added for fun.

Once she'd controlled herself, Ruby said, "No." She put her hand on Penelope's arm and, looking into those eyes, those beautiful eyes, answered, "The man who said it was Theodor—"

"Well, there you are!" The two women looked up to see a sunburned man in golf attire standing over them.

"Jerry! Oh, honey! This is my friend, Ruby!"

It seemed that Jerry and his insurance buddies had also had a few drinks while out on the golf course. As they converged on the bar with their golf caps, sunglasses, and white golf shirts, they looked like a gaze of hungry raccoons.

The arrival of the men marked a line in Ruby's memory of what happened that evening; the alcohol really kicked in at that point. Things started to get a bit hazy; she remembered bits and pieces, snapshots of things . . .

*Ruby remembered that the guys chatted very briefly about their round of golf. Then there was talk of dinner. The insurance company folks had reservations for a buffet-style thing in town, which Penelope didn't seem too keen on. And after that, the men were going to have a poker night. "Typical bullshit," Penelope said a bit loudly. Jerry frowned but didn't disagree.*

*It seemed to Ruby that Penelope was pretending to be drunker than she actually was—maybe to get out of the dinner? Then again, Ruby was feeling pretty drunk too, so maybe it wasn't a bluff. For her part, Ruby was also hungry; she hadn't eaten since lunch the day before, and then after she drank too much with Sammy, and his friend Eddie, and all those goddamned tequila shots . . .*

*Ruby looked around for a waiter to get some appetizers. While she was trying to order—her Spanish wasn't working for some reason—more people came, the wives. Suddenly, eight couples were standing around, and another table got pulled up to theirs, scraping noisily and metallically across the floor, to make room for the ladies, who all sat down.*

*And a glass fell and broke, but the waiters cleaned it up.*

*Then there was ceviche in huge glasses and fried shrimp. And then a woman named Joan with fake blonde hair and big fake tits asked Ruby where she was from.*

*And Ruby replied, "San Francisco."*

*And Joan asked, "No, I mean* from.*"*

*And Ruby said, "Well, technically, Sausalito."*

*And then Joan asked, "Is that in Vietnam?"*

*And everyone broke out laughing.*

*And Joan laughed too . . .* the stupid bitch.

*Ruby thought for a moment about the best way to kill her. On the table before her were several forks and dull knives. There were also a couple of large glass beer mugs . . . slamming one into Joan's face might not kill her, but it would definitely wipe that stupid grin off her face.*

*Then the bus arrived, and there was confusion, and purses were picked up, and chairs moved again. Then most everyone went to the dinner in town and the poker night.*

*There were just three of them left. Penelope, Ruby, and a black lady. Shannon? Sharon? Her husband sold life insurance too. But she—Sharon/Shannon—hated these events because of people like Joan. And then they made fun of Joan until they realized their references to Vietnam and Charlie, and Joan as one of Charlie's Angels, might be offensive to other guests. So, they stopped.*

*Then Ruby went to the bar and asked the waiter for cigarettes even though she hadn't smoked in years—in Spanish, which she found to her satisfaction was now working brilliantly. And he told her he could get* Maria. *But Ruby didn't know* Maria; *she just wanted cigarettes. So, she asked him if* Maria *sold the cigarettes. Then she remembered that* Maria *was marijuana in Spanish, and she laughed and laughed by herself. She wanted to tell Penelope and Sharon/Shannon . . . but then she forgot because she had to decide about the pot. And she decided that Penelope and Sharon/Shannon were too straight for weed and that she was too drunk. Finally, she said no, asking for Marlboro Lights, but they only had Camel Lights. So, she said, "Fine, fuck it," but in Spanish—or maybe in English—and she lit up.*

*Then she was back at the table, and Shannon/Sharon had a cigarette, one for the road, and then she was gone. And it wasn't that late, only 9:30 p.m., but it felt much later.*

*Then it was really quiet in the bar all of a sudden, and there was a nice breeze.*

*Then Ruby was in the hallway fumbling in her purse for her room key. Then she and Penelope were sitting on the floor in Ruby's room, drinking vodka and Sprite out of the minibar. Ruby was using a glass with some water in it for an ashtray. And Penelope was smoking too.*

*Then Penelope turned on the radio and found a rock and roll station. Van Halen came on, and Ruby thought it was cool that she knew them and that she loved Eddie's impish smile, but she didn't say it out loud. Then Ruby looked at Penelope and asked her if she knew that her eyes were beautiful, and Ruby told her to never let go of her dreams.*

*And Penelope thanked her and said something about her daughter, and Jerry, and what time was it? And then Penelope said something about Jerry again and how much she loved him. And then Penelope kissed Ruby.*

And *that moment* . . . for that one brief moment, Ruby felt completely sober; or at least that was Ruby's clearest memory of the night.

*Ruby was filled with so much desire that she wanted to explode . . . for this woman who she had only known for a few hours. Her heart was pounding. She could feel the music on her skin,* in her skin. *And she kissed Penelope, or Penelope kissed her. And she tasted cigarettes and Sprite, and Penelope's tongue was cold from the ice. And Ruby had never really wanted a woman, ever. And then she thought of Kong and how she loved him, but not like that. Like a brother. But she thought how under the right circumstances, she'd let him fuck her if it would make him happy. Because she wanted him to be happy. Then there was a blur of body parts, and emotions, and scents, and tingling, and Ruby's heart pounding harder, and her hands were in Penelope's hair, and Penelope's skin was so soft—and the skin of Penelope's torso was hot with stored the heat from the sun, but the flesh on her ass was cool, and her swimsuit was still damp somehow—and she tasted like salt and sweat and then Penelope's head was between Ruby's legs, and oh, God, and Ruby felt unbearable amazing heat inside and everywhere, and she needed more, and she hated Arvin, and she hated old man Cho, and she hated that she had killed so many people, and she hated ever having had Mr. Park's dick inside her, and she hated feeling so dirty, and she was glad he was dead, and then she was crying, and she didn't want it to end, but she knew that it would, so she cried more and harder because it wasn't fair and then she was sobbing in Penelope's arms . . .*

At 3:00 a.m., Ruby sat on an ottoman on her balcony in only a bathrobe, smoking a cigarette. The sliding glass door to the bedroom was open. Penelope was asleep.

She'd been thinking about the evening. Everything. She'd never really been attracted to women. Not like that. Sure, she appreciated beauty, the human form. She knew a nice set of tits when she saw them, but she'd never felt desire like . . . a shiver ran from her crotch through her belly and up her spine, like when you're finishing peeing. She shivered with it and smirked.

*What a fucking mess, Yi . . .* Still smirking and shaking her head, she was about to crush out the cigarette when she felt Penelope's presence.

"Can I?" she said as she sat down. Ruby handed her what remained of her cigarette, and Penelope used it to light a new one, then offered Ruby's back to her.

She shook her head, so Penelope crushed it out.

Penelope took a deep drag, then exhaled. "I . . . I don't usually—" she began.

"I've never—" Ruby turned and said.

"Me either, never. This is the first . . ." Penelope stopped. Then after a moment, she added, "Makes you kind of rethink things . . ."

"No shit?!" Ruby scoffed. "Right?"

Penelope held her cigarette upright, studying the ember. She blew on it gently, and it intensified into a bright orange. Then, she patted Ruby's right leg and said, "I better get back to my room. I'll just tell Jerry we were girl-talkin'."

She offered Ruby the cigarette, and she accepted. Penelope stood and headed back inside. Ruby kept looking straight ahead, but she could see the light from the room behind her shift and change as Penelope moved around, getting dressed.

"I'm gonna go now," Penelope said through the sliding glass doors.

Ruby just raised her right hand and waved without turning around. She waited until she heard the *ta-tonk* of the front door to her room closing, then she went inside, climbed into bed, bathrobe and all, and went to sleep.

The next morning, on the floor, just in front of the door, she found a sheet of hotel stationery with Penelope's contact information scrawled on it.

*Such elegant handwriting.*

# PART SIX

## THE SNAKE YOU DON'T KILL TODAY

# CHAPTER SEVENTY-FOUR

Mary pulled up to Abby's house at 10:00 a.m. the next morning. She parked on the street and saw Art in the driveway, tinkering with his motorcycle. He left the bike on its kickstand and walked over to greet her.

"Mornin', Mary," he smiled.

"How are you, Art?"

"I'm good. Excited, actually!" He gave her a chaste hug in greeting. "Abby's out running some errands. She'll be back in a bit."

"Yeah. She said she'd be out. Thanks again for agreeing to teach me today."

"Yeah, sure. I never knew you were interested in bikes," Art looked over at the Ducati SportClassic in the driveway. "Try as I might, I just can't get Abby interested. She calls my bike the 'organ donor machine.'"

Mary laughed. "I've spent a lot of time on four-wheelers. And dirt bikes as a kid. Street bikes have always kind of intrigued me, but I never made the time for it, I guess."

"Well, you're gonna have tons of time now . . ." Art paused, foot in his mouth. "I mean, that . . . now that you're getting rid . . . gonna be . . ." He put his hands on his hips as he stammered, looking around for someone to help him out, but Abby was nowhere in sight, ". . . single."

Mary put her hand on his arm. "It's okay, Art. It's a divorce, not cancer."

Art smiled with relief and shrugged. "Sorry. I'm better at accounting than at the people stuff."

"Well, I hope you're better at motorcycles than the people stuff, or I'm screwed."

Art laughed enthusiastically, so much so that he snorted. “Oh. Sorry about that.” He cleared his throat. “Come on. Let me show you the basics. I’ve got a helmet for you. Bought it for Abby. Never been used . . . like those baby shoes . . .” He chuckled.

Mary cringed and shook her head at the Hemingway reference.

As they walked up the drive, she took in the motorcycle she’d be learning to ride. She had to admit the bike was beautiful. The parts that were painted were all bright red. Everything else was either metal or black—rubber tires, leather seat. The lettering of the word *Ducati* on the tank had a cool retro look to it that Mary loved.

This wasn’t the type of bike she would be riding as a part of her plan. Art’s bike was far more aggressive. If she could master riding this beast, she’d have no problem with the motorcycle she was planning to use. She spent all that Saturday morning with Art, initially just driving up and down the street, practicing getting the bike moving in first gear. She loved Art, despite his social issues. And she found that he was a masterful teacher.

Mary learned that much like driving a stick shift, the gears were simple to manage once you got going in first. The trick was easing off the clutch while giving the beast gas with the throttle. It was all about coordination. Once it got going, shifting gears—coordinating the clutch in her left hand, throttle in her right, and her left foot on the gear shift—was not that big a deal.

By the time Abby showed up around 1:00 p.m., Mary was comfortable running the Ducati up and down the street and going around the block. She was also dripping with sweat. While she was moving, the breeze helped, but the helmet, long pants, jacket, and gloves generated a lot of heat when at a standstill. Abby saw how Mary looked when she arrived and brought out a large pitcher of lemonade.

“Break time!” she shouted as she served three glasses.

“So, how’s she doin’?” Abby asked.

“She’s a natural. She nailed the friction point on the clutch real quick. Once you get that, it’s just repetition. Practice. Practice. Practice.”

“How you feelin’?” Abby asked Mary, who had gulped down her glass of lemonade and was serving herself another.

“I think I’m ready to take it on the highway,” she replied.

Abby looked at Art, whose lips were tightly pursed. He began nodding slowly. “So, the only thing you’ve got to remember is that everything we’ve talked about applies even more as you go faster. You need to stay attached to the bike,” Art crouched, demonstrating the proper riding position. “You lean; it leans.” He leaned as he explained. "You're centered; it's centered. And direction is critical—wherever you're looking, that's where you're going to go." Art pointed at his eyes with two fingers, then away from himself. "So look only where you want to go. Don't look where you don't want to go."

Marry nodded. "Sounds like good advice in general."

"*Be water, my friend*," Abby added snarkily.

Art shook his head. "It's a good thing you don't ride, Abb. You just don't have the—"

"—proper frame of mind, yada, yada." Abby punched Art in the arm. "Go for it, girl. We'll be here when you get back."

Mary mounted the Ducati and rode down the street, as she had dozens of times that day, and took a right. This time, however, instead of taking the next right and completing a circuit around the block, she continued straight and steered towards the ramp onto Mopac highway. Once she was on the onramp, she shifted, she realized, for the first time, into third gear . . . and accelerated. As the revs increased, she cycled through gears, weaving through traffic, the sound of the wind rushing past competing with and soon overcoming the roar of the engine vibrating between her legs. This wasn't just transportation; there was something visceral, even sexual, about riding this machine. She was flying.

Mary suddenly realized she'd been in the left lane for a while now, zipping past trucks, minivans, and sedans. She looked down and was shocked to see the speedometer pegging 108 miles per hour. Her initial instinct was to cut the throttle and brake. But she remembered everything Art had told her, and instead, she eased off the throttle gently and downshifted until she was at the speed limit. She found an exit, turned around, and headed back to Art and Abby's.

"So, all good?" Art asked as Mary removed her helmet and dismounted.

"Oh, my GOD!!!! WOW!!!! Just . . . WOW!!!!!" As she shouted, she realized how quiet everything had gotten now that she wasn't moving anymore.

Art laughed, covering his ears. Abby also laughed, though her eyes gave away that while the thrill of the ride and the moment they were sharing might be amazing, there was a dark undercurrent. She knew that, for Mary, learning to ride was a means to an end. A very specific end.

* * *

Right about the time that Mary was flying down Mopac, Johnny's mobile phone rang. It was the call he'd been dreading. He was sitting on the sofa at Karen's place. She was out at work, showing some clients a house.

"Hello."

"You're late, Johnny. I still have no documents signed by your partner. I have been extremely patient. The mediation was yesterday. Where. Is. My. Money?"

Johnny stood up. He liked to pace when he talked on the phone. Especially when he was nervous.

"I've got great news, Eddie! Everything worked out just like I planned. I just need a little time." Although Johnny had made his best effort to sound confident, the end of that last statement had sounded weak.

Sick Eddie sighed heavily into the phone.

"How much is a little, Johnny?"

"My lawyer says that there's some processes. The decree has to be signed by the judge. Then the other lawyer, Pringle, he's the one on the estate, he has to . . . do something legal too . . . with the judge, after we send him copies of the decree, that is. Then the insurance company will pay—"

"Hold on. Hold on. Hold on," Sick Eddie interrupted. "Are you fuckin' with me, Johnny? You told me before that you *couldn't* pay me because Nellie's life insurance wasn't any good."

"No, no, no," Johnny insisted. "Not *that* insurance. This is different insurance. For the painting."

Johnny paused. He could hear Sick Eddie breathing.

"Explain."

"See, Nellie had this painting that was stolen. And the insurance is going to pay. And in the mediation, we signed an agreement that I get all that money. Five million dollars. So, it won't be any problem," Johnny explained. "It's . . . all good."

"Five million. Okay. When?"

Johnny cleared his throat. "Well, like my lawyer said . . . the processes, the decree—"

"Johnny?! When? Give. Me. A. Date."

"Graves, my lawyer, said for sure by spring. Latest . . ." Johnny cringed, "May."

Silence.

Silence.

Silence.

"You. Stupid. Fuck."

Johnny said nothing. He could hear clacking on the line. *Typing?*

"Do you know how much money you'll owe me in May, with interest?"

Johnny could've kicked himself. He still hadn't bought that damned calculator. But it was only six months. How much could it be? Besides, he'd always been pretty good at guesstimating.

"Two million?" he guessed.

"Try three-point-nine million," Sick Eddie chuckled. "You fucking idiot."

Johnny's legs felt weak. He sat on the sofa, and an involuntary "Huh?" escaped his lips.

"Wait a minute," Sick Eddie said. "Insurance on a painting? Are you talking about that Monet? The one you offered me as collateral?"

"Yeah," Johnny said.

"So, you think you're going to collect five million dollars on a painting you stole? And that's how you're going to pay me . . . *NEXT YEAR!!!???*"

"I'm sorry, Eddie. But . . . what if I give you the painting? It's gotta be worth—"

"I told you Johnny. No one gets two strikes."

"But, Eddie. I promise—"

"You're a dead man walking, Johnny."

The line went dead.

# CHAPTER SEVENTY-FIVE

A critical element of Mary's plan lay on the table in front of her. She was back at home getting organized. Before her was a black and gray camouflage-patterned nylon bag, about twenty-two inches long. As Mary unzipped the bag, she remembered Grandma Nellie and thought it sad and ironic that she would be using a rifle Nellie had bought for protection to avenge her murder.

Inside the bag, torn down into three parts, was one of Grandma Nellie's many "bug-out" guns. This particular one was a Bergara BA13. It was a well-made firearm, its main strength as far as Mary's plan being that it could be taken apart into smaller pieces—the longest measuring only 20 inches—for ease of transport. She couldn't afford to be spotted with a rifle slung over her shoulder on her way to kill Johnny.

Mary put the rifle together and took it apart several times, as much to refresh her memory as to make sure that the pieces all came together as they should. The rifle was clean, spotless. Nellie was a stickler for that sort of thing.

Inside the bag was also a box of ammunition, .30-06. The weapon was perfect for the plan in most respects. There were only two issues. First, this rifle was a one-shot weapon. This meant that she had to hit her target on the first shot, or she'd have to reload. Second, she hadn't fired the rifle in more than a year. Firearm safety—and prudence—dictated that she should take it out and shoot some practice rounds. But she didn't think she should risk being seen out at a firing range practicing with a .30-06 . . . not when, if everything went according to plan, her husband would shortly be accidentally shot with a round of the same caliber.

Mary zipped up the bag and placed it inside a black backpack. Inside the backpack was a handheld GPS for navigation, camouflage hunting clothes, a camo neck gaiter, a cap, and boots. After zipping up the backpack, she neatly placed it inside a small, hard-shelled, carry-on size suitcase, to which she then added various essentials for her weekend spa getaway, including a swimsuit and other casual clothing.

# CHAPTER SEVENTY-SIX

"You sure about this?" Abby asked. She was driving her minivan, an older model vehicle that, important to Mary, didn't have a GPS system, and thus could not be geolocated. Mary was in the passenger's seat. They'd left Fredericksburg at 10:00 a.m. It was Friday, November 6, and they were halfway to their destination near Dallas. The total trip time was approximately three hours.

Mary sat for a few moments, staring ahead. Then took a deep breath before speaking. "I don't think I have any other choice, Abby. I mean, yeah, at first, a big part of my motivation was probably . . . anger. I was just pissed off that Johnny could . . ." she took another deep breath, and her voice trembled slightly as she resumed, "he could cut Nellie's life short like that . . . just for money, or control, or whatever it is he was after. But, after I got over being pissed off—" She turned and looked at Abby. "The thing is, if I do *nothing*, he'll get away with it." She turned and looked forward. "I know . . . deep down inside, I *know* that he did it. Johnny killed her." Mary paused, looking out the window to her right. Then she turned back to Abby. "But I also know there are just bits and pieces of evidence, all of it circumstantial. Smarts, luck, or whatever, he did a good enough job covering his tracks. I don't think the police have enough to go on. And even if they did, I don't think there's any way a jury will convict him."

Mary shook her head. "But even if they did convict him, assume for a moment that they did . . . I can't be sure that he'd get the death penalty. And if he does, when? Even if he ends up on death row, how long does that take? When would they *actually* kill him? After how many years? How many appeals? How much time will he spend living in prison, watching TV, eating, reading, breathing . . ." Mary turned to her friend and said slowly, "He doesn't deserve to breathe, Abby."

Abby nodded, lips pursed. Her thoughts were interrupted by her phone's GPS, "*In two miles, take exit 359 on the right.*" She glanced at the display, then said, "We're about five minutes out from the gas station."

"You want anything other than water?" Mary asked.

Abby hesitated for a moment, then said, "I'm tempted to say smokes . . ." She glanced sideways at Mary.

"Yeah," Mary nodded. "Me too . . ."

They pulled into the gas station and stopped next to one of the fuel pumps. While Abby dealt with gas, Mary went into the convenience store. She was dressed in a bright red dress and made it a point to browse slowly through the store, pausing in front of each security camera she saw. As she went, she collected a bottle of sparkling water, a bottle of plain water, a bottle of Coke Zero, and a bag of Corn Nuts. At the counter, she asked the clerk, a young Asian woman, for two packs of American Spirit Turquoise and a lighter.

Abby came in while she was paying and walked through the store, making sure to pass in front of all the cameras she could see. She could hear Mary, at a distance, chatting up the clerk. As she bagged everything up, Abby sidled up next to Mary and picked up the tail end of their conversation.

"Well, you stick to it, Grace. You're almost done. And one day, you'll look back and tell your kids about the days when you worked at a gas station and went to college at the same time. That is just *so* admirable," Mary said, reaching up and taking the offered bag.

"Thank you, Miss . . ." the clerk looked down at Mary's credit card, and her eyes grew wide, "Miracle? Is that really your name, Miracle? So very lucky!"

Mary laughed. "Oh, you have no idea, Grace. You take good care of yourself. We'll make sure," she looked for a moment at Abby as she spoke, "to stop here on the way back to Austin. Hopefully, we'll get to see each other again!"

As they drove away from the station, Abby said, "Nicely done. She'll definitely remember you."

"She's from northern China. Came here to stay with family. Works there full time, and she's getting her EMT certification at the same time." There was a bit of irony in Mary's tone as she concluded, "Said she wants to save lives . . ."

# CHAPTER SEVENTY-SEVEN

"So, this guy is *back on the market!*" shouted Shawn, holding out a half-empty beer bottle. "Cheers!"

The four men were outside the hunting cabin near a Weber grill, three seated in lawn chairs, one cooking.

"Whaddya mean, back on?" Craig jibed. "That would mean at some point he was *off* the market!" He clinked his bottle against Shawn's and guffawed at his own joke.

Shawn joined in Craig's laughter, "Too-shay, buddy!!!"

Johnny held out his bottle, smiling broadly. He was happy to be the center of attention. He'd arrived at the hunting lease just ten minutes earlier. It was located just north of San Saba, Texas. The guys were already several brewskis into lunch, which consisted of grilled kielbasa sausage and assorted brands of beer.

After all the stress of the past few weeks, Johnny was finally relaxing; his ribs were bothering him less, he was going to be a rich man, and he was going hunting. It didn't get any better than this.

Gary was manning the grill. He raised his own beer from a distance. "Just look at the smile on that bastard's face! You give Karen a nice ride before coming up here?"

Johnny grinned, nodding in an exaggerated manner while saying, "A gentleman never tells."

All the men laughed.

"So, seriously, Miracle-Man, when's it official?" Shawn asked.

Johnny swallowed a mouthful of beer. "About a week out . . . it's all just formalities now. The mediator judge laid down the law. Sharp guy. Told her and her lawyer that a jury would easily see how much I'd done around the vineyard. No way she could keep everything. Made her agree to give me five million, man. Five mother-fucking million!"

Shawn nodded, standing up, and raising his beer yet again, with an overly serious look and tone, said, "Seriously, gents. Here's to Johnny, Jonathan Sebastian Miracle, who . . ." he made a humping motion with his hips, "worked his ass off at the Crab-ass Vineyards!"

Johnny threw a piece of sausage at Shawn. All the men laughed.

# CHAPTER SEVENTY-EIGHT

A little over an hour later, Mary and Abby were checking into the Four Seasons Resort in Las Colinas, a little town just outside of Dallas.

"I see you ladies are with us for two nights," said the desk agent, an Indian woman in her mid-twenties. "You're booked in one of our Premier Villas, overlooking the golf course, with two double beds. Sounds like a great girls' weekend."

"We've been friends since longer than I can remember, honey. Leavin' the husbands and kids and getting a little 'me time' in!" Abby replied.

"Good for you both! And I see you have some spa treatments booked; that's tomorrow at one p.m., as well as dinner reservations for tomorrow night. Do you need dinner reservations for tonight?"

Abby shook her head. "Naw. We drove all day. Just gonna do room service tonight, unwind." Then she added in a sing-songy voice, "Have some wine . . . Sleep in late mañana . . . Then," she went up an octave, "spa day!"

Mary nodded in agreement.

"Well, that sounds great," the desk attendant replied. "Anything you need, my name is Candace." She gave them their room keys.

As she did, Mary said, "Oh, shoot! Abby, I forgot the bubbles!" She turned and said, "Candace, is there a wine store nearby? We wanted some champagne for tonight . . ." she smiled sheepishly, lowering her voice slightly, "but not at Four Seasons prices."

Candace nodded conspiratorially and said, "There's a strip mall literally across the road, just go left on Bryson Nelson Way. You can't miss it."

Mary and Abby knew this; they'd chosen this hotel for a specific reason, scouting the area online before making the hotel reservation.

"Why don't you go get settled, shower, and such? I'll run over and take care of it," Abby volunteered.

"Awww . . . Are you sure?" Mary asked. "That is so sweet of you!"

Mary thanked Candace, and while Abby headed out to the car, Mary took her and Abby's rolling bags to their room, insisting on handling the luggage herself. Once there, Mary quickly unpacked her bag. The clothes she piled neatly on the bed. She also removed from the suitcase the burner phone she'd bought as a part of her scheme. It was currently turned off.

She left the nylon bag with the rifle and the black backpack in the suitcase, locking it shut with the built-in combination lock and placing it in the closet. She then changed out of the red dress into blue jeans and an olive-green shirt and put on a blue baseball cap. She wore old work boots. The look she was going for was somewhere between 'landscaping supervisor' and 'weekend gardener.' She put the *Do not disturb* hanger on the door to the room.

Then she put the burner phone in one front pocket. She removed a thick white envelope from her purse, which she stuffed in her other pocket. Last, she plugged in her regular phone and left it charging on the desk. If her phone was later traced for geolocation data, it would appear that she'd arrived at the hotel and stayed in the room.

Each Premier Villa had its own private lawn and firepit area overlooking the golf course. Mary put on sunglasses and went out the sliding glass door, careful to make sure there were no security cameras. She walked around the hotel's east side to meet Abby down on Bryson Nelson Way.

"All good?" Abby asked as Mary got in the minivan.

"I think so. I didn't see any cameras, kept my head down."

"Okay," Abby said as she accelerated. They drove about five minutes to an apartment complex, where Abby let Mary out of the car. Abby then put "Wine near me" in her phone's GPS.

"Oh shoot," she chuckled. "I missed my turn."

Mary smiled. "Wish me luck."

While Abby drove back to the liquor store Candace had recommended, Mary turned on the burner phone and hit redial. On the third ring, the call was answered.

"Yep?"

"Hi, Sam? This is Gail. We spoke last week about the motorcycle. I'm here

. . . I think . . . at your complex."

"You're early," Sam replied. "You out front?"

"At the entrance," Mary said. "There's a fountain."

"Sit tight then; I'll be there in five."

Mary waited.

A red car passed, leaving the complex.

Ten minutes later, she heard another vehicle approaching the exit. It was a man on a motorcycle, a Kawasaki KLR650. As he pulled up, she saw that he was carrying a helmet, his left arm threaded through the facemask. He stopped next to her and dismounted.

"There she is," he said, then extended his hand and shook hers. "Sam," he smiled.

"She's perfect," Mary reacted. "My boyfriend's been wanting one for ages."

"So," Sam said, "this is all the paperwork you need for the title change," he held out an envelope toward her.

Mary dug into her pocket and pulled out her envelope. "Thirty-five hundred dollars cash, like we said."

They traded, and while Mary pretended to review the paperwork, Sam counted the cash.

"And you're sure you want this helmet? It's old and kinda smelly . . ."

Mary laughed. "It's fine. If my boyfriend saw me leave the house with a helmet, he'd know something was up."

"Man, I wish I had a girlfriend like you!" Sam said, smiling a bit too broadly.

Mary held out her hand, and he handed her the helmet. The key was still in the ignition.

"You sure you . . ."

"I got it," Mary said, pulling on the helmet, then mounting the bike. She turned the ignition, and the bike started right up. She saw, to her satisfaction, that the tank was full, while she heard Sam saying, "I filled her up for ya."

Mary put the bike in gear. She gave Sam a thumbs up and a small wave with her right hand, gripped the throttle, gave the bike some gas, and headed out of the apartment complex.

# CHAPTER SEVENTY-NINE

Johnny decided to call it a night earlier than the others; this was his first real break in a while.

Since Nellie died, things had been hectic—first one thing, then another. Well, really, even before she died. He still felt a slight pang of guilt when he thought about the old woman, which he tried to avoid doing as much as possible.

*She lived a good, long life,* he'd told himself repeatedly. *We all gotta die of something.* He sighed. *Fuck it . . . water under the bridge . . .*

He unpacked his gear, laying out his clothes for the next morning's hunt. He was on autopilot, thinking about what he would do next in his life.

*Karen's a nice lady . . . but the guys are right. I'm young, good-looking, now I'm rich . . . I can do better. I oughta get outta Smallsville, Texas. Maybe go to Austin or San Antonio—lots of hot, rich ladies there . . .*

He stripped down to boxer shorts and put on a t-shirt to sleep in. While he brushed his teeth, he looked at himself in the bathroom mirror. He clenched the toothbrush in his teeth and flexed his biceps in the mirror. *Still got it, man. Ripped as shit!* He smiled at himself, nodding. *Yep. San Antonio. Maybe find myself a rich Latina . . . with a weak heart.* He made a face at himself in the mirror, putting his hands on either cheek and opening his mouth in a big "O" like the Munch-inspired scream emoji; then he smiled. *That was dark, Miracle-Man. Very dark.*

He winked at his reflection, set his phone alarm for 4:30 a.m., and went to bed.

# CHAPTER EIGHTY

After leaving the apartment complex on the Kawasaki, Mary drove back towards the hotel, but instead of turning onto the property, she continued up the road to the strip mall where the liquor store was located. She parked the motorcycle there, leaving the helmet hanging on the handlebars. She'd seen this before and always wondered why people didn't steal the helmets. She hoped it would be there when she came back.

She walked for about ten minutes, returning to her hotel room using the same route she'd left by. Abby was already back in the room. She had unpacked and changed into comfy clothes. She had opened the champagne and had a half-empty flute in her hand.

"How's the bike?" she asked.

"Fine. Much easier to handle than the Ducati. And more . . . upright? Not as aggressive."

Abby nodded.

Mary changed clothes as well.

"Want one?" Abby asked, holding out her champagne glass.

"Just one," she replied. "Then I'm gonna try to get some sleep. Long day tomorrow."

As they sipped bubbly, Mary and Abby ran through the details of Mary's plan one more time. It was simple enough. But even simple plans can go wrong.

At 5:30 p.m., Abby placed a room service order for two. When the food arrived, Mary nibbled a little hummus and salad. She wasn't very hungry.

At 7:00 p.m., Mary took five milligrams of melatonin, put on her eye covers, and went to bed while Abby read.

* * *

At midnight, Mary's phone alarm rang. She turned it off on the first ring and rolled out of bed.

Abby was still awake.

"You didn't get any sleep?" Mary asked.

Abby shook her head. "Couldn't. Too tense. Edgy . . . Just thinkin'."

"Hmmm." Mary rubbed her eyes.

Ten minutes later, Mary was dressed in olive green pants, a black t-shirt, a denim jacket, and her work boots. She had the camouflage clothes, neck gaiter, and cap in her backpack, which also contained the nylon bag with the rifle.

"Well . . ." Mary said, looking at Abby.

"Like I said, I was thinkin'. You sure about this, girl? I mean, this shit is about as real as it gets."

"Are you saying I shouldn't do this?"

"I just . . . Lord knows he deserves it, but . . ." Abby lowered her voice to a whisper even though they were alone, "it's still murder."

Mary whispered as well. "Abby, Johnny poisoned and killed Nellie. My grandmother. What would you do if someone did that to Art? And you knew the system wouldn't do anything, that justice would never be served?"

Abby nodded with lips tight. She sighed. "I just can't believe it's come to this. That we're *doing* this . . ."

Mary eyes blazed. "*You're* doing *nothing*," she hissed. "Remember that! And if I get caught, what do you say?!"

Abby rolled her eyes. "That all you told me was that you were goin' to see him to try and reconcile. To try and get back together."

"Exactly. That's all you know. Okay?"

Abby nodded. "Okay. Well, good luck." She opened her arms and gave Mary a hug. The two friends held each other for a few moments.

"All right, then," Mary said. "See you later."

"I'll be there. On time."

Mary headed for the sliding glass door, then paused and turned. "Thank you, again. I love you, Abby."

Abby nodded, putting her hands on her heart, then blew Mary a kiss. "Be smart. Be safe. I love you too."

The night was eerily quiet as Mary walked back around the building. The parking lot at the strip mall was almost empty. As she approached the motorcycle, she was relieved to find the helmet still hanging where she'd left it. She put on the backpack and removed the key from her pocket. The bike started right up, and she rode out of the parking lot and then in a southwestern direction.

Johnny had repeatedly regaled Mary with stories of his hunting exploits. As a result, although she'd never hunted with him, she had a general idea of what went on. And she knew where Shawn's hunting lease was located—near San Saba—as they had been there once for an overnight barbecue Shawn had thrown for friends and their spouses.

Her three-hour journey was uneventful.

When she got to the hunting lease entrance, she slowed to confirm it was the right place, then rode about a mile past until she found a bend in the road where she could hide the motorcycle behind trees.

Mary then hiked back up the road, entering the property by climbing through the fencing about fifty yards before reaching the entry gate. She stuck to the trees as she followed a path parallel to the dirt road leading to the hunting cabin. Once she could see the cabin through the trees, she found a vantage point behind a large oak. She removed the rifle scope from the backpack and used it like a telescope to take a closer look at the cabin. It was dark. No movement. It was 3:40 a.m. Mary kept an eye on the cabin while she changed into the camouflage gear, then packed away her riding clothes before making herself comfortable as she waited for the guys to wake up.

# CHAPTER EIGHTY-ONE

At 4:30 a.m., several phone alarms went off inside the hunting cabin. The previous silence was soon filled with grunts, farts, and creaking as the guys roused from sleep and dressed for their first day of hunting.

Gary turned on the lights and started coffee.

Johnny's ribs were better, but as he was going to be moving around quite a bit, he popped two ibuprofen before putting on his hunting clothes. Soon, the cabin smelled of coffee, bacon, and eggs as Gary whipped up a quick breakfast for the four. Johnny heated a couple of corn tortillas in the microwave and gobbled down two breakfast tacos.

"All right," Shawn said, holding out a fist with four coffee swizzle sticks sticking up evenly, though each stick was a different length. The hunting buddies used this method to decide who got to hunt in which location on the lease.

"I can't lose these days," Johnny said, smiling and holding up a whole swizzle stick, the longest of the four. "I'll take the deer blind at Guppy's Pond."

"Of course you will," Gary said. "I'll take Dead Man's."

"Midway," Craig said.

"Shit," Shawn said, holding up the smallest swizzle stick. "BFE . . ." BFE stood for Bum Fuck Egypt, the deer blind at the other end of the property and the longest walk from the cabin.

At approximately 5:00 a.m., the guys exited the cabin and headed to their different hunting spots. As they did, they were unaware that they were being watched.

Johnny's walk was the shortest of the four. He crossed the dirt road that led from the highway to the cabin and then crossed a small field into a creek bed which he followed east, away from the highway, for about four hundred yards to a water tank fed by a well. Deer and other animals came to the tank for water, and there was a deer feeder about twenty yards away. Johnny trudged up through trees to the deer blind, which lay slightly uphill about eighty yards from the tank and feeder area. He climbed up into the blind and got settled in.

Mary had watched the four men exit the cabin and immediately identified Johnny. As he peeled off from the rest of the group and followed the creek bed, Mary had kept an eye on him, using the scope of her rifle as he got further out. She needed to know where he was going to set up while keeping enough distance between them that he didn't spot her.

As he passed the water tank, she watched him turn to head up the hill; anticipating his path, she scanned the area above until she spotted the deer blind. She could barely see the bottom of the blind through the trees. It was painted gray and green camo. Mary scanned back along his path, trying to choose the best spot to set up. As she did, she saw another hunter who had already passed the water tank and was continuing along the creek bed. Mary couldn't tell which of the others it was, as she'd been more focused on Johnny.

All four wore camo and safety vests when they left the cabin. Deer cannot see long wave-length colors well, like red and orange. For safety, hunters wear bright orange vests that don't stand out to deer but identify them to other hunters as 'not prey.' For some reason, this guy had taken off his safety vest. Mary watched him as he kept walking up the creek bed until he disappeared from view. Then she began to move in Johnny's direction.

About a hundred yards before the water tank, she exited the creek bed, hiking up into the trees about ten yards, just enough to find cover. Then she crept along until she was about fifty yards from the tank.

Given Johnny's location, she had two choices. She could continue up the hill to try and position herself to shoot him when he left the deer blind, or she could wait where she was. From her position, if deer came to feed or drink—and Johnny killed one—she could shoot him when he came down to claim his prize. It would be a fifty-yard shot. Very doable. If no deer came—or if Johnny shot and missed—his most likely path back to the cabin was the route he had just taken, and she would be there waiting for him.

She decided that the safe bet was to wait down where she was. She found a spot next to a fallen tree. There, she unpacked the rest of the rifle, assembled it, and loaded a single .30-06 cartridge.

Then, she made herself comfortable once more, and waited.

# CHAPTER EIGHTY-TWO

Mary didn't have to wait long.

She'd been in position for about twenty minutes when she heard a gunshot. It sounded as though it came from up around the deer blind. She scanned using the scope but couldn't see any deer. Maybe Johnny was shooting in another direction?

*Shit . . .*

The first shot was followed by two more gunshots in quick succession from the same area but of a different timbre, either from a different weapon or shooting in a different direction.

*What the hell?*

The first shooter fired again, and then the second fired twice more.

The last shot was followed by someone exclaiming, "*FUCK!*"

Mary heard another shot, then rustling. It sounded as though someone was rapidly making their way through the trees. She followed the sound with her eyes until she saw the hunter she'd seen before, the one without the safety vest, break out of the trees on the hilly side of the creek, then cross the water, disappearing into the trees on the other side.

Although he'd scrambled across the creek in only seconds, he'd taken long enough for Mary to make out a few details. His right hand still gripped a hunting rifle. His other arm hung useless by his side, his hunting shirt stained dark. The man had been shot. As he passed into the trees, he looked back over his shoulder, and Mary saw that he had a tattoo that came up his neck onto his face; she couldn't tell exactly what the tattoo was. Just as he disappeared into the trees, Mary spun to the right as she heard a voice scream.

"You're goin' down, motherfucker!"

She knew that voice; it was Johnny. It had come from up and to the right. From the sound of it, he was out in the open. As his voice echoed through the trees, she realized that while she'd been distracted watching the other man, Johnny must have exited the blind and started down towards the creek.

"I'm gonna send you back to Sick Eddie in pieces!" he shouted.

Mary's neck felt tight and her palms began to sweat. She began scanning frantically trying to locate him as from the sound of it, he was coming closer.

* * *

Johnny was over the shock of having been shot at. He was in a rage. He'd seen the shot that hit Javier, and he was going to finish him off.

*It's payback time!*

He had been comfortably set up in the deer blind, focused on the feeder and water tank, visualizing the appearance of a large buck down by the creek—Johnny believed he could call animals with his mind—when he'd heard movement off to the right. It wasn't the sound of movement that piqued his curiosity but the immediate silence afterward. In his experience, most animals don't suddenly stop moving when they make noise. That was predatory . . . human behavior.

He'd carefully slipped into a prone position and crawled his way around to look over to the side where he'd heard the noise start and stop. After a few moments of scanning, waiting for movement, he'd spotted Javier, Sick Eddie's enforcer, the guy that had broken his ribs. Javier was moving carefully towards the blind, carrying a rifle. At that distance, Johnny couldn't tell what type, but it was clear to Johnny that Javier was up to no good.

Johnny found Javier in his scope and waited. When the man stopped next to a tree, about thirty yards out, and pointed his rifle in Johnny's direction, Johnny's belly tightened. This was for real. Sick Eddie was going to take him out . . .

*No one fucks with the Miracle-Man!*

Johnny exhaled slowly, but just as he squeezed the trigger, Javier dropped to the ground. He must have seen something—a reflection from Johnny's scope? The barrel of the rifle?

The first shot missed.

Javier fired back wildly—one bullet hit the deer blind, and the other went wide. Johnny's second shot found its target. He saw Javier recoil from the impact to his shoulder. On reflex, the goon squeezed off two more rounds before he started yelling, struggled to his feet, and down the hill, leaving his rifle behind. Johnny fired again, but the shot went wide.

Adrenaline coursed through Johnny. Rage. Blood lust. His enemy was wounded and unarmed. There was no way he was letting him get away. He scrambled down the ladder to the deer blind and gave chase.

* * *

Mary could hear Johnny moving through the trees. He was close but moving downhill. While this was not how she'd planned things, she knew that if he followed the wounded man, his path would bring him down to the creek. She looked up and down the creek as well as she could from where she was positioned. All clear. She crawled down on her knees and one hand, carrying the rifle in the other, looking both ways as she went. Once she reached the creek bed, she lay prone, positioning herself to shoot down the funnel formed by the creek's banks when Johnny crossed.

She waited and listened.

"Fucker's not getting a dime from me after this . . . You hear me, asshole?! You can tell that sonofabitch I said so!" Johnny was coming closer to the creek.

Mary continued to listen for her husband's movements. Her muscles tensed as she realized that the sounds were coming toward her.

*Johnny was coming toward her.*

She had anticipated that he would follow the other man's path, but maybe he hadn't seen where his quarry had gone.

If Johnny came near, she would be easily visible.

The rustling stopped.

Could he see her?

*Had* he seen her?

She heard a twig snap—up and away from her.

Suddenly, Johnny appeared. His face contorted, wild with anger. He emerged from the trees, crouched low, and moved quickly into a sitting position on the ground, his back against the water tank, putting it between him and the downhill side of the creek.

Then he turned and rose onto one knee, resting his rifle on top of the tank, looking through his scope, scanning through the woods, hunting the wounded man.

He was oblivious to the fact that he was now completely exposed to Mary's position.

* * *

Mary stared through her scope, centering the crosshairs on Johnny's head. Her lizard brain was firing adrenaline, and her heart rate was rising. She took a deep breath, inhaling for four counts, holding it for four, and exhaling for four more.

One bullet.

One shot.

As she lined him up in her sights . . . she realized . . . she wasn't looking at a paper target. She was looking at another human being.

Johnny.

Her husband.

The man she had once loved and made love with. The guy who had shown her the sunrise in Mexico and proposed to her to the sound of "Solamente Una Vez." The man she had promised to love, honor, and cherish.

Johnny, who had cried at the end of *Marley and Me*.

Mary felt her energy dissipating. Her stomach hollow. Her resolve fading . . .

In a flash, she remembered the last time she had fired on another living creature—the rattler. But that was a snake. This was Johnny . . . As she remembered the rattler, she also remembered the weekend Nellie died. And she remembered what her grandmother always said, "The *snake* you don't kill today may kill *you* tomorrow."

Mary looked down the scope; Johnny was still scanning the trees for the wounded man. He was looking away from her but then, slowly, his head turned, following the contours of the creek bed towards Mary, his face still contorted with anger.

Mary breathed slowly in and out.

Johnny squinted in her direction. He was now looking right at her.

She was wearing camo, but she realized that she had lowered her neck gaiter for comfort as she made her way down to the creek, and she hadn't put it back up over her face.

She saw the jolt of recognition in Johnny's eyes as he realized what he was seeing; his wife, in a sniper position, pointing a rifle at him. Mary gently hugged the butt of the weapon tighter into her shoulder, becoming one with the tool. She lowered the crosshairs a smidge, from Johnny's head to his chest; a much larger target, which she knew that, when hit with a large caliber like a .30-06, would almost always be lethal. It's every sniper's preferred target zone.

Johnny shifted his body toward her, quickly raising his rifle, aiming at her as his lips twisted into a bitter smile and his eyes glimmered with hate.

Mary slowly exhaled and gently squeezed the trigger. The end of the rifle barrel erupted in tandem with a deafening *boom* just as she saw the muzzle flare from her husband's rifle.

She flinched instinctively, bracing for the impact.

# CHAPTER EIGHTY-THREE

A .30-06 bullet exiting a rifle breaks the speed of sound. Two such gunshots simultaneously fired—two simultaneous sonic booms—are enough to jolt everything nearby into stunned silence. Several startled birds' wings fluttered as they fled the scene. The rest, squirrels, lizards, insects, even the leaves in the trees, all seemed to pause in reverent awe at the physics of what had just occurred. Two projectiles propelled by controlled explosions to over 760 miles per hour passed within inches of one another, traveling in opposite directions.

For the nearby fauna, the auditory shock was soon overridden by another sense, olfactory, as the metallic scent of fresh blood tainted the air. As birds began to chirp and sing again, squirrels to peek, insects to crawl, a sharp but distinct *CLACK* sound stood out from the rest of the natural sounds, something mechanical and artificial.

Mary's one shot was spent. She rolled over twice downhill, then crawled into the tree line. As she did, her mind was assessing; everything seemed fine, all her body parts were functioning, and she felt no pain.

*Johnny missed me . . .*

*I'm ALIVE!*

What she wasn't sure of was whether her bullet had found its target. She struggled to load another shell into the rifle. Her hands were shaking almost uncontrollably, but she had the presence of mind to pocket the spent shell. She raised her neck gaiter, covering the bottom half of her face. Then she raised the rifle, taking cover behind a tree trunk, pointing towards Johnny, and using the scope to seek him out.

*If I did shoot him, he was shooting at me too. So, it was self-defense . . . kind of.*

She tried to slow her breathing. Her heart was pounding. As she pointed the rifle, looking for Johnny, she tried to engage larger muscle groups to keep the weapon steady. He was still hiding by the water tank. As she leaned right, she could make out his leg, and, next to it, the barrel of his rifle. Carefully, she edged towards the creek and saw that Johnny's rifle lay on the rocky creek bed. That must have been the *CLACK* she'd heard, his rifle clattering on the stone.

As she edged forward, she saw her husband leaning back in a seated position against the water tank, a dark stain in the center of his trunk still expanding over his belly and onto his legs. He was staring, dead-eyed, into the distance.

Staying low, Mary moved up the creek bed towards him, rifle ready, just close enough to confirm that he was indeed dead. Then, she looked upstream and saw the trail of blood splatter the other hunter had left as he went into the woods.

No sign of him.

She edged back into the trees on the downhill side of the creek and leaned against a mid-sized oak for cover, putting it between her and where the wounded man had gone.

Her breathing was still strained.

*Now what, Mary?*

The normal thing would be to assist the wounded. But first things first.

*Who was that guy?*

*Why was he shooting it out with Johnny?*

*Is he even alive? Does he have another weapon, a gun, or a knife?*

*How long until Johnny's friends come to see what all the shooting was about?*

The last thing she needed was witnesses of any kind.

She decided it was best to retreat. So, staying low, she retrieved her backpack and then jogged back the way she'd come.

# CHAPTER EIGHTY-FOUR

Mary returned to the motorcycle without incident. She started it up and began her return trip. The route she was taking back to the hotel was different, however. After about forty-five minutes, she turned off Highway 67 onto the smaller FM 200. She pulled over a moment to confirm her route on the handheld GPS, then continued down the road about a mile until she found the turn north that took her up to the bank of the Brazos River.

She took the bike offroad and went along the bank about a hundred yards, looking left and right to confirm that she was alone. Then she stopped the bike and put it up on its kickstand, leaving the motor running. She quickly opened the backpack and removed the three parts of the rifle, which she threw into the river along with the spent shell casing and three extra bullets she had brought along just in case. She took the opportunity to change out of her camo gear back into civilian clothes. Then she hopped on the bike and retraced her path back to Highway 67.

An hour later, Mary exited the highway for the last leg, taking several smaller roads heading towards the southwest side of Lake Worth. As she rode along Heron Drive, she felt a sense of relief when she saw Abby's minivan waiting on the side of the road, as planned. She rode past the minivan and turned offroad, slowly making her way through the rough terrain until she reached the edge of the lake and found a spot that looked deep enough to cover the bike. There, she pushed the motorcycle into the water, then walked back to the minivan.

# CHAPTER EIGHTY-FIVE

On the ride back to the hotel, Mary told Abby how everything had gone down. While they talked, she changed into gym clothes that Abby brought with her: leggings, a sports bra, a t-shirt, and running shoes.

"Are you sure you heard right? Sick Eddie? What kind of name is that?"

"That's what it sounded like."

"What could he owe him money for?" Abby asked.

"Beats me," Mary replied. "I know Johnny likes to bet on football now and then, but it's never been big money."

Abby shook her head. "Well, he must be into this Eddie guy for a lot if he was trying to kill him."

"Good news is that it really creates a mess forensics-wise. Someone else's blood out there, and all. Whoever Johnny was shooting at will definitely be the prime suspect."

When they got to the hotel at just before 10:30 a.m., they went down to the restaurant for breakfast—not because they were hungry, but to strengthen their alibi. At one p.m., the two friends went to the hotel spa for their scheduled treatments. More champagne. Mani-pedis. Facials. Then massages. Mary fell asleep during her facial and again during her massage. She was exhausted. They were done with everything at about 4:30. They returned to their room, showered, and dressed for dinner.

The dining room in the hotel's restaurant was crowded.

Abby ordered a bottle of rosé to go with the salmon salads they both ordered. The friends made a show of having a great time, chatting up their waitress, and having her take a photo of them together, all the while waiting for Mary's phone to ring. The call came with dessert, at eight p.m., just as a slice of cheesecake and death by chocolate (which Mary had ordered) arrived.

Mary looked at her phone.

UNKNOWN.

"Should I take this?" she asked Abby gayly.

Abby shrugged. "I guess."

"Hello?"

"Mrs. Mary Miracle, please?"

"This is she."

"This is Sheriff Alan Watts with the San Saba County Sheriff's Department, ma'am."

"Okay?"

"I'm afraid I have some bad news," the voice said.

Mary stood up from the table, looking concerned.

"What kind of bad news?" she said loudly. She signaled with her hand for Abby to give her a moment and walked out of the restaurant into the lobby. Abby followed her. Several guests noted the friends walking out.

"I'm afraid there's been an accident," the caller took a deep breath. "Your husband is dead, ma'am."

"What?" Mary whispered into the phone, then raised her voice. "What do you mean . . . dead?"

Mary stood within earshot of the concierge desk, and the attendant looked up. Abby was right next to her.

"Can I ask where you are?"

"I'm up in Dallas, well, near Dallas . . . Las Colinas. For the weekend. But . . . what happened?" Mary began thinking about Grandma Nellie, dying in her arms. Grandma Nellie, who loved her so much . . . trying to stir up tears.

"He was shot, ma'am. We're not sure exactly by who or how it happened. Appears to have been a hunting accident. Best as we can tell right now. He was found on a lease near his deer blind."

"My God . . . poor Johnny. When?" The tears began to flow. Abby asked the concierge for tissues, which he quickly provided.

"Sometime today. Hard to pin down exactly. His friends found him around four p.m. The M.E. will know more. We've taken him to the San Saba County morgue." The sheriff paused, speaking in a muffle to someone nearby.

"Once they're done with the autopsy, we can release the body to you for—

"

"I . . . well . . . I don't know. We're . . ." Mary sat down in a lobby chair. "We're getting divorced, you see . . . So . . . Oh, God! Poor Johnny!" Mary broke down crying.

Abby held her friend. By this point, several people in the hotel lobby were surreptitiously watching the scene, whispering amongst themselves.

Mary cried a bit longer, then composed herself, sniffling.

"I'm sorry," she said.

"It's all right, ma'am. It's terrible news. I understand."

"I just don't know if I'm the right person . . . If I should be the one . . . With the divorce and all? Maybe his father?"

"That makes sense, ma'am, given the situation. His friends only had your phone number. Do you—"

"Sure, hold on."

Mary gave the sheriff Johnny's father's phone number. The sheriff offered his condolences, and the call ended.

"Oh God, Abby!" Mary exclaimed.

"Let's go upstairs, hon."

Mary nodded. "Poor Johnny . . ."

Abby waved at the concierge. "Just have them put dinner on the room."

"Of course, ma'am. So very sorry . . ."

Abby caught up with Mary, and the two friends returned to their room for the night.

# CHAPTER EIGHTY-SIX

Abby turned the TV on to a twenty-four-hour news station and turned up the volume. She drew the curtains.

Still, the friends spoke in whispers.

"Looked legit to me," Abby said.

Mary sighed. "Good. Thanks. Lots of witnesses."

"Well, better call Beavers," Abby said.

Mary nodded. "It still seems to me like that's what I would do if this had really been an accident . . . don't you think?"

Abby nodded and sat down on the bed as Mary called.

"Hello, Betsy?"

"Don't tell me you're having second thoughts *now*? There's nothing we can do at this point," Beavers said with quite a lot of 'I told you so' in her voice.

"No . . . It's not . . . It's . . ." Mary stammered. "It's Johnny. I just got a call . . ."

Abby nodded, giving her a thumbs up.

Mary paused, making a sniffling sound. "I just got a call from the sheriff in . . . San Saba, I think? He said Johnny's dead."

"Oh, my God! How did . . . Wait. Wasn't he going hunting this weekend?"

"Yes. I think that's right. They said they thought it was an accident. He got shot."

There was a pause.

"Why are you calling me?"

Mary told Beavers about not wanting to be responsible for the body, which Beavers agreed was the right decision. "But I was worried because he also asked *where I was*."

"Where *are* you?"

"In Dallas. Well, nearby . . . Las Colinas. I'm calling you from my hotel. I was getting away for the weekend with a girlfriend of mine. At the Four Seasons."

"Okay. Good. When did you get there?"

"Yesterday."

"And she can corroborate your location?"

"We drove up together. In her car. Been here together since."

"Anyone else seen you?"

"We were at the spa most of the day."

"Okay. Good. Well, I don't do criminal law. But if you hear from the sheriff again, or any law enforcement for that matter, you call me immediately. You got that?"

"Okay, got it."

There was a pause, then Beavers said, "This raises an interesting legal question. I'm sorry, I don't mean to be insensitive or callous . . . we can talk about it later . . ."

"No, that's okay," Mary responded. "What question?"

"Well, I'm just thinking . . . Even though you agreed to give Johnny the Monet insurance money, that agreement is basically just a contract . . . in his favor. Since he died while you two were still married . . . legally, as his wife, you inherit everything he owned, including the rights under that contract. So technically, you are now a widow, and *you* get the insurance money. I mean, his family may want to fight over it if it comes to that, but I think, legally, you're on very solid ground."

Mary paused, then simply said, "Poor Johnny . . ."

"I'm sorry. This isn't the right time to bring this up. It's just the lawyer in me. I am so sorry for your loss, Mary. If there's anything I can do for you, don't hesitate to call me."

Mary ended the call.

# CHAPTER EIGHTY-SEVEN

The following morning, Abby went down to the front desk at ten to check out.

"I am so sorry to hear about your friend," Candace said.

"Thank you," Abby replied. "It's tough. She had a rough night, so we figured we'd head on back a little sooner than planned."

"I understand completely," Candace said, printing out the bill. "I told my manager, and he said to comp the dinner last night. For what that's worth . . ."

"Aw . . . Thank you so much . . ."

Abby and Mary drove back to Fredericksburg. They were silent most of the way. Abby put on a local Austin station once they were close to town, and during the top-of-the-hour news summary, Johnny was mentioned on the air. Just a blip.

> *The San Saba sheriff's department confirms that a Fredericksburg man was shot and killed yesterday in an apparent hunting accident in the Hill Country. This marks the first fatality of the 2015 hunting season.*

"So, now what?" Abby asked.

"Well, I gotta finish getting my apartment organized. Then get ready for law school . . ."

"That'll keep you busy."

"Meanwhile, I guess . . . just lay low."

"If I hear from anyone," Abby said, "I'll call you."

"But let's assume that everything is bugged, phone, text, email . . ."

"Goes without saying," Abby acknowledged. "How do you . . . feel?"

Mary shrugged. "He got what he deserved, Abby."

They pulled up to Mary's apartment at a little after one o'clock. Mary got her suitcase, and Abby got out to help, giving Mary one of her famous 'Abby hugs.' And a kiss on the cheek.

"See you soon, girl," Abby said.

"You will." Mary started toward her door, then turned and said, "I love you, Abby. You're a good friend. My best friend."

Abby sashayed forward and gave Mary another enveloping hug, and as they separated, wiped away tears. "I love you too, Mary."

Just as they were about to part ways, Mary's phone rang.

# CHAPTER EIGHTY-EIGHT

Karen Kline poured herself another glass of red wine. She had started drinking at around nine that Sunday morning when she'd heard the news about Johnny on TV. She'd cried at first. Then she'd taken the Monet out from its hiding place to console herself.

Johnny had told her that the stolen artwork would fetch at least a million dollars.

*Well, at least he left me rich!*

She'd finished off the first bottle; the glass she'd just poured was what remained of the second bottle. She'd started drinking because of *poor Johnny.* She'd kept drinking to summon the courage for the phone call she knew she needed to make. Karen was good at pretending. She knew that a real friend of Mary's, having heard the news about Johnny, would call her. And Karen had been pretending for so long, all she really had was pretense. But she was nervous about the call. She wanted to sound natural. Normal.

For the fourth time, she trudged up the stairs to her bedroom as she felt it would be easier to call from there. This time, she would do it.

Her mobile phone in one hand and her wineglass in the other, Karen looked at herself in the full-length mirror that hung on the door to her closet. She was wearing the emerald green lace babydoll she'd slept in. She looked good, and that made her feel sexy and strong. She needed to feel that right now.

"Aargh!" she yelled. "Okay. Let's do this!"

Mary answered on the third ring.

"Hello, Karen."

"Hi. Mary . . . I was just calling because I heard about Johnny . . . How are you? Terrible, I guess," Karen was gushing. Maybe slurring just a little. "I know you guys were getting a divorce and all, but still . . . I'm so sorry."

"Thanks, Karen. I appreciate that."

Mary sounded a bit cool. Had she found out about Karen and Johnny? Or about the real estate flip scheme? Karen had been listed as a realtor on the paperwork for both deals . . .

"Well, tell me if it's *too soon* . . . But, now that you're single, we can go out . . . Like old times? Two single chicks! That'd be fun," Karen gushed some more, trying and failing to walk the line between encouraging and enthusiastic.

"You know, Karen . . . I could forgive the real estate part of this whole mess. I mean, it's only money. And it worked out fine for me, so, you know, no harm, no foul. And I could forgive you screwing my husband; I mean, you always did have that trashy streak. And, Lord knows, Johnny screwed enough strippers that it's pretty clear his taste ran in that direction. What I can't get over is that you'd call me up to offer condolences and not fess up. That you would just try to pretend like nothing happened. It's like you don't even want to be forgiven. Like you don't have the balls to say you screwed up and you're sorry."

Karen stood for a moment in stunned silence. She hadn't prepared for an angry Mary. She hadn't expected that. Then, she exploded.

"Oh, fuck off, Mary!" Karen screeched. "See, that's what you don't get! You've always expected everyone to come and bow down before *THE GREAT MARY!* Of course you don't care about the money 'cause you've always had it. You never had to fight tooth and nail like I did to get by! And as for Johnny. Honey! I only fucked him because I was bored. And he fucked me for the same reason—because *YOU BORED HIM!* I don't think he'd gotten his rocks off the way I did for him in years, the poor bastard. So, no. I'm not going to apologize. You should apologize to me! You stole David from me . . ." Karen was crying now, but she kept going. "It's *YOUR FAULT* I got pregnant! Hell, you even had to ruin prom for me. You and that bitch Mrs. Shoe. You should apologize to *me!* You're a toxic person, Mary. Toxic! You always have been. And your toxicity is finally coming home to roost. Your husband's dead, your grandmother's dead, and you're *ALL ALONE!* So, fuck you, Mary! *FUCK OFF AND DIE!*"

Karen was standing in front of the mirror. There was spittle all over the glass from her yelling, and she saw that she'd spilled some red wine on her white rug. She was panting, listening, waiting for Mary to respond.

"Oh God, Karen. Honey, you need help . . ."

It took a moment for Karen to register the change in voice. Then, it clicked.

"Abby?" she asked.

"Honey, yeah . . ."

"I told you, Abby," Mary's voice affirmed.

"Karen, I . . . I think we better go," Abby said. "Goodbye."

"No, you don't, you fat bitch! You don't hang up on me! I hang up on you!" Karen looked at the phone. The line was dead. Karen was boiling. She took a slurp from her wineglass, then went to the bathroom and soaked a towel in water. Kneeling on all fours, she dabbed at the spilled wine, trying to remove the stain. As she did, she sobbed.

When she was done, she sat on the bed, leaning against the headboard. Mindlessly drinking from the wine glass. On the wall, next to her bedroom door, hung the Monet. She'd hung it using Johnny's tools.

"Who has the last laugh, bitch!" Karen said out loud. "Cheers!"

She raised her glass.

To no one.

# CHAPTER EIGHTY-NINE

Not long after Karen's call to Mary, Walter Gripke answered his phone on the second ring. He was at the grocery store buying toilet paper. He answered only because it was Sheriff Strauss calling.

"You watchin' the news?" Strauss asked.

"Nope," Gripke replied. "What'd I miss?"

"Your cold case just got a lot colder."

"Aw, great! Now what?"

Earlier that week, Gripke had gotten the results from the DNA lab tests on all of the articles from Zeke Fulton's truck that he'd sent away for analysis. There were several items that came back positive with Fulton's DNA on them. And that was it. Nothing else. A dead end.

"Johnny Miracle's dead."

"No shit! What happened?"

"Huntin' accident, from the sound of it."

"Damn. First Nellie, now him. Lotta people dyin' around Mrs. Miracle," Gripke mused.

"Didn't you tell me you had a hunch about ole Johnny?"

"Yeah, I dunno. When I chatted him up at the barbecue, he seemed . . . *interested* in the whole Fulton thing. Asked me for my card. My gut tells me he knew something he wasn't sayin'."

"Well, he ain't sayin' nothin' no more. That's for sure!" Strauss chuckled. "Just thought you'd wanna know."

"Where'd it happen?"

"San Saba. You gonna give 'em a call and get details?" Strauss asked.

"Sure am."

“Well, good luck with that. I admire your tenacity, Walt. But, sometimes, cold is cold, and there ain’t nothin’ to be done about it. But you keep on pluggin’, buddy. That’s why—”

“Yeah, yeah. I know. That’s why I get paid the big bucks . . .”

Strauss laughed loudly, then ended the call with, “Have a great rest of your weekend!”

Gripke put the phone back in his pocket. He knew that there was something there. A connection between Fulton and that vineyard. Maybe Gomez? Maybe old Nellie? He was sure Mary knew something. Just like he knew Johnny had been holding back on him.

But one of the first lessons he’d learned years ago as a master-at-arms in the Navy still held true: “It’s not about what you know. It’s about what you can prove.”

# CHAPTER NINETY

Saturday night, Sick Eddie had not slept well. He was concerned. Javier hadn't called in as agreed. He'd lain in bed, eyes wide open, thinking. *There's no way that son of a bitch could've got one up on Javier! That would truly be a 'miracle.'*

Javier, of course, was replaceable. But Sick Eddie never liked losing employees. It reflected poorly on him. Besides, the two men had history.

*Javier knows too much about my business. I hope he's okay, and just laying low. Or, if things went south, probably best if he's dead . . . worst case would be if he somehow got caught in the act.*

On the Sunday morning after the shooting, Sick Eddie went to work as he normally would, promoting Leo, who ran the front door, to office door duty. Later that day, he heard on the news that Johnny Miracle was dead.

*So Javier got him. Well, that's something.*

Throughout the day, Sick Eddie kept his phone close by. No calls came in from Javier.

Monday morning, while watching the early morning news, Sick Eddie saw a new report.

> *A shocking development in the hunting death of Jonathan Miracle that police previously ruled an accident. Authorities confirm that a second body has been found nearby. Another man, Javier Palenque, was found dead by a gunshot wound about a mile from the body of Jonathan Miracle. Police are now considering the case a double homicide. The shooting occurred on a hunting lease near San Saba, Texas, and police are asking anyone with information to please call the number on the screen below.*

Sick Eddie knew he would be getting a visit from the police once they tracked down where Javier had worked. He let Leo know to be ready. Then, as he'd planned, he called Clive Connard.

"Clive, I was so sorry to hear the news about your friend, Johnny."

"Yeah, yeah. Me too. Terrible thing. Can't be too safe out there," Clive responded. He obviously hadn't heard the latest. He still thought the shooting had been a hunting accident.

"Well, given the circumstances, I doubt that Johnny will be repaying his debt to me," Sick Eddie said. "I know my lawyer contacted you about putting the vineyard in an entity. I just wanted to call myself to assure you that once you sign everything, our respective percentage ownership will not change. Although I will be president of the corporation, I will look out for both our best interests. I simply need your agreement to this minor legal modification to ensure my investment is protected."

Clive cleared his throat. "I'm sorry, but I don't see how this is my problem, Mr. de la Rosa. With all due respect, I didn't borrow the money from you; Johnny did." Clive was formal and respectful in tone. He'd heard stories about Sick Eddie.

"The thing is, Clive, my money went to buy that vineyard based on some very specific representations that Johnny made about when I'd get that money back. And about my return on investment. Representations were made about screwing his wife on the price and flipping the property to a guy named Rosenbaum . . . and Johnny told me that all of this was your idea."

Clive was silent.

"All respect to the recently departed, Johnny wasn't smart enough to put that flip deal together on his own. As the idea was yours, and Johnny ain't around to pay up, in my book, that means you inherited my debt."

Clive remained silent.

"But, hey, I get that you don't see it that way. We'll just have to agree to disagree. If you change your mind, you've got my number."

Clive sighed with relief when the call ended.

The following day, when Clive walked out of his house to go to work, he found his Cadillac sitting in his driveway where he'd left it, destroyed. All the windows were smashed, the doors were dented and spray-painted, the tires slashed, and the inside was full of horse manure. And, resting dead on the center on the hood was a single bullet: a .30-06.

Clive borrowed his wife's car to go to the office. Once there, he called Sick Eddie, asking him when would be convenient to sign everything. That afternoon, they met in Clive's upstairs conference room. The documents that Clive signed put the vineyard into an entity owned 100% by Edward de la Rosa but provided that if the vineyard sold, proceeds from the sale would be split fifty-fifty.

"I thought you said our ownership interests would stay the same?" Clive moped. "My deal with Johnny was 75/25 . . ."

"That was my offer yesterday, Clive. Which you chose not to accept. I didn't choose to be in the grape business, man. You can appreciate that, right?"

Clive nodded, signing the last pages reluctantly. "Are you going to put the vineyard up for sale, then? So we can cash out sometime soon?"

"Not just yet, Clive. Now that I'm in it, I kinda want to enjoy it for a bit, you know?"

Clive nodded. "Have you given any thought to who's going to run things for you?"

"For *us*, Clive. You're my partner," Sick Eddie smiled. "Who was running it before?"

"Johnny and this guy Pedro."

"Give me his number," Sick Eddie said. "Not Johnny's . . . the one that's still alive."

Clive obliged as Sick Eddie's lawyer collected all the papers.

They shook hands. "I'm so glad we were able to reach an accommodation here, Clive. You're a good friend," Sick Eddie said.

Clive's new business partner and his lawyer then left the room.

# CHAPTER NINETY-ONE

For the next week, nothing significant happened. As Abby and Mary had discussed, they laid low. Mary later heard that Johnny's father had his son cremated and held a small ceremony in Buda. Mary was not invited and did not attend.

About a week and a half after Johnny died, Mary received a call from a San Saba County Sheriff's Department deputy, asking for details as to her whereabouts the weekend that Johnny died.

"Can I have a few moments of your time?" he asked.

Just as Mary was about to reply, she saw that Abby was calling her as well. Mary declined the call. She gave the deputy a high-level rundown of the events of the weekend. That she drove up to Dallas with Abby on Friday. That they had stayed at the Four Seasons for a girls' weekend, including a spa session. That she received the call from the sheriff when they were having dinner at the restaurant the evening of the accident.

The deputy seemed uninterested, perfunctory.

"I already checked with the hotel, ma'am," he told her. "They confirmed you were there during all the relevant times."

"Do you want my friend Abby's number?" Mary asked.

"I've got it. Already talked to her. Just before I called you. Everything seems to check out all right. I'm sorry to bother you."

"I heard about another man being shot nearby . . . on the news. Was that related to Johnny's . . . situation?" she asked.

"I really can't get into that, ma'am. It's an ongoing investigation is all I can say."

Once she hung up, Mary called Abby.
"I just got a call from the sheriff's department," Mary said.
"Me too."
"I guess they're still not sure if Johnny's death was an accident?"
"Sounds like it," Abby replied.
"Poor Johnny."
"Yeah, poor Johnny."
The friends maintained the charade when they talked by phone or texted.

# CHAPTER NINETY-TWO

Mary still had some Johnny-related items pending to take care of. But, wisely, she waited through the holidays for things to quiet down.

Two weeks before she was to resume law school, she sat at the Starbucks in Fredericksburg, sipping on a grande mocha and waiting. She noted a couple of locals discreetly pointing and whispering. She was glad to be living full time in Austin, away from the small-town gossips.

It was noon, and she saw the woman she was waiting for coming towards her.

"Well, there you are, and don't you look nice?" Mary stood and gave Kitty Clark a hug.

"Well, bless your heart, hon. Thank you!" The Rhinestone Realtor pulled up a chair and sat down. Kitty made a point of removing her right earbud for the conversation. "And I am so sorry for your loss!"

"Thank you. It's . . ." Mary sighed. "Even though our marriage was ending, still . . . you spend so much time with someone . . . I mean, you just don't wish an end like that on anyone, you know?" Mary said.

"I know. Even despite everything else, it's still so sad. He was sooo young."

Mary nodded.

"That said, it doesn't forgive what him and Clive tried to pull on you, with the vineyard. I mean, I'm sorry he's dead and all. But right is right, and fair is fair." Kitty reached out and took Mary's hand. "Us gals need to stick together. If men think they can walk all over us, well, they got another thing comin'."

"That's actually what I wanted to talk to you about."

"Mm-hmm." Kitty nodded. "Go on."

"Well, if you hadn't come to me and told me that Johnny was cutting a side deal with Clive on selling me the vineyard—"

Kitty raised her hand and interrupted, "Sweetie, you never would've taken two million for that land. Knowin' you like I do now—"

"Now, hold on. Let me finish." Kitty rolled her eyes coyly and sat back. Mary continued, "Johnny was out to screw me on that deal, and he failed in large part because you gave me a heads up. I really appreciate that. And I wanted to thank you properly."

Mary reached under the table and passed Kitty a medium-sized shopping bag.

"Oh, honey," Kitty fanned herself with her hand. "You're gonna make me cry! You really didn't have to." Kitty half stood and hugged Mary.

"Go on and open it."

Kitty did and removed a brand-new Louis Vuitton purse. "Oh, my God! *Loo-ee Veeeton*. I. Love. It."

"I figure it'll come in handy once you break off on your own."

"Tell me about it. I have just about had it working for that Clive. And, you should know, somethin's up with your vineyard. You ever hear of Edward de la Rosa? Ring a bell?"

Mary shook her head but made a mental note. *Edward de la Rosa? Sick Eddie?*

"Well, apparently, Clive and this guy are partners in the vineyard now, fifty-fifty. For what that's worth."

Mary nodded. More interesting information.

"Well, aren't you going to look inside?" Mary gazed at the purse. "There's a little something in there to help you launch your real estate career."

Kitty looked at Mary suspiciously, opened the purse, then slammed it closed, looking around them both to see if anybody was watching. "Shut the fuck up!" she whispered. "Are you crazy?"

Mary laughed.

"Seriously, woman! How much . . . I can't accept this." Kitty put the purse on the table and pushed it towards Mary.

Mary pushed it back.

"Listen, Kitty. Karen was the listing agent on the deal, but since Clive didn't have a broker, I didn't have to pay a buyer's commission. So, I want you to have it. You earned it."

"But that's . . ." Kitty lowered her voice and whispered, "what . . . a hundred . . . a hundred twenty thousand dollars???"

Mary nodded.

"Oh, shit, girl . . ." Kitty began to cry.

Mary handed her a tissue, which she used to dab at her eyes. Then she reached out for Mary's hand. "Thank you, you sweet, sweet woman. Thank you!"

# CHAPTER NINETY-THREE

Mary had another debt to settle. She was at Betsy Beavers's law office, waiting in a large conference room just off the reception lobby. She watched the comings and goings through the windows overlooking the lobby. Finally, she saw her guests arrive. They stopped at reception, and a moment later, Betsy Beavers came out and led them into the conference room.

"I will leave you to your business," she said, pushing a button on the wall. Electric privacy shades hummed down, covering the windows.

Once everyone was seated, Mary smiled. Across the table from her was Nick Rosenbaum. Seated at the head of the table between them was his mother, an elegant petite lady. And standing at the far end of the room, refusing a chair, was the biggest man Mary had ever seen. A giant.

Mary began, "Mrs. Rosenbaum—"

"Please," interrupted the woman, smiling. "Call me Ruby."

"Ruby, thank you again for your help, you and Nick both, in getting the vineyard sold," Mary said.

Nick raised his hands in protest. "Look, Mary. When Mom told me what she wanted me to do, well, this isn't my . . . kind of thing. Not my style of—"

"Hush, dear," Ruby interrupted. "Nicholas is a good son. He's sharp as a tack. Wharton MBA. Et cetera. Et cetera. He's done great work with our vineyards. But," she sighed, "he *is* a man. And he doesn't know what we women have to endure. Thankfully, he knows when to listen to the voice of experience, don't you, dear?"

"Yes, Mother," Nick said, rolling his eyes at Mary.

"That said," Ruby continued, "business is business. This was an accommodation only, dear—"

"Oh, yes!" Mary exclaimed. "I have a check here," she handed Ruby an envelope, "for two hundred and fifty thousand dollars. I added a bit for your trouble."

Ruby's eyes turned to steel. "The escrow money we lost was only two hundred thousand, dear. Our deal was that you would repay *that* amount."

Mary felt as though each word were a finger poking her in the chest. She blanched. She felt afraid of this little woman. Physically afraid.

Several moments of uncomfortable silence passed. Nobody moved.

Then Ruby's face softened. "Of course, I am overreacting. You're young."

Nick cleared his throat.

Mary realized she'd been holding her breath and tremulously exhaled.

"You are trying to show gratitude." Ruby reached out and gently patted her arm. She smiled broadly.

Mary suddenly felt warm inside. Loved. *How the hell does she do that?*

"I did what I did to help you out of principle. For Nellie—not for money. But," she nodded, "I see that you're young and that you mean well. So, I won't take offense. That said, a deal is a deal. Nicholas," Ruby handed her son the envelope without taking her eyes off Mary, "after you deposit the check, please wire back the extra fifty thousand."

"Yes, Mother."

"Now, there is one other matter we need to deal with . . ." Ruby looked at her son and Kong.

"We'll be right outside."

The two men left the room, closing the door behind them.

Ruby continued. "Shortly after you married Johnny, Nellie called me because she was concerned about him. And, among other things, specifically about the Monet. I gave her two pieces of advice, both of which she followed. The first was to take out insurance on the painting. The second was slightly more devious but not uncommon in the art world.

"Nellie sent me various photos of the painting, and I had a professional make a replica. When it was done, I sent it to Nellie, and she hung it over the fireplace, sending me the original for safekeeping. It's in my safe. I can continue to hold it for you or deliver it wherever you direct."

Mary's eyes welled with tears. The painting, her family heirloom—Nellie's Monet. It wasn't gone after all. *Gandy was right . . . Johnny had stolen a fake!*

"But . . . why didn't you tell me sooner?" Mary asked.

"Well, given that the painting was 'stolen,'" Ruby made air quotes with her fingers, "and, given its value, I wouldn't put it past the police to tap your phone. I thought it better to discuss this face-to-face. There was no rush, after all . . . so now you can decide whether you want to keep the painting *and* the insurance money."

"There's five million dollars insurance on it," Mary confirmed.

"A very nice windfall."

"But I couldn't do that," Mary protested.

"Why not?"

"Well . . . it wasn't stolen."

"But dear, the insurance company thinks it was."

"Wouldn't that be . . . fraud?"

Ruby stared at Mary momentarily, then slowly shook her head and said, "I really just do not understand your generation."

Mary had no idea what to do about the insurance money. But, given that she was going to be going to law school and living in an apartment for a few years, she asked Ruby to continue to hold the painting for her for the time being, to which she agreed.

"Very well then, I would like to wrap up the final part of our deal, if you would be so kind as to give Kong directions?"

Mary nodded, and the two left the conference room. She shared the address Ruby needed with Kong.

"I will say my goodbyes now," Ruby said. "However, Nicholas has another meeting in about an hour. Is there a coffee shop nearby?"

"Just down the street," Mary said.

"Good. You two go and get some coffee," Ruby commanded. "You're clearly attracted to one another. Explore that. Maybe there's something there . . . I want to be able to enjoy my grandchildren. I'm not getting any younger. And neither are the two of you."

Mary's eyes widened, and she blushed.

Nick shook his head, shrugged, and smiled at Mary.

# CHAPTER NINETY-FOUR

Ruby sat in the back seat of a rented Mercedes-Benz as Kong drove west out of Austin. She was feeling nostalgic, as was appropriate. So many years had passed.

She remembered the first time she'd set eyes on Penelope Duran in that turquoise one-piece swimsuit. So many years ago. They'd kept in touch after their little tryst in Cabo. Penelope was married, of course, so anything more than friendship was impossible, but she had been that—a good friend.

They could have been more, maybe. But their timing was bad. Penelope's husband, Jerry, died in 1993. By that time, Ruby had married Stanley Rosenbaum and was raising Nicholas. Ruby chuckled to herself.

*Star-crossed lovers, we.*

When Jerry died, Ruby consoled Penelope and advised her when asked what she should do with the life insurance money. Penelope was enamored with country life. She'd always wanted to live on the land.

"Follow your dreams, Penelope. If not now, when?"

"But I don't know the first thing about vineyards, Ruby. Besides, isn't it more of a man's game?"

Ruby had laughed. "If there's one thing I've learned in life: no man, no matter how smart or strong, can compete with a motivated woman. You can do this."

Following Ruby's advice, Penelope had used the insurance proceeds to invest in a vineyard. She had adapted well to Texas, even shortening her name to Nellie, something the locals seemed more comfortable with.

Over the years, the time between Ruby and Nellie's phone calls grew longer. But they still tried to keep in touch. Ruby recalled when she had last called Nellie to catch up.

*"Hello. May I speak to Nellie, please?"*

*"Nope. She's dead . . . Uh . . . Who is this? Can I help you?"*

Ruby had simply hung up. Nellie had told her all about Johnny. And she was pretty confident that was who had answered. Still, she wanted to know exactly what had happened. So, she called several more times until, finally, Mary answered.

*"I'm an old friend of your grandmother's, Mary. Actually, when your grandfather died, I was the one that helped her find the land for the vineyard and get organized."*

Mary told Ruby all about Nellie's passing. Ruby shared *some* of her memories of Nellie. And, because Ruby's family was in the wine business, Mary had asked her what she thought about Clive's first offer to buy the vineyard.

*"Well, dear. My sense for the Texas real estate market is a bit rusty, but off the top of my head . . . that sounds like a really shitty offer."*

*"You don't know the half."* Mary told Ruby what Kitty had reported about Clive and Johnny's deal and about Johnny getting a commission on the sale of *her* land.

Ruby sat quietly for a few moments, then said, *"My dear, if you will let me help you, I can try to see to it that you get fair market value for your land."*

The plan was simple. Mary would list the property for sale. Then, the Rosenbaums would contact the realtor, make a higher offer that was too attractive for the market, start a bidding war, and attempt to drive up Clive's offer.

*"He'll either bid more or simply go away."*

It was worth a shot, and they agreed to give it a go.

Neither expected Clive and Johnny to conceal the Rosenbaums' offer from Mary and to try to flip the vineyard for a profit.

*"Now, what do I do?"* Mary had asked on a subsequent call.

*"My dear, this is perfect. You just hold out for four million dollars from that Connard fellow. There's two million dollars between our offer and that four million. Let greed work in your favor,"* Ruby told Mary.

She'd been right.

Ruby shook her head. *Men are so predictable. Greedy ones, more so.*

Ruby had to put two hundred thousand in escrow, knowing she would lose it. But the deal was rich enough for Mary that she was willing to take that risk and reimburse Ruby.

Ruby's thoughts were interrupted by Kong, "The vineyard is to the left, Ruby Yi."

"Thank you, Kong. Could you stop . . . just by the front?"

Kong parked the Mercedes to the side of the front gate. Ruby rolled down her window and took a look at what she could see from the road. As far as Ruby knew, it was all owned by Clive Connard now. The big Crabapple Creek Vineyard sign was still there. She'd seen it in photos. As she studied the place, a truck pulled up to the gate. It had a large Crabapple Creek Vineyard logo painted on the door. A good-looking Mexican man was driving.

*Pedro Gomez, no doubt,* thought Ruby. Nellie had spoken of him often, but Ruby had never met him or even seen a photo. *Nice to put a face to the name.*

The gates opened, and the truck drove in.

"Okay. Let's go."

Ten minutes later, they had parked at their final stop—the address Mary had given her. Ruby walked along with Kong holding her arm, the spike heels of her Louboutins sinking into the soft loam.

"Here we are," Kong said. He left her and stepped a few yards away.

Ruby looked down at the headstone. She'd never been in a cemetery. Not even when Arvin Cho died. She'd not gone to his funeral—she'd claimed she was too devastated.

Ruby Rosenbaum *née* Yi had killed more men than she cared to remember. She'd negotiated with mobsters, bribed politicians, killed her first husband, built a real estate empire, remarried, and raised a son. She'd begun this adventure of life without anything except faith in herself. And over time, life confirmed that she could trust almost no one. She'd learned to believe in only a few things.

That money *could* be made without hurting others. But that cheating is a part of life. And that it's better to be in on the game than not.

She'd also come to believe in God—a God who forgave sins. A God who forgave all the bad she'd done. She couldn't prove it, but she chose to believe it because believing it was more pleasant than not. Believing it allowed her to sleep at night, most nights anyway.

*They say it's a lucky person who can count their friends on the fingers of one hand.*

*That I can do.*

As Ruby stood in the presence of her only two friends, Kong and Nellie, she looked down at the words carved on the tombstone.

*Penelope (Nellie) Duran*
*1949 – 2015*
*A Motivated Woman*

Ruby thought back to her beautiful, freckle-faced friend. She could still see her as she'd been in Cabo, as if it were only yesterday . . . smiling, full of life.

"Let's go, Kong."

She took the big man's arm and walked carefully in the loam. Her posture was relaxed, her arm loosely gripping Kong's as she studied the scenery. Taking everything in.

She turned, looked up at him, her voice warm, and asked, "Do you want to be buried or cremated?"

Kong paused for a moment, then looked at her askance, and replied, "Why *exactly* are you asking me this, Ruby Yi?"

And Ruby laughed, until tears came.

# CHAPTER NINETY-FIVE

Mary had one final Johnny Miracle-related problem she needed to resolve. The Monet insurance claim. While it had originally seemed very straightforward, something about Ruby Yi—what she had said, how the woman was and acted—had made Mary doubt her initial instinct. She'd been brooding over the issue ever since.

Law school was starting in less than a week. Mary had already bought her books. She'd given herself until the start of classes to decide, and she wasn't any closer to an answer. She went for a walk around campus to think, almost an hour, trying to decide what to do about the insurance money. Being on the law school campus was very apropos. This was, after all, a legal question. A question about what was fair. What was just.

She was conflicted. The 'right thing' legally was to refuse the insurance payout. Now that she knew the Monet hadn't been stolen and that Ruby was keeping it for her, she would be committing fraud if she didn't tell the insurance company. And it's not like she needed the money. After paying the estate taxes, she had netted almost two-and-a-half million dollars on the vineyard sale. That was more than most people retired on. She was rich, and her life was just beginning.

So why did Ruby think she was crazy to refuse the money?

*It* is *five million dollars. . .*

Mary could imagine seven-point-five-million dollars in the bank. She could do a lot of good with that kind of money. And to collect it, all she had to do was . . . nothing. Just keep her damned mouth shut. It was very tempting.

She finished her walk and headed home. That evening, she had a wedge salad for dinner, with fried pork belly and blue cheese dressing along with two glasses of red wine. She went to bed with the insurance money still on her mind. She tossed and turned, periodically checking the time on her phone. At 3:00 a.m., she was still wide awake.

She gave up on sleep, got up, and made herself peppermint tea. It was dark out, though the moon lit the night sky. She could hear cars sporadically passing below her apartment window—so different from country life. She sat on the sofa, legs curled under her, a large mug of hot tea resting warmly on her belly.

*What would Nellie do?*

As she ran once again through different justifications for taking or refusing the cash, Mary realized, *Actually, I'm asking the wrong question. Grandma Nellie would tell me that herself.*

*". . . you have to do you,"* she recalled Nellie telling her. *I am not a child anymore. It's not about what 'my grandma' would have done.*

*This is about what kind of person I am.*

She thought back over the major events of her life, those things she felt had shaped her as a person: losing her mother; growing up without a father; the blessing of living with Grandma Nellie; her close friends; her marriage to Johnny; and, what she would call for the rest of her life, "all the shit that happened after Nellie died." There was some pretty bad stuff in there.

*My grandmother made me an accessory after the fact to the murder of Zeke Fulton and I kept that secret from the police, my lawyer, and even my best friend. I lied to them all.*

*I trusted Johnny with that secret . . . and I shouldn't have. I was completely wrong about him. And I never told Nellie or Pedro about any of that.*

*I forged a letter from my grandmother to keep the Monet insurance money out of Johnny's hands.*

*I told Johnny at the mediation that he could have the insurance money when I knew that he'd never see a dime, because I was going to kill him.*

*I dragged my best friend into the murder plot, making her an accessory to the crime.*

*I killed my husband.*

Her thoughts lingered on Johnny. Possibly her greatest crime. She tried again to feel something for him: sadness, pity. She remembered the morning they met in Mexico. The night he proposed. Their wedding day. But it was no good. All of those used-to-be fond memories were ruined forever by what he had become: Grandma Nellie's killer. He not only took her grandmother from her. That was horrible enough. But he also forever ruined all those good memories—he had corrupted a huge chunk of her adult life.

*He was a horrible person . . .*

*Killing him may have been illegal. But was it wrong?*

Mary pondered, and as she did slowly shook her head. What she was asking was a moral question. A question about principles. Not just a question about the law, but a question about justice, which Mary was beginning to understand is not necessarily the same thing.

*Johnny deserved what he got. I killed Johnny. . . because he was a horrible person. He* **chose** *to be. He would have gotten away with killing Nellie if it wasn't for me. He deserved to die. He deserved worse. After everything he took from me, I've taken everything I can from him. In fact, I'm going to keep Johnny's name: Mary Miracle. I'm going to wear his name for the rest of my life like a fucking scalp. . . as a reminder to me of who I am and what I'm capable of.*

Mary recalled when she saw Johnny through her rifle scope—just before shooting him. How his face had been contorted by rage—rage against the man who was shooting at him: against Palenque *and* Sick Eddie. Until he saw her. Then his rage turned to recognition, and a glimmer of surprise in his eyes said, *"Wow . . . you figured it all out. And here you are. I didn't think you had it in you."*

And that was when she understood why she was struggling with this decision about the insurance money. She wasn't the same person anymore. There had been a tectonic shift in her.

The old Mary *couldn't* take the money. The old Mary *didn't* have it in her. But then, the old Mary *couldn't* have killed Johnny either. All that had changed.

Like a snakeskin, Mary had shed her old self. But she still hadn't gotten used to who the new Mary was. Regardless, just like the line between love and hate, there was a line between the Mary before, and the Mary after. And she knew that the change was due to one moment, one critical act that had divided her life into a *before* and an *after*: killing Johnny Miracle.

*I now know that I've 'got it in me' to do whatever I want. Whatever I choose to do, I am capable of doing. Even killing. I* do *have it in me.*

*Before killing Johnny, I wouldn't even have considered keeping the insurance money. I would have been afraid to do it. I didn't have it in me. Now, I know I can. I know that I am capable of that, and of much worse.*

Mary nodded. She felt liberated. Because she understood that from that day forward who she was as a person would be defined not by what life threw at her, but by her choices, her actions. It was with this in mind that Mary Miracle recalled with clarity—for what would not be the last time in her life—the moment she *decided* to kill her husband and how that decision made a new woman of her. A stronger woman. A better woman.

*From this point forward, I will not be a good person because I am afraid to do bad things. I will be a good person because I have no fear—because I know* I am capable of doing bad things, *but I choose not to. I will choose to do good.*

*Killing Johnny was the right thing to do. It was illegal, but it was just. Righteous.*

*But there's nothing righteous about taking the insurance money.*

*I still have the Monet. Grandma Nellie saw to that. I'm not entitled to the insurance money. I don't deserve it.*

*I can always earn money. I don't need to steal it.*

*I'll call Gandy tomorrow and withdraw the insurance claim on the Monet.*

For the first time in a long time, Mary felt at peace. Secure. Confident. She knew in her gut that this was the right decision.

Mary got up from the sofa. She stretched and yawned. She rinsed her teacup in the sink, turned out the lights, and, with newfound trust in herself and peace in her heart, she went to bed.

As she lay in bed, Mary Miracle felt alone, but not lonely; somehow, she felt connected, a part of everything, positioned right where she should be in the scheme of things. She stretched her legs, hugged her pillow, and fell soundly asleep.

# AFTERWORD

Today is July 19, 2023. It's 8:40 AM and I am in my home office in Dallas, Texas. I've been up since 4:00 a.m.

Five minutes ago, I typed the last keystroke on the final version of Killing Johnny Miracle.

Before sending it off to my editor, I decided that now is the perfect time to write to you, dear reader, and share a few brief thoughts with you.

First off, thanks so much for taking the time to read this book. These days, life is very demanding of our time, and I consider it a privilege when folks share hours of their valuable time with me and my crazy stories.

I sometimes get asked how these books come into being, so I thought I would share a little bit of that info here for anyone who's interested.

Each book starts with a general concept, and then two or three fun ideas that I think would make the story interesting or different from what's already out there. This book was no exception. I had several ideas knocking about in the back of my head for a new book. It turns out that not all of them would fit into one book. Only a part of what I was originally planning actually made it into this novel. Still, the main arc is there:

. . . a story about how a strong young woman finds her moral compass and life path while the universe is throwing buckets of shit at her.

This was the story I wanted to write.

**How long did it take you to write this book?**

The first draft of Killing Johnny Miracle was written in ten days during Covid. Our youngest child had broken his arm mountain biking, so I flew up to visit him. He was fine physically; the trip was really more about moral support.

This trip to see our son was smack dab in the middle of the pandemic. As a result, I had to quarantine for 10 days before I could see him. So I camped out in a hotel and wrote for 10 hours a day while surviving on room service and afternoon walks on the shores of Lake Geneva. 100 hours of writing later, the first draft of the book that you are holding was done. That was on October 21, 2020.

That also was, as is the case with any book, just the beginning.

Since that first draft back in 2020, the book has been through eighteen revisions by me, including four revisions that were completed after getting feedback from four different editors. Along the way, the book has been read multiple times by my loving wife, my trusty beta readers, and my reliable, often cruel, but always honest (and usually right), focus group.

**Are any of the characters based on people in real life?**

The answer to that is yes and no (typical lawyer). There is no character in this novel who is based solely on someone who I actually know. But there are always bits and pieces of characters that are drawn from real life. What I can say, without naming names, is that when I am thinking about certain character traits, I think of certain people. For example, Karen the narcissist in the novel is based loosely on a specific person in the sense that I know a very narcissistic female and when I thought about how Karen would react to something, I thought of that person (when she reads this, being the narcissist that she is, she'll know I'm talking about her). The same holds true for Johnny. He's a self-centered, not too bright, frat boy type. I've known a few of those over the years and drew from that experience when writing Johnny.

**How did you choose the setting—Fredericksburg, Texas?**

I was born and raised in South Texas. Although I am first generation U.S. on my mother's side—she came over from Cuba when Fidel Castro took power—I am fifth generation south Texas on my father side. I've spent most of my life in Texas, and a significant chunk of that in Austin.

While living in Austin, we visited Fredericksburg numerous times. We even looked for property there at one point, considering something along the lines of what Nellie decided to do—buying some land and growing some grapes. The Texas Hill Country is a beautiful part of the state, an area I'm very familiar with, and a setting I've wanted to use for a story for some time now.

Although this is a crime thriller on its face, there are a lot of elements to the story that are decidedly western. The whole "losing the ranch to the tax man" is a classic western story arc. The evil landowner (Clive Connard) is another western staple, and the climactic shoot out obviously comes from that tradition as well. Fredericksburg felt like the perfect place for a story like this—a modern day western.

**There are a lot of sayings, proverbs, quotes in this novel. Was that intentional and which ones are original?**

The novel was built around Nellie's motto, which at the end of the story we learn actually originated with Ruby Yi: No man, no matter how smart or strong, can compete with a motivated woman. The proverbial element to the novel grew from that seed and as I look back I do see a lot of them in the book. Those original to J.K. Franko include the above, and those set forth below.

The snake you don't kill today may kill you tomorrow.

It's a divorce, not cancer.

Pretty isn't permanent.

The thin line between love and hate is self-deception.

Blood only flows in one direction.

And, of course, Hamlet never said:

Oh, to be a shirt upon those boobs. . .

* * *

One small request from me to you. Word of mouth is still the best way we independent authors have to grow our readership.

If you enjoyed *Killing Johnny Miracle*, please tell other people.

Gift someone a copy.

A review on Amazon would be great. If you're not comfortable writing a long review, write a very short one. Even a couple of words with an honest star rating is much appreciated.

# ACKNOWLEDGEMENTS

Thank you to my wife Raquel for support, input, reading early versions of this novel and not being overly critical of the weak points while giving me great feedback on how to make the story better. You are an amazing partner and I love you.

Thanks to my beta readers, Mercedes Perote and Sara Bensadon, Ph.D. Your input and encouragement is invaluable.

Thanks to my focus group participants—Francesca Marturano Pratt, Cheryl Green, Renee Freeman Owens, and Lisa Hall—who devoted a significant chunk of their time to providing feedback leading to significant improvements in the story.

Thank you to author, designer, artist, and marketing guru Tony Marturano for all his work and support in bringing this project to fruition.

# ABOUT J.K. FRANKO

J.K. Franko was born, raised, and over-educated (B.A. Philosophy, J.D. Law, M.B.A. Business) in Texas.

He is the author of the internationally acclaimed revenge crime thrillers—the Roy Cruise Series.

Franko lives in Dallas with his wife and five or six dogs.

## ALSO BY J.K. FRANKO

What would YOU do if someone hurt the one you love?

J.K. Franko's thrilling crime and retribution series is AVAILABLE NOW from Amazon sites worldwide.

**TURN THE PAGE FOR A SPECIAL PREVIEW OF BOOK 1!**

Thus shall you punish wrongdoers.
So that all who hear of your actions shall tremble and cease to do evil.
You must show no pity: Life shall pay for life, eye for eye,
tooth for tooth, hand for hand, foot for foot.

DEUTERONOMY 19: 19-21

# PROLOGUE

When I try to piece together how this whole mess began, a part of me thinks it may have started over thirty years ago. At least the seeds were planted that far back, in the early 1980s. What happened then, at that summer camp in Texas, set the stage for everything that was to come.

Odd, how something so remote in time and geography continues to impact me here, today.

Sometimes I try to imagine her, how she felt—that eleven-year-old girl—as she ran, stumbling and tripping through the woods that night. I try to put myself in her shoes. When I do, I wonder if she was frightened.

Did she understand the consequences of what she'd gotten herself into? I imagine it felt otherworldly to her, like a dream. But not a good dream. No, one of the bad ones—the ones that make your heart machine-gun as you try to outrun some dark thing that's chasing you. But the faster you try to run, the slower you go, your legs feeling leaden, clumsy, useless. Panic sets in. Tears of frustration form.

Fear takes hold and won't let go. You open your mouth to scream but realize, to your horror, that you're paralyzed. It's not that you can't scream; you can't even breathe. Not a dream—a nightmare.

Then again, all that may simply be my imagination. It could just be me projecting what I might have felt onto Joan.

Maybe she wasn't scared at all.

True, it was dark out. The night smelled of rain, but there was no lightning, only the far-off rumble of thunder hinting at a distant storm. There were no trail lights, no visibility but for the moon peeking out intermittently from behind a patchwork of clouds. But, Joan had been down this trail before. She was running toward the main cabin.

She had been at Camp Willow for almost two full weeks. She had been up and down that trail at least ten times a day, every day. Of course, that was during the day, and always with her buddy, or a camp counselor (the children called them troop leaders).

Joan had never been on the trail at night. And never alone.

Maybe I imagine Joan was scared because, as an adult, I believe that she should have been. I would have been terrified.

Adults know that evil flourishes in the dark.

The woods aren't a safe place for a little girl to be alone during the day. But at night?

Any experienced hiker will tell you that the forest changes at night. Landmarks look different. Depth perception suffers, even in young eyes.

By day, a copse of crape myrtles to the side of a trail is obvious. The bright fuchsia flowers stand in stark contrast to the greys, browns, and greens of the surrounding trees and foliage.

Turning right at the crape myrtles leads you back to the main camp. If you miss the turn, the trail continues to wind down until it reaches the scenic overlook that drops fifty feet to the river and jagged rocks below.

By day, those fuchsia flowers would be impossible to miss. But at night that landmark would simply blend into the background.

You see, there are no pretty pink flowers in the woods at night.–

By now, you're probably wondering what Joan was doing out alone in the middle of the night. What could make her leave the safety of her cabin without her buddy? And why was she running?

To answer that, I have to tell you a little bit about her first.

Joan was a cute, bright little girl. Those who didn't know her well might mistake her curious nature for precociousness. But she wasn't. In fact, she was respectful and responsible, as older sisters tend to be.

She was also one of those children who aren't afraid to speak their mind. That is how her parents had raised her. She came from one of those kinds of families where the parents speak to their children as though they are adults. And the kids do the same. No pussyfooting around.

Joan was clear about what she believed, too. She didn't scare easily.

She didn't start out scared that night. She started out curious. Sneaking around after lights-out. Snooping. She called it "spying."

It's natural in young children, this behavior. Visceral. Primordial. If you have children, you know what I'm talking about. Evolution has hardwired something into kids that says: *We must learn how to spy on others. How to gather "secret" information. How to stalk. We must learn to be predator, or we will become prey.*

It's a part of growing up. It's all fun and games.

But there is a stark line that divides games from reality.

Joan crossed that line as she approached the cabin she planned to spy on.

She knew these kids. She'd been watching them for the last couple of days, eavesdropping at lunch, that kind of thing. She'd overheard them talking, but she couldn't believe what they were planning was true.

If it was, she had to do something.

You see, Joan was raised with clearly defined notions of right and wrong. She went to Bible study. And Grandma had read to her, when Mom and Dad weren't around, from the Old Testament. About Satan and Original Sin. Grandma had taught her that there were certain things that were mystical, sacred, and dangerous. You just didn't play around with them.

Joan crept up quietly, purposefully between pools of light. Once she reached the cabin, she paused. She could hear voices. Even though it was well past lights out, there was definitely something going on in there.

Carefully, she raised herself just enough to see inside the screened window, then quickly lowered herself. She'd seen them—she wasn't sure if they could see her, if they were looking in her direction or not.

She listened closely, trying to make out what they were doing. But the only thing she could hear was the hammering of her heart against her ribcage, the ringing of the blood in her ears. She placed her hands over her mouth to silence the breath that was coming so quick and shallow that she was starting to feel giddy.

She slowly peeked in the window again, and saw that no one was looking in her direction. Her eyes had already adjusted to the dark. Even so, it took a few moments for her brain to register what was going on, and a few more seconds to actually understand what she was seeing.

Joan's mouth fell open. She couldn't believe what was happening, what they were doing. She gaped, involuntarily holding her breath, staring.

There were rules at Camp Willow. What campers could and couldn't do.

What Joan witnessed went way beyond breaking camp rules. She was shocked. Stunned. And she was angry. This wasn't just wrong. It was evil.

You'd go to hell for it.

She had to make it stop.

"I'm gonna tell!"

For one brief moment, everything froze. The woods went quiet.

The three words hung in the air.

A screech broke the silence, followed by the flapping of wings as a frightened creature of some sort flew from its roost. At the same moment, the kids in the cabin turned in unison and gawked at the source of the scream.

Joan looked at them. She knew them. As she looked from one to the other, and they stared at her, Joan realized that she was outnumbered.

She turned and fled as fast as her feet would carry her. As she did, she heard a girl's voice hiss in a loud whisper, "Joan, wait!"

Joan ignored her and ran away, toward the main cabin. She felt strong, energized, full of purpose. But as I told you before, the trail was dark. The moonlight came and went. A storm was brewing in the distance. There were strange noises all around her. Shadows formed menacing shapes along the path.

And Joan was alone.

They say that when accidents happen it is usually not any one thing that goes wrong, but rather, it is the cumulative effect of multiple failure modes. For little Joan, the adrenaline, the darkness, the disorientation, and the lack of depth perception—all of these factors—probably combined and led to a very bad outcome. This is what the sheriff later told Joan's parents.

Joan was lucky at first. Despite the odds, she didn't miss the turn on the trail. She didn't miss the crape myrtles. Joan took the correct path and was headed straight for the main cabin. Until she stumbled on a root and fell, hard.

Really hard.

Her knee smashed into the ground, taking the brunt of the fall. The impact knocked off her left shoe.

Joan started crying. Quietly, so no one could hear. She tried to collect herself and rolled up into a sitting position, rocking and holding her knee. Moving it gently. Assessing the damage.

A flash of lightning startled her, but also gave her enough light to see that her shoe was only a few feet away.

She tried to stop crying.

She wanted her mommy. Wanted to be home. She wished she hadn't been spying. Wished she hadn't seen what she'd seen.

But, she also felt deep down inside that everything would be okay. She knew that Jesus would protect her because she was a good girl.

The moon peeked out from behind the clouds. In the light, Joan crawled toward her shoe. As she did, through her tears, Joan saw movement.

Shadows taking human form.

They appeared, one at a time.

The kids she'd been spying on.

* * *

**END PREVIEW.**

**BOOK 1 – EYE FOR EYE**

**AVAILABLE NOW FROM AMAZON**

Made in the USA
Monee, IL
18 September 2023

03c51ab7-f599-48dc-a40a-5b9da9398991R01